LEGACY F

Out there on the other worlds, the ones defying any restriction, there was much to be proud of. Fiume, where the gas giants were being dismantled to build a vast shell around the star, with an inner surface capable of supporting life. Milligan, whose colonists were experimenting with truly giant wormholes which they hoped could reach other galaxies. Oranses, home to the original sinners, condemned by the Vatican for their project of introducing communal sentience to every living thing on their planet, every worm, insect, and stalk of grass, thus creating Gaia in all her majesty.

All this glorious playground was our heritage, a gift from the youth of today to their sulking, inward-looking parents. . .

—from "Watching Trees Grow"
by Peter F. Hamilton

"A clever mystery, a fascinating premise, and a rewarding resolution."

—*Science Fiction Chronicle* on
"Watching Trees Grow"

FUTURES

FOUR NOVELLAS

PETER F. HAMILTON * STEPHEN BAXTER
PAUL McAULEY * IAN McDONALD

EDITED AND WITH AN INTRODUCTION BY PETER CROWTHER

ASPECT®

WARNER BOOKS

An AOL Time Warner Company

WARNER BOOKS EDITION

Cover design by Don Puckey
Cover illustration by Jim Burns

This edition is published by arrangment with Gollancz, an imprint of the Orion Publishing Group.

Warner Books, Inc.
1271 Avenue of the Americas
New York, NY 10020

Visit our Web site at
www.twbookmark.com.

For information on Time Warner Trade Publishing's online publishing program, visit www.ipublish.com.

An AOL Time Warner Company

Printed in the United States of America

First Warner Books Printing: December 2001

10 9 8 7 6 5 4 3 2 1

Contents

Introduction by Peter Crowther vii

Watching Trees Grow 1
by Peter F. Hamilton

Reality Dust 109
by Stephen Baxter

Making History 181
by Paul J. McAuley

Tendeléo's Story 267
by Ian McDonald

The Infinite Frontier

An Introduction by Peter Crowther

Let's talk about space:

Well, it makes a kind of sense, you've either *bought* this book (Hurrah!) or you're thumbing through it—maybe *thinking* about buying it, maybe just hanging around until the counter queue disappears so you can hit on the assistant you've been eyeing up for the past few weeks, or maybe you've just ducked into a bookstore and you're waiting for the rain to stop. Whichever, you've still picked up what is, to all intents and purposes (given the fairly obvious packaging), a science fiction book, so we'll take it as read you've got *some* kind of interest in space.

So we'll move forward a little.

Do you remember who first *took* you into space? Because, let's face it, we've all *been* up there, either via the printed page, the movie theater or the TV set. So who was that person into whose care you entrusted your imagination . . . saying, albeit silently, "Here I am . . . make my senses spin and my jaw drop . . . *feed* me Wonder!"?

If it was by the printed page then maybe it was in the capable hands of H. G. Wells or Jules Verne, with their futuristic visions of space travel, in cumbersome rockets whose trajectory and power source were a little shaky even then, around about a century ago for most of those marvelous tales. Or maybe it was the pulp-fictioneers, those penny-a-word scribes who filled page after page of exotic planetary locations usually populated by scantily-clad females and horrible monsters (boy, it must have been tough being a girl on some of those orbiting rocks . . . at least until the torn-suited Earth astronaut crash-landed to save the day).

Maybe it was the likes of the "serious" writers . . . guys like Isaac Asimov, with his agoraphobic investigator, his robotic hordes and the mind-boggling read that were the *Foundation* books; and Ray Bradbury, with his homespun humanistic homilies of interstellar needles descending onto the Martian quilt and poverty-line families constructing soapbox rockets in their back yards; and Arthur C. Clarke, with his barroom fables from the White Hart and the short story "The Sentinel" that became *2001: A Space Odyssey.*

In fact, maybe it *was* film—the sight of Spielberg's mother ship descending onto the mountain-top or the spectacle of the alien toddler bursting out of John Hurt's stomach—or TV (Joseph Stefano's insectoid Zanti misfits from *The Outer Limits*, perhaps . . . or the scene when one of the folks in Rod Serling's *Twilight Zone* diner reveals he's a Martian) that lit the fire in your soul and set you dreaming about *out there.*

There are so many writers and artists and directors who, year upon year, decade upon decade, have continued the craft, fashioning their own voices and their own ideologies, that it's a genre in which, no matter where you start into it, it's eminently possible—and frequently *essential*—to travel back to earlier works for further entertainment and enlightenment.

As we've been told through our TV sets for more than 30 years, space may well be the final frontier.

Of course there's Time to be unraveled yet, *and* Immortality, but the vastness of space—with its seemingly infinite possibilities of worlds, cultures, environments, eco structures and so on—invariably strikes the loudest chord in the minds of fiction readers and movie-watchers the world over. And no matter how far we manage to progress into the void, that frontier will still be there . . . the line just being constantly rubbed out and redrawn again and again, each time a little further away.

Although I've spent much of the last 10 or 12 years involved with horror, dark fantasy and even crime—both writing it and editing anthologies of the stuff—science fiction (or, more specifically, space fiction) was my first love . . . fed from the British black and white reprints of full-color American comic books such as *Mystery In Space* or curled up on a sofa listening to the BBC's radio renditions of Charles Chilton's *Journey Into Space*.

But it was Patrick Moore who first took me into space via a *book*.

The year was 1958, and it was probably my first hardcover . . . bought by my parents for Christmas (it's neatly inscribed in my mother's handwriting, penned, I'm sure, little realizing the effect such a gift was to have on her son) a book entitled *Peril on Mars*, written by the great astronomer himself. It was wonderful stuff and I had no hesitation in scribbling down the titles of the three earlier adventures of Maurice Gray and his friends on the Red Planet. I've since had the opportunity of acknowledging that formative experience by commissioning an Introduction from Patrick for *Mars Probes*, an anthology of new stories about our closest planetary neighbor to be published in the US in late 2001—it's always nice to square the books and repay your dues, no matter how long it takes.

Anyway, back in the 1950s and hungry for more science fictional inspiration, I haunted the bookshops and quickly discovered Angus McVicar's *Lost Planet* series, featuring young Jeremy Grant, and E. C. Eliott's tales of Kemlo and his friends on Satellite Belt K. And then on to H. G. Wells's *The War of the Worlds*—which I had already read as a *Classics Illustrated* and so knew the story—and Edgar Rice Burroughs's *Princess of Mars* and its many sequels.

After that, courtesy of my English Language tutor at Leeds Grammar School, came Ray Bradbury's *The Illustrated Man* . . . in which "Kaleidoscope", a one-act tale of a doomed astronaut adrift in the void, brought the concept of space travel firmly into the realms of the possible—even the probable—and, paradoxically, its downbeat finale made the prospect of such adventure even more attractive than the ray-gun variety of SF favored by the comic books and the once-so-called "juvenile" adventures.

From then I was firmly hooked.

As I grew older and more adventurous and demanding in my reading, the emphasis on space gave way to *terra firma* tales set sometimes in possible futures, sometimes in the present and occasionally on an alternate version of Earth on which accepted historical facts and events had been altered . . . sometimes subtly and sometimes not. Thus it was that the science—or simply the developmental and speculative possibilities inherent in this brave and frequently audacious brand of literature—wove its spell.

Now I can enjoy the so-called hard science (quite an achievement for someone who regularly marvels at both car and computer—and even, when the muse hides for a while, my desk lamp—when they obligingly respond to the flicking of a switch) just as much as the space opera of, say, E. E. Smith's Lensman books and old issues of *Amazing* and *Fantastic*.

All of these still grace my crowded bookshelves, though old faithfuls such as some of the ones I've already mentioned and the likes of Carey Rockwell's adventures of Tom Corbett, Space Cadet are (despite, in the latter, the exemplary technical assistance of Willey Ley) a little more mannered today than they seemed to be all those years ago. But mannered or not, they all make up a glorious confusion of adventures and stories set both on Earth and on worlds near and far, and in strange futures . . . realities populated by fantastic creatures and barely recognizable versions of ourselves. And every single word on every page continues to fight the good fight and carry forward the baton of imaginative fiction.

The quartet of novellas in *Futures*, the second in what will be a continuing series of the very best in long short fiction, comes from four writers working at the forefront of British science fiction . . . four writers who have carried that baton of imagination with tremendous vigor.

There are echoes of many of the authors I've already mentioned—and a whole lot more—in these four great works.

I could say that, for me at least, Ian McDonald's latest tale of the rampaging alien infestation known as the Chaga and, specifically, of its effects on the life of a young East African girl, calls to mind much of J. G. Ballard's work circa *The Drowned World*; that Stephen Baxter's consideration of godhood and immortality on one of Saturn's moons in the sixth millennium seems a touch reminiscent of Arthur C.

Clarke's almost mystical parables of Mankind's true destiny set against a backdrop of supposed future utopias; that Peter F. Hamilton's centuries-long murder investigation conducted, as forensic science develops, by descendants of the Roman Empire on an alternate Earth, carries the feel of both Agatha Christie's Hercule Poirot tales and the Gil Hamilton stories of Larry Niven; and that Paul McAuley's epoch-stretching, post–Quiet War saga of politics, upheaval and opera at the edge of the solar system features all the very best in hard science *and* future history as exemplified by Isaac Asimov's Foundation cycle.

But that's just my take—yours may well be entirely different: just as we all bring different things *to* the reading process, so too do we *take away* different things when that process has been completed.

All that *is* certain is that great writing is here in these pages . . . great invention and great characterization, too—finally laying to rest (if such a ceremony were really needed anymore) the hoary old chestnut that SF cares less about humanity and personal relationships than it does about detailing the workings of a rocket's engines. And you're due for some of the most wonderful and disconcerting suggestions as to what may lie ahead for the human race.

In their introduction to the 1992 edition of *The Encyclopedia of Science Fiction*, John Clute and Peter Nicholls rightly recognize that the secret history of SF is bigger on the inside than it is on the outside . . . and the further in you go, the bigger it gets. Science fiction is more popular now than ever before: moreover, having at last escaped the withering stigma imposed by the constraints of the old pulp magazines in terms of both content and execution, it's finally finding warmer receptions in the one-time frosty corridors occupied by the *literati*—as surely evidenced by John Updike's recent *Toward the End of Time.*

What the great supporters of the field have always said is true: science fiction is the literature of ideas. Here are four more . . . but they are four covering a whole host of styles and images and approaches to the field.

Space Opera, Future Civilizations, Alien Invasions, Scientific Advancement, Political Chicanery, Human Relationship and even Police Procedural—they're all here. But then they *would* be . . . because those are what science fiction is all about. So no matter who took you into space the first time, you're about to go again . . . in the safe hands of four of the best interstellar pilots in the galaxy. Enjoy the trip.

Peter Crowther
November 2000

Watching Trees Grow

Peter F. Hamilton

One

Oxford, England AD 1832

If I was dreaming that night I forgot it the instant when that blasted telephone woke me with its shrill two-tone whistle. I fumbled round for the bedside light, very aware of Myriam shifting and groaning on the mattress beside me. She was seven months pregnant with our child, and no longer appreciated the calls which I received at strange hours. I found the little chain dangling from the light, tugged it, and picked up the black bakelite handset.

I wasn't surprised to have the rich vowels of Francis Haughton Raleigh rolling down the crackly line at me. The family's old *missi dominici* is my immediate superior. Few others would risk my displeasure with a call at night.

"Edward, my boy," he growled. "So sorry to wake you at this ungodly hour."

I glanced at the brass clock on the chest of drawers; its luminous hands were showing quarter past midnight. "That's all right, sir. I wasn't sleeping."

Myriam turned over and gave me a derisory look.

"Please, no need to call me, *sir*. The thing is, Edward, we have a bit of a problem."

"Where?"

"Here in the city, would you believe. It's really the most damnable news. One of the students has been killed. Murdered, the police seem to think."

I stopped my fidgeting, suddenly very awake. Murder, a concept as difficult to grasp as it was frightening to behold. What kind of pre-Empire savage could do that to another person? "One of ours?"

"Apparently so. He's a Raleigh, anyway. Not that we've had positive confirmation."

"I see." I sat up, causing the flannel sheet to fall from my shoulders. Myriam was frowning now, more concerned than puzzled.

"Can we obtain that confirmation?" I asked.

"Absolutely. And a lot more besides. I'm afraid you and I have been handed the family jurisdiction on this one. I'll pick you up in ten minutes." The handset buzzed as the connection ended.

I leaned over and kissed Myriam gently. "Got to go."

"What is it? What's happened?"

Her face had filled with worry. So much so that I was unable to answer in truth. It wasn't that she lacked strength. Myriam was a senior technical nurse, seeing pain and suffering every day at the city clinic—she'd certainly seen more dead bodies than I ever had. But blurting out this kind of news went against my every instinct. Obscurely, it felt to me as though I was protecting our unborn. I simply didn't want my child to come into a world where such horror could exist. *Murder*. I couldn't help but shiver as I pulled on my shirt, cold fingers making a hash of the small pearl buttons. "Some kind of accident, we think. Francis and I have to investigate. I'll tell you in the morning." When, the Blessed Mary willing, it might be proved some ghastly mistake.

My leather attaché case was in the study, a present from my mother when I passed my legal exams. I had been negligent in employing it until now, some of its fine brass implements and other paraphernalia had never even been taken from their compartments. I snatched it up as if it were some form of security tool, its scientific contents a shield against the illogicality abroad in the city that night.

I didn't have a long wait in the lobby before Francis's big black car rolled up outside, crunching the slushy remnants of last week's snowfall. The old man waited patiently while I buckled the safety restraint straps around my chest and shoulders before switching on the batteries and engaging the gearing toggle. We slipped quietly out onto the cobbled street, powerful yellow headlamps casting a wide fan of illumination.

The apartment which Myriam and I rent is in the city's Botley district, a pleasant area of residential blocks and well-tended parks, where small businesses and shops occupy the ground floors of most buildings. The younger, professional members of the better families had taken to the district, their nannies filling the daytime streets with prams and clusters of small excitable children. At night it seemed bleaker somehow, lacking vitality.

Francis twisted the motor potentiometer, propelling the car up to a full twenty-five miles an hour. "You know, it's at times like this I wish the Roman Congress hadn't banned combustion engines last year," he grumbled. "We could be there in half a minute."

"Batteries will improve," I told him patiently. "And petroleum was dangerous stuff. It could explode if there were an accident."

"I know, I know. Lusting after speed is a Shorts way of

thinking. But I sometimes wonder if we're not being too timid these days. The average citizen is a responsible fellow. It's not as if he'll take a car out looking to do damage with it. Nobody ever complains about horseriding."

"There's the pollution factor as well. And we can't afford to squander our resources. There's only a finite amount of crude oil on the planet, and you know the population projections. We must safeguard the future, we're going to spend the rest of our lives there."

Francis sighed theatrically. "Well recited. So full of earnest promise, you youngsters."

"I'm thirty-eight," I reminded him. "I have three accredited children already." One of which I had to fight to gain family registration for. The outcome of a youthful indiscretion with a girl at college. We all have them.

"A child," Francis said dismissively. "You know, when I was young, in my teens in fact, I met an old man who claimed he could remember the last of the Roman Legionaries withdrawing from Britain when he was a boy."

I performed the math quickly in my head. It could be possible, given how old Francis was. "That's interesting."

"Don't patronize, my boy. The point is, progress brings its own problems. The world that old man lived in changed very little in his lifetime—it was almost the same as the Second Imperial Era. While today, our whole mindset, the way we look at our existence, is transformed every time a new scientific discovery drops into our lap. He had stability. We don't. We have to work harder because of that, be on our guard more. It's painful for someone of my age."

"Are you saying today's world makes murder more likely?"

"No. Not yet. But the possibility is there. Change is always a domino effect. And the likes of you and I must be conscious of that, above all else. We are the appointed guardians, after all."

"I'll remember."

"And you'll need to keep remembering it as well, not just for now, but for centuries."

I managed to prevent my head from shaking in amusement. The old man was always going on about the uncertainties and dangers of the future. Given the degree of social and technological evolution he'd witnessed in the last four hundred years, it's a quirk which I readily excuse. When he was my age the world had yet to see electricity and water mains; medicine then consisted of herbs boiled up by old women in accordance with lore already ancient in the First Imperial Era. "So what do we know about this possible murder?"

"Very little. The police phoned the local family office, who got straight on to me. The gentleman we're talking about is Justin Ascham Raleigh; he's from the Nottingham Raleighs. Apparently, his neighbor heard sounds coming from his room, and thought there was some kind of fight or struggle going on. He alerted the lodgekeepers. They opened the room up and found him, or at least a body."

"Suspicious circumstances?"

"Very definitely yes."

We drove into the center of Oxford. Half past midnight was hardly late by the city's standards. There were students thronging the tree-lined streets, just starting to leave the cafes and taverns. Boisterous, yes; I could remember my own time here as a student, first studying science, then later law. They shouted as they made their way back to their residences and colleges; quoting obscure verse, drinking from the neck of bottles, throwing books and bags about . . . one group was even having a scrum down, slithering about on the icy pavement. Police and lodgekeepers looked on benignly at such activity, for it never gets any worse than this.

Francis slowed the car to a mere crawl as a bunch of revelers ran across the road ahead. One young man mooned us before rushing off to merge with his laughing friends. Many of them were girls, about half of whom were visibly pregnant.

"Thinks we're the civic authorities, no doubt," Francis muttered around a small smile. "I could show him a thing or two about misbehaving."

We drew up outside the main entrance to Dunbar College. I hadn't been inside for well over a decade, and had few memories of the place. It was a six-story building of pale yellow stone, with great mullioned windows overlooking the broad boulevard. Snow had been cleared from the road and piled up in big mounds on either side of the archway which led into the quad. A police constable and a junior lodgekeeper were waiting for us in the lodgekeeper's office just inside the entranceway, keeping warm by the iron barrel stove. They greeted us briskly, and led us inside.

Students were milling uneasily in the long corridors, dressed in pajamas, or wrapped in blankets to protect themselves from the cool air. They knew something was wrong, but not what. Lodgekeepers dressed in black suits patrolled the passages and cloisters, urging patience and restraint. Everyone fell silent as we strode past.

We went up two flights of spiraling stone stairs, and along another corridor. The chief lodgekeeper was standing outside a sturdy wooden door, no different to the twenty other lodgings on that floor. His ancient creased face registered the most profound sadness. He nodded as the constable announced who we were, and ushered us inside.

Justin Ascham Raleigh's accommodation was typical of a final year student—three private rooms: bedroom, parlor and study. They had high ceilings, wood paneled walls dark with age, long once-grand curtains hanging across the windows. All the interconnecting doors had been opened, allowing us to see the corner of a bed at the far end of the little suite. A fire had been lit in the small iron grate of the study, its embers still glowing, holding off the night's chill air.

Quite a little group of people were waiting for us. I glanced at them quickly: three student-types, two young men and a girl, obviously very distressed; and an older man in a jade-green police uniform, with the five gold stars of a senior detective. He introduced himself as Gareth Alan Pitchford, his tone somber and quiet. "And I've heard of you, sir. Your reputation is well established in this city."

"Why thank you," Francis said graciously. "This is my deputy, Edward Bucahanan Raleigh."

Gareth Alan Pitchford bestowed a polite smile, as courteous as the situation required, but not really interested. I bore it stoically.

"So what have we got here?" Francis asked.

Detective Pitchford led us into the study. Shelving filled with a mixture of academic reference books and classic fiction covered two walls. I was drawn to the wonderfully detailed star charts which hung upon the other walls, alternating with large photographs of extravagant astronomical objects. A bulky electrically powered typewriter took pride of place on a broad oak desk, surrounded by a litter of paper and open scientific journals. An ordinary metal and leather office chair with castors stood behind the desk, a gray sports jacket hanging on its back.

The body was crumpled in a corner, covered with a navy-blue nylon sheet. A considerable quantity of blood had soaked into the threadbare Turkish carpet. It started with a big splash in the middle of the room, laying a trail of splotches to the stain around the corpse.

"This isn't pretty," the detective warned as he turned down the sheet.

I freely admit no exercise in self control could prevent me from wincing at what I saw that moment. Revulsion gripped me, making my head turn away. A knife was sticking out of Justin Ascham Raleigh's right eye; it was buried almost up to the hilt.

The detective continued to pull the sheet away. I forced myself to resume my examination. There was a deep cut across Justin Ascham Raleigh's abdomen, and his ripped shirt was stained scarlet. "You can see that the attacker went for the belly first," the detective said. "That was a disabling blow, which must have taken place about here." He pointed to the glistening splash of blood in the middle of the study. "I'm assuming Mr. Raleigh would have staggered back into this corner and fallen."

"At which point he was finished off," Francis said matter-of-factly. "I would have thought he was dying anyway from the amount of blood lost from the first wound, but his assailant was obviously very determined he should die."

"That's my belief," the detective said.

Francis gave me an inquiring look.

"I agree," I stuttered.

Francis gestured weakly, his face flush with distaste. The sheet was pulled back up. Without any spoken agreement, the three of us moved away from the corpse to cluster in the doorway leading to the parlor.

"Can we have the full sequence of events, please?" Francis asked.

"We don't have much yet," the detective said. "Mr. Raleigh and five of his friends had supper together at the Orange Grove restaurant earlier this evening. It lasted from half past seven to about ten o'clock, at which point they left and separated. Mr. Raleigh came back here to Dunbar by himself around twenty past ten—the lodgekeepers confirm that. Then at approximately half past eleven, his neighbor heard an altercation, then a scream. He telephoned down to the lodgekeeper's office."

I looked from the body to the door which led back out into the corridor. "Was no one seen or heard to leave?"

"Apparently not, sir," the detective said. "The neighbor came straight out into the corridor and waited for the lodgekeepers. He didn't come in here himself, but he swears no one came out while he was watching."

"There would be a short interval," I said. "After the scream he'd spend some time calling the lodgekeepers—a minute or so."

"People must have been using the corridor at that time," the detective said. "And our murderer would have some blood on their clothes. He'd be running too."

"And looking panicked, I'll warrant," Francis said. "Someone would have seen them and remembered."

"Unless it was the neighbor himself who is the killer," I observed.

"Hey!" one of the students barked. "Don't talk about me as if I'm a piece of furniture. I called the lodgekeepers as soon as I heard the scream. I didn't bloody well kill Justin. I *liked* him. He was a top chap."

"Peter Samuel Griffith," the detective said. "Mr. Raleigh's neighbor."

"I do apologize," Francis said smoothly. "My colleague and I were simply eliminating possibilities. This has left all of us rather flustered, I'm afraid."

Peter Samuel Griffith grunted in acknowledgment.

I looked straight at the detective. "So if the murderer didn't leave by the front door . . ."

Francis and I pulled the curtains back. Justin Ascham Raleigh's rooms looked inward over the quad. They were in a corner, where little light ventured from the illuminated pathway crossing the snow-cloaked lawn. Mindful of possible evidence, I opened my case and took out a pair of tight-fitting rubber gloves. The latch on the window was open. When I gave the iron frame a tentative push it swung out easily. We poked our heads out like a pair of curious children at a fairground attraction. The wall directly outside was covered with wisteria creeper, its ancient gnarled branches twisted together underneath a thick layer of white ice crystals; it extended upwards for at least another two floors.

"As good as any ladder," Francis said quietly. "And I'll warrant there's at least a dozen routes in and out of Dunbar that avoid the lodgekeepers."

The detective took a look at the ancient creeper encircling the window. "I've heard that the gentlemen of Dunbar College do have several methods of allowing their lady friends to visit their rooms after the gates are locked."

"And as the gates weren't locked at the time of the murder, no one would have been using those alternative routes. The murderer would have got out cleanly," Francis said.

"If we're right, then this was a well planned crime," I said. If anything, that made it worse.

Francis locked his fingers together, as if wringing his hands.

He glanced back at the sheet-covered corpse. "And yet, the nature of the attack speaks more of a *crime passionelle* than of some cold plot. I wonder." He gazed back at the students. "Mr. Griffith we now know of. How do the rest of these bedraggled souls come to be here, Detective Pitchford?"

"They're Mr. Raleigh's closest friends. I believe Mr. Griffith phoned one as soon as he'd called the lodgekeeper."

"That was me," the other young man said. He had his arm thrown protectively round the girl, who was sobbing wretchedly.

"And you are?" Francis asked.

"Carter Osborne Kenyon. I was a good friend of Justin's; we had dinner together tonight."

"I see. And so you phoned the young lady here?"

"Yes. This is Bethany Maria Caesar, Justin's girlfriend. I knew she'd be concerned about him, of course."

"Naturally. So do any of you recall threats being made against Mr. Raleigh? Does he have an equivalent group of enemies, perhaps?"

"Nobody's ever threatened Justin. That's preposterous. And what's this to you, anyway? The police should be asking these questions."

The change in Francis's attitude was small but immediate, still calm but no longer so tolerant. And it showed. Even Carter Osborne Kenyon realized he'd made a big gaffe. It was the kind of switch that I knew I would have to perfect for myself if I ever hoped to advance through the family hierarchy.

"I am the Raleigh family's senior representative in Oxford," Francis said lightly. "While that might seem like an enviable sinecure from your perspective, I can assure you it's not all lunches and cocktail parties with my fellow fat old men doing deals that make sure the young work harder. I am here to observe the official investigation, and make available any resource our family might have that will enable the police to catch the murderer. But first, in order to offer that assistance I have to understand what happened, because we will never let this rest until that barbarian is brought to justice. And I promise that if it was you under that sheet, your family would have been equally swift in dispatching a representative. It's the way the world works, and you're old enough and educated enough to know that."

"Yeah, right," Carter Osborne Kenyon said sullenly.

"You will catch them, won't you?" Bethany Maria Caesar asked urgently.

Francis became the perfect gentleman again. "Of course we will, my dear. If anything in this world is a certainty, it's that. I will never rest until this is solved."

"Nor me," I assured her.

She gave both of us a small smile. A pretty girl, even through her tears and streaked make up; tall and lean, with blonde hair falling just below her shoulders. Justin had been a lucky man. I could well imagine them hand in hand walking along some riverbank on a summer's eve. It made me even more angry that so much *decency* had been lost to so many young lives by this vile act.

"Thank you," she whispered. "I really loved him. We've

been talking about a long term marriage after we left Oxford. I can't believe this . . . *any* of this."

Carter Osborne Kenyon hugged her tighter.

I made an effort to focus on the task in hand. "We'd like samples of every specimen the forensic team collects from here, fibers, hair, whatever," I told the detective. The basic procedures which had been reiterated time and again during my investigator courses at the family institute. Other strategies were invoked by what I saw. I lowered my voice, turning slightly away from the students so I could speak my mind freely, and spare them any further distress at this time. "And it might be a good idea to take blood samples from people in the immediate vicinity as well as any suspects you might determine. They should all be tested for alcohol or narcotics. Whoever did this was way off balance."

"Yes, sir," the detective said. "My team's already on its way. They know what they're doing."

"That's fine," Francis said. His look rebuked me. "If we could also sit in on the interviews, please."

"Certainly."

The Oxford City police station was less than a mile from Dunbar College. When Francis and I reached it at one o'clock there were few officers on duty. That changed over the next hour as Gareth Alan Pitchford assembled his investigator team with impressive competence. Officers and constables began to arrive, dressed in mussed uniforms, bleary-eyed, switching on the central heating in unused offices, calling down to stores for equipment. A couple of canteen staff came in and started brewing tea and coffee.

The building's Major Crime Operations Center swung

into action as Gareth Alan Pitchford made near continuous briefings to each new batch of his recruits. Secretaries began *clacking* away on typewriters; detectives pinned large scale maps of Oxford on the wall; names were hurriedly chalked up on the blackboard, a confusing trail of lines linking them in various ways; and telephones built to a perpetual chorus of whistles.

People were brought in and asked to wait in holding rooms. The chief suspects, though no one was impolite enough to say it to their faces. Gareth Alan Pitchford soon had over thirty young men and women worrying away in isolation.

"I've divided them into two categories," he told the Operations Center. "Dunbar students sharing the same accommodation wing; physically close enough to have killed Raleigh, but for whom there is no known motive, just opportunity. And a batch of his closest friends. We're still waiting for the last one of them to arrive, but I gather the uniform division has not located him. First off, I want the doctor to collect blood samples from all of them before the interviews start; if this is a drug or alcohol induced crime we'll need to be quick to catch the evidence."

Standing discreetly at the back of the room, I watched the rest of the officers acknowledge this. It was as though they were willing that to be the solution. Like me, they didn't want a world where one normal, unaffected person could do this to another.

"Wrong approach," Francis muttered quietly to me.

"In what way?" I muttered back.

"This slaying was planned; methodically and cleverly. Drugs or alcohol implies spur of the moment madness. An irrational act to which there would have been witnesses. You mark my words—there won't be a fingerprint on either the knife or the window."

"You may be right."

"When Pitchford starts the interviews, I want us to attend those with Justin's friends. Do I need to tell you why?"

"No." It was at times like this I both appreciated and resented the old man's testing. It was an oblique compliment that he thought I had the potential to succeed him eventually; but it was irritating in equal proportion that I was treated as the office junior. "Whoever did this had to know Justin, which means the friends are the only genuine suspects."

"Glad to see all those expensive courses we sent you on haven't been totally wasted," Francis said. I heard a reluctant note of approval in his voice. "The only other suspect I can think of is a Short. They don't value life as much as we do."

I kept my face composed even though I could not help but regard him as an old bigot at heart. Blaming the Shorts for everything from poor harvests to a tire puncture was a prejudice harking back to the start of the Second Imperial Era, when the roots of today's families were grown amid the Sport Of Emperors. Our march through history, it would seem, isn't entirely noble.

The interview room was illuminated by a pair of hundred-watt bulbs in white ceramic shades. A stark light in a small box of a room. Glazed amber tiles decorated the lower half of the walls, adding to the chill atmosphere. The only door was a sturdy metal affair with a slatted grate halfway up.

Peter Samuel Griffith sat behind the table in a wooden chair, visibly discomforted by the surroundings. He was holding a small sterile gauze patch to the needle puncture in his arm where the police doctor had taken a sample of his blood. I used my pencil to make a swift note reminding myself to collect such samples for our family institute to review.

Detective Gareth Alan Pitchford and a female stenographer sat opposite Mr. Griffith while Francis and myself stood beside the door, trying to appear inconspicuous.

"The first thing which concerns me, obviously, is the timing of events," the detective said. "Why don't you run through them again for me, please?"

"You've heard it all before," Peter Samuel Griffith said. "I was working on an essay when I heard what sounded like an argument next door."

"In what way? Was there shouting, anything knocked about?"

"No. Just voices. They were muffled, but whoever was in there with Justin was disagreeing with him. You can tell, you know."

"Did you recognize the other voice?"

"No. I didn't really hear it. Whoever they were, they spoke pretty quietly. It was Justin who was doing the yelling. Then he screamed. That was about half past eleven. I phoned the lodgekeepers."

"Immediately?"

"More or less, yes."

"Ah, now you see, Peter, that's my problem. I'm investigating a murder, for which I need hard facts; and you're giving me *more or less*. Did you phone them immediately? It's not a crime that you didn't. You've done the right thing, but I must have the correct details."

"Well, yeah . . . I waited a bit. Just to hear if anything else happened. That scream was pretty severe. When I couldn't hear anything else, I got really worried and phoned down."

"Thank you, Peter. So how long do you think you waited?"

"Probably a minute, or so. I . . . I didn't know what to do at first; phoning the lodgekeepers seemed a bit drastic. I mean, it could just have been a bit of horsing around that had gone wrong. Justin wouldn't have wanted to land a chum in any trouble. He was a solid kind of chap, you know."

"I'm sure he was. So that would have been about, when . . . ?"

"Eleven thirty-two. I know it was. I looked at the clock while I was calling the lodgekeepers."

"Then you phoned Mr. Kenyon straight away?"

"Absolutely. I did have to make two calls, though. He wasn't at his college, his roommate gave me a number. Couldn't have taken more than thirty seconds to get hold of him."

"What did you tell him?"

"Just that there was some sort of trouble in Justin's room, and the lodgekeepers were coming. Justin and Carter are good friends, *best* friends. I thought he'd want to know what was going on. I'd realized by then that it was serious."

"Most commendable. So after you'd made the phone call to Mr. Kenyon you went out into the corridor and waited, is that right?"

"Yes."

"How long would you say it was between the scream and the lodgekeepers arriving?"

"Probably three or four minutes. I'm not sure exactly, they arrived pretty quick once I got out into the corridor."

The detective turned round to myself and Francis. "Anything you want to ask?"

"No, thank you," Francis said before I could answer.

I have to say it annoyed me. The detective had missed points—like had there been previous arguments, how was he sure it was Justin who screamed, was there anything valuable in the room, which other students had been using the corridor and could confirm his whole story? I kept my silence, assuming Francis had good reason.

Next in was Carter Osborne Kenyon, who was clearly suffering from some kind of delayed shock. The police provided him with a mug of tea, which he clamped his hands around for warmth, or comfort. I never saw him drink any of it at any time during the interview.

His tale started with the dinner at the Orange Grove that evening, where Justin's other closest friends had gathered: Antony Caesar Pitt, Christine Jayne Lockett, and Alexander Stephan Maloney. "We did a lot of things together," Carter said. "Trips to the opera, restaurants, theater, games . . . we even had a couple of holidays in France in the summer—hired a villa in the South. We had good times." He screwed his eyes shut, almost in tears. "Dear Mary!"

"So you'd known each other as a group for some time?" Gareth Alan Pitchford asked.

"Yes. You know how friendships are in college; people cluster together around interests, and class too, I suppose. Our families tend to have status. The six of us were a solid group, have been for a couple of years."

"Isn't that a bit awkward?"

"What do you mean?"

"Two girls, four men."

Carter gave a bitter laugh. "We don't have formal membership to the exclusion of everyone else. Girlfriends and boyfriends come and go, as do other friends and acquaintances; the six of us were a core if you like. Some nights there could be over twenty of us going out together."

"So you'd known Justin for some time; if he could confide in anyone it would be you or one of the others?"

"Yeah."

"And there was no hint given, to any of you, that he might have been in trouble with somebody, or had a quarrel?"

"No, none."

"What about amongst yourselves—there must have been some disagreements?"

"Well, yes." Carter gave his tea a sullen glare, not meeting the detective's look. "But nothing to kill for. It was stupid stuff . . . who liked what play and why, books, family politics, restaurant bills, sports results, philosophy, science—we chewed it all over; that's the kind of thing which keeps every group alive and interesting."

"Name the worst disagreement Justin was currently involved in."

"Bloody hell!"

"Was it with you?"

"No!"

"Who then?"

Carter's hands tightened round the mug, his knuckles whitening. "Look, it's nothing really. It's always happening."

"What is?"

"Okay, you didn't hear this from me, but Antony likes to gamble. I mean, we all do occasionally—a day at the races, or an evening at a casino—just harmless fun, no big money involved. But with Antony, it's getting to be a problem. He plays cards with Justin. He's been losing quite heavily recently. Justin said it served him right, that Antony should pay more attention to statistics. He was a legal student, he should know better, that there is no such thing as chance."

"How much money?"

Carter shrugged. "I've no idea. You'll have to ask Antony. But listen, Antony isn't about to kill for it. I know Justin, he'd never allow it to get that far out of control."

"Fair enough," the detective said. "Do you know if Justin had anything worth stealing?"

"Something valuable?" Carter appeared quite perplexed by the idea. "No. We're all students. We're all broke. Oh, don't get me wrong, our families support us here; the allowance is adequate for the kind of life we pursue, but nothing more. Ask Antony," he added sourly.

"I wasn't thinking in terms of cash, possibly an heirloom he kept in his room?"

"Nothing that I ever saw, and I've been in there a thousand times. I promise you, we're here only for our minds. Thoughts are our wealth. Which admittedly made Justin the richest of us all—his mind was absolutely chocka with innovative concepts. But nothing a thief could bung in his swag bag." He pantomimed a catching thought, his beefy hands flapping round his head.

"I thought Justin was an astrophysicist," Francis said.

"He was."

"So what ideas could he have that were valuable?"

"Dear Mary." Carter shot Francis a pitying look. "Not industrial ideas, machinery and trinkets for your factories. Original thoughts. Pure science, that was his playground. He was hinting that he'd come up with one fairly radical notion. His guaranteed professorship, he called it."

"Which was?"

"I haven't a clue. He never really explained any of his projects to us. Justin could be very conservative, in both senses. The only thing I know is, it involved spectrography . . . you know, picking out the signature of specific elements by their emission spectrum. He was running through a collection of photographs from the observatory archives. I could help him a little with that—spectrography is simple physics. We were speculating on how to improve the process, speed it up with automation, some kind of electromechanical contraption. But we never got past a few talks in the bar."

"Did he write any of this project down?" the detective asked. "Keep notes, a file?"

"Not as far as I know. As I said, a fanciful speculation in its early stages. Talk to any science stream student and you'll get something similar; we all have our pet theories that will rock the universe if they're proven."

"I see." The detective dabbed the tip of his pencil on his lips. "How long had Mr. Raleigh and Miss Caesar been an item?"

"Oh, for at least a year. 'Bout time too, they'd been flirting ever since I met them. Bit of a relief when they finally got it together, know what I mean? And they were so well suited. It often helps when you're friends for a while first. And they're both bright sparks." He smiled ruefully. "There. If you want a qualifier for our group, I suppose that's it. We're all top of the league in what we do. Except for dear old Chris, of course. But she's still got the intellect. Gives as good as she gets every time."

Gareth Alan Pitchford rifled through his notes. That'll be Christine Jayne Lockett?"

"Yeah. She's our token artist. The rest of us are science stream, apart from Antony; he's law. Chris dropped out of the formal route after she got pregnant. Loves life in the garret. Thinks it's romantic. Her family don't share the opinion, but she gets by."

"What is your field of study? Francis asked.

Carter glanced up, surprised, as if he'd forgotten the two of us were there. "Nuclear engineering. And a hell of a field it is, too. Do you know the Madison team in Germany is only a few years from building a working atomic reactor? Once that happens and we build commercial reactors to generate electricity, the world will never burn another lump of coal ever again. Isn't that fantastic! It's the science of the future." He stopped, apparently in pain. "That's what Justin and I always argued about. Damn!"

"Justin disagreed with you about atomic power? I thought he was an astrophysicist."

"He was. That's why he disagreed. Damn silly stargazer. He kept insisting that fusion was the way forward, not fission. That one day we'd simply tap the sun's power directly. What a beautiful dream. But that was Justin for you. Always went for the high concept."

"Can you tell me roughly what time you got the phone call from Mr. Griffin telling you something was wrong?" the detective asked.

"That's easy enough. It was just after half past eleven."

"I see. And where were you?"

Carter's face reddened slightly. "I was with Chris in her studio. We went back there together after the meal."

"I see. Was that usual?"

"Sometimes I'd go there, yeah. Nothing unusual about it."

"What exactly is your relationship with Miss Lockett? Her number was the first which your roommate gave to Mr. Griffith."

"We have a thing. It's casual. Not serious at all. Is this relevant?"

"Only in that it gives you and her a definite location at the time of the murder."

"Location . . ." His eyes widened. "You mean an alibi."

"Yes. Providing Miss Lockett confirms it."

"Bloody hell, you're serious, aren't you?"

"Absolutely. So tell me what you did after receiving the phone call from Mr. Griffith."

"I went straight to Dunbar. Hailed a cab. It took about twenty minutes. They'd found the body by that time of course. I think you were there yourself by then."

"I probably was."

"You said you went straight to Dunbar College from Miss Lockett's studio," I said. "When did you call Miss Caesar?"

"As soon as I got to Dunbar. The police were everywhere, so I knew it was a real mess. I used Peter's phone before I went into Justin's room."

"Where was she?"

"At her room in Uffers . . . Uffington College."

"And she arrived straight away?" Gareth Alan Pitchford asked.

"You know she did. You were the one who let us in to Justin's rooms, remember? Uffers is only just down the road from Dunbar, it's less than four minutes' walk away. I expect she ran."

"Okay." The detective closed his notebook. "Thank you

very much. We'll need to talk to you again, of course. I'll have a car run you home."

"I'll stay, thanks. I want to be with the others when you've finished interviewing them."

"Of course."

It was Antony Caesar Pitt who followed Carter into the interview room. By that time it was close to three o'clock in the morning. A Caesar family representative came in with him; Neill Heller Caesar. Younger than Francis, dressed in a very expensive gray business suit. There was no way of telling what an inconsiderate hour it was from his deportment; he was shaved, wide awake, and friendly with the police. I envied that ability to insinuate himself into the situation as if his presence was an essential component of the investigation. Another goal to aim for. People like us have to be as smooth as a beach stone.

The world calls us representatives, but negotiators would be more accurate. We're the deal makers, the oil in the cogs of the Roman Congress. Families, that is the big ones like mine who originated from the Sport of Emperors, can hardly venture into physical conflict when we have a dispute amongst ourselves. Violence is going the same way as Shorts, bred out of our existence. Instead, you have us.

Families have their own internal codes of behavior and conduct, while the Roman Congress provides a framework for overall government. So when two families collide over anything—a new invention, access to fresh resources—people like Francis and Neill Heller Caesar sit down together and thrash out an agreement about distribution and equal rights. Two hundred years ago, when the Americas were opened up, the major disputes were over what territories each family should have to settle, which is when our profession matured. These days, the big quarrels mostly concerns economic matters—inevitable given the way the whole world is hurtling headfirst into scientific industrialization.

But representation of family interests also goes right down to a personal individual level. To put it in First Era crudity, we were there that night to make damn sure the police caught whoever killed one of us. While Neill Heller Caesar was there to ensure his family members weren't pressured into confessing. Unless of course they were guilty. For all our differences, no family would tolerate or cover up for a murderer.

Neill Heller Caesar shook hands with both of us, giving me an equal amount of respect. As flattery went, I have to admit he scored a partial success.

"Hope you don't mind my sitting in," he said pleasantly. "There are two of our flock involved so far. Best to make sure they conduct themselves correctly now. Could save a lot of time later on. I'm sure everyone wants this appalling incident cleared up as soon as possible. My condolences, by the way."

"Thank you," Francis said. "I'm most gratified that you're here. The more people working on this investigation, the faster it will be solved. Hope you can manage the crowding. I don't believe this room was built with such a large audience in mind."

"Not a problem." Neill Heller Caesar sat down next to Antony, giving the young man a reassuring smile. Antony needed the gesture. He had obviously had quite a night; his tie was unknotted, hanging around his collar, his jacket was crumpled, and there were several stains on the fabric. Apart from that he came over as perfectly average, a short man with broad shoulders, who kept himself fit and healthy.

"You had dinner with Mr. Raleigh and your other friends this evening?" Gareth Alan Pitchford asked.

"That's right." Antony Caesar Pitt's voice was strained, attempting defiant contempt. He couldn't quite pull it off, lacking the internal confidence to make it real. He searched round his jacket pockets and pulled out a silver cigar case. Selecting one of the slim cigars and lighting it was another attempt at conveying calm nerves. He took a deep drag.

"I understand the dinner finished around ten o'clock. Where did you go after that?"

"To some friends."

"And they are . . . ?"

"I'd rather not say, actually."

The detective smiled thinly. "I'd rather you did."

Neill Heller Caesar put a friendly hand on Antony's leg. "Go ahead." It was an order more forceful than any the detective could ever make.

Antony exhaled a thick streamer of smoke. "It's a club I go to occasionally. The Westhay."

"On Norfolk Street?"

"Yes."

"Why were you there?"

"It's a club. Why does anyone go to a club?"

"For a dance and a pleasant evening, usually. But this is different. People go to the Westhay, Mr. Caesar, because there's an unlicensed card game there most evenings. I understand you're a gambling man."

"I enjoy a flutter. Who doesn't? It's not as if having a game with friends is a major crime."

"This is not the vice division; I don't care about your personal shortcomings, I'm investigating the murder of your friend. How long were you there?"

Antony chewed the cigar end. "I finished just after one. They wiped me out, and believe me you don't ask for credit at the Westhay. It's strictly cash only. I walked back to my college and your constables were waiting for me. But look, even if I give you the names of the guys I was playing with it won't do you any good. I only know first names, and they're not going to admit even being there."

"That's not your concern right now, Mr. Pitt. I gather you and Mr. Raleigh played cards on a regular basis."

"For Mary's sake! I wouldn't kill Justin over a couple of hundred pounds."

"The detective spread his hands wide. "Did I say you would?"

"You implied it."

"I'm sorry if that's the impression you received. Do you know of anyone who had any kind of dispute with Mr. Raleigh?"

"No. Nobody. Justin was genuinely a great guy."

The detective leaned back in his chair. "So everyone tells us. Thank you, Mr. Pitt. We will probably need to ask you more questions at some other time. Please don't leave the city."

"Sure." Antony Caesar Pitt straightened his jacket as he got up, and gave Neill Heller Caesar a mildly annoyed glance.

One of the station's secretaries came in as Antony left. She handed a clipboard to Gareth Alan Pitchford. His expression of dismay deepened as he flicked through the three flimsy sheets of paper which it held.

"Bad news?" Francis inquired.

"It's the preliminary forensic report."

"Indeed. Were there any fingerprints on the knife?"

"No. Nor were there any on the window latch. The site team is now dusting all three rooms. They'll catalog each print they find."

"And work through a process of elimination," Francis said. "The only trouble with that is, the prints belonging to all Justin's friends will quite legitimately be found in there."

"That's somewhat premature, isn't it?" Neill Heller Caesar said. "You've no idea how many unknown prints they'll find at this stage."

"You're right, of course."

I could tell how troubled Francis was. I don't know why. He must have been expecting negatives like that in the report: I certainly was.

"You have a problem with it?" Neill Heller Caesar asked him.

"No. Not with the report. It's the way Justin's friends are all saying the same thing: he had no enemies. Indeed, why should he? A young man at university, what could he have possibly done to antagonize someone so?"

"Obviously something."

"But it's so out of character. Somebody must have noticed the reason."

"Perhaps they did, and simply aren't aware of it."

Francis nodded reluctantly. "Maybe." He gave the detective a glance. "Shall we continue."

Interestingly from my point of view, Neill Heller Caesar elected to stay in the interview room. Maloney didn't have any family representative sit in with him. Not that the Maloneys lacked influence; he could have had one there with the proverbial click of a finger. It made me wonder who had made the call to Neill. I scribbled a note to ask the police later. It could be guilt, or more likely, anxiety.

Alexander Stephan Maloney was by far the most nervous of the interviewees we'd seen. I didn't consider it to be entirely due to his friend being murdered. Something else was bothering him. The fact that *anything* could distract him at such a time I found highly significant. The reason became apparent soon enough. He had a very shaky alibi, claiming he was working alone in one of the laboratories in the Leighfield chemistry block.

"Number eighteen," he said. "That's on the second floor."

"And nobody saw you there?" Gareth Alan Pitchford asked, a strong note of skepticism in his voice.

"It was quarter to eleven at night. Nobody else is running long-duration experiments in there right now. I was alone."

"What time did you get back to your rooms?"

"About midnight. The college lodgekeepers can confirm that for you."

"I'm sure they will. How did you get back from the laboratory to the college?"

"I walked. I always do unless the weather is really foul. It gives me the opportunity to think."

And you saw no one while you were walking?"

"Of course I saw people. But I don't know who any of them were. Strangers on a street going home to bed. Look, you can ask my professor about this. He might be able to confirm I was there when I said I was."

"How so?"

"We're running a series of carbon accumulators, they have to be adjusted in a very specific way, and we built that equipment ourselves. There are only five people in the world who'd know what to do. If he looks at it in the morning he'll see the adjustments were made."

"I'd better have a word with him, then, hadn't I?" the detective said. He scrawled a short note on his pad. "I've asked all your friends this question, and got the same answer each time. Do you know if Justin had any enemies?"

"He didn't. Not one."

There was silence in the interview room after he left. All of us were reflecting on his blatant nerves, and his non-existent alibi. I kept thinking it was too obvious for him to have done it. Of course not all the suspects would have alibis: they didn't part after their dinner believing they'd need one. Ask me what I was doing every night this past week, and I'd be hard pressed to find witnesses.

Christine Jayne Lockett bustled into the interview room. I say bustled because she had the fussy motions that put me in mind of some formidable maiden aunt. When she came into a room everyone knew it. When she spoke, she had the tone and volume which forced everyone to listen. She was also quite attractive, keeping her long hair in a high style. Older than the others, in her mid twenties, which gave her a certain *air.* Her lips always came to rest in a cheerful grin. Even now, in these circumstances, she hadn't completely lost her bonhomie.

"And it started out as such a beautiful day," she said wistfully as she settled herself in the chair. Several necklaces chinked and clattered at the motion, gold pagan charms and crucifixes jostling against each other. She put a small poetry book on the table. "Do you have any idea who did it, yet?"

"Not as such," Gareth Alan Pitchford said.

"So you have to ask me if I do. Well I'm afraid I have no idea. This whole thing is so incredible. Who on earth would want to kill poor Justin? He was a wonderful man, simply wonderful. All of my friends are. That's why I love them, despite their faults. Or perhaps because of them."

"Faults?"

"They're young. They're shallow. They have too many opinions. They're easily hurt. Who could resist the company of such angels?"

"Tell me about Justin. What faults did he have?"

"Hubris, of course. He always thought he was right. I think that's why dear Bethany loved him so much. That First Era saying: 'differences unite.' Not true. She's a strong-willed girl as well. How could a strong person ever be attracted to a weak one—tell me that. They were so lucky to have found each other. Nobody else could win her heart, not for lack of trying you understand."

"Really?" Gareth Alan Pitchford couldn't shade the interest in his voice. "She had admirers?"

"You've seen her. She's gorgeous. A young woman of beauty, complemented by a fiercely sharp mind. Of course she had admirers, by the herd."

"Do you have names?"

"Men would ask to buy her a drink every time we went into a tavern. But if you mean persistent ones, ones that she knew . . . Alexander and Carter were both jealous of Justin. They'd both asked her out before she and Justin became lovers. It always surprised me that they managed to remain friends. A man's ego is such a weak appendage, don't you think."

"I'm sure. Did this jealousy last? Were either of them still pursuing her?"

"Not actively. We were all friends, in the end. And nothing I saw, no wistful gazes, or pangs of lust, would cause this. I do know my friends, Detective Pitchford, and they are not capable of murder. Not like this."

"Who is, then?"

"I have no idea. Somebody from the First Imperial Era? One might still be alive."

"If so, I've not heard of them, but I'll inquire. Do you know if Justin had antagonized anyone? Not necessarily recently," he added, "but at any time since you knew him."

"His self-confidence put a lot of people off. But then all of us have that quality. It's not a characteristic which drives someone to murder."

"Mr. Kenyon claims he was with you after the dinner at the Orange Grove. Is this true?"

"Perfectly true. We went back to my apartment. It was after ten, and baby-sitters are devilishly expensive in this city."

"The baby-sitter can confirm this?"

"Your officers already took her statement. We arrived back at about quarter past ten."

"And after that? You were together for the rest of the night?"

"Right up until Carter got the phone call, yes. We drank some wine, I showed him my latest piece. We talked. Not for long, mind you. We hadn't even got to bed before he dashed off." Her fingers stroked at the book's leather cover. "What a dreadful, dreadful day."

Gareth Alan Pitchford glanced round at all of us after Christine left, his expression troubled. It was as if he was seeking our permission for the interview we all knew couldn't be avoided. Neill Heller Caesar finally inclined his head a degree.

Bethany Maria Caesar had regained some composure

since I saw her in Justin's rooms. She was no longer crying, and her hair had been tidied up. Nothing could be done about her pallor, nor the defeated slump of her shoulders. A sorrowful sight in one so young and vibrant.

Neill Heller Caesar hurriedly offered her a chair, only just beating me to it. She gave him a meek smile and lowered herself with gentle awkwardness, as if her body weighed more than usual.

"I apologize for having to bring you in here, Miss Caesar," the detective said. "I'll be as brief as possible. We just have a few questions. Formalities."

"I understand." She smiled bravely.

"Where were you at ten thirty this evening?"

"I'd gone back to my rooms at Uffington after the meal. There was some lab work which I needed to type up."

"Lab work?"

"I'm taking biochemistry. It's a busy subject right now, so much is opening up to us. It won't be long now before we understand the genetic molecule; that's the heart of life itself. Oh. I'm sorry. I'm rambling. It just takes my thought away from . . ."

This time I was the one who chivalrously offered a glass of water. She took it gratefully, a small flustered smile touching her lips. "Thank you. I suppose I must have got to Uffers just after ten. The lodgekeepers should be able to tell you the exact time. They sign us in at night."

"Of course. Now what about Justin. You were closest to him, did you know if he was embroiled in any kind of antagonism with someone? Some wild incident? A grudge that wouldn't go away?"

"If you'd ever met Justin you wouldn't have to ask that. But no . . . he hadn't annoyed anyone. He wasn't the type;

he was quiet and loved his subject. Not that we were hermits. We went out to parties, and he played a few games for the college, but not at any level which counted. But we were going to make up for all that time apart after . . ." She tugged a handkerchief out of her sleeve and pressed it against her face. Tears leaked out of tightly closed eyes.

"I believe that's sufficient information for now," Neill Heller Caesar said, fixing the detective with a pointed gaze. Gareth Alan Pitchford nodded his acceptance, clearly glad of the excuse to end the questioning. Neill Heller Caesar put his arm round Bethany's trembling shoulders, and helped guide her from the interview room.

"Not much to go on," the detective muttered gloomily once she was outside. "I'd welcome any suggestions." He looked straight at Francis, who was staring at the closed door.

"Have patience. We simply don't have enough information yet. Though I admit to being mystified as to any possible motive there could be for ending this young man's life in such a terrifying way. We do so desperately need to uncover what it was that Justin encountered which led to this."

"I have a good team," the detective said, suddenly bullish. "You can depend on our investigation to uncover the truth."

"I don't doubt it," Francis said with a conciliatory smile. "I think my colleague and I have seen enough for tonight. Why don't we reconvene tomorrow—or rather later this morning, to review the case so far. The remaining interviews should be over by then, and forensic ought to have finished with Justin's room."

"As you wish," the detective said.

Francis said nothing further until we were safely strapped

up in his car and driving away from the station. "So, my boy, first impressions? I often find them strangely accurate. Human instinct is a powerful tool."

"The obvious one is Alexander," I said. "Which in itself would tend to exclude him. It's too obvious. Other than that, I'm not sure. None of them has any apparent motive."

"An interesting comment in itself."

"How so?"

"You—or your subconscious—haven't included anyone else on your suspect list."

"It must be someone he knows," I said, a shade defensively. "If not his immediate coterie, then someone else who was close. We can start to expand the list tomorrow."

"I'm sure we will," Francis said.

It seemed to me that his mind was away on some other great project or problem. He sounded so disinterested.

MURDER. It was the banner scored big and bold across all the street corner newspaper placards, most often garnished with adjectives such as *foul, brutal*, and *insane*. The vendors shouted the word in endless repetition, their scarves hanging loosely from their necks as if to give their throats the freedom necessary for such intemperate volume. They waved their lurid journals in the air like some flag of disaster to catch the attention of the hapless pedestrians.

Francis scowled at them all as we drove back to the police station just before lunchtime. The road seemed busier than usual, with horse-drawn carriages and carts jostling for space with cars. Since the law banning combustion engines, electric vehicles were growing larger with each new model; the newest ones were easily recognizable, with six wheels supporting long bonnets that contained ranks of heavy batteries.

"Those newspapers are utter beasts," he muttered. "Did you hear, we've had to move Justin's parents from their home so they might grieve in peace? Some reporter tried to pretend he was a relative so he could get inside for an interview. Must be a Short. What is the world degenerating into?"

When we arrived at the station it was besieged with reporters. Flashbulbs hissed and fizzled at everyone who hurried in or out of the building. Somehow Francis's angry dignity managed to clear a path through the rabble. Not that we escaped unphotographed, or unquestioned. The impertinence of some was disgraceful, shouting questions and comments at me as if I were some circus animal fit only to be provoked. I wished we could have taken our own photographs in turn, collecting their names to have them hauled before their senior editors for censure.

It was only after I got inside that I realized our family must have interests in several of the news agencies involved. Commerce had become the driving force here, overriding simple manners and decency.

We were shown directly to Gareth Alan Pitchford's office. He had the venetian blinds drawn, restricting the sunlight and, more importantly, the reporters' view inside. Neill Heller Caesar was already there. He wore the same smart suit and shirt that he'd had on for the interviews. I wondered if he'd been here the whole time, and if we'd made a tactical error by allowing him such freedom. I judged Francis was making the same calculation.

The detective bade us sit, and had one of his secretaries bring round a tray with fresh coffee.

"You saw the press pack outside," he said glumly. "I've had to assign officers to escort Justin's friends."

"I think we had better have a word," Francis said to Neill Heller Caesar. "The editors can be relied upon to exert some restraint."

Neill Heller Caesar's smile lacked optimism. "Let us hope so."

"What progress?" I inquired of the detective.

His mood sank further. "A long list of negatives, I'm afraid. I believe it's called the elimination process. Unfortunately, we're eliminating down to just about nothing. My team is currently piecing together the movements of all the students at Dunbar preceding the murder, but it's not a promising avenue of approach. There always seems to be several people in the corridor outside Mr. Raleigh's room. If anyone had come out, they would have been seen. The murderer most likely did use the window as an exit. Forensic is going over the wisteria creeper outside, but they don't believe it to be very promising."

"What about footprints in the snow directly underneath the window?"

"The students have been larking about in the quad for days. They even had a small football game during that afternoon, until the lodgekeepers broke it up. The whole area has been well trampled down."

"What about someone going into the room?" Francis asked. "Did the students see that?"

"Even more peculiar," the detective admitted. "We have no witness of anyone other than Mr. Raleigh going in."

"He was definitely seen going in, then?" I asked.

"Oh yes. He chatted to a few people in the college on his way up to his room. As far as we can determine, he went inside at about ten past ten. That was the last anyone saw him alive."

"Did he say anything significant to any of those people he talked to? Was he expecting a guest?"

"No. It was just a few simple greetings to his college mates, nothing more. Presumably the murderer was waiting for him."

"Justin would have kept those windows closed yesterday," I said. "It was freezing all day. And if the latch was down, they'd be very difficult to open from the outside, especially by anyone clinging to the creeper. I'm sure a professional criminal could have done it, but not many others."

"I concur," Francis said. "It all points to someone he knew. And knew well enough to open a window for them to get in."

"That's a very wild assumption," Neill Heller Caesar said. "Someone could simply have gone to his room hours earlier and waited for him. There would have been several opportunities during the day when there was nobody in that corridor outside. I for one refuse to believe it was in use for every second of every minute during the entire afternoon and evening."

"The method of entry isn't too relevant at this time," the detective said. "We still have absolutely no motive for the crime." I resisted giving Francis a glance. I have to say I considered the method of entry to be extremely relevant. A professional break-in opened up all sorts of avenues. As did Justin opening the window for a friend.

"Very well," Francis said levelly. "What is your next step?"

"Validating the alibis of his closest friends. Once I'm satisfied that they are all telling the truth, then we'll get them back in for more extensive interviews. They knew him best, and one of them may know something without realizing it. We need to review Mr. Raleigh's past week, then month. Six months if that's what it takes. The motive will be there somewhere. Once we have that, we have the murderer. How they got in and out ceases to be an issue."

"I thought all the alibis were secure, apart from Maloney's," Neill Heller Caesar said.

"Maloney's can probably be confirmed by his professor," the detective said. "One of my senior detectives is going out to the chemistry laboratory right away. Which leaves Antony Caesar Pitt with the alibi most difficult to confirm. I'm going to the Westhay Club myself to see if it can be corroborated."

"I'd like to come with you," I said.

"Of course."

"I'll go to the chemistry laboratory, if you don't mind," Neill Heller Caesar said.

Touché, I thought. We swapped the briefest of grins.

Unless you knew exactly where to go, you'd never be able to locate the Westhay. Norfolk Street was an older part of Oxford, with buildings no more than three or four stories. Its streetlights were still gas, rather than the sharp electric bulbs prevalent through most of the city. The shops and businesses catered for the lower end of the market, while most of the houses had been split into multiple apartments, shared by students from minor families, and young manual workers. I could see that it would be redeveloped within fifty years. The area's relative lack of wealth combined with the ever-rising urban density pressure made that outcome inevitable.

The Westhay's entrance was a wooden door set between a bicycle shop and bakery. A small plaque on the wall was the only indication it existed.

Gareth Alan Pitchford knocked loudly and persistently until a man pulled back a number of bolts and thrust an unshaven face round the side. It turned out he was the manager. His belligerence was washed away by the detective's badge, and we were reluctantly allowed inside.

The club itself was upstairs, a single large room with bare floorboards, its size decrying a grander purpose in days long gone. A line of high windows had their shutters thrown back, allowing broad beams of low winter sunlight to shine in through the grimy, cracked glass. Furniture consisted of sturdy wooden chairs and tables, devoid of embellishments like cushioning. The bar ran the length of one wall, with beer bottles stacked six deep on the mirrored shelving behind. A plethora of gaudy labels advertised brands which I'd never heard of before. In front of the bar, an old woman with a tight bun of iron-gray hair was sweeping the floor without visible enthusiasm. She gave us the most fleeting of glances when we came in, not even slowing her strokes.

The detective and the manager began a loud argument about the card game of the previous evening, whether it ever existed and who was taking part. Gareth Alan Pitchford was pressing hard for names, issuing threats of the city licensing board, and immediate arrest for the suspected withholding of information, in order to gain a degree of compliance.

I looked at the cleaning woman again, recalling one of my lectures at the investigatory course: a line about discovering all you need to know about people from what you find in their rubbish. She brushed the pile of dust she'd accrued into a tin pan, and walked out through a door at the back of the bar. I followed her, just in time to see her tip the pan into a large corrugated metal bin. She banged the lid down on top.

"Is that where all the litter goes?" I asked.

She gave me a surprised nod.

"When was it emptied last?"

"Two days ago," she grunted, clearly thinking I was mad.

I opened my attaché case, and pulled on some gloves. Fortunately the bin was only a quarter full. I rummaged round through the filthy debris it contained. It took me a while sifting through, but in among the cellophane wrappers, crumpled paper, mashed cigarettes ends, shards of broken glass, soggy beer mats, and other repellent items, I found a well-chewed cigar butt. I sniffed tentatively at it. Not that I'm an expert, but to me it smelled very similar to the one which Antony Caesar Pitt had lit in the interview room. I dabbed at it with a forefinger. The mangled brown leaves were still damp.

I dropped the cigar into one of my plastic bags, and stripped my gloves off. When I returned to the club's main room, Gareth Alan Pitchford was writing names into his notebook; while the manager wore the countenance of a badly frightened man.

"We have them," the detective said in satisfaction. He snapped his notebook shut.

I took a train down to Southampton the following day. A car was waiting for me at the station. The drive out to the Raleigh family institute took about forty minutes.

Southampton is our city, the same way Rome belongs to the Caesars, or London to the Percys. It might not sprawl on such grand scales, or boast a nucleus of Second Era architecture, but it's well-ordered and impressive in its own right. With our family wealth coming from a long tradition of seafaring and merchanteering, we have built it into the second largest commercial port in England. I could see large ships nuzzled up against the docks, their stacks churning out streamers of coal smoke as the cranes moved ponderously beside them, loading and unloading cargo. More ships were anchored offshore, awaiting cargo or refit. It had only been two years since I was last in Southampton, yet the number of big ocean-going passenger ships had visibly declined since then. Fewer settlers were being ferried over to the Americas, and even those members of families with established lands were being discouraged. I'd heard talk at the highest family councils that the overseas branches of the families were contemplating motions for greater autonomy. Their population was rising faster than Europe's, a basis to their claim for different considerations. I found it hard to believe they'd want to abandon their roots. But that was the kind of negotiation gestating behind the future's horizon, one that would doubtless draw me in if I ever attained the levels I sought.

The Raleigh institute was situated several miles beyond the city boundaries, hugging the floor of a wide rolling valley. It's the family's oldest estate in England, established right at the start of the Second Era. We were among the first families out on the edge of the Empire's hinterlands to practice the Sport of Emperors. The enormous prosperity and influence we have today can all be attributed to that early accommodation.

The institute valley is grassy parkland scattered with

trees, extending right up over the top of the valley walls. At its heart are more than two dozen beautiful ancient stately manor houses encircling a long lake, their formal gardens merging together in a quilt of subtle greens. Even in March they retained a considerable elegance, their designers laying out tree and shrub varieties in order that swathes of color straddled the land whatever the time of year.

Some of the manors have wings dating back over nine hundred years, though the intervening time has seen them accrue new structures at a bewildering rate until some have become almost like small villages huddled under a single multifaceted roof. Legend has it that when the last of the original manors was completed, at least twelve generations of Raleighs lived together in the valley. Some of the buildings are still lived in today. For indeed I grew up in one; but most have been converted to cater for the demands of the modern age, with administration and commerce becoming the newest and greediest residents. Stables and barns contain compartmentalized offices populated by secretaries, clerks, and managers. Libraries have undergone a transformation from literacy to numeracy, their leather-bound tomes of philosophy and history replaced by ledgers and records. Studies and drawing rooms have become conference rooms, while more than one chapel has become a council debating chamber. Awkley Manor itself, built in the early fourteen hundreds, has been converted into a single giant medical clinic, where the finest equipment which science and money can procure tends to the senior elders.

The car took me to the carved marble portico of Hewish Manor, which now hosted the family's industrial science research faculty. I walked up the worn stone steps, halting at the top to take a look round. The lawns ahead of me swept down to the lake, where they were fringed with tall reeds. Weeping willows stood sentry along the shore, their denuded branches a lacework of brown cracks across the white sky. As always a flock of swans glided over the black waters of the lake. The gardeners had planted a new avenue of oaks to the north of the building, running it from the lake right the way up the valley. It was the first new greenway for over a century. There were some fifty of them in the valley all told, from vigorous century-old palisades, to lines of intermittent aged trees, their corpulent trunks broken and rotting. They intersected each other in a great meandering pattern of random geometry, as if marking the roads of some imaginary city. When I was a child, my cousins and I ran and rode along those arboreal highways all summer long, playing our fantastical games and lingering over huge picnics.

My soft sigh was inevitable. More than anywhere, this was home to me, and not just because of a leisurely childhood. This place rooted us Raleighs.

The forensic department was downstairs in what used to be one of the wine vaults. The arching brick walls and ceiling had been cleaned and painted a uniform white, with utility tube lights running the length of every section. White-coated technicians sat quietly at long benches, working away on tests involving an inordinate amount of chemistry lab glassware.

Rebecca Raleigh Stothard, the family's chief forensic scientist, came out of her office to greet me. Well into her second century, and a handsome woman, her chestnut hair was only just starting to lighten towards gray. She'd delivered an extensive series of lectures during my investigatory course, and my attendance had been absolute, not entirely due to what she was saying.

I was given a demure peck on the check, then she stepped back, still holding both of my hands, and looked me up and down. "You're like a fine wine, Edward," she said teasingly. "Maturing nicely. One decade soon, I might just risk a taste."

"That much anticipation could prove fatal to a man."

"How's Myriam?"

"Fine."

Her eyes flashed with amusement, "A father again. How devilsome you are. We never had boys like you in my time!"

"Please. We're still very much in your time."

I'd forgotten how enjoyable it was to be in her company. She was so much more easygoing than dear old Francis. However, her humor faded after we sat down in her little office.

"We received the last shipment of samples from the Oxford police this morning," she said. "I've allocated our best people to analyze them."

"Thank you."

"Has there been any progress?"

"The police are doing their damnedest, but they've still got very little to go on at this point. That's why I'm hoping your laboratory can come up with something for me, something they missed."

"Don't place all your hopes on us. The Oxford police are good. We only found one additional fact that wasn't in their laboratory report."

"What's that?"

"Carter Osborne Kenyon and Christine Jayne Lockett

were imbibing a little more than wine and spirits that evening."

"Oh?"

"They both had traces of cocaine in their blood. We ran the test twice, there's no mistake."

"How much?"

"Not enough for a drug induced killing spree, if that's what you're thinking. They were simply having a decadent end to their evening. I gather she's some sort of artist?"

"Yes."

"Narcotic use is fairly common amongst the more Bohemian sects, and increasing."

"I see. Anything else?"

"Not a thing."

I put my attaché case on my knees, and flicked the locks back. "I may have something for you." I pulled the bag containing the cigar butt from its compartment. "I found this in the Westhay Club, I think it's Antony Caesar Pitt's. Is there any way you can tell me for sure?"

"Pitt's? I thought his alibi had been confirmed?"

"The police interviewed three people, including the manager of the Westhay, who all swear he was in there playing cards with them."

"And you don't believe them?"

"I've been to the Westhay, I've seen the manager and the other players. They're not the most reliable people in the world, and they were under a lot of pressure to confirm whether he was there or not. My problem is that if he was there that evening the police will thank them for their statement and their honesty and let them go. If he wasn't, there could be consequences they'd rather avoid. I know that sounds somewhat paranoid, but he really is the only one of the friends who had anything like a motive. In his case, the proof has to be absolute. I'd be betraying my responsibility if I accepted anything less."

She took the bag from me, and squinted at the remains of the cigar which it contained.

"It was still damp with saliva the following morning," I told her. "If it is his, then I'm prepared to accept he was in that club."

"I'm sorry, Edward, we have no test that can produce those sort of results. I can't even give you a blood type from a saliva sample."

"Damn!"

"Not yet, but one of my people is already confident he can determine if someone has been drinking from a chemical reaction with their breath. It should deter those wretched cab drivers from having one over the eight before they take to the roads if they know the police can prove they were drunk on the spot. Ever seen a carriage accident? It's not nice. I imagine a car crash is even worse."

"I'm being slow this morning. The relevance being?"

"You won't give up. None of us will, because Justin was a Raleigh, and he deserves to rest with the knowledge that we will not forget him, no matter how much things change. And change they surely do. Look at me, born into an age of leisured women, at least those of my breeding and status. Life was supposed to be a succession of grand balls interspersed with trips to the opera and holidays in provincial spa towns. Now I have to go out and earn my keep."

I grinned. "No you don't."

"For Mary's sake, Edward; I had seventeen fine and healthy children before my ovaries were thankfully exhausted in my late nineties. I need something else to do after all that child rearing. And, my dear, I always hated opera. This, however, I enjoy to the full. I think it still shocks mummy that I'm out here on the scientific frontier. But it does give me certain insights. Come with me."

I followed her the length of the forensic department. The end wall was hidden behind a large freestanding chamber made from a dulled metal. A single door was set in the middle, fastened with a heavy latch mechanism. As we drew closer I could hear an electrical engine thrumming incessantly. Other harmonics infiltrated the air, betraying the presence of pumps and gears.

"Our freezer," Rebecca announced with chirpy amusement.

She took a thick fur coat from a peg on the wall outside the chamber, and handed me another.

"You'll need it," she told me. "It's colder than those fridges which the big grocery stores are starting to use. A lot colder."

Rebecca told the truth. A curtain of freezing white fog tumbled out when she opened the door. The interior was given over to dozens of shelves, with every square inch covered in a skin of hard white ice. A variety of jars, bags, and sealed glass dishes were stacked up. I peered at their contents with mild curiosity before hurriedly looking away. Somehow, scientific slivers of human organs are even more repellent than the entirety of flesh.

"What is this?" I asked.

"Our family's insurance policy. Forensic pathology shares this freezer with the medical division. Every biological unknown we've encountered is in here. One day we'll have answers for all of it."

"And one day the Borgias will leave the Vatican," I said automatically.

Rebecca placed the bag on a high shelf, and gave me a confident smile. "You'll be back."

Two
Manhattan City AD 1853

It was late afternoon as the SST came in to land at Newark aerodrome. The sun was low in the sky, sending out a red gold light to soak the skyscrapers. I pressed my face to the small port, eager for the sight. The overall impression was one of newness, under such a light it appeared as though the buildings had just been erected. They were pristine, flawless.

Then we cruised in over the field's perimeter, and the low commercial buildings along the side of the runway obscured the view. I shuffled my papers into my briefcase as we taxied to the reception building. I'd spent the three-hour flight over the Atlantic re-reading all the principal reports and interviews, refreshing my memory of the case. For some reason the knowledge lessened any feeling of comfort. The memories were all too clear now: the cold night, the blood-soaked body. Francis was missing from the investigation now, dead these last five years. It was he, I freely admit, who had given me a degree of comfort in tackling the question of who had killed poor Justin Ascham Raleigh. Always the old *missi dominici* had exuded the air of conviction, the epitome of an irresistible force. It would be his calm persistence that would unmask the murderer, I'd always known and accepted that. Now the task was mine alone.

I emerged from the plane's walkway into the reception lounge. Neill Heller Caesar was waiting to greet me. His physical appearance had changed little, as I suppose had mine. Only our styles were different; the fifties had taken on the air of a colorful radical period that I wasn't altogether happy with. Neill Heller Caesar wore a white suit with flares that covered his shoes. His purple and green cheesecloth shirt had rounded collars a good five inches long. And his thick hair was waved, coming down below his shoulders. Tiny gold-rimmed amber sunglasses were perched on his nose.

He recognized me immediately, and shook my hand. "Welcome to Manhattan," he said.

"Thank you. I wish it was under different circumstances."

He prodded the sunglasses back up his nose. "For you, of course. For myself, I'm quite glad you're here. You've put one of my charges in the clear."

"Yes. And thank you for the cooperation."

"A pleasure."

We rode a limousine over one of the bridges into the city itself. I complimented him on the height of the buildings we were approaching. Manhattan was, after all, a Caesar city.

"Inevitable," he said. "The population in America's northern continent is approaching one and a half billion—and that's just the official figure. The only direction left is up."

We both instinctively looked at the limousine's sunroof.

"Speaking of which: how much longer?" I asked.

He checked his watch. "They begin their descent phase in another five hours."

The limousine pulled up outside the skyscraper which housed the Caesar family legal bureau in Manhattan. Neill Heller Caesar and I rode the lift up to the seventy-first floor. His office was on the corner of the building, its window walls giving an unparalleled view over ocean and city alike. He sat behind his desk, a marble-topped affair of a stature equal to the room as a whole, watching me as I gazed out at the panorama.

"All right," I said. "You win. I'm impressed." The sun was setting, and in reply the city lights were coming on, blazing forth from every structure.

He laughed softly. "Me too, and I've been here fifteen years now. You know they're not even building skyscrapers under a hundred floors any more. Another couple of decades and the only time you'll see the sun from the street will be a minute either side of noon."

"Europe is going the same way. Our demographics are still top weighted, so the population rise is slower. But not by much. Something is going to have to give eventually. The Church will either have to endorse contraception, or the pressure will squeeze us into abandoning our current restrictions." I shuddered. "Can you imagine what a runaway expansion and exploitation society would be like?"

"Unpleasant," he said flatly. "But you'll never get the Borgias out of the Vatican."

"So they say."

Neill Heller Caesar's phone rang. He picked it up and listened for a moment. "Antony is on his way up."

"Great."

He pressed a button on his desk, and a large wall panel

slid to one side. It revealed the largest TV screen I'd ever seen. "If you don't mind, I'd like to keep the Prometheus broadcast on," he said. "We'll mute the sound."

"Please do. Is that thing color?" Our family channel had only just begun to broadcast in the new format. I hadn't yet availed myself with a compatible receiver.

His smile was the same as any boy given a new football to play with. "Certainly is. Twenty-eight-inch diameter, too—in case you're wondering."

The screen lit up with a slightly fuzzy picture. It showed an external camera view, pointing along the fuselage of the Prometheus, where the silver gray moon hung over it. Even though it was eight years since the first manned spaceflight, I found it hard to believe how much progress the Joint Families Astronautics Agency had made. Less than five hours now, and a man would set foot on the moon!

The office door opened and Antony Caesar Pitt walked in. He had done well for himself over the intervening years, rising steadily up through his family's legal offices. Physically, he'd put on a few pounds, but it hardly showed. The biggest change was a curtain of hair, currently held back in a ponytail. There was a mild frown on his face to illustrate his disapproval at being summoned without explanation. As soon as he saw me the expression changed to puzzlement, then enlightenment.

"I remember you," he said. "You were one of the Raleigh representatives assigned to Justin's murder. Edward, isn't it?"

"That's helpful," I said.

"In what way?"

"You have a good memory. I need that right now."

He gave Neill Heller Caesar a quick glance. "I don't

believe this. You're here to ask me questions about Justin again, aren't you?"

"Yes."

"For Mary's sake! It's been twenty-one years."

"Yes, twenty-one years, and he's still just as dead."

"I appreciate that. I'd like to see someone brought to justice as much as you. But the Oxford police found nothing. Nothing! No motive, no enemy. They spent weeks trawling through every tiny little aspect of his life. And with you applying pressure they were thorough, believe me. I should know, with our gambling debt I was the prime suspect."

"Then you should be happy to hear, you're not any more. Something's changed."

He flopped down into a chair and stared at me. "What could possibly have changed?"

"It's a new forensic technique." I waved a hand at the television set. "Aeroengineering isn't the only scientific discipline to have made progress recently, you know. The families have developed something we're calling genetic fingerprinting. Any cell with your DNA in it can now be positively identified."

"Well good and fabulous. But what the hell has it got to do with me?"

"It means I personally am now convinced you were at the Westhay that night. You couldn't have murdered Justin."

"The Westhay." He murmured the name with an almost sorrowful respect. "I never went back. Not after that. I've never played cards since, never placed a bet. Hell of a way to get cured." He cocked his head to one side, looking up at me. "So what convinced you?"

"I was there at the club the following morning. I found a cigar butt in the rubbish. Last month we ran a genetic fingerprint test on the saliva residue, and cross referenced it with your blood sample. It was yours. You were there that night."

"Holy Mary! You kept a cigar butt for twenty-one years?"

"Of course. And the blood, as well. It's all stored in a cryogenic vault now along with all the other forensic samples from Justin's room. Who knows what new tests we'll develop in the future."

Antony started laughing. There was a nervous edge to it. "I'm in the clear. Shit. So how does this help you? I mean, I'm flattered that you've come all this way to tell me in person, but it doesn't change anything."

"On the contrary. Two very important factors have changed thanks to this. The number of suspects is smaller, and I can now trust what you tell me. Neill here has very kindly agreed that I can interview you again. With your permission, of course."

This time the look Antony flashed at the family representative was pure desperation. "But I don't have anything new to tell you. Everything I knew I told the police. Those interviews went on for *days*."

"I know. I spent most of last week reading through the transcripts again."

"Then you know there's nothing I can add."

"Our most fundamental problem is that we never managed to establish a motive. I believe it must originate from his personal or professional life. The murder was too proficient to have been the result of chance. You can give me the kind of access I need to Justin's life to go back and examine possible motives."

"I've given you access, all of it."

"Maybe. But everything you say now has more weight attached. I'd like you to help."

"Well sure. That's if you're certain you can trust me now. Do you want to wire me up to a polygraph as well?"

I gave Neill Heller Caesar a quick glance. "That won't be necessary."

Antony caught it. "Oh great. Just bloody wonderful. OK. Fine. Ask me what the hell you want. And for the record, I've always answered honestly."

"Thank you. I'd like to start with the personal aspect. Now, I know you were asked a hundred times if you'd seen or heard anything out of the ordinary. Possibly some way he acted out of character, right?"

"Yes. Of course. There was nothing."

"I'm sure. But what about afterwards, when the interviews were finished, when the pressure had ended. You must have kept on thinking, reviewing all those late night conversations you had over cards and a glass of wine. There must have been something he said, some trivial non sequitur, something you didn't bother going back to the police with."

Antony sank down deeper into his chair, resting a hand over his brow as weariness claimed him. "Nothing," he whispered. "There was nothing he ever said or did that was out of the ordinary. We talked about everything men talk about together, drinking, partying, girls, sex, sport; we told each other what we wanted to do when we left Oxford, all the opportunities our careers opened up for us. Justin was a template for every family student there. He was almost a stereotype, for Mary's sake. He knew what he wanted; his field was just taking off, I mean . . ." He waved at the TV screen. "Can you get anything more front line? He was going to settle down with Bethany, have ten kids, and gaze at the stars for the rest of his life. We used to joke that by the time he had his three hundredth birthday he'd probably be able to visit them, all those points of light he stared at through a telescope. There was *nothing* unusual about him. You're wasting your time with this, I wish you weren't, I really do. But it's too long ago now, even for us."

"Can't blame me for trying," I said with a smile. "We're not Shorts, for us time is always relevant, events never diminish no matter how far away you move from them."

"I'm not arguing," he said weakly.

"So what about his professional life? His astronomy?"

"He wasn't a professional, he was still a student. Every week there was something that would excite him; then he'd get disappointed, then happy again, then disappointed . . . That's why he loved it."

"We know that Justin had some kind of project or theory which he was working on. Nobody seemed to know what it was. It was too early to take it to his professor, and we couldn't find any notes relating to it. All we know is that it involved some kind of spectrography. Did he ever let slip a hint of it to you?"

"His latest one?" Antony closed his eyes to assist his recall. "Very little. I think he mentioned once he wanted to review pictures of supernovae. What for, I haven't got the faintest idea. I don't even know for certain if that was the new idea. It could have been research for anything."

"Could be," I agreed. "But it was a piece of information I wasn't aware of before. So we've accomplished something today."

"You call that an accomplishment?"

"Yes. I do."

"I'd love to know what you call building the Channel Tunnel."

My smile was pained. Our family was the major partner in that particular venture. I'd even been involved in the preliminary negotiations. "A nightmare. But we'll get there in the end."

"Just like Justin's murder?"

"Yes."

Three

Ganymede AD 1920

My journey out to Jupiter was an astonishing experience. I'd been in space before, of course, visiting various low Earth orbit stations which are operated by the family, and twice to our moonbase. But even by current standards, a voyage to a gas giant was considered special.

I took a scramjet-powered spaceplane from Gibraltar spaceport up to Vespasian in its six-hundred-mile orbit. There wasn't much of the original asteroid left now, just a ball of metal-rich rock barely half a mile across. Several mineral refineries were attached to it limpet-fashion, their fusion reactor cooling fins resembling black peacock tails. In another couple of years it would be completely mined out, and the refineries would be maneuvered to the new asteroids being eased into Earth orbit.

A flotilla of industrial and dormitory complexes drifted around Vespasian, each of them sprouting a dozen or more assembly platforms. Every family on Earth was busy constructing more micro-gravity industrial systems and long-range spacecraft. In addition to the twenty-seven moonbases, there were eight cities on Mars and five asteroid colonies; each venture bringing some unique benefit from the purely scientific to considerable financial and economic reward. Everyone was looking to expand their activities to some fresh part of the solar system, especially in the wake of the Caesar settlement claim.

Some of us, of course, were intent on going further still. I saw the clearest evidence of that as the *Kuranda* spiraled up away from Earth. We passed within eight thousand miles of what the planetbound are calling the Wanderers Cluster. Five asteroids in a fifty-thousand-mile orbit, slowly being hollowed out and fitted with habitation chambers. From Earth they appeared simply as bright stars performing a strange slow traverse of the sky. From the *Kuranda* (with the aid of an on-board video sensor) I could clearly see the huge construction zones on their surface where the fusion engines were being fabricated. If all went well, they would take two hundred years to reach Proxima Centuri. Half a lifetime cooped up inside artificial caves, but millions of people had applied to venture with them. I remained undecided if that was a reflection of healthy human dynamism, or a more subtle comment on the state of our society. Progress, if measured by the yardstick of mechanization, medicine, and electronics, seemed to be accelerating at a rate which even I found perturbing. Too many people were being made redundant as new innovations came along, or AIs supplanted them. In the past that never bothered us—after all who wants to spend four hundred years doing the same thing. But back then it was a slow transition, sliding from occupation to occupation as fancy took you. Now such migrations were becoming forced, and the timescale shorter. There were times I even wondered if my own job was becoming irrelevant.

The *Kuranda* took three months to get me to Jupiter,

powered by low-temperature ion plasma engines, producing a small but steady thrust the whole way. It was one of the first of its class, a long-duration research and explorer ship designed to take our family scientists out as far as Neptune. Two hundred yards long, including the propellant tanks and fusion reactors.

We raced round Jupiter's pale orange cloudscape, shedding delta-V as captain Harrison Dominy Raleigh aligned us on a course for Ganymede. Eight hours later when we were coasting up away from the gas giant, I was asked up to the bridge. Up is a relative term on a spaceship which wasn't accelerating, and the bridge is at the center of the life-support section. There wasn't a lot of instrumentation available to the three duty officers, just some fairly sophisticated consoles with holographic windows and an impressive array of switches. The AI actually ran *Kuranda*, while people simply monitored its performance and that of the primary systems.

Our captain, Harrison Dominy Raleigh, was floating in front of the main sensor console, his right foot Velcroed to the decking.

"Do we have a problem?" I asked.

"Not with the ship," he said. "This is strictly your area."

"Oh?" I anchored myself next to him, trying to comprehend the display graphics. It wasn't easy, but then I don't function very well in low gravity situations. Fluids of every kind migrate to my head, which in my case brings on the most awful headaches. My stomach is definitely not designed to digest floating globules of food. And you really would think that after seventy-five years of people traveling through space that someone would manage to design a decent freefall toilet. On the plus side, I'm not too nauseous during the aerial maneuvers that replace locomotion, and I am receptive to the anti-wasting drugs developed to counter calcium loss in human bones. It's a balance which I can readily accept as worthwhile in order to see Jupiter with my own eyes.

The captain pointed to a number of glowing purple spheres in the display, each one tagged by numerical icons. "The Caesars have orbited over twenty sensor satellites around Ganymede. They provide a full radar coverage out to eighty thousand miles. We're also picking up similar emissions from the other major moons here. No doubt their passive scans extend a great deal further."

"I see. The relevance being?"

"Nobody arrives at any of the moons they've claimed without them knowing about it. I'd say they're being very serious about their settlement rights."

"We never made our voyage a secret. They have our arrival time down to the same decimal place as our own AI."

"Which means the next move is ours. We arrive at Ganymede injection in another twelve hours."

I looked at those purple points again. We were the first non-Caesar spaceship to make the Jupiter trip. The Caesars sent a major mission of eight ships thirteen years ago; which the whole world watched with admiration right up until commander Ricardo Savill Caesar set his foot on Ganymede and announced to his massive television audience that he was claiming not only Ganymede, but Jupiter and all of its satellites for the Caesar family. It was extraordinary, not to say a complete violation of our entire world's rationalist ethos. The legal maneuvering had been going on ever since, as well as negotiations amongst the most senior level of family representatives in an attempt to get the Caesars to repudiate the claim. It was a standing joke for satirical show comedians, who got a laugh every time about excessive greed and routines about one person one moon. But in all that time, the Caesars had never moved from their position that Jupiter and its natural satellites now belonged to them. What they had never explained in those thirteen years is why they wanted it.

And now here we were. My brief wasn't to challenge or antagonize them, but to establish some precedents. "I want you to open a communication link to their primary settlement," I told the captain. "Use standard orbital flight control protocols, and inform them of our intended injection point. Then ask them if there is any problem with that. Treat it as an absolutely normal everyday occurrence . . . we're just one more spaceship arriving in orbit. If they ask what we're doing here: we're a scientific mission and I would like to discuss a schedule of geophysical investigation with their Mayor. In person."

Harrison Dominy Raleigh gave me an uncomfortable grimace. "You're sure you wouldn't like to talk to them now?"

"Definitely not. Achieving a successful Ganymede orbit is not something important enough to warrant attention from a family representative."

"Right then." He flipped his headset mike down, and instructed the AI on establishing a communication link.

It wasn't difficult. The Caesars were obviously treading as carefully as we were. Once the *Kuranda* was in orbit, the captain requested spaceport clearance for our ground to orbit shuttle, which was granted without comment.

The ride down was an uneventful ninety minutes, if you were to discount the view from the small, heavily-shielded ports. Jupiter at a quarter crescent hung in the sky above Ganymede. We sank down to a surface of fawn-colored ice pocked by white impact craters and great *sulci*, clusters of long grooves slicing through the grubby crust, creating broad river-like groupings of corrugations. For some reason I thought the landscape more quiet and dignified than that of Earth's moon. I suppose the icescape's palette of dim pastel colors helped create the impression, but there was definitely an ancient solemnity to this small world.

New Milan was a couple of degrees north of the equator, in an area of flat ice pitted with small newish craters. An undisciplined sprawl of emerald and white lights covering nearly five square miles. In thirteen years the Caesars had built themselves quite a substantial community here. All the buildings were freestanding igloos whose base and lower sections were constructed from some pale yellow silicate concrete, while the top third was a transparent dome. As the shuttle descended toward the landing field I began to realize why the lights I could see were predominately green. The smallest igloo was fifty yards in diameter, with the larger ones reaching over two hundred yards; they all had gardens at their center illuminated by powerful lights underneath the glass.

After we landed, a bus drove me over to the administration center in one of the large igloos. It was the Mayor, Ricardo Savill Caesar himself, who greeted me as I emerged from the airlock. He was a tall man, with the slightly flaccid flesh of all people who had been in a low-gravity environment for any length of time. He wore a simple gray and turquoise one-piece tunic with a mauve jacket, standard science mission staff uniform. But on him it had become a badge of office, bestowing that extra degree of authority. I could so easily imagine him as the direct descendant of some First Era Centurion commander.

"Welcome," he said warmly. "And congratulations on your flight. From what we've heard, the *Kuranda* is an impressive ship."

"Thank you," I said. "I'd be happy to take you round her later."

"And I'll enjoy accepting that invitation. But first it's my turn. I can't wait to show off what we've done here."

Thus my tour began; I believe there was no part of that igloo into which I didn't venture at some time during the next two hours. From the life support machinery in the lower levels to precarious walkways strung along the carbon reinforcement strands of the transparent dome. I saw it all. Quite deliberately, of course. Ricardo Savill Caesar was proving they had no secrets, no sinister apparatus under construction. The family had built themselves a self-sustaining colony, capable of expanding to meet their growing population. Nothing more. What I was never shown nor told, was the reason why.

After waiting as long as politeness required before claiming I had seen enough we wound up in Ricardo Savill Caesar's office. It was on the upper story of the habitation section, over forty feet above the central arboretum's lawn, yet the tops of the trees were already level with his window. I could recognize several varieties of pine and willow, but the low gravity had distorted their runaway growth, giving them peculiar swollen trunks and fat leaves.

Once I was sitting comfortably on his couch he offered me some coffee from a delicate china pot.

"I have the beans flown up and grind them myself," he said. "They're from the family's estates in the Caribbean. Protein synthesis might have solved our food supply problems, but there are some textures and tastes which elude the formulators."

I took a sip, and pursed my lips in appreciation. "That's good. Very good."

"I'm glad. You're someone I think I'd like to have on my side."

"Oh?"

He sat back and grinned at me. "The other families are unhappy to say the least about our settlement claim on this system. And you are the person they send to test the waters. That's quite a responsibility for any representative. I would have loved to sit in on your briefing sessions and hear what was said about us terrible Caesars."

"Your head would start spinning after the first five hours," I told him, dryly. "Mine certainly did."

"So what is it you'd like your redoubtable ship and crew to do while they're here?"

"It is a genuine scientific mission," I told him. "We'd like to study the bacterial life you've located in the moons here. Politics of settlement aside, it is tremendously important, especially after Mars turned out to be so barren."

"I certainly have no objection to that. Are we going to be shown the data?"

"Of course." I managed to sound suitably shocked. "Actually, I was going to propose several joint expeditions. We did bring three long-duration science station vehicles with us that can be deployed on any of the lunar surfaces."

Ricardo Savill Caesar tented his forefingers, and rested his chin on the point. "What kind of duration do these vehicles have?"

"A couple of weeks without resupply. Basically they're

just large caravans we link up to a tractor unit. They're fully mobile."

"And you envisage dispatching a mission to each moon?"

"Yes. We're also going to drop a number of probes into Jupiter to investigate its structural composition."

"Interesting. How far down do you believe they can reach?"

"We want to examine the supercritical fluid level, the surface of it at least."

He raised an eyebrow. "I shall be most impressed if your probe design is good enough to reach that level. The furthest we've ever reached is seven hundred kilometers down."

"Our engineers seem quite confident it can be reached. The family has always given solid-state science a high priority."

"A kind of mechnological machismo."

"I suppose so."

"Well, this is all very exciting. I'm very keen to offer you our fullest cooperation and assistance. My science team has been looking forward to your arrival for months. I don't think they'll be disappointed. Fresh angles are always so rewarding, I find."

I showed him a satisfied nod. This stalemate was the outcome with the highest probability according to our council strategists. We'd established that our family was free to roam where it chose on any of the moons, but not to stay. Which meant the most popular, if somewhat whimsical theory, was unlikely. Several senior family councils had advanced the notion that the Caesars had discovered high-order life out here, and wanted to keep it for themselves. After all, since they found bacteria in the undersurface seas of both

Ganymede and Europa, then more complex life was an ultra-remote possibility. Personally, I had always considered that just too far fetched. More curiously, Ricardo Savill Caesar hadn't objected to us probing Jupiter itself. The second most likely theory was that they'd found something of extraordinary value in its atmosphere. Again unlikely. There had been dozens of robot probes sent here in the decades before their flight. Which put me far enough down the list to start considering alien spaceships and survivors of Atlantis. Not an enjoyable prospect for any rational man. But as Ricardo Savill Caesar wasn't giving anything away, my options were reducing. It was an annoying challenge. He knew that I knew the reason for the settlement claim had to be staring right at me. I simply couldn't see it.

I told myself it didn't matter. I never expected to catch it straight away, and we were due to stay at Jupiter for six months. There was plenty of time.

"Then we're all done bar the details," I said. "I'll get my AI to link to your AI. I'm sure they can organize schedules and personnel rosters between them."

He raised his cup in happy salute. "I'm sure they can. I'll authorize a link to the *Kuranda* immediately."

"There is one other thing. A small matter."

"Oh?"

"I'd like to see someone while I'm here. One of your deputies, in fact. It relates to an old investigation of mine. There are one or two points I need to clear up with her."

"Who are we talking about?"

"Bethany Maria Caesar. I gather she's on Io."

"Yes," he said cautiously. "She runs the science team there."

His abrupt shift in attitude was fascinating. It was as

though I'd suddenly won a point in our game of words and nuances. If only I could have worked out how I'd done that. All I'd said was her name. "You don't object to me talking to her, do you?"

"Not at all. If it isn't confidential, what is this old investigation, exactly?"

"A murder."

"Good Lady Mary. Really?"

"As I say, it's an old one. However, I have a new theory I'd like to run past her."

The Io science outpost was nothing like New Milan. It consisted of two dozen cylindrical compartments resting on concrete cradles sunk deep into the carmine-colored crust; they were all plugged into each other like some array of antique electronic components. For years they'd suffered from the exhalations of the volcano. Its furious sulfur emission clouds had gently drizzled down, staining their metallic-white casings with a thin film of dirty amber colloid which dribbled round the exterior to drip from the belly. But for all its functionalism, the Caesars had certainly chosen a location with a view. One of the compartments had an observation gallery, aligned so that its curving windows looked directly out at the distant sulfur volcano, which appeared as a dark conical silhouette rising out of the horizon.

I waited for Bethany Maria Caesar at one of the refractory tables in the gallery, staring straight out at the volcano through the gritty, smeared windows, hoping I would get to see an eruption. The only evidence of any seismic activity was the occasional tremor which ran through the compartment, barely enough to create a ripple in my teacup.

"Hello, Edward, it's been a long time."

I would never have recognized her. This woman standing before me bore only the faintest resemblance to that beautiful, distraught girl I'd sat with through innumerable interviews eight decades ago. She looked, for want of a better word, old. Her face was lined with chubby wrinkles that obscured the features I once knew; nor was there any more of that glowing blonde hair—she'd had a crew cut so severe it barely qualified as stubble, and that was grayish. The tunic she wore was loose-fitting, but even that couldn't disguise her stooped posture.

She put both hands on the table and lowered herself into a chair opposite me with a slight wheeze. "Quite a sight, aren't I?"

"What happened?" I asked, appalled. No briefing file had mentioned any sort of accident or chronic illness.

"Low gravity happened, Edward. I can see your face is all puffed up with fluid retention, so you already know a fraction of the suffering possible. Content yourself with that fraction. Low gravity affects some people worse than others, a lot worse. And after thirteen years' constant exposure, I'm just about off the scale."

"Dear Mary! I don't know what you Caesars want with Jupiter, but nothing is worth abusing yourself like this. Come home, back to Earth."

Her smile alluded to a wisdom denied me. "This is my home. Jupiter is the frontier of humanity."

"How can you say that? It's killing you."

"Life!" the word was spat out. "Such a treacherous gift."

"A precious gift," I countered.

"Ah yes. Poor old Justin. I was quite surprised when I

saw you were the representative the Raleighs were sending. You caused me quite a little trip down memory lane."

"I won't lie to you, you're not my primary reason for being here."

"Ha. The great mystery of our time. What can those wicked Caesars want with Jupiter? Had any luck working it out yet?"

"None at all. But we'll get there in the end."

"I'm sure you will. Devote enough processing power to any problem, and ultimately it will be solved."

"That's more like the Bethany I remember."

"I doubt it. This is experience talking. We have more AIs per head of population up here than anywhere on Earth. Every scrap of research data is analyzed and tabulated—our knowledge base is expanding at a rate we can barely keep track of. And we can devote so much of ourselves to understanding it. We don't have to worry so much about our physical requirements. The AIs take care of that for us; they run the food synthesis plants, the cybernetics factories, administration. I consider my life here to be my liberation, Edward. I don't have to concern myself with the mundane anymore. I can use my mind full time."

"Then I'm glad for you. You've found something new out here. AI utilization on Earth is causing no end of problems. They can take over the running of just about all mechanical operations and do it with increased efficiency. Industry and utility provision are discarding more and more human operatives. We're seeing large-scale patterns of unemployment evolving. And it brings a host of social unrest with it. There's more petty crime than there ever used to be; psychologists need counseling they have such a heavy workload these days. People are starting to question the true worth of introducing AIs."

"I'm sure there will be temporary problems thrown up by AI integration. You never get smooth transitions of this magnitude. Moving to a leisure-based society is going to be hard for a people who are so set in their ways. The penalty for a long life is the increasing resistance to change. The familiar is too easy and comfortable for it to be discarded quickly. And the families are very familiar with their life as it is. But the change will happen. If we have a purpose it is to think and create; that's our uniqueness. Any non-sentient animal can build a nest and gather food. Now this march through progress has finally started to relieve us of that physical distraction. I mean, that's what we were doing it for in the first place, right? Once you set out to determine how the universe works, then as a species there's no turning back. We're freefalling to the plateau, Edward."

"The plateau?"

"The moment at which science has explained everything, and machines are perfect. After that, human life becomes one long summer afternoon picnic. All we do then is think, dream, and play."

"I can't quite see that myself."

"That's a shame. You must adapt or die, Edward. I took you as someone bright enough to surmount that last hurdle and climb up there to the plateau. Perhaps the Sport of Emperors wasn't the blessing we like to believe, at least, not for everyone. The original Caesars were so certain they were doing the right thing with their gift for all the Empire. They'd bred stables of gladiators for generations, evolving their speed and strength until they were invincible in the arena. Only age slowed and weakened them. It was such a short leap to breed for longevity, and what a political weapon that was. The one thing everybody always wants. But the life they bred for in the children of the Empire was longer than nature ever intended. And messing with nature however crudely is always dangerous. Humans change their environment. That is our true nature. The cycle of life and death, of constant renewal, is nature's way of adapting us as a species to the freshness we create for ourselves."

"Are you saying I've outlived my usefulness?"

"I don't know, Edward. Can you give up everything you've lived for in order to face the unknown? Or are you going to watch trees grow as the same old seasons wash past you to no effect?"

"That's what you believe you're doing by living out here, is it?"

"I enjoy change. It's the most magnificent challenge."

"You have the luxury of enjoying it."

Her laugh was a fluid-clogged cackle. "Oh Edward, so single minded. You and I are alive, which is more than can be said for Justin. I have to admit, I'm very curious. What can you possibly have to add to the matter at this stage?"

I waved a hand at the curving windows, with their slim reinforcement mesh of carbon strands. That particular carbon allotrope was the reason the glass could be so thin, one of the new miracles we took so much for granted. "Carbon 60."

"How the hell can pentospheres possibly be connected to Justin's murder? We only discovered the stuff ten years ago . . . Oh. Mary, yes! It was Alexander, wasn't it? He was the one who found it."

"I hope so."

"*Hope?*"

"Carbon 60 is an awesome substance. There are so many theoretical applications, from ultrastrength fibers to superconductivity. It's being incorporated into just about every process and structure we use. And they're still finding new uses on a daily basis."

"So?"

"So I need to know about Justin's great project, the one he was working on when he was killed. Was he studying supernovae for carbon signatures?"

"Heavens." She sat back and gave me an admiring look. "You really don't give up, do you?"

"No."

"We only found out that carbon 60 existed in stellar nebulae after we—or rather Alexander—produced it in a laboratory. What you're saying is that it could have happened the other way round, aren't you? That some astronomer found traces, proof that it physically existed, and chemists worked at synthesizing it afterwards."

"It's certainly possible. The existence of carbon 60 has been postulated for a long time; I traced an early reference back to 1815—it was some very speculative paper on theoretical molecular structures. Justin might have had the idea carbon could be produced by stellar events, and found the spectral signature."

"And Alexander, who was a chemist, immediately realized the practical use such a find would have, and killed him for it. Then when a decent interval had passed, in this case, ninety years, he miraculously produces the elusive substance in his lab, to the enormous benefit of his family who have lauded him ever since. Who would possibly suspect any connection with a tragic murder all that time ago? And . . ." She gave a start. "Alexander never had an air tight alibi for that night, plus he was working on carbon at the time. Yes, I can see why you've invested so much effort into this."

"I've never been able to find out what Justin was working on," I said. "Even you said you weren't sure. But considering the state you were in after his murder, you weren't even sure what day it was. And you've had a long time to reflect on everything he ever said to you."

"I'm sorry, Edward, you've had a wasted trip."

"You don't know?" I couldn't keep the bitterness from my voice. It had been a desperately long shot. But it was the first possible lead I'd got in sixty-seven years.

"I know exactly what Justin was working on," she said sorrowfully. "I just didn't want to tell anyone at the time."

"Why?" I demanded, suddenly furious. "Information like that was critical to the investigation."

"No it wasn't. Don't you understand anything? I loved him, I really did. And he had a crazy theory. He thought there might be life in space. Bacteria that floated through the void like interstellar dust clouds, propelled by solar wind. That's the spectral signature he was looking for, not carbon 60. He said it was possible all our plagues came from outer space—that was why our immune system always takes time to respond, because each one was new to our planet. He believed all that back in the 1830s. Holy Mary, what a brilliant mind."

"But—"

"Yes I *know*," she snapped at me. "He was right, damnit. He was absolutely right. And I was on the mission which proved it beyond any doubt. We're convinced the bacterial life we found on Ganymede and Europa originated from space—there's evidence for it all over the Jovian system. Do you have any idea how painful that was for me after so many years? It's not an irony, it's a tragedy. And I can't tell anybody he thought of it first, because there's no proof. He'll never get the credit he deserves, and that's my fault."

"So why didn't you tell us at the time?" I asked.

"To protect his memory. I didn't want people laughing at my beautiful lover. He was too precious to me for that. I wouldn't have been able to stand it. And they would have done it, the newspapers would have ridiculed him, because it was all too fantastic back then. Invasion of the space flu! I wanted to give him some dignity. He deserved that much."

I sighed in defeat. She was right, I'd put a lot of hope on her confirming my theory. "I don't suppose I can blame you for protecting him. In fact, I'd probably do the same thing."

She rested her hand on mine as another little tremor ran through the gallery. "What will you do now?"

"Me? Complete the *Kuranda* mission, then go home and get on with my life. My changeable life, that is."

Her heavy, wrinkled cheeks lifted in a melancholy smile. "Thank you, Edward. It's nice to know that someone else cared about him."

Four

Raleigh Family Institute AD 1971

The lone oak tree was over two hundred years old, its upper half broken long ago, leaving just an imposing stump to support several sturdy boughs. Rich emerald moss was creeping into the wrinkly bark around the base. I settled down in the cusp of a forking root and looked back down the sloping grassland toward the lake. My FAI shrank to a discrete soap bubble beside my head, emission functions on standby, isolating me from the digital babble of family business. It left my own thoughts free to circulate quietly in my head. It was a lovely day, the sun rising above the valley walls, already warm enough to burn off the dew. Buttercups and daisies starred the thick grass, their tiny petals already fully open, receptive. As always, the vista allowed me considerable serenity.

I made a point of taking a walk around the institute grounds every day, unless the weather was truly awful of course. And it could be on occasion. Climate control was one thing we hadn't got round to implementing. I was glad about that—there should be some unpredictability in our lives. I suppose that's why I enjoyed the grounds so much. They were wholly natural. Since I was appointed to the senior family council eight years ago, I'd made damn sure that the only trees planted in the institute valley had been genuine genotypes—same went for the rest of the flora.

A folly, perhaps. But on the rare occasions when anyone questioned me about it, I maintained that it was a valid cultural enclave, and what I was doing was essential preservation. Now that our urban areas were depopulating, everyone wanted to enjoy their own little piece of the rural idyll. Farming had been in a solid decline ever since food synthetics became available at the start of the century. The individual farms which carried on were run by cantankerous old conservationists, or simply families who were determinedly clinging to the old ways. There weren't many such anachronisms—they didn't take up much land area, so it didn't affect the joint council's overall habitation development strategy. As a result, abandoned farmland right across the country was being reinvented as the kind of pastoral woodland that only ever existed in the most romanticized notions of pre–First Era history. Everybody who left the city wanted their own forest, complete with a glade that had a pool fed by a babbling brook, where their mock First Era villa could be sited. Nobody wanted to wait a hundred years for the trees to grow, so reformatted DNA varieties were the *grande* fashion, taking just a couple of years to grow sixty or seventy feet, then slowing into a more natural growth model. It struck me as strange, as if our new biononic technology had infected us with different mental patterns; as society matured we were slowly reverting to a Short mentality. Everything had to be *now*, as if there were no tomorrow other than the awesome potential future which Bethany Maria Caesar established for us in nineteen sixty three.

My FAI expanded, chiming melodically. I still used the

old interface mode, despite the ease of modern direct sensory linkages. It was, I suspected, a quiet personal admission that Bethany Maria Caesar had been right those many years ago back on Io when she claimed that resistance to evolution was derived from age. None of my great-great-great-great grandchildren had shown any recalcitrance in being fitted with interfaces, nor demonstrated any psychological harm resulting from them. Not that I could hold my own childhood up as any kind of template to the modern world. However, I remained aloof. When you've had to upgrade through as many different types of interfaces and operating programs as I have you remain profoundly skeptical as to how long the latest is going to last before it achieves obsolescence. Best you stay with the one you found most comfortable for a few decades.

It was Rebecca Raleigh Stothard's face that filled the FAI. I might have guessed, there weren't many people my AI would allow to intrude on my private time. Her holographic image grinned at me, conjuring up a host of most pleasurable memories. Rebecca had undergone DNA reset five years ago, reverting her physiological age to her mid-twenties. She'd been an attractive woman when we had our first dalliance a hundred years ago; now she was simply angelic.

"I thought you'd like to be the first to hear," she said. "The Neuromedical Protocol Commission have cleared the procedure, effective from twelve-thirty p.m. Rome mean time today."

"Yes!" the word hissed out from my lips. Given what turbulent times we were living in, it was wholly unjustified for me to feel so elated at such a small piece of news. Yet that didn't prevent me from laughing out loud. "I've finally brought it to an end."

"The Borgias are still in the Vatican," she said primly.

"Show a little confidence. It has to be the pair of them."

"I hope so," she said. There was a note of concern to her voice. "I'd hate to think you were becoming obsessional."

"You know as well as I do the percentage of my time which this case occupies is so small it can't even be measured. This is simply the satisfaction of a job seen through to its end. Besides, I owe it to Francis."

"I know. So what's next?"

"I'll start the ball rolling, and haul her in. Is the system on-line here?"

"Give me three days to complete installation." She winked, and her image vanished. The FAI remained on active status.

The light right across the valley suddenly and silently quadrupled in intensity, turning a vivid violet hue. My iris filters closed, and I looked straight up. A brilliant star was burning in the eastern quadrant of the sky, the backwash of energy from a starship initiating its compression drive. Violet drifted into turquoise which in turn began the shade into emerald. I still think the spectral wash from a compression drive is among the most wondrous sights we have ever created, even if it is an accidental by-product. It wouldn't last, of course. The first generation of faster-than-light starships were crude affairs, creating their own individual wormhole down which to fly. The families were cooperating on the project to construct exotic matter, which would be able to hold wormholes open permanently. That had to qualify as one of the more favorable signs of recent years—even at the height of the crazed sixties we managed to retain enough sense to see the necessity of such collaboration. Even the Caesars joined with us.

Every time I thought of the negotiations I was involved in to revamp the old Joint Families Astronautics Agency I also remembered my trip to Jupiter, and marveled at how we were so incapable of seeing the utterly obvious. Size hid their goal from us. But how could we have possibly known we had to think so big?

Bethany Maria Caesar called her murdered lover a visionary, but compared to her he was blind. As soon as she began her work on biononic systems back in eighteen fifty she had realized what would happen should she eventually be successful. The self-replicating biononics she envisaged would be the pinnacle of molecular engineering machinery, organelle-sized modules that could assemble single atoms into whatever structure an AI had designed and, equally important, disassemble. Cluster enough of them together like some patch of black lichen, and they would eat their way through any ore, extracting the atoms you required for whatever project you had in mind. They could then weave those atoms into anything from quantum wire and pentospheres to iron girders and bricks. That included food, clothes, houses, starships . . . Quite literally, anything you could think of and manage to describe to your AI.

The human race stopped working for a living. Just as she said. Or prophesied, depending on your opinion of her.

The human race had stopped dying, too. Specific medical versions of biononic modules could travel through the human body, repairing damaged cells. They could also reset DNA.

Amongst all the upheaval, it was our view and attitude toward commodities which underwent the most radical of all our revisions. From valuing all sorts of gems and precious metals and rare chemicals, we had switched to valuing just one thing: matter. Any matter. It became our currency and our obsession. It didn't matter what atom you owned, even if it was only hydrogen—especially hydrogen if you were a Caesar. Fusion could transform it into a heavier element, one which a biononic module could exploit. Every living person in the solar system had the potential to create whatever they wanted, limited only by personal imagination and the public availability of matter.

And the Caesars had the greatest stockpile of unused matter in the solar system: Jupiter. That's how far ahead they were thinking once Bethany spurred them on. The population pressures we'd been facing were nothing compared with what was about to be unleashed. A race of semi-immortals with the potential to increase their numbers at a near exponential rate simply by using the old-fashioned natural method of reproduction—never mind artificial wombs and cloning techniques.

To think, when I was young, I used to worry that our early petrol engine cars would use up all the oil reserves. Within weeks of Bethany's biononic modules coming online family spaceships charged off across the solar system to lay claim to any and every chunk of matter a telescope had ever detected. The most disgraceful, shameful year of post Second Era history. A year of madness and greed, when all our rationality seemed to crumble before the forces of avarice. The Crisis Conference of '65 managed to calm things down a little. Thankfully, every family rejected the Rothchild claim on the sun. And the rest of the solar system was apportioned almost equally. We Raleighs came out of it with Titan as well as a joint claim—with 15 other families—

on Saturn. But the Caesars still had Jupiter, consolidating their position as the foremost human family. And the FTL starship project was born, the agreement most accredited with easing the tension.

The function of family councils changed to that of resource allocators, enabling us to enforce the original legal framework that underpinned civilization. Controlling the distribution of raw matter was economics stripped down to its crudest level. But it worked, after a fashion, allowing us to retain order and balance. Given the circumstances, it was a better outcome than I would have predicted.

The last of the compression drive's scarlet light drained away from the sky, taking with it the strange double shadows cast by the oak. I began instructing the FAI to contact a senior representative of the Lockett family.

Christine Jayne Lockett was a stark reminder that I really ought to get myself reset. Men always suffer from the same casual illusion that we simply became more handsome as we matured, and were increasingly desirable as a result. What tosh.

When she walked into my office in the Meridor Manor all I could see was the bitterness leaking from her face. It spoiled her features, a near-permanent scowl highlighting the wrinkles accumulating around her eyes and across her cheeks. Her hair was still long, but not cared for with any great enthusiasm. And the clothes she wore were at least a century out of date; they looked hand made, and badly at that. Paint flecked her hands, lying thick under short, cracked nails.

The small file of personal data which my AI had

collected for me told of how she now lived out in the countryside in a naturalist community. They grew their own food, made their own utensils, smoked their hallucinogenics, and generally avoided contact with the rest of their family. No biononics were allowed across the threshold of their compound, although they did have a net interface to call for medical help if any of their number had an accident.

She stalked over to my desk and thrust her face up against mine. "Oppressive bastard! Who the hell do you think you are? How dare you have me arrested and forced away from my home like this. I've done nothing wrong." It was almost a scream.

The Lockett family representative who was accompanying her gave me a tired grimace. Apparently Christine Jayne Lockett had refused point blank to use an airpod, insisting she traveled by groundcar. It had taken them eight hours to drive to the institute from northern England.

"Oh yes you have."

My voice was so cold she recoiled.

"You and Carter Osborne Kenyon are the only people left on my suspect list," I said. "And now I'm finally going to discover the truth."

"But Carter was with me for the whole evening."

I directed a mirthless smile at her. "Yes."

It took a moment for the implication to sink in. Her mouth widened in astonishment. "Holy Mary, you think we did it together, don't you? You think we killed that poor, poor boy."

"The rest of the alibis all check out. You two provided each other's alibi. It's the only weak link left."

"You utter shit!" She sat down heavily in my visitor's chair, staring at me with malice and disbelief. "So you wait all this time until you're some super duper big shot, and exploit your position to pressure my family into handing me over to you, all so you can erase a blemish on your record." Her gaze switched to her family representative. "Gutless coward!" she snarled at him. "The Locketts aren't this feeble that we have to kiss Raleigh ass when they tell us. You're supposed to protect me from this kind of victimization. I've got strong links to the elder council, you know. Give me a bloody telephone, I'm going to hang you bastards out to dry."

"Your family council agreed to my interviewing you," I said.

"Then I'm taking this to the Roman Congress itself. I have rights! You can't throw me in prison because you've failed to pin this on anyone else. Why didn't you bring Carter here, eh? I'll bet the Kenyons wouldn't stand for being shoved around by the likes of you."

"Firstly, Carter is on the *Aquaries*, they're out exploring stars twenty light-years away, and won't be back for another year. Secondly, you're not under arrest, you're here to be interviewed. Thirdly, if what I suspect is true, Carter will be arrested the moment he docks at New Vespasian."

"Interview me? Mary, how dumb is this? I Did Not Murder Justin. Which part of that don't you understand? Because that's all I'm saying."

"It's not that simple any more, not these days."

My FAI floated over to her, and expanded to display a sheet of text. She waved dismissively at it. "I don't use them. What does it say?"

"It's a ruling from the Neuromedical Protocol Commission, clearing a new design of biononic for human application. This particular module takes direct sensory integration a stage further, by stimulating selected synapses to invoke a deep access response."

"We all stopped speaking Latin at the end of the First Era."

"All right, Christine, it's really very simple. We can read your memories. I'm going to send you down to our laboratory, wire you up to a great big machine, and watch exactly what happened that night on a high-resolution, home theater-sized color screen. And there's not a thing you can do to stop me. Any further questions?"

"Bloody hell! Why, Edward? What do you believe was our motive?"

"I have no idea, although this procedure will enable me to trace it through associative location. All I've got left to go on now is opportunity. You and Carter had that."

Her stubborn scowl vanished. She sat there completely blank-faced for a couple of seconds, then gave me a level smile. "If you believe it, then go right ahead."

On a conscious level I kept telling myself she was bluffing, that it was one last brave gesture of defiance. Unfortunately, my subconscious was not so certain.

The family's forensic department had come up in the world over the last century. No longer skulking in the basement of Hewish Manor, it now occupied half the third floor. Laboratories were crypts of white gloss surfaces, populated by AI pillars with transparent sensor domes on top. Technicians and robots moved around between the units, examining and discussing the results. The clinic room which we had been allocated had a single bed in the middle, with four black boxy cabinets around it.

Rebecca greeted us politely and ushered Christine to the bed. Strictly speaking, Rebecca was a clinical neurologist these days rather than a forensic doctor, but given how new the application was she'd agreed to run the procedure for me.

As with all biononic systems, there's never anything to actually see. Rebecca adjusted a dispenser mechanism against the nape of Christine's neck, and introduced the swarm of modules. The governing AI guided their trajectory through the brain tissue, controlling and regulating the intricate web they wove within her synaptic clefts. It took over an hour to interpret and format the information they were receiving, and map out the activation pathways within her cerebrum.

I watched the primary stages with a growing sense of trepidation. Justin's murder was one of the oldest active legal files the Raleighs had. The weight of so many years was pressing down on this moment, seeking resolution. If we couldn't solve this now, with all our fantastic technological abilities at my disposal, then I had failed him, one of our own.

Rebecca eventually ordered me to sit down. She didn't actually say "be patient" but her look was enough.

An FAI expanded in the air across one end of the clinic room, forming into a translucent sheet flecked with a moiré storm of interference. Color specks flowed together. It showed a hazy image of an antiquated restaurant viewed at eye level. On the couch Christine moaned softly, her eyes closed, as the memory replayed itself inside her skull, a window into history.

"We're there," Rebecca said. She issued a stream of instructions to the AI.

That March night in eighteen thirty-two played out in front of me, flickering and jerking like a home movie recorded on an antique strip of film. Christine sat at a table with her friends in the middle of the Orange Grove. Young, beautiful, and full of zest, their smiles and laughter making me ache for my own youth. They told each other stories and jokes, complained about tutors, gossiped about students and university staff, argued family politics. After the waiter brought their main course they went into a giggling huddle to decide if they should complain about the vegetables. More wine was ordered. They became louder.

It was snowing when they collected their coats and left. Tiny flecks of ice adding to the mush of the pavement. They stood as a group outside the restaurant, saying their good-byes, Christine kissing everybody. Then with Carter's arm around her shoulder, the pair of them made their way through Oxford's freezing streets to the block where she had her artist's garret.

There was the baby-sitter to pay and show out. Then the two of them were alone. They stumbled into her studio, and kissed for a long time, surrounded by Christine's outré paintings. There wasn't much to see of that time, just smears of Carter's face in badly blurred close up. Then she went over to an old chest of drawers, and pulled a stash of cocaine out from a jewelry box. Carter was already undressing when she turned back to him.

They snorted the drugs, and fondled and groped at each other in an ineffectual manner for what seemed an age. The phone's whistling put an end to it. Christine staggered over to answer it, then handed it to Carter. She watched with a bleary focus as his face showed first annoyance then puzzlement and finally shock. He slammed the handset down and scooped up his clothes. A clock on the studio wall said twenty-six minutes to twelve.

I couldn't move from the clinic seat. I sat there with my head in my hands, not believing what I'd just seen. It had to be faked. The Locketts had developed false memory implantation techniques. They'd corrupted our institute AIs. Christine had repeated the alibi to herself for so long it had become stronger than reality. Aliens traveled back in time to alter the past.

"Edward."

When I looked up, Christine Jayne Lockett was staring down at me. There was no anger in her expression. If anything, she was pitying me.

"I wasn't joking when I said I knew people on our elder council," she said. "And let me tell you, you arrogant bastard, if this . . . this *mental rape* had been in connection with any other case, I would have kicked up such a stink that your whole family would disown you. The only reason I won't is because I loved Justin. He was my friend, and I'll never forget him for bringing a thread of happiness into my life. I wanted his murderer caught back then, and I want it just as bad now."

"Thank you," I whispered feebly.

"Are you going to give up?"

My smile was one of total self pity. "We're reaching what Bethany called the plateau, the end of scientific progress. I've used every method we know of to find the murderer. Every one of them has failed me. The only thing left now that could solve it is time travel, and I'm afraid our physicists are all pretty much agreed that's just a fantasy."

"Time travel," she said contemptuously. "You just can't see beyond your fabulous technology, can you? Your reliance is sickening. And what use is it when it comes down to the things that are genuinely important?"

"Nobody starves, nobody dies," I snapped at her, abruptly infuriated with her poverty-makes-me-morally-superior attitude. "I notice your happy stone-age colony isn't averse to using our medical resources any time something nasty happens."

"Yes, we fall back on technological medicine. We're neither ignorant, nor stupid. We believe technology as sophisticated as ours should be used as a safety net for our lives, not as an integral part, or ruler, as you choose. The simple way we live allows us to return to nature without having to endure the struggle and squalor of the actual stone age. For all things there is a balance, and you have got it badly wrong. Your society is exploiting the universe, not living in harmony with it. The way we live allows our minds to prosper, not our greed."

"While the way we live allows dreams to become reality. We are a race without limits."

"Without physical limits. What use is that, Edward? What is the ultimate reason to give everyone the power of a god? Look at you, what you're doing—you hoard entire planets in readiness for the day when you can dismantle them and fabricate something in their place. What? What can possibly need building on such a scale? Explore the universe by all means, I'm sure there are miracles and marvels out there just as great as the one we've created for ourselves. But at the end of the day, you should come home to your family and your friends. That's what's truly important."

"I'm glad you've found a way to live with what we've achieved. But you're in a minority. The rest of us want to grab the opportunity this time has gifted us with."

"You'll learn," she said. "After all, you've got eternity."

Five
Earth Orbit AD 2000

My flyer ripped up through the ionosphere like a fish leaving water. The gravatonic and magnetic flux lines which knotted around the little craft tugged a braided haze of auroral streamers out behind us, looking for all the world like some ancient chemical rocket exhaust. Once clear of the atmosphere's bulk, I increased the acceleration to twenty gees, and the slender scintillating strand was stretched to breaking point. Wispy photonic serpents writhed back down toward the planet as we burst free.

I extended my perceptual range, tracking the multitude of flyers falling in and out of the atmosphere all around me. They blossomed like silver comets across my consciousness, dense currents of them arching up from the Earth in a series of flowing hoops with every apex reaching precisely six hundred miles above the equator. The portal Necklace itself, which occupied that orbit, was visualized by nodes of cool jade light sitting atop the hoops. Each of them was nested at the center of a subtle spatial distortion, lensing the light outward in curving ephemeral petals.

The flyer soared round in a flat curve, merging with the traffic stream that was heading for the Tangsham portal a thousand miles ahead of me. Africa's eastern coastline drifted past below, its visual clarity taking on a dreamlike quality, perfectly resolved yet impossibly distant. I watched it dwindle behind the flyer as all the wretched old emotions rose to haunt me again. Although I'd never quite had the courage to deactivate the Justin Ascham Raleigh file in the wake of the debacle which was Christine's memory retrieval, I'd certainly abandoned it in my own mind. I couldn't even remember giving my cybershadow the order to tag all the old suspects and watch for any status change within the global dataspace.

Yet when the information slipped into my mind as I awoke that morning I knew I could never ignore it. Whatever would Francis have said?

I kept the flyer's forward perception primary as we approached the portal. The circle of exotic matter had a breadth of nine hundred yards, the rim of a chasm that could be seen only from one direction. Its pseudofabric walls glowed green where they intersected the boundaries of normal space-time, forming a tunnel that stretched off into middle-distance. Two lanes of flyers sped along its interior in opposite directions, carrying people to their new world and their hoped-for happiness.

I wished them well, for the next portal led to Nibeza, one of the Vatican-endorsed societies, with complex proscriptions built into its biononics. Essentially they were limited to medical functions and providing raw materials for industry, everything else had to be built the hard way. A society forever frozen on the cusp of the nineteen sixties, where people are kept busy doing their old jobs.

Fully half of the new worlds were variants on the same theme, the only difference being in the level of limitations imposed on their biononics. There were even some deactivated portals now; those that had been used to establish the Restart worlds. There were no biononics on such planets, nor even the memory of them. The new inhabitants had their memories wiped, awakening on arrival to the belief they had traveled there in hibernation sleep on an old slower-than-light colony ship that left Earth in the nineteen forties. They remained free to carry on their lives as though the intervening years had never happened.

I believe it was our greatest defeat that so many of us were unable to adjust naturally to our new circumstances, where every thought is a treasure to be incubated. It was a failure of will, of self confidence, which prevented so many from taking that next psychological step. The adjustment necessary was nothing like the re-education courses which used to mark our race's waves of scientific progress; an adaptation which could be achieved by simply going back to school and learning new skills. To thrive today you had to change your attitude and look at life from a wholly new perspective. How sad that for all its triumphs, the superb society we had constructed and systematically labored to improve for two thousand years was unable to provide that inspiration for everyone at the end.

But as I'd been told so many times, we now had the time to learn, and this new phase of our existence had only just begun. On the Earth below, nearly a third of the older adults spent their time daysleeping. Instead of the falsehood of enforced technological limitation on colony worlds, they immersed themselves in perfectly activated memories of the old days, trading such recollections amongst themselves for those blissful times spent in a simpler world. The vast majority, so they said, relished the days of childhood or first romances set in the age of horse drawn carriages and sailing ships.

Maybe one day they would tire of their borrowed times and wake from their unreality to look around anew at what we have achieved. For out there on the other worlds, the ones defying any restriction, there was much to be proud of. Fiume, where the gas giants were being dismantled to build a vast shell around the star, with an inner surface capable of supporting life. Milligan, whose colonists were experimenting with truly giant wormholes which they hoped could reach other galaxies. Oranses, home to the original sinners, condemned by the Vatican for their project of introducing communal sentience to every living thing on their planet, every worm, insect, and stalk of grass, thus creating Gaia in all her majesty. All this glorious playground was our heritage, a gift from the youth of today to their sulking, inward-looking parents.

My flyer soared out of the traffic stream just before we passed over the rim of the Tangsham portal. I directed it round the toroid of exotic matter to the station on the other side. The molecular curtain over the hangar complex entrance parted to let us through, and we alighted on one of the reception platforms. Charles Winter Hutchenson, the station chief, came out to meet me. The Hutchensons are one of our partners in Tangsham, a settlement which is endeavoring to transform people into starvoyagers, a species of immense biomechanical constructs that will spend eternity exploring space. Placing a human mind into the core of such a vessel is simple enough, but its psychology must undergo considerable adaptation to be comfortable with such a body. Yet as I saw on my approach to the portal, there was no shortage of people wishing to join the quest. The solid planets in the

Tangsham star system were ringed with construction stations, fed by rivers of matter extracted from asteroids and gas giants. Energy converter nodules had been emplaced deep within the star itself to power such colossal industrial endeavor. It was a place of hard science; there was little of nature's beauty to be found there.

"Pleasure to welcome you on board," Charles Winter Hutchenson said warmly. "I didn't know elder representatives concerned themselves with incidents like this."

"I have several motives," I confessed. "I met Carter Osborne Kenyon a long time ago. Attending to him now is the least I can do. And he is one of the senior nuclear engineers on the project, he's entitled to the best service we can provide. Is he back yet?"

"Yes. He arrived about an hour ago. I halted the transshipment as you asked."

"Fine. My cybershadow will take care of the official casework for us. But I'd like to assess the requirements in person first."

"Okay. This way." He led me over to a cathedral-sized cargo hall where the stasis chamber was being kept. It was a translucent gray cylinder suspended between two black glass slabs. The outline of a prone human figure was just visible inside.

My cybershadow meshed me with the chamber's control AI, and I instructed it to give me a status review. Carter Osborne Kenyon wasn't in a good condition. There had been an accident on one of Tangsham's construction stations; even with our technological prowess, machinery isn't flawless. Some power relays had surged, plasma temperature had doubled, there had been a blow-out. Metal was vaporized as the errant plasma jet cut its way through several sheets of decking. Loose panels had swung about, one of them catching Carter a severe blow. The left side of his body had been badly damaged. Worse than that, the edge of the metal had cracked his skull open, pulping the brain tissue inside. It would have been fatal in an earlier age. He was certainly clinically dead before he hit the ground. But the emergency systems had responded efficiently. His body had immediately been sealed in stasis, and microdrones had swept the area, gathering up every cell that had splashed across the floor and nearby walls. The cells were subsequently put in stasis with him.

We had all the component parts, they just had to be reassembled properly. His genome would be read, and each damaged cell repaired, identified, then replaced in its correct location. It could be done on Tangsham, but they would have to commit considerable resources to it. While Earth, with its vast elderly population, retained the greatest level of medical expertise among all of the settled worlds, and subsequently devoted the highest percentage of resources to the field. That concentration of knowledge almost meant our software and techniques remained far ahead of everyone else. Carter's best chance for a full reanimation and recovery was with us.

"The damage is within our accepted revival limits," I told Charles Winter Hutchenson. "I'll authorize the procedure and take him back with me to the institute clinic."

The station chief seemed glad that the disruption to his routine was being dealt with so propitiously. He instructed the cargo hall's gravity field to refocus, and the stasis chamber bobbed up into the air, then slid away to my flyer's hold.

I left the portal, and guided the flyer directly to the Raleigh institute. It wasn't just the physical cell structure of

Carter's brain which the medical technicians would repair, his memories too would have to be re-established. That was the part of him I was most interested in salvaging. It was as close to time travel as I would ever get.

With the sensorium integration routines developed for the daysleepers I would be able to drop right into his world. I would be there, observing, listening, and tasting, right from the very first time he met Justin Ascham Raleigh during that initial freshers week, until the night of the murder. And unlike him, I wouldn't view those moments through sentiment—I'd be scouring every second for anomalies, hints of out of character behavior, the misplaced nuance of a single word.

There were three and a half solid years to reconnoiter. I wasn't just examining the time they were in each other's presence. Anything that was said and done during that time could prove crucially relevant. Even his dreams might provide a clue.

It would take a while. There were so many resources I had to supervise and negotiate over, I couldn't schedule much current time to the case, maybe an hour a week. But I'd waited this long now. Time was no longer a relevant factor.

Six

Eta Carinae AD 2038

The deepflight ship eased out of the wormhole portal and twisted smoothly to align itself on the habitat disk. Two light years away, Eta Carinae had inflated across half of the universe. Its blue-white ejecta lobes were webbed with sharp scarlet lines as the outer plasma envelope slowly radiated away their incredible original temperature. The entire edifice was engulfed in a glowing crimson corona that bristled with spiky gas jets slowly dissipating out toward the stars. Fronds of dark cold dust eddied around it at a greater distance, the remnants of earlier explosive activity.

Eta Carinae is one of the most massive, and therefore unstable, stars in the galaxy. It is almost the most dauntingly elegant. I could appreciate why the transcendients had chosen to base themselves here, ten thousand light-years away from Earth. Despite its glory, an ever-present reminder of matter's terrible fragility. Such a monster could never last for more than a few million years. Its triumphant end will come as a detonation that will probably be seen from galactic superclusters halfway toward the edge of infinity.

How Justin Ascham Raleigh would have loved this.

The habitat appeared in our forward sensors. A simple white circle against the swirling red fogs of the hulking sky. Two hundred miles across, it was alone in interstellar space apart from its companion portal. One side flung out towers and spires, alive with sparkling lights. The other was apparently open to space, its surface undulating gently with grassy vales and meandering streams. Forests created random patches of darker green that swarmed over the low hills.

"We have landing clearance," Neill Heller Caesar said.

"Have they changed the governing protocols?" I asked. I wasn't unduly nervous, but I did want this case to go to its absolute completion.

He paused, consulting his cybershadow. "No. The biononic connate acknowledges our authority."

The deepflight ship slid through the habitat's atmospheric boundary without a ripple. We flew along an extensive valley, and alighted at its far end, just before the central stream broke up into a network of silver runnels that emptied into a deep lake. There was a small white villa perched on the slope above the stream, its roof transparent to allow the inhabitants an uninterrupted view of Eta Carinae.

I followed Neill Heller Caesar across the spongy grass, impressed by how clean and natural the air smelled. A figure appeared in the villa's doorway and watched us approach.

It was so inevitable, I considered, that this person should be here of all the places in the universes we had reached. The transcendent project was attempting to imprint a human mind on the fabric of space-time itself. If they succeeded we would become as true angels, creatures of pure thought, distracted by nothing. It was the final liberation to which Bethany Maria Caesar had always aspired.

She smiled knowingly at me as I came through the gate in the white picket fence surrounding her garden. Once again, the elegant twenty-year-old beauty I'd seen in Justin's rooms at Dunbar College. I could scarcely remember the wizened figure who'd talked to me on Io.

"Edward Bucahanan Raleigh." She inclined her head in a slight bow. "So you never gave up."

"No."

"I appreciate the pursuit of a goal, especially over such a length of time. It's an admirable quality."

"Thank you. Are you going to deny it was you?"

She shook her head. "I would never insult you like that. But I would like to know how you found out."

"It was nothing you could have protected yourself from. You see, you smiled."

"I smiled?"

"Yes. When my back was turned. I've spent the last thirty years reviewing Carter's memories of his time at Oxford; accessing a little chunk of them almost every day. I'd gone over everything, absolutely everything, every event I considered remotely relevant was played again and again until I was in danger of becoming more like him than he ever was himself. It all amounted to nothing. Then I played his memories right to the bitter end. That night when Francis and I arrived at Justin's rooms, I asked detective Pitchford to take blood samples from all of you. He was rather annoyed about it, some junior know-it-all telling him how to do his job. Quite rightly, too. And that was when you smiled. I couldn't see it, but Carter did. I think he must have put it down to you being amused by Pitchford's reaction. But I've seen you smile like that on one other occasion. It was when we were on Io and I asked you to come back to

Earth because of the way low gravity was harming you. I asked you because I didn't understand then what the Caesars wanted with Jupiter. You did. You'd worked out in advance what would happen when biononics reached their full potential and how it could be used to your advantage. You were quite right, too, that particular orthodox branch of your family has already consumed Ganymede to build their habitats, and they show no sign of slowing their expansion."

"So I smiled at you."

"Yes. Both times you were outsmarting me. Which made me wonder about the blood sample. I had your sample taken out of stasis and analyzed again. The irony was, we actually had the relevant test back in eighteen thirty. We just never ran it."

"You found I had excessive progestin in my blood. And I smiled because your request confirmed the investigation would go the way I'd extrapolated. I knew I'd be asked for a sample by the police, but it was a risk I was prepared to take, because the odds of anyone making a connection from that to the murder were almost non-existent."

"The most we'd be likely to ask was how you got hold of an illegal contraception. But then you were a biochemist, you were probably able to make it in the lab."

"It wasn't easy. I had to be very careful about equipment usage. The church really stigmatizes contraception, even now."

"Like you say, using it still wasn't a reason to murder someone. Not by itself. Then I wondered why you were taking contraception. Nearly a third of the girls at university became pregnant. They weren't stigmatized. But then they're free to come back in fifty or seventy years after they've finished having children, and pick up where they left off. Not you though. I believed you were suffering from low-gravity deterioration on Io because I had no reason to think differently."

"Of course you didn't," she said disdainfully. "Everybody thinks the Sport of Emperors just bred the families for long life. But the Caesars were much cannier and crueler than that. There are branches of the family bred to reinforce other traits."

"Like intelligence. They concentrated on making you smart at the expense of longevity."

"Very astute of you, Edward. Yes, I'm a Short. Without biononic DNA reset I wouldn't have lived past a hundred and twenty."

"You couldn't afford time off from university to have children. It would have taken up half of your life, and you could already see where the emerging sciences were leading. That century was the greatest age of discovery and change we've ever had. It would never be repeated. And you might have been left behind before biononics reached fruition. No problem for us, but in your case being left behind might mean death."

"He didn't care," she said. Her eyes were closed, her voice a pained whisper. "He loved me. He wanted us to be together forever and raise twenty children."

"Then he found out you weren't going to have children with him."

"Yes. I loved him, too, with all my heart. We could have had all this future together, if he'd just made an allowance for what I was. But he wouldn't compromise, he wouldn't listen. Then he threatened to tell my college if I didn't stop taking the progestin. I couldn't believe he would betray me like that. I would have been a disgrace. The college would have sent me away. I didn't know how much value the Caesars would place on me, not back in those days, before I'd proved myself. I didn't know if they'd cover for me. I was twenty-one and desperate."

"So you killed him."

"I sneaked up to his room that night to ask him one last time. Even then he wouldn't listen. I actually had a knife in my hand, and he still said no. He was such a traditionalist, a regular bloke, loyal to his family and the world's ideology. So, yes, I killed him. If I hadn't, today wouldn't exist."

I looked up at the delicate strata of red light washing across the sky. What a strange place for this to finally be over. I wondered what Francis would make of it all. The old man would probably have a glass of particularly fine claret, then get on with the next case. Life was so simple when he was alive.

"It would," I said. "If not you, then someone else would have reached the breakthrough point. You said it yourself, we were freefalling to the plateau."

"All this does put us in an extremely awkward position," Neill Heller Caesar said. "You are the inventor of biononics, the mother of today's society. But we can hardly allow a murderer to go around unpunished, now can we."

"I'll leave," she said. "Go into exile for a thousand years or whatever. That way nobody will be embarrassed, and the family won't lose any political respect."

"That's what you want," I said. "I cannot agree to that. The whole reason that we have family command protocols built in to biononics is to ensure that there can be no radical breakaways. Nobody is able to set up by themselves and inflict harm on the rest of us. Humanity even in its current state has to be able to police itself, though the occasions where such actions are needed are thankfully rare. You taking off by yourself, and probably transcending into a pure energy form is hardly an act of penance. You killed a member of my family so that you could have that opportunity. Therefore, it must be denied you." My cybershadow reported that she issued a flurry of instructions to the local biononic connate. It didn't acknowledge. Neill Heller Caesar had kept his word. And I marveled at the irony in that. Justice served by an act of trust, enacted by a personality forged in a time where honesty and integrity were the highest values to which anyone could aspire. Maybe the likes of he and I did have something valid to contribute to everything today's youngsters were busy building.

Bethany Maria Caesar stiffened as she realized there was to be no escape this time. No window with a convenient creeper down which to climb. "Very well," she said. "What do you think my punishment should be? Am I to hang from the gallows until I'm dead."

"Don't be so melodramatic," Neill Heller Caesar told her. "Edward and I have come to an agreement which allows us to resolve this satisfactorily."

"Of course you have," she muttered.

"You took Justin's life away from him," I said. "We can produce a physical clone of him from the samples we kept. But that still won't be *him*. His personality, its uniqueness is lost to us forever. When you're dealing with a potentially immortal being there could be no crime worse. You have wasted his life and the potential it offered; in return you will be sentenced to exactly that same punishment. The difference is, you will be aware of it."

Was that too cruel of me? Possibly. But then consider

this: I once knew a man who knew a man who had seen the Empire's legionaries enforcing Rome's rule at the tip of a sword. None of us is as far removed from barbarism as we like to think.

Seven
Life Time

Bethany Maria Caesar was taken from the Eta Carinae habitat on our deepflight ship. We disembarked her on a similar habitat in Jupiter orbit which the Caesars had resource funded. She is its sole inhabitant. None of its biononics will respond to her instructions. The medical modules in her body will continue to reset her DNA. She will never age nor succumb to disease. In order to eat, she must catch or grow her own food. Her clothes have to be sewn or knitted by herself. Her house must be built from local materials, which are subject to entropy hastened by climate, requiring considerable maintenance. Such physical activities occupy a great deal of her time. If she wishes to continue living she must deny herself the luxury of devoting her superb mind to pure and abstract thoughts. However, she is able to see the new and wondrous shapes which slide fluidly past her region of space, and know her loss.

Her case is one of the oldest to remain active within our family thoughtcluster. One day, when I've matured and mellowed, and the Borgias have left the Vatican, I may access it again.

Reality Dust

Stephen Baxter

An explosion of light: the moment of her birth.

She cried out.

A sense of self flooded through her body. She had arms, legs; her limbs were flailing. She was *falling,* and glaring light wheeled about her.

But she remembered another place: a black sky, a world—no, a *moon*—a face before her, smiling gently. *This won't hurt. Close your eyes.*

A name. *Callisto.*

But the memories were dissipating.

"No!"

She landed hard, face down, and she was suffused by sudden pain. Her face was pressed into dust, rough, gritty particles, each as big as a moon to her staring eyes.

The flitter rose from liberated Earth like a stone thrown from a blue bowl. The little cylindrical craft tumbled slowly as it climbed, sparkling, and Hama Druz marvelled at the beauty of the mist-laden, subtly curved landscape below him, drenched as it was in clear bright sunlight.

But the scars of the Occupation were still visible. Away from the great Conurbations, much of the land still glistened silver-gray where starbreaker beams and Qax nanoreplicators had chewed up the surface of the Earth, life and rocks and all, turning it into a featureless silicate dust.

"But already," he pointed out eagerly, "life's green is returning. Look, Nomi, there, and there . . ."

His companion, Nomi Ferrer, grunted skeptically. "But that greenery has nothing to do with edicts from your Interim Coalition of Governance, or all your philosophies. That's the worms, Hama, turning Qax dust back into soil. Just the worms, that's all."

Hama would not be put off. Nomi, once a ragamuffin, was an officer in the Green Army, the most significant military force yet assembled in the wake of the departing Qax. She was forty years old, her body a solid slab of muscle, with burn marks disfiguring one cheek. And, in Hama's judgment, she was much too sunk in cynicism.

He slapped her on the shoulder, "Quite right, And that's how we must be, Nomi: like humble worms, content to toil in the darkness, to turn a few scraps of our land back the way they should be. That should be enough for any life!"

Nomi just snorted.

The two-seat flitter began to descend toward a Conurbation. Still known by its Qax registration of 11729, the Conurbation was a broad, glistening sprawl of bubble-dwellings blown from the bedrock, and linked by the green-blue of umbilical canals. Hama saw that many of the dome-shaped buildings had been scarred by fire, some even cracked open. But the blue-green tetrahedral sigil of free Earth had been daubed on every surface.

A shadow passed over the Conurbation's glistening

rooftops. Hama shielded his eyes and squinted upward. A fleshy cloud briefly eclipsed the sun. It was a Spline ship: a living starship kilometers across, its hardened epidermis pocked with monitor and weapon emplacements. He suppressed a shudder. For generations the Spline had been the symbol of Qax dominance. But now the Qax had gone, and this last abandoned Spline was in the hands of human engineers, who sought to comprehend its strange biological workings.

On the outskirts of the Conurbation there was a broad pit scooped out of the ground, its crudely scraped walls denoting its origin as post-Occupation: human, not Qax. In this pit rested a number of silvery, insectile forms, and as the flitter fell further through the sunlit air, Hama could see people moving around the gleaming shapes, talking, working. The pit was a shipyard, operated by and for humans, who were slowly rediscovering yet another lost art; for no human engineer had built a spacecraft on Earth for three hundred years.

Hama pressed his face to the window—like a child, he knew, reinforcing Nomi's preconception of him—but to Lethe with self-consciousness. "One of those ships is going to take us to Callisto. imagine it, Nomi—a moon of Jupiter!"

But Nomi scowled. "Just remember *why* we're going there: to hunt out jasofts—criminals and collaborators. It will be a grim business, Hama, no matter how pretty the scenery."

The flitter slid easily through the final phases of its descent, and the domes of the Conurbation loomed around them.

There was a voice, talking fast, almost babbling.

"There is no time. There is no space. We live in a universe of static shapes. Do you see? Imagine a grain of dust that represents all the particles in *our* universe, frozen in time. Imagine a stupendous number of dust grains, representing all the possible shapes the particles can take. This is reality dust, a dust of the Nows. And the dust fills a realm of instants." A snapping of fingers. "There. There. There. Each moment, each juggling of the particles, a new grain. The reality dust contains all the arrangements of matter there could ever be. Reality dust is an image of eternity . . ."

She lay there, face pressed into the dirt, wishing none of this was happening.

Hands grabbed her, by shoulder and hip. She was dragged, flipped over on her back. The sky above was dazzling bright.

She cried out again.

A face loomed, silhouetted. She saw a hairless scalp, no eyebrows or lashes. The face itself was rounded, smoothed over, as if unformed. But she had a strong impression of great age.

"This won't hurt," she whispered, terrified. "Close your eyes."

The face loomed closer. "Nothing here is real." The voice was harsh, without inflection. A man? "Not even the dust."

"Reality dust," she murmured.

"Yes. Yes! It is reality dust. If you live, remember that."

The face receded, turning away.

She tried to sit up. She pressed her hands into the loose dust, crushing low, crumbling structures, like the tunnels of worms. She glimpsed a flat horizon, a black, oily sea, forest-covered hills. She was on a beach, a beach of silvery, dusty sand. The sky was a glowing dome. The air was full of mist;

she couldn't see very far, in any direction, as if she were trapped in a glowing bubble.

Her companion was mid-sized, his body shapeless and sexless. He was dressed in a coverall of a nondescript color. He cast no shadow in the bright diffuse light.

She glanced down at herself. She was wearing a similar coverall. She fingered its smooth fabric, baffled.

He was walking slowly, limping, as though exhausted. Walking away, leaving her alone.

"Please," she said.

Without stopping, he called back, "If you stay there you'll die."

"What's your name?"

"Pharaoh. That is all the name I have left, at any rate."

She thought hard. Those sharp birth memories had fled, but still . . . "*Callisto*. My name is Callisto."

Pharaoh laughed. "Of course it is."

Without warning, pain swamped her right hand.

She snatched it to her chest. The skin felt as if it had been drenched in acid.

The sea had risen, she saw, and the black, lapping fluid had covered her hand. Where the fluid had touched, the flesh was flaking away, turning to chaotic dust, exposing sketchy bones that crumbled and fell in thin slivers.

She screamed. She had only been here a moment, and already such a terrible thing had happened.

Pharaoh limped back to her. "Think beyond the pain."

"I can't—"

"*Think*. There is no pain."

And, as he said it, she realized it was true. Her hand was gone, her arm terminating in a smooth, rounded stump. But it didn't hurt. How could that be?

"What do you feel?"

". . . Diminished," she said.

"Good," he said. "You're learning. There is no pain here. Only forgetting."

The black, sticky fluid was lapping near her legs. She scrambled away. But when she tried to use her missing right hand she stumbled, falling flat.

Pharaoh locked his hand under her arm and hauled her to her feet. The brief exertion seemed to exhaust him; his face smoothed further, as if blurring. "Go," he said.

"Where?"

"Away from the sea." And he pushed her, feebly, away from the ocean.

She looked that way doubtfully. The beach sloped upward sharply; it would be a difficult climb. Above the beach there was what looked like a forest, tall shapes like trees, a carpet of something like grass. She saw people moving in the darkness between the trees. But the forest was dense, a place of colorless, flat shadows, made gray by the mist.

She looked back. Pharaoh was standing where she had left him, a pale, smoothed-over figure just a few paces from the lapping, encroaching sea, already dimmed by the thick white mist.

She called, "Aren't you coming?"

"Go."

"I'm afraid."

"Asgard. Help her."

Callisto turned. There was a woman, not far away, crawling over the beach. She seemed to be plucking stray grass blades from the dust, cramming them into her mouth. Her face was a mask of wrinkles, complex, textured—a stark contrast to Pharaoh's smoothed-over countenance. Her voice querulous, she snapped, "Why should I?"

"Because I once helped you."

The woman got to her feet, growling.

Callisto quailed. But Asgard took her good hand and began to haul her up the beach.

Callisto looked back once more. The oil-black sea lapped thickly over a flat, empty beach, Pharaoh had gone.

As they made their way to Hama's assigned office, Nomi drew closer to Hama's side, keeping her weapons obvious.

The narrow corridors of Conurbation 11729 were grievously damaged by fire and weaponry—and they were scars inflicted not by Qax, but by humans. In some places there was even a smell of burning.

And the corridors were crowded; not just with former inhabitants of the Qax-built city, but with others Hama couldn't help but think of as *outsiders*.

There were ragamuffins—like Nomi herself—the product of generations who had waited out the Occupation in the ruins of ancient human cities, and other corners of wilderness Earth. And there were returned refugees and traders, the descendants of people who had fled to the outer moons and even beyond the Solar System to escape the Qax's powerful, if inefficient, grasp. Some of these returned space travelers were exotic indeed, with skin darkened by the light of other stars, and frames made spindly or squat by other gravities—even eyes replaced by Eyes, mechanical supplements. And most of them had *hair:* hair sprouting wildly from their heads and even their faces, in colors of varying degrees of outrage. They made the Conurbation's Occupation-era inhabitants, with their drab monkish robes and shaven heads, look like characterless drones.

The various factions eyed each other with suspicion, even hostility; Hama saw no signs of unity among liberated mankind.

Hama's office turned out to be a spacious room, the walls lined with data slates. It even had a natural-light window, overlooking a swathe of the Conurbation and the lands beyond.

This prestigious room had once, of course, been assigned to a jasoft—a human collaborator administering Earth on behalf of the Qax—and Hama felt a deep reluctance to enter it. For Hama, up to now, the liberation had been painless, a time of opportunity and freedom, like a wonderful game. But that, he knew, was about to change.

Hama Druz, twenty-five years old, had been assigned to the Commission for Historical Truth, the tribunal appointed to investigate and try collaboration crimes. His job was to hunt out jasofts.

Some of these collaborators were said to be *pharaohs*, kept alive by Qax technology, perhaps for centuries . . . Some, it was said, were even survivors of the pre-Occupation period, when human science had advanced enough to beat back death. If the jasofts were hated, the pharaohs had been despised most of all; for the longer they had lived, the more loyalty they owed to the Qax, and the more effectively they administered the Qax regime. And that regime had become especially brutal after a flawed human Rebellion more than a century earlier.

Hama, accompanied by Nomi, would spend a few days here, acquainting himself with the issues around the collaborators. But to complete his assignment he would have to travel far beyond the Earth: to Jupiter's moon, Callisto, in fact. There—according to records kept during the Occupation by the jasofts themselves—a number of pharaohs had fled to a science station maintained by one of their number, a man named Reth Cana.

For the next few days Hama worked through the data slates assembled for him, and received visitors, petitions, claimants. He quickly learned that there were many issues here beyond the crimes of the collaborator class.

The Conurbation itself faced endless problems day to day. The Conurbations had been deliberately designed by the Qax as temporary cities. It was all part of the grand strategy of the latter Occupation; the Qax's human subjects were not to be allowed ties of family, of home, of loyalty to anybody or anything—except perhaps the Occupation itself.

The practical result was that the hastily-constructed Conurbation was quickly running down. Hama read gloomily through report after report of silting-up canals and failing heating or lighting and crumbling dwelling-places. There were people sickening of diseases long thought vanished from the planet—even hunger had returned.

And then there were the wars.

The aftermath of Qax's withdrawal—the overnight removal of the government of Earth after three centuries—had been extremely difficult. In less than a month humans had begun fighting humans once more. It had taken a chaotic half-year before the Interim Coalition had coalesced, and even now, around the planet, brushfire battles still raged against warlords armed with Qax weaponry.

And it had been the jasofts, of course, who had been the focus of the worst conflicts. In many places jasofts, including pharaohs, had been summarily executed. Elsewhere the jasofts had gone into hiding, or fled off-world, or had even fought back.

The Interim Coalition had quelled the bloodshed by promising that the collaborators would be brought to justice before the new Commission for Historical Truth. But Hama—alone in his office, poring over his data slates—knew that justice was easier promised than delivered. How were shortlived humans—dismissively called *mayflies* by the pharaohs—to try crimes whose commission might date back centuries? There were no witnesses save the pharaohs themselves; no formal records save those maintained under the Occupation; no testimony save a handful of legends preserved through the endless dissolutions of the Conurbations; not even any physical evidence since the Qax's great Extirpation had wiped the Earth clean of its past.

What made it even more difficult, Hama was slowly discovering, was that the jasofts were *useful*.

It was a matter of compromise, of practical politics. The jasofts knew how the world worked, on the mundane level of keeping people alive, for they had administered the planet for centuries. So some jasofts—offered amnesties for cooperating—were discreetly running parts of Earth's new, slowly-coalescing administration, just as they had under the Qax.

And meanwhile, children were going hungry.

Hama had, subtly, protested against his new assignment.

He felt his strength lay in philosophy, in abstraction. He longed to rejoin the debates going on in great constitutional conventions all over the planet, as the human race, newly liberated from the Qax, sought a new way to govern itself.

But his appeal against reassignment had been turned down. There was simply too much to do now, too great a mess to clear up, and too few able and trustworthy people available to do it.

It was so bad, in fact, that some people were openly calling for the return of the Qax. *At least we were kept warm and fed under the Qax. At least there were no bandits trying to rob or kill us. And there were none of these disgusting ragamuffins cluttering up the public places . . .*

As he witnessed the clamor of the crowds around the failing food dispensers, Hama felt a deep horror—and a determination that this should not recur. And yet, to his shame, he looked forward to escaping from all this complexity to the cool open spaces of the Jovian system.

It was while he was in this uncertain mood that the pharaoh sought him out.

Asgard led her to the fringe of the forest. There, ignoring Callisto, she hunkered down and began to pull at strands of grass, ripping them from the ground and pushing them into her mouth.

Callisto watched doubtfully. "What should I do?"

Asgard shrugged. "Eat."

Reluctantly, Callisto got to her knees. Favoring her truncated arm, it was difficult to keep her balance. With her left hand she pulled a few blades of the grass stuff from the dust. She crammed the grass into her mouth and chewed. It was moist, tasteless, slippery.

She found that the grass blades weren't connected to roots. Rather they seemed to blend back into the dust, to the tube-like structures there. Deeper into the forest's gathering darkness the grass grew longer, plaiting itself into ropy vine-like plants. And deeper still she saw things like trees looming tall.

People moved among the trees, digging at the roots with their bare hands, pushing fragments of food into their faces.

"My name," she said, "is Callisto."

Asgard grunted. "Your dream-name."

"I remembered it."

"No, you *dreamed*."

"What is this place?"

"It isn't a place."

"What's it called?"

"It has no name!" Asgard held up a blade of grass. "What color is this?"

"Green," Callisto said immediately . . . but that wasn't true. It wasn't green. What color, then? She realized she couldn't say.

Asgard laughed, and shoved the blade in her mouth.

Callisto looked down the beach. "What happened to Pharaoh?"

Asgard shrugged. "He might be dead by now. Washed away by the sea."

"Why doesn't he come up here, where it's safe?"

"Because he's weak. Weak and mad."

"He saved me from the sea."

"He helps all the newborns."

"Why?"

"How should I know? But it's futile. The ocean rises and falls. Every time it comes a little closer, higher up the beach. Soon it will lap right up here, to the forest itself."

"We'll have to go into the forest."

"Try that and Night will kill you."

Night? Callisto looked into the forest's darkness, and shuddered.

Asgard eyed Callisto with curiosity, no sympathy. "You really are a newborn, aren't you?" She dug her hand into the dust, shook it until a few grains were left on her palm. "You know what the first thing Pharaoh said to *me* was? 'Nothing is real.' "

"Yes—"

" 'Not even the dust. *Because every grain is a whole world.*' " She looked up at Callisto, calculating.

Callisto gazed at the sparkling grains, wondering, baffled, frightened.

Too much strangeness.

I want to go home, she thought desperately. But where, and what, is home?

Two women walked into Hama's office: one short, squat, her face a hard mask, and the other apparently younger, taller, willowy. They both wore bland, rather scuffed Occupation-era robes—as he did—and their heads were shaven bare.

The older woman met his gaze steadily. "My name is Gemo Cana. This is my daughter. She is called Sarfi."

Hama eyed them with brief curiosity.

This was a routine appointment. Gemo Cana was, supposedly, a representative of a citizens' group concerned about details of the testimony being heard by the preliminary hearings of the Truth Commission. The archaic words of family—*daughter, mother*—were still strange to Hama, but they were becoming increasingly more common, as the era of the Qax cadres faded from memory.

The daughter, Sarfi, averted her eyes. She looked very young, and her face was thin, her skin sallow.

He welcomed them with his standard opening remarks. "My name is Hama Druz. I am an advisor to the interim Coalition and specifically to the Commission for Historical Truth. I will listen to whatever you wish to tell me and will help you any way I can; but you must understand that my role here is not formal, and—"

"You're tired," Gemo Cana said.

"What?"

She stepped forward and studied him, her gaze direct, disconcerting. "It's harder than you thought, isn't it? Running an office, a city—a world. Especially as you must work by persuasion, consent." She walked around the room, ran a finger over the data slates fixed on the walls, and paused before the window, gazing out at the glistening rooftops of the Conurbation, the muddy blue-green of the canals. Hama could see the Spline ship rolling in the sky, a wrinkled moon. She said, "It was difficult enough in the era of the Qax, whose authority, backed by Spline gunships, was unquestionable,"

"And," asked Hama, "how exactly do you know that?"

"This used to be my office."

Hama reached immediately for his desktop.

"Please." The girl, Sarfi, reached out toward him, then seemed to think better of it. "Don't call your guards. Hear us out."

He stood. "You're a jasoft, Gemo Cana."

"Oh, worse than that," Gemo murmured. "I'm a *pharaoh* . . . You know, I have missed this view. The Qax knew what they were doing when they gave us jasofts the sunlight."

She was the first pharaoh Hama had encountered face to face. Hama quailed before her easy authority, her sense of dusty age; he felt young, foolish, his precious philosophies half-formed. And he found himself staring at the girl; he hadn't even known pharaohs could have children.

Deliberately he looked away, seeking a way to regain control of the situation. "You've been in hiding."

Gemo inclined her head. "I spent a long time in this office, Hama Druz. Longer than you can imagine. I always knew the day would come when the Qax would leave us exposed."

"So you prepared."

"Wouldn't you? I was doing my duty. I didn't want to die for it."

"Your duty to Qax occupiers?"

"No," she said, a note of weariness in her voice. "You seem more intelligent than the rest; I had hoped you might understand that much. It was a duty to mankind, of course. It always was."

He tapped a data slate on his desk. "*Gemo Cana*. I should have recognized the name. You are one of the most hunted jasofts. Your testimony before the Commission—"

She snapped. "I'm not here to surrender, Hama Druz, but to ask for your help."

"I don't understand."

"I know about your mission to Callisto. To the enclave there. Reth has been running a science station since before the Occupation. Now *you* are going out there to close him down."

He said grimly, "These last few years have not been a time for science."

She nodded. "So you believe science is a luxury, a plaything for easier times. But science is a thread in the tapestry of our humanity—a thread Reth had maintained. Do you even know what he is doing out there?"

"Something to do with life forms in the ice—"

"Oh, much more than that. Reth has been exploring the nature of reality—*seeking a way to abolish time itself.*" She smiled coolly. "I don't expect you to understand. But it has been a fitting goal, in an era when the Qax sought to obliterate human history—to abolish the passage of time from the human consciousness . . ."

He frowned. *Abolishing time?* Such notions were strange to him, meaningless. He said, "We have evidence that the science performed on Callisto was only a cover—that many pharaohs fled there during the chaotic period following the Qax withdrawal."

"Only a handful. There only ever was a handful of us, you know. And now that some have achieved a more fundamental escape, into death, there are fewer than ever."

"What do you *want?*"

"I want you to take us there."

"To Callisto?"

"We will remain in your custody, you and your guards. You may restrain us as you like. We will not try anything—*heroic*. All we want is sanctuary. They will kill us, you see."

"The Commission is not a mob."

She ignored that. "I am not concerned for myself, but for my daughter. Sarfi has nothing to do with this; she is no jasoft."

"Then she will not be harmed."

Gemo just laughed.

"You are evading justice, Gemo Cana."

She leaned forward, resting her hands on the desk nonchalantly; this really had been her office, he realized. "*There is no justice here,*" she hissed. "How can there be? I am asking you to spare my daughter's life. Later, I will gladly return to face whatever inquisition you choose to set up."

"Why would this *Reth* help you?"

"His name is Reth Cana," she said. "He is my brother. Do you understand? Not my cadre sibling. *My brother.*"

Gemo Cana; Reth Cana.

In the Qax world, families had been a thing for ragamuffins and refugees, and human names had become arbitrary labels; the coincidence of names had meant nothing to Hama. But to these ancient survivors, a shared name was a badge of kinship. He glanced at Gemo and Sarfi, uneasy in the presence of these close primitive ties, of mother and brother and daughter.

Abruptly the door opened; Nomi Ferrer walked in, reading from a data slate. "Hama, your ship is ready to go. But I think we have to . . ." She looked up, took in the scene at a glance. In an instant she was at Gemo's side, with a laser pistol pressed against the pharaoh's throat. "Gemo Cana," she hissed. "How did you get in here?"

Sarfi stepped toward Nomi, hands fluttering like birds.

Hama held up his hand. "Nomi, wait."

Nomi was angered. "Wait for what? Standing orders, Hama. This is a Category One jasoft who hasn't presented herself to the Commission. I should already have killed her."

Gemo smiled thinly. "It isn't so easy, is it, Hama Druz? You can theorize all you want about justice and retribution. But here in this office, you must confront the reality of a mother and her child."

Sarfi said to Hama, "If your guard kills my mother, she kills me too."

"No," said Hama. "We aren't barbarians. You have nothing to fear—"

Sarfi reached out and swept her arm down at the desk—no, Hama saw, startled; her arm passed *through* the desk, briefly breaking up into a cloud of pixels, boxes of glowing color.

"You're a Virtual' he whispered.

"Yes. And do you want to know where I live?" She stepped up to her mother and pushed her hand into Gemo's skull.

Gemo observed his lack of comprehension. "You don't know much about us, do you, even though you presume to judge us? . . . Hama, pharaohs do not breed true."

"Your daughter was mortal?"

"The Qax's gift was ambiguous. We watched our children grow old and die. That was our reward for serving the Qax; perhaps your Commission will accept that historical truth. And when she died—"

"When she died, you downloaded her into your *head?*"

"Nowhere else was safe," Gemo said. "And I was glad to, umm, make room for her. I have lived a long time; there were memories I was happy to shed . . ."

Nomi said harshly, "But she isn't your daughter. She's a copy."

Gemo closed her eyes. "But she's all I have left."

Sarfi looked away, as if ashamed.

Hama felt moved, and repelled, by this act of obsessive love.

There was a low concussion. The floor shuddered.

Nomi Ferrer understood immediately. "Lethe. That was an explosion."

Hama could hear running footsteps, cries. The light

dropped, as if some immense shadow were passing over the sky. Hama ran to the window.

All around the Conurbation, ships were lifting, hauled into the sky by silent Qax technology, an eerie rising of ballooning metal flanks. But they entered a sky that was already crowded, darkened by the rolling, meaty bulk of a Spline craft.

Hama quailed from the brute physical reality of the erupting conflict. And he knew who to blame. "It's the jasofts," he said. "The ones taken to orbit to help with the salvaging of the Spline. They took it over. And now they've come here, to rescue their colleagues . . ."

Gemo smiled, squinting up at the sky. "Sadly, stupidity is not the sole prerogative of mayflies. This counter-coup cannot succeed. And then, when this Spline no longer darkens the sky, your vengeance will not be moderated by show trials and bleats about justice and truth . . ."

Sarfi pressed her hands to her face.

Hama stared at Gemo. "*You knew.* You knew this was about to happen. You timed your visit to force me to act."

"It's all very complicated, Hama Druz," Gemo said softly, manipulating. "Don't you think so? Get us out of here—all of us—and sort it out later."

Nomi pulled back the pharaoh's head. "You know what I think? I think you're a monster, pharaoh. I think you killed your daughter, long ago, and stuck her in your head. An insurance against a day like today."

Gemo, her face twisted by Nomi's strong fingers, forced a smile. "Even if that were true, what difference would it make?" And she gazed at Hama, waiting for his decision.

Obeying Nomi's stern voice commands, the ship rose sharply. Hama felt nothing as shadows slipped over his lap.

This small craft, commissioned to take Hama to Jupiter's moons, was little more than a translucent hemisphere. In fact it would serve as a lifedome, part of a greater structure waiting in Earth orbit to propel him across the Solar System. The three of them, plus Sarfi, were jammed into a cabin made for two. The Virtual girl was forced to share the space already occupied by Hama and Gemo. Where her projection intersected their bodies it dimmed and broke up, and she averted her face; Hama was embarrassed by this brutal indignity.

The ship emerged from its pit and rushed beneath the looming belly of the spline; there was a brief, ugly moment of fleeing, crumpled flesh, oozing scars meters long, glistening weapon emplacements dug in like stab wounds.

The air was crowded, Ships of all sizes cruised above Conurbation 11729, seeking to engage the Spline. Hama saw, with a sinking heart, that one of the ancient, half-salvaged ships had crashed back to Earth. It had made a broad crater, a wound in the ground circled by burning blown-silicate buildings. Already people had died today, irreplaceable lives lost forever.

The ship reached clear sky and soared upward. Earth folded over into a glowing blue abstraction, pointlessly beautiful, hiding the gruesome scenes below; the air thinned, the sky dimming through violet, to black.

The lifedome began to seek out the orbiting angular structure that would carry it to the outer planets.

Hama began to relax, for the first time since Gemo had revealed herself. Despite everything that had happened he was relieved to leave behind the complication of the Conurbation; perhaps in the thin light of Jupiter the dilemmas he would have to face would be simpler.

Sarfi gasped.

A vast winged shape sailed over the blue hide of Earth, silent, like a predator.

Hama's heart sank at the sight of this new, unexpected intruder. What now?

Nomi said softly, "Those wings must be hundreds of kilometers across."

"Ah," said Gemo. "just like the old stories. The ship *is* like a sycamore seed . . . But none of you remembers *sycamore trees,* do you? Perhaps you need us, and our memories, after all."

Nomi said, anger erupting, "People are dying down there because of your kind, Gemo—"

Hama placed a hand on her arm. "Tell us, pharaoh. Is it Qax?"

"Not Qax," she said. "*Xeelee.*" It was the first time Hama had heard the name. "That is a Xeelee nightfighter," said Gemo. "The question is—what does it want here?"

There was a soft warning chime.

The ship shot away from Earth. The planet dwindled, closing on itself, becoming a sparkling blue bauble, a bauble over which a black-winged insect crawled.

Callisto joined the community of foragers.

Dwelling where the forest met the beach, the people ate the grass, and sometimes leaves from the lower branches, even loose flaps of bark. The people were wary, solitary. She didn't learn their names—if they had any—nor gained a clear impression of their faces, their sexes. She wasn't even sure how many of them there were here.

Not many, she thought.

Callisto found herself eating incessantly. With every mouthful she took she felt herself grow, subtly, in some invisible direction—the opposite to the diminution she had suffered when she lost her hand to the burning power of the sea. There was nothing to drink—no fluid save the oily black ink of the ocean, and she wasn't tempted to try that. But it didn't seem to matter.

Callisto was not without curiosity.

The beach curved away, in either direction. Perhaps this was an island, poking out of the looming black ocean.

There was no bedrock, not as far as she could dig. Only the drifting, uniform dust.

There were structures in the dust: crude tubes and trails, like the markings of worms or crabs. The grass *emerged*, somehow, coalescing from looser dust formations. The grass grew sparsely on the open beach, but at the fringe of the forest it gathered in dense clumps. In some tufts the long blades wove together until they merged, forming more substantial, ropy plants.

Tiring of Asgard's cold company, she plucked up her courage and walked away from the beach, deeper into the forest.

Away from the lapping of the sea and the wordless rustle of the foraging people, it grew dark, quiet. Grass ropes wrapped around her legs, tugging, yielding with reluctance as she passed. This was a drab, still, lifeless place, she thought. In a bush like this there ought to be texture: movement, noise, scent. So, anyhow, her flawed memories dimly protested.

She found a thick, solid mass, like a tree root. It was a tangle of grassy ropes, melding into a more substantial whole. She followed it. The root soon twined around another, and then another, the whole soon merging into a snaking cylinder broad enough to walk on. And from all around her more such giant roots were converging, as if she were approaching some great confluence of life.

At last the roots left the ground before her and rose up in a thick, twisted tangle, impossible to penetrate.

She peered up. The root stems coalesced into a thick unified trunk. It was a "tree" that rose above the surrounding vegetative mass and into the light of the sky. But a low mist lay heavily, obscuring her view of the tree's upper branches.

She felt curiosity spark.

She placed her hand on the knotted-up lower trunk, then one foot, and then the other. The stuff of the tree was hard and cold.

At first the climbing was easy, the components of the "trunk" loosely separated. She found a way to lodge her bad arm in gaps in the trunk so she could release her left hand briefly, and grab for a new handhold before she fell back. But as she climbed higher the ropey sub-trunks grew ever more tangled.

High above her the trunk soared upward, daunting, disappearing into the mist. But she thought she made out branches arching through the mist, high above the surrounding vegetation. When she looked down, she saw how the "roots" of this great structure dispersed over the forest floor, branching into narrower trees and vine-thin creepers and at last clumps of grass, dispersing into the underlying dust. She felt unexpectedly exhilarated by this small adventure—

There was a snarl, of greed and anger. It came from just

above her head. She quailed, slipped. She finished up dangling by her one hand.

It was human. Or, it might once have been human. It must have been four, five times her size. It was naked, and it clung to the tree above her, upside down, so that a broad face leered, predator's eyes fixed on her, its limbs were cylinders of muscle, its chest and bulging belly massive, weighty. And it was male: an erection poked crudely between its legs.

It thrust its mouth at her, hissing. She could smell blood on its breath.

She screamed and lost her grip.

She fell, sliding down the trunk. She scrabbled for purchase with her feet and her one good hand. She slammed repeatedly against the trunk, and the wind was knocked out of her.

Above her, the beast receded, still staring into her eyes.

When she reached the ground, ignoring the aches of battered body and torn feet, she blundered away, running until she reached the openness of the beach.

For an unmeasured time she lay on the beach, drawing comfort from the graininess of the dust.

The craft was called a GUTship.

As finally assembled, it looked something like a parasol of iron and ice. The canopy of the parasol was the habitable lifedome, and the "handle" was the GUTdrive unit itself, embedded in a block of asteroid ice which served as reaction mass. The shaft of the parasol, separating the lifedome from the drive unit, was a kilometer-long spine of metal bristling with antennae and sensors.

The design was centuries old.

The ship itself had been built long before the Occupation, and lovingly maintained by a colony of refugees who had seen out the Qax era huddled in the asteroid belt. In a hundred subtle ways the ship showed its age. Every surface in the lifedome was scuffed and polished from use, the soft coverings of chairs and bunks were extensively patched, and many of the major systems bore the scars of rebuilding.

GUT, it seemed, was an acronym for Grand Unified Theory. Once, Gemo whispered, unified-theory energy had fueled the expansion of the universe itself. In the heart of each GUTdrive asteroid ice was compressed to conditions resembling the initial singularity—the Big Bang. There, the fundamental forces governing the structure of matter merged into a single superforce. When the matter was allowed to expand again, the phase energy of the decomposing superforce, released like heat from condensing steam, was used to expel asteroid matter as a vapor rocket . . .

Remarkable, exotic, strange; this might be a primitive ship compared to a mighty Spline vessel, but Hama had never dreamed that mere humans had once mastered such technologies.

But when they were underway, with the lifedome opaqued over and all the strangeness shut out, none of that mattered. To Hama it was like being back in the Conurbations, in the enclosed, claustrophobic days before the Occupation was lifted. A deep part of his mind seemed to believe that way lay beyond these walls—occupied Earth, or endless universe—did not matter so long as he was safe and warm. He felt comfortable in his mobile prison—and was guilty to feel that way.

But everything changed when they reached Callisto.

They entered a wide, slow orbit around the ice moon.

The sun was shrunk to the tiniest of discs by Jupiter's remoteness, five times as far as Earth from the central light. When Hama held up his hand it cast sharp, straight shadows, the shadows of infinity, and he felt no warmth.

And through this rectilinear, reduced light, Callisto swam.

The satellite was like a dark, misty twin of Earth's Moon. its surface was crowded with craters—even more so than the Moon's, for there were none of the giant lava-flood seas that smoothed over much lunar terrain. The largest craters were complex structures, plains of pale ice surrounded by multiple arcs of folded and cracked land, like ripples frozen into shattered ice and rock. Some of these features were the size of continents, large enough to stretch around this lonely moon's curved horizon, evidently the result of immense, terrifying impacts.

But these great geological sculptures were oddly smoothed out, the cracks and ripples reduced to shallow ridges. Unlike the rocky Moon, Callisto was made of rock and water ice. Over billions of years the ice had suffered viscous relaxation; it flowed and slumped. The most ancient craters had simply subsided, like great geological sighs, leaving these spectacular palimpsests.

"The largest impact structure is called Valhalla," Gemo was saying. "Once there were human settlements all along the northern faces of the circular ridges. All dark now, of course—save where Reth has made his base."

Nomi grunted, uninterested in tourism. "Then that's where we land."

Hama gazed out at this silent sculpture of ice and time. "Remarkable," he said. "I never imagined—"

Gemo said caustically, "You are a drone of the Occupation. You never even saw the sunlight, you never imagined a universe beyond the walls of your Conurbation, you have never lived. You have no *memory*. And yet you presume to judge. Do you even know why Callisto is so-called? It is an ancient myth. Callisto was a nymph, beloved of Zeus and hated by jealous Hera, who metamorphosed her into a bear . . ." She seemed to sense Hama's bafflement. "Ah, but you don't even remember the *Gree-chs,* do you?"

Nomi confronted her. "*You* administered the Extirpation, pharaoh. Your arrogance over the memories you took from us is—"

"Ill-mannered," Hama said smoothly, and he touched Nomi's shoulder, seeking to calm the situation. "A lack of grace that invalidates her assumption of superiority over us. Don't concern yourself, Nomi. She condemns herself and her kind every time she speaks."

Gemo glared at him, full of contempt.

But now Jupiter rose.

The four of them crowded to see. They bobbed in the air like balloons, thrust into weightlessness now that the drive was shut down.

The largest of planets was a dish of muddy light, of cloudy bands, pink and purple and brown. Where the bands met, Hama could see fine lines of turbulence, swoops and swirls like a lunatic watercolor. But a single vast storm disfigured those smooth bands, twisting and stirring them right across the southern hemisphere of the planet, as if the whole of Jupiter were being sucked into some vast central maw.

As perhaps it was. There was a legend that, a century before, human rebels called the Friends of Wigner had climaxed their revolt by escaping *back through time,* across thousands of years, and had hurled a black hole into the heart of Jupiter. The knot of compressed spacetime was already distorting Jupiter's immense, dreamy structure, and in perhaps a million years would destroy the great world altogether. It was a fantastic story, probably no more than a tale spun for comfort during the darkest hours of Occupation.

Still, it was clear that *something* was wrong with Jupiter. Nobody knew the truth—except perhaps the pharaohs, and they would say nothing.

Hama saw how Sarfi, entranced, tried to rest her hand against the lifedome's smooth transparency. But her hand sank into the surface, crumbling, and she snatched it away quickly. Such incidents seemed to cause Sarfi deep distress—as if she had been programmed with deep taboos about violating the physical laws governing "real" humans. Perhaps it even hurt her when such breaches occurred.

Gemo Cana did not appear to notice her daughter's pain.

The lifedome neatly detached itself from the ship's drive section and swept smoothly down from orbit. Hama watched the moon's folded-over, crater-scarred landscape flatten out, the great circular ramparts of Valhalla marching over the close horizon.

The lifedome settled to the ice with the gentlest of crunches.

A walkway extended from a darkened building block, and nuzzled hesitantly against the ship. A hatch sighed open.

Hama stood in the hatchway. The walkway was a transparent, shimmering tube before him, concealing little of the silver-black morphology of the collapsed landscape beyond. The main feature was the big Valhalla ridge, of course. Seen this close it was merely a rise in the land, a scarp that marched to either horizon: it would have been impossible to tell from the ground that this was in fact part of a great circular rampart surrounding a continent-sized impact scar, and Hama felt insignificant, dwarfed.

He forced himself to take the first step along the walkway.

The gravity here was about an eighth of Earth's, comparable to the Moon's, and to walk through Callisto's crystal stillness was enchanting; he floated between footsteps in great bounds.

Gemo mocked his pleasure. "We are like *Armm-stron* and *All-dinn.*"

Nomi growled, "More *Gree-chs,* pharaoh?"

Reth Cana was waiting to meet them at the end of the walkway.

He was short, squat, with a crisp scalp of white hair, and he wore a practical-looking coverall of some papery fabric. He was scowling at them, his face a round wrinkled mask.

Beyond him, Hama glimpsed extensive chambers, dug into the ice, dimly lit by a handful of floating globe lamps—extensive, but deserted.

But Hama's gaze was drawn back to Reth. *He looks like Gemo.*

Gemo stepped forward now, and they faced each other, brother and sister separated for centuries. Stiffly, they embraced. They were like copies of each other, subtly morphed.

Sarfi hung back, watching, hands folded before her.

Hama felt excluded, almost envious of this piece of complex humanity. How must it be to be bound to another person by such strong ties—for life?

Reth stepped away from his sister and inspected Sarfi. Without warning he swept his clenched fist through the girl's belly. He made a trail of disrupted pixels, like a fleshy comet. Sarfi crumpled over, crying out.

The sudden brutality shocked Hama.

Reth laughed. "A Virtual? I didn't suspect you were so sentimental, Gemo."

Gemo stepped forward, her mouth working. "But I remember your cruelty."

Now Reth faced Hama. "And this is the one sent by Earth's new junta of children."

Hama shrank before Reth's arrogance and authority. His accent was exotic—antique, perhaps; there was a rustle of history about this man. Hama tried to keep his voice steady. "I have a specific assignment here, sir—"

Reth snorted. "My work, a project of centuries, deals with the essence of reality itself. It is an achievement of which you have *no* understanding. If you had a glimmer of sensitivity you would leave now. Just as, if you and your mayfly friends had any true notion of duty, you would abandon your petty attempts at governing."

Nomi growled. "You think we got rid of the Qax just to hand over our lives to the likes of you?"

Reth glared at her. "Can you really believe that *we* would have administered the withdrawal of the Qax with more death and destruction than *you* have inflicted?"

Hama stood straight. "I'm not here to discuss hypotheticals with you, Reth Cana. We are pragmatic. If your work is in the interest of the species—"

Reth laughed out loud; Hama saw how his teeth were discolored, greenish. "*The interest of the species.*" He stalked about the echoing cavern, posturing. "Gemo, I give you the future. If this young man has his way, science will be no more than a weapon! . . . And if I refuse to cooperate with his *pragmatism?*"

Nomi said smoothly, "Those who follow us will be a lot tougher. Believe it, jasoft."

Gemo listened, stony-faced.

"Tomorrow," Reth said to Hama. "Twelve hours from now. I will demonstrate my work, my results. But I will not justify it to the likes of you; make of it what you will." And he swept away into shadows beyond the fitful glow of the hovering globe lamps.

Nomi said quietly to Hama, "Reth is a man who has spent too long alone."

"We can deal with him," Hama said with more confidence than he felt.

"Perhaps. But *why* is he alone? Hama, we know that at least a dozen pharaohs came to this settlement before the Occupation was ended, and probably more during the collapse. Where are *they?*"

Hama frowned. "Find out."

Nomi nodded briskly.

The oily sea lapped even closer now. The beach was reduced to a thin strip, trapped between forest and sea.

She walked far along the beach. There was nothing different, just the same dense forest, the oily sea. Here and there the sea had already covered the beach, encroaching into the forest, and she had to push into the vegetation to make further progress. Everywhere she found the tangle of roots and vine-like growths. Where the rising liquid had touched, the grasses and vines and trees crumbled and died, leaving bare, scattered dust.

The beach curved around on itself.

She was on an island. At least she had learned that much. Eventually, she supposed, that dark sea would rise so high it would cover everything. And they would all die.

There was no night. When she was tired, she rested on the beach, eyes closed.

There was no time here—not in the way she seemed to remember, on some deep level of herself: no days, no nights, no change. There was only the beach, the forest, that black oily sea, lapping ever closer, all of it under a shadowless gray-white sky.

She looked inward, seeking herself. She found only fragments of memory: an ice moon, a black sky—a face, a girl's perhaps, delicate, troubled. She didn't like to think about the face. It made her feel—complex. Lonely. Guilty.

She asked Asgard about time.

Asgard, gnawing absently on a handful of bark chips, ran a casual finger through the reality dust, from grain to grain. "There," she said. "Time passing. From one moment to the next. For we, you see, are above time."

"I don't understand."

"Of course you don't. A blade of grass is a shard of story. Where the grass knits itself into vines and trees, that story deepens. And if *I* eat a grass blade I absorb its tiny story, and it becomes mine. So Pharaoh said. And I don't know who told *him*. Do you see?"

"No," said Callisto frankly.

Asgard just looked at her, apathetic, contemptuous.

There was a thin cry, from the ocean. Callisto shaded her eyes, looked that way.

It had been a newborn, thrust arbitrarily into the air, just as Callisto had been. But this newborn had fallen, not to the comparative safety of the dust, but direct into the sea. She—or he—made barely a ripple on that placid black surface. Callisto saw a hand raised briefly above the sluggish meniscus, the flesh already dissolving, white bones curling.

And then it was gone, the newborn lost.

Callisto felt a deep horror.

Now, as she looked along the beach, she saw dark masses—a mound of flesh, the grisly articulation of fingers—fragments of the suddenly dead, washed up on this desolate beach. This had happened before, she realized. Over and over.

Asgard sat apathetically, chewing on her bark.

Is this it? Callisto wondered. Must I sit here like Asgard, waiting for the rising ocean of death to claim me?

She said, "We can't stay here."

"No," Asgard agreed reluctantly. "No, we can't."

Hama, with Reth and Gemo, rode a platform of metal deep into the rocky heart of Callisto.

The walls of the pressurized shaft, sliding slowly upward, were lined with slick transparent sheets, barring them from the ice. Hama reached out with a fingertip. The wall surface was cold and slippery, lubricated by a thin sheet of condensation from the chill air. There were no signs of structure, of strata in the ice; here and there small bores had been dug away from the shaft, perhaps as samples.

Callisto was a ball of dirty water ice. Save for surface impacts, nothing had happened to this moon since it accreted from the greater cloud that had formed the Jupiter system. The inner moons—Io, Europa, Ganymede—were heated, to one degree or another, by tidal pumping from Jupiter. So Europa, under a crust of ice, had a liquid ocean; and Io was driven by that perennial squeezing to spectacular volcanism. But Callisto had been born too far from her huge parent for any of that gravitational succor. Here, the only heat was a relic of primordial radioactivity; here there had been no geology, no volcanism, no hidden ocean.

Nevertheless, it seemed, Reth Cana had found life here. And, as the platform descended, Reth's cold excitement seemed to mount.

Nomi Ferrer was pursuing her own researches, in the settlement and out on the surface. But she had insisted that Hama be escorted by a squat, heavily-armed drone robot. Both Reth and Gemo ignored this silent companion, as if it were somehow impolite of Hama to have brought it along.

Nor did either of them mention Sarfi, who hadn't accompanied them. To Hama it did not seem human to disregard one's daughter, Virtual or otherwise. But then, what was human about a near-immortal traitor to the race? What was human about Reth, this man who had buried himself alone in the ice of Callisto, obsessively pursuing his obscure project, for decade after decade?

Even though the platform was small and cramped, Hama felt cold and alone; he suppressed a shiver.

The platform slowed, creaking, to a halt. He faced a chamber dug into the ice.

Reth said, "You are a kilometer beneath the surface. Go ahead. Take a look."

Hama saw that the seal between the lip of the circular platform and the roughly-cut ice was not perfect. He felt a renewed dread at his reliance on ancient, patched-up technology. But, suppressing hesitation, he stepped off the platform and into the ice chamber.

With a whir of aged bearings, the drone robot followed him.

Hama stood in a rough cube perhaps twice his height. It had been cut out of the ice, its walls lined by some clear glassy substance; it was illuminated by two hovering light globes. There was a knot of instrumentation, none of it familiar to Hama, along with a heap of data slates, some emergency equipment, and scattered packets of food and water. This was a working place, impersonal.

Reth stepped past him briskly. "Never mind the gadgetry; you wouldn't understand it anyhow . . . *Look.*" And he snapped his fingers, summoning one of the floating globes. It came to hover at Hama's shoulder.

Hama leaned close to inspect the cut-away ice. He could see texture: the ice was a pale, dirty gray, polluted by what looked like fine dust grains—and, here and there, it was stained by color, crimson and purple and brown.

Reth had become animated. "I'd let you touch it," he breathed. "But the sheeting is there to protect *it* from *us*—not the other way around. The biota is much more ancient, unevolved, fragile than we are, the bugs on your breath might wipe it out in an instant. The prebiotic chemicals were probably delivered here by comet impacts during Callisto's formation. There is carbon and hydrogen and nitrogen and oxygen. The biochemistry is a matter of carbon-carbon chains and water—*like* Earth's, but not precisely so. Nothing *exactly* like our DNA structures . . ."

"Spell it out," Gemo said casually, prowling around the gadgetry. "Remember, Reth, the education of these young is woefully inadequate."

"This is life," Hama said carefully. "Native to Callisto."

"Life—yes," Reth said. "The highest forms are about equivalent to Earth's bacteria. But—native? I believe the life forms here have a common ancestor, buried deep in time, with Earth life—and with the more extravagant biota of Europa's buried ocean, and probably the living things found elsewhere in the Solar System. Do you know the notion of panspermia? Life, you see, may have originated in one place, perhaps even outside the System, and then was spread through the worlds by the spraying of meteorite-impact debris. And everywhere it landed, life embarked on a different evolutionary path."

"But here," Hama said slowly, fumbling to grasp these unfamiliar concepts, "it was unable to rise higher than the level of a bacterium?"

"There is no room," said Reth. "There is liquid water here: just traces of it, soaked into the pores between the grains of rock and ice, kept from freezing by the radiogenic heat. But energy flows thin, and replication is very slow—spanning thousands of years." He shrugged. "Nevertheless there is a complete ecosystem . . . Do you understand? My Callisto bacteria are rather like the cryptoendoliths found in some inhospitable parts of the Earth. In Antarctica, for instance, you can crack open a rock and see layers of green life, leaching nutrients from the stone itself, sheltering from the wind and the desolating cold: communities of algae, cyanobacteria, fungi, yeast—"

"Not any more," Gemo murmured, running a finger over control panels. "Reth, the Extirpation was very thorough, an effective extinction event; I doubt if any of your cryptoendoliths can still survive."

"Ah," said Reth. "A pity."

Hama straightened up, frowning. He had come far from the cramped caverns of the Conurbations; he was confronting life from another world, half a billion kilometers from Earth. He ought to feel wonder. But these pale shadows evoked only a kind of pity. Perhaps this thin, cold, purposeless existence was a suitable object for the obsessive study of a lonely, half-mad immortal.

Reth's eyes were on him, hard.

Hama said carefully, "We know that before the Occupation the Solar System was extensively explored, by *My-kal Puhl* and those who followed him. The records of those times are lost—or hidden," he said with a glance at the impassive Gemo. "But we do know that everywhere the humans went, they found life. Life is commonplace. And in most places we reached, life has attained a much higher peak than *this*. Why not just catalog these scrapings and abandon the station?"

Reth threw up his arms theatrically. "I am wasting my time. Gemo, how can this mayfly mind possibly grasp the subtleties here?"

She said dryly, "I think it would serve you to try to explain, brother!" She was studying a gadget that looked like a handgun mounted on a floating platform. "This, for example."

When Hama approached this device, his weapon-laden drone whirred warningly. "What is it?"

Reth stalked forward. "It is an experimental mechanism based on laser light, which . . . It is a device for exploring the energy levels of an extended quantum structure!" He began to talk, rapidly, lacing his language with phrases like "spectral lines" and "electrostatic potential wells," none of which Hama understood.

At length Gemo interpreted for Hama.

"Imagine a very simple physical system—a hydrogen atom, for instance. I can raise its energy by bombarding it with laser light. But the atom is a quantum system, it can only assume energy levels at a series of specific steps. There are simple mathematical rules to describe the steps. This is called a 'potential well.' "

As he endured this lecture, irritation slowly built in Hama; it was clear there was much knowledge to be reclaimed from these patronizing, arrogant pharaohs.

"The potential well of a hydrogen atom is simple," said Reth rapidly. "The simplest quantum system of all. It follows an inverse-square rule. But I have found the potential wells of much more complex structures—"

"Ah," said Gemo. "Structures embedded in the Callisto bacteria."

"Yes." Reth's eyes gleamed. He snatched a data slate from a pile at his feet. A series of numbers chattered over the slate, meaning little to Hama, a series of graphs that sloped sharply before dwindling to flatness: a portrait of the mysterious "potential wells," perhaps.

Gemo seemed to understand immediately. "Let me." She took the slate, tapped its surface and quickly reconfigured the display. "Now, look, Hama: the energies of the photons that are absorbed by the well are proportional to this series of numbers."

1. 2. 3. 5. 7. 11. 13 . . .

"Prime numbers," Hama said.

"Exactly," snapped Reth. "Do you see?"

Gemo put down the slate and walked to the ice wall; she ran her hand over the translucent cover, as if longing to touch the mystery that was embedded there. "So inside each of these bacteria," she said carefully, "there is a quantum potential well that encodes prime numbers."

"And much more," said Reth. "The primes were just the key, the first hint of a continent of structures I have barely begun to explore." He paced back and forth, restless, animated. "Life is never content simply to subsist, to cling on. Life seeks rooms to spread. That is another commonplace, young man. But here, on Callisto, there was no room: not in the physical world; the energy and nutrients were simply too sparse for that. And so—"

"Yes?"

"And so they grew *sideways,*" he said. "And they reached orthogonal realms we never imagined existed."

Hama stared at the thin purple scrapings and chattering primes, here at the bottom of a pit with these two immortals, and feared he had descended into madness.

. . . 41. 43. 47. 53. 59 . . .

In a suit no more substantial than a thin layer of cloth, Nomi Ferrer walked over Callisto's raw surface, seeking evidence of crimes.

The sun was low on the horizon, evoking highlights from the curved ice plain all around her. From here, Jupiter was forever invisible, but Nomi saw two small discs, inner moons, following their endless dance of gravitational clockwork.

Gemo Cana had told her mayfly companions of how the Jovian system had once been. She told them of Io's mineral mines, nestling in the shadow of the huge volcano Babbar Patera. She told them of Ganymede: larger than Mercury, heavily cratered and geologically rich—the most stable and heavily populated of all the Jovian moons. And Europa's icy crust had sheltered an ocean hosting life, an ecosystem much more complex and rewarding than anybody had dreamed. "They were *worlds*. Human worlds. All gone now, shut down by the Qax. But remember . . ."

Away from the sun's glare, lesser stars glittered, surrounding Nomi with immensity.

But it was a crowded sky, despite that immensity. Crowded and dangerous. For—she had been warned by the Coalition—the Xeelee craft that had glowered over Earth was now coming *here*, hotly pursued by a Spline ship retrieved from the hands of jasoft rebels and manned by Green Army officers. What would happen when that miniature armada got here, Nomi couldn't imagine.

The Xeelee were legends of a deep-buried, partly extirpated past. And perhaps they were monsters of the human future. The Xeelee were said to be godlike entities so aloof that humans might never understand their goals. Some scraps of Xeelee technology, like starbreaker beams, had fallen into the hands of "lesser" species, like the Qax, and transformed their fortunes. The Xeelee seemed to care little for this—but, on occasion, they intervened.

To devastating effect.

Some believed that by such interventions the Xeelee

were maintaining their monopoly on power, controlling an empire which, perhaps, held sway across the Galaxy. Others said that, like the vengeful gods of humanity's childhood, the Xeelee were protecting the "junior races" from themselves.

Either way, Nomi thought, it's insulting. Claustrophobic. She felt an unexpected stab of resentment. We only just got rid of the Qax, she thought. And now, this.

Gemo Cana had argued that in such a dangerous universe, humanity needed the pharaohs. "Everything humans know about the Xeelee today, every bit of intelligence we have, was preserved by the pharaohs. I refuse to plead with you for my life. But I am concerned that you should understand. We pharaohs were not—dynastic tyrants. We fought, in our way, to survive the Qax Occupation, and the Extirpation. For we are the wisdom and continuity of the race. Destroy us and you complete the work of the Qax for them, finish the Extirpation. Destroy us and you destroy your own past—which we preserved for you, at great cost to ourselves."

Perhaps, Nomi thought. But in the end it was the bravery and ingenuity of one human—*a mayfly*—that had brought down the Qax, not the supine compromising of the jasofts and pharaohs.

She looked up toward the sun, toward invisible Earth. I just want a sky clear of alien ships, she thought. And to achieve that, perhaps we will have to sacrifice much.

Reth Cana began to describe where the Callisto bugs had "gone."

"There is no time," he whispered. "There is no space.

This is the resolution of an ancient debate—do we live in a universe of perpetual change, or a universe where neither time nor motion exists? Now we understand. Now we know we live in a universe of static shapes. Nothing exists but the particles that make up the universe—that make up *us*. Do you see? And we can *measure* nothing but the separation between those particles.

"Imagine a universe consisting of a single elementary particle, an electron perhaps. Then there could be no space. For space is only the separation between particles. Time is only the measurement of changes in that separation. So there could be no time.

"Imagine now a universe consisting of *two* particles . . ."

Gemo nodded. "Now you can have separation, and time."

Reth bent and, with one finger, scattered a line of dark dust grains across the floor. "Let each dust grain represent a distance—a configuration of my miniature two-particle cosmos. Each grain is labeled with a single number: the separation between the two particles." He stabbed his finger into the line, picking out grains. "*Here* the particles are a meter apart; *here* a micron; *here* a light-year. There is one special grain, of course: the one that represents zero separation, the particles overlaid. This diagram of dust shows all that is important about the underlying universe—the separation between its two components. And every possible configuration is shown at once, from this god-like perspective."

He let his finger wander back and forth along the line, tracing out a twisting path in the grains. "And here is a history: the two particles close and separate, close and separate. If they were conscious, the particles would think they were embedded in time, that they are coming near and far. But we can see that their universe is no more than dust grains, the lined-up configurations jostling against each other. It feels like time, inside. But from outside, it is just—sequence, a scattering of instants, of reality dust."

Gemo said, "Yes. 'It is utterly beyond our power to measure the change of things by time. Quite the contrary, time is an abstraction at which we arrive by means of the changes of things.'" She eyed Hama. "An ancient philosopher. *Mach*, or *Mar-que* . . ."

"If the universe has three particles," said Reth, "you need *three* numbers. Three relative distances—the separation of the particles, one from the other determine the cosmos's shape. And so the dust grains, mapping possible configurations, would fill up three-dimensional space—though there is still a unique grain, representing the special instant where all the particles are joined. And with four particles—"

"There would be six separation distances," Hama said. "And you would need a six-dimensional space to map the possible configurations."

Reth glared at him, eyes hard. "You are beginning to understand. Now. Imagine a space of stupendously many dimensions." He held up a dust grain. "Each grain represents one configuration of all the particles in our universe, frozen in time. This is reality dust, a dust of the Nows. And the dust fills *configuration space,* the realm of instants. Some of the dust grains may represent slices of our own history." He snapped his fingers, once, twice, three times. "There. There. There. Each moment, each juggling of the particles, a new grain, a new coordinate on the map. There is one grain that represents the coalescing of all the universe's particles into a single point. There are many more grains representing chaos—darkness—a random, structureless shuffling of the atoms.

"Configuration space contains all the arrangements of matter there could ever be. It is an image of eternity." He waved a fingertip through the air. But if I trace out a path from point to point—"

"You are tracing out a history," said Hama. "A sequence of configurations, the universe evolving from point to point."

"Yes. But *we* know that time is an illusion. In configuration space, all the moments that comprise our history exist simultaneously. *And all the other configurations that are logically possible also exist,* whether they lie along the track of that history or not."

Hama frowned. "And the Callisto bugs—"

Reth smiled. "I believe that, constrained in this space and time, the Callisto lifeforms have started to explore the wider realms of configuration space. Seeking a place to play."

Nomi turned away from the half-buried human township. She began to toil up the gentle slope of the ridge that loomed above the settlement. This was one of the great ring walls of the Valhalla system, curving away from this place for thousands of kilometers, rising nearly a kilometer above the surrounding plains.

The land around her was silver and black, a midnight sculpture of ridges and craters. There were no mountains here, none at all; any created by primordial geology or the impacts since Callisto's birth had long since subsided, slumping into formlessness. There was a thin smearing of black dust over the dirty white of the underlying ice; the dust was loose and fine-grained, and she disturbed it as she passed, leaving bright footprints.

"Do you understand what you're looking at?"

The sudden voice startled her; she looked up.

It was Sarfi. She was dressed, as Nomi was, in a translucent protective suit, another nod to the laws of consistency that seemed to bind her Virtual existence. But she left no footprints, nor even cast a shadow.

Sarfi kicked at the black dust, not disturbing a single grain. "The ice sublimes—did you know that? It shrivels away, a meter every ten million years—but it leaves the dust behind. That's why the human settlements were established on the north side of the Valhalla ridges. There it is just a shade colder, and some of the sublimed ice condenses out. So there is a layer of purer ice, right at the surface. The humans lived off ten-million-year frost . . . You're surprised I know so much. Nomi Ferrer, I was dead before you were born. Now I'm a ghost imprisoned in my mother's head. But I'm *conscious*. And I am still curious."

Nothing in Nomi's life had prepared her for this conversation. "Do you love your mother, Sarfi?"

Sarfi glared at her. "She preserved me. She gave up part of herself for me. It was a great sacrifice."

Nomi thought, You resent her. You resent this cloying, possessive love. And all this resentment bubbles inside you, seeking release. "There was nothing else she could have done for you."

"But I died anyway. I'm not *me*. I'm a download. I don't exist for me, but for *her*. I'm a walking, talking construct of her guilt." She stalked away, climbing the slumped ice ridge.

Gemo started to argue detail with her brother. How was it possible for isolated bacteria-like creatures to form any kind of sophisticated sensorium?—but Reth believed there were slow pathways of chemical and electrical communication, etched into the ice and rock, tracks for great slow thoughts that pulsed through the substance of Callisto. Very well, but what of quantum mechanics? The universe was *not* made up of neat little particles, but was a mesh of quantum probability waves—Ah, but Reth imagined quantum probability lying like a mist over his reality dust, constrained by two things: the geometry of configuration space, as acoustic echoes are determined by the geometry of a room; and something called a "static universal wave function," a mist of probability that governed the likelihood of a given Now being experienced . . .

Hama closed his eyes, his mind whirling.

Blocky pixels flickered across his vision, *within* his closed eyes. Startled, he looked up.

Sarfi was kneeling before him; she had brushed her Virtual fingertips through his skull, his eyes. He hadn't even known she had come here.

"I know it's hard to accept," she said. "My mother spent a long time making me understand. You just have to open your mind."

"I am no fool," he said sharply. "I can imagine a map of all the logical possibilities of a universe. But it would be just that—a map, a theoretical construct, a thing of data and logic. It would not be a *place*. The universe doesn't *feel* like that. I feel time passing. I don't experience disconnected instants, Reth's dusty reality."

"Of course not," said Reth. "But you must understand that everything we know of the past is a record embedded in the present—the fossils and geology of Earth, so cruelly obliterated by the Qax, even the traces of chemicals and electricity in your own brain that comprise your memory, maintaining your illusion of past times . . . Gemo, may I—"

Gemo nodded, unsmiling.

Reth tapped a data slate. Sarfi froze, becoming a static, inanimate sculpture of light. Then, after perhaps ten seconds, she melted, began to move once more.

She saw Hama staring at her. "What's wrong?"

Reth, ignoring her, said, "The child contains a record of her own shallow past, embedded in her programs and data stores. She is unaware of the intervals of time when she is frozen, or deactivated. If I could start and stop you, Hama Druz, you would wake protesting that your memories contained no gaps. But your memories themselves would have been frozen. I could even chop up your life and rearrange its instants in any way I chose; at each instant you would have an intact set of memories, a record of a past, and you would believe yourself to have lived through a continuous consistent reality.

"And thus the maximal-reality dust grains contain *embedded within themselves* a record of the eras which "preceded" them. Each grain contains brains, like yours and mine, with "memories" embedded in them, frozen like sculptures. And history emerges in configuration space because those rich grains are then drawn, by a least-energy matching principle, to the grains which "precede" and "follow" them . . . You see?"

Sarfi looked to Gemo. "Mother? What does he mean? . . ."

Gemo watched her clinically. "Sarfi has been reset many times, of course," she said absently. "I had no wish to see her grow old, accreted with worthless memory. It was rather like an Extirpation, you see. The Qax sought to reset humanity, to abolish the memory of the race. In the ultimate realization, we would have become a race of children, waking every day to a fresh world, every day a new creation. It was cruel, of course. But, theoretically, intriguing. Don't you think?"

Sarfi was trembling.

Now Reth began telling Gemo, rapidly and with enthusiasm, of his plans to explore his continent of configurations. "No human mind could apprehend that multidimensional domain unaided, of course. But it can be modeled, with metaphors—rivers, seas, mountains. It is possible to *explore* it . . ."

Hama said, "But, if your meta-universe is static, timeless, how could it be experienced? For experience depends on duration."

Reth shook his head impatiently. He tapped his data slate and beckoned to Sarfi. "Here, child."

Hesitantly, she stepped forward.

She trailed a worm-like tube of light, as if her image had been captured at each moment in some invisible emulsion.

She emerged, blinking, at the other end of the tube, and looked back at it, bewildered.

"Stop these games," Hama said tightly.

"You see?" Reth said. "Here is an evolution of Sarfi's structure, but mapped in space, not time. But it makes no difference to Sarfi. Her memory at each frozen instant contains a record of her walking across the floor toward me—doesn't it, dear? And thus, in static configuration space, sentient creatures could have experiences, afforded them by the evolution of information structures across space."

Hama turned to Sarfi. "Are you all right?"

"What do you think?"

"I think Reth may be insane," he said.

She stiffened, pulling back. "Don't ask me. I'm not even a mayfly, remember?"

"It is a comforting philosophy, Hama," Gemo said. "Nothing matters, you see: not even death, not even the Extirpation. For we persist, each moment exists forever, in a great universe . . ."

It was a philosophy of decadence, Hama thought angrily. A philosophy of morbid contemplation, a consolation for ageless pharaohs as they sought to justify the way they administered the suffering of their fellow creatures. No wonder it appealed to them so much.

Gemo and Reth talked on, more and more rapidly, entering realms of speculation he couldn't begin to follow.

Callisto told Asgard what she was intending to do.

She walked along the narrowing beach, seeking scraps of people, of newborns and others, washed up by the pitiless black sea.

She picked up what looked like a human foot. It was oddly dry, cold, the flesh and even the bones crumbling at her touch.

She collected as many of these hideous shards as she could hold, and toiled back along the barren dust.

Then she worked her way through the forest back to the great tree, where she had encountered the creature called Night. She paused every few paces and pushed a section of corpse into the ground. She covered each fragment over with ripped-up grass and bits of bark.

"You're crazy," Asgard said, trailing her, arms full of dried, crumbling flesh and bone.

"I know," Callisto said. "I'm going anyway."

Asgard would not come far enough to reach the tree itself. So Callisto completed her journey alone.

Once more she reached the base of the tree. Once more, her heart thumping hard, she began to climb.

The creature, Night, seemed to have expected her. He moved from branch to branch, far above, a massive blur, and he clambered with ferocious purpose down the trunk.

She scrambled hurriedly back to the ground.

He followed her—but not all the way to the ground. He clung to his trunk, his broad face broken by that immense, bloody mouth, hissing at her.

She glowered back, and took a tentative step toward the tree. "Come get me," she muttered. "What are you waiting for?" She took a piece of corpse (a *hand*—briefly her stomach turned), and she hurled it up at him.

He ducked aside, startled. But he swiveled that immense head. As the hand descended he caught it neatly in his scoop of a mouth, crunched once and swallowed it whole. He looked down at her with new interest.

And he took one tentative step toward the ground.

"That's it," she crooned. "Come on. Come eat the flesh. Come eat *me*, if that's what you want—"

Without warning he leapt from the trunk, immense hands splayed.

She screamed and staggered back. He crashed to the ground perhaps an arm's length from her. One massive fist slammed into her ankle, sending a stab of pain that made her cry out.

If he'd landed on top of her he would surely have crushed her.

The beast, winded, was already clambering to his feet.

She got to her feet and ran, ignoring the pain of her ankle.

Night followed her, his lumbering four-legged pursuit slow but relentless. As she ran she kicked open her buried caches of body parts. He snapped them up and gobbled them down, barely slowing. The morsels seemed pathetically inadequate in the face of Night's giant reality.

She burst out onto the open beach, still running for her life. She reached the lip of the sea, skidding to a halt before the lapping black liquid. Her plan had been to reach the sea, to lure Night into it.

But when she turned, she saw that Night had hesitated on the fringe of the forest, blinking in the light. Perhaps he was aware that she had deliberately drawn him here.

He stepped forward deliberately, his immense feet sinking into the soft dust. There was no need for him to rush.

Callisto was already exhausted, and, trapped before the sea, there was nowhere for her to run.

Now that he was out in the open she saw how far from the human form he had become, with his body a distorted slab of muscle, a mouth that had widened until it stretched around his head. And yet scraps of clothing clung to him, the remnants of a coverall of the same unidentifiable color as her own. Once this creature, too, had been a newborn here, landing screaming on this desolate beach.

He towered over her, and she wondered how many unfortunates he had devoured to reach such proportions.

Beyond his looming shoulder, she could see Asgard, pacing back and forth along the beach.

"Great plan," Asgard called. "Now what?"

"I—"

Night raised up on his hind legs, huge hands pawing at the air over her head. He roared wordlessly, and bloody breath gushed over her.

Close your eyes, Callisto thought. *This won't hurt.*

"No," Asgard said. She took a step toward the looming beast, began to run.

"No, no, *no!*" With a final yell she hurled herself at his back.

He looked around, startled, and swiped at Asgard with one giant paw. She was flung away like a scrap of bark, to land in a heap on the dust. But Night, off-balance, was stumbling backward, back toward the sea.

When his foot sank into the oily ocean, he looked down, as if surprised.

Even as he lifted his leg from the fluid the flesh was drying, crumbling, the muscles and bone sloughing away in layers of purple and white. He roared his defiance, and cuffed at the sea—then gazed in horror at one immense hand left shredded by contact with the entropic ooze.

He began to fall, slowly, ponderously. Without a splash, the fluid opened up to accept his immense bulk. He was immediately submerged, the shallow fluid flowing eagerly over him.

In one last burst of defiance he broke the surface, mouth open, his flesh dissolving. His face was restored, briefly, to the human, his eyes a startling blue. He cried out, his voice thin: "*Reth!*"

The name sent a shiver of recognition through Callisto.

Then he fell back, and was gone.

She hurried to Asgard.

Asgard's chest was crushed, she saw immediately, imploded to an implausible degree, and her limbs were splayed around her at impossible angles. Her face was growing smooth, featureless, like a child's, beautiful in its innocence. Her gaze slid over Callisto.

Callisto cradled Asgard's head. "This won't hurt," she murmured. "Close your eyes."

Asgard sighed, and was still.

"Let me tell you about pharaohs," Nomi said bitterly.

Hama listened in silence.

They stood on the Valhalla ridge, overlooking the old, dark settlement; the brightest point on the silver-black surface of Callisto was their own lifedome.

Nomi said, "This was just after the Qax left. I got this from a couple of our people who survived, who were *there*. There was a nest of the pharaohs, in one of the biggest Conurbations—one of the first to be constructed, one of the oldest. The pharaohs retreated into a pit, under the surface dwellings. They fought hard; we didn't know why. They had to be torched out. A lot of good people, good *mayflies,* died that day. When our people had dealt with the pharaohs, shut down the mines and drone robots and booby-traps . . . after all that, they went into the pit. It was dark. But it was warm, the air was moist, and there was movement everywhere. Small movements. And, so they say, there was a smell. Of *milk*—"

Nomi was silent for a long moment; Hama waited.

"Hama, I can't have children. I grew up knowing that. So maybe I ought to find some pity for the pharaohs. They don't breed true—like Gemo and Sarfi. But Sarfi is the exception, I think. Sometimes their children *are* born with Qax immortality. But—"

"Yes?"

"But they don't grow. They stop developing, at the age of two years or one year or six months or a month; some of them even stop growing before they are ready to be born, and have to be plucked from their mothers' wombs.

"And that was what our soldiers found in the pit, Hama. Racked up like specimens in a lab, hundreds of them. Must have been accumulating for centuries. Plugged into machines, mewling and crying."

"Lethe." Maybe Gemo is right, Hama thought; maybe the pharaohs really have paid a price we can't begin to understand.

"The pit was torched . . ."

Hama thought he saw a shadow pass across the sky, the scattered stars. "Why are you telling me this, Nomi?"

Nomi pointed. "There's a line of shallow graves over there. Not hard to find, in the end."

"Ah."

"The killings seemed to be uniform, the same method every time. A laser to the head. The bodies seemed peaceful," Nomi mused. "Almost as if they welcomed it."

He had killed them. Reth had killed the other pharaohs who came here, one by one. But why?

And why would an immortal welcome death? Only if—his mind raced—only if she were promised a better place to go—

Everything happened at once.

A shadow, unmistakable now, spread out over the stars: a hole in the sky, black as night, winged, purposeful. And, low toward the horizon, there was a flare of light.

"Lethe," said Nomi softly. "That was the GUTship. It's *gone*—just like that."

"Then we aren't going home." Hama felt numb; he seemed beyond shock. ". . . Help me. Oh, help me . . ."

A form coalesced before them, a cloud of blocky pixels.

Hama made out a sketch of limbs, a face, an open, pleading mouth. It was Sarfi, and she wasn't in a protective suit. Her face was twisted in pain; she must be breaking all her consistency overrides to have projected herself to the surface like this.

Hama held out his gloved hands, driven by an impulse to hold her; but that, of course, was impossible.

"Please," she whispered, her voice a thin, badly-realized scratch. "It is Reth. He plans to kill Gemo."

Nomi set off down the ridge slope in a bouncing low-G run.

Hama said to Sarfi, "Don't worry. We'll help your mother—"

Now he saw anger in that blurred, sketchy face. "To Lethe with her! Save *me* . . ."

The pixels dispersed into a meaningless cloud, and winked out.

Callisto reached the great tree.

The trunk soared upward, a pillar of rigid logic and history and consistency. She slapped its hide, its solidity giving her renewed confidence. And now there was no Night, no lurking monster, waiting up there to oppose her.

With purpose, ignoring the aches of her healing flesh and torn muscles, she began to climb.

As she rose above the trunk's lower tangle and encountered the merged and melded upper length, the search for crevices became more difficult, just as it had before. But she was immersed in the rhythm of the climb, and however high she rose there seemed to be pocks and ledges molded into the smooth surface of the trunk, sufficient to support her progress.

Soon she had far surpassed the heights she had reached that first time she had tried. The mist was thick here, and when she looked down the ground was already lost: the great trunk rose from blank emptiness, as if rooted in nothingness.

But she thought she could see shadows, moving along the trunk's perspective-dwindled immensity: the others from the beach, some of them at least, were following her on her unlikely adventure.

And still she climbed.

The trunk began to split into great arcing branches that pushed through the thick mist. She paused, breathing deeply. Some of the branches were thin, spindly limbs that dwindled away from the main trunk. But others were much more substantial, great highways that seemed anchored to the invisible sky.

She picked the most solid-looking of these upper branches, and continued her climb.

Impeded by her damaged arm, her progress was slow but steady. It was actually more difficult to make her way along this tipped-over branch than it had been to climb the vertical trunk. But she was able to find handholds, and places where she could wrap her limbs around the branch.

The mist thickened further until she could see nothing around her but this branch: no sky or ground, not even the rest of this great tree, as if nothing existed but herself and the climb, as if the branch came from the mist and finished in the mist, a strange smooth surface over which she must toil forever.

And then, without warning, she broke through the mist.

In a pit dug into the heart of Callisto, illuminated by a single hovering globe lamp, Gemo Cana lay on a flat, hard pallet, unmoving.

Her brother stood hunched over her, working at her face with gleaming equipment. "This won't hurt. Close your eyes . . ."

"Stop this!" Sarfi ran forward. She pushed her hands into Gemo's face, crying out as the pain of consistency violation pulsed through her.

Gemo turned, blindly. Hama saw that a silvery mask had been laid over her eyes, hugging the flesh there. "Sarfi? . . ."

Nomi stepped forward, laser pistol poised. "Stop this obscenity."

Reth wore a mask of his own, a smaller cap that covered half his face; the exposed eye peered at them, hard, suspicious, calculating. "Don't try to stop us. You'll kill her if you try. *Let us go,* Hama Druz."

Nomi raised her pistol at his head.

But Hama touched the soldier's arm. "Not yet."

On her pallet, Gemo Cana turned her head blindly. She whispered, "There's so much you don't understand."

Hama snapped, "You'd better make us understand, Reth Cana, before I let Nomi here off the leash."

Reth paced back and forth. "Yes—technically, this is a kind of death. But not a single one of the pharaohs who passed through here did it against his or her will."

Hama frowned. " 'Passed through'?"

Reth stroked the metal clinging to Gemo's face; his sister turned her head in response. "The core technology is an interface to the brain via the optic nerve. In this way I can connect the quantum structures which encode human consciousness to the structures stored in the Callisto bacteria—or rather, the structures which serve as, umm, a gateway to configuration space . . ."

Hama started to see it. "You're attempting to download human minds into your configuration space."

Reth smiled. "It was not enough, you see, to study configuration space at second-hand, through quantum structures embedded in these silent bacteria. The next step had to be direct apprehension by the human sensorium."

"The next step in what?"

"In our evolution, perhaps," Reth murmured. "With the help of the Qax, we have banished death. Now we can break down the walls of this shadow theater we call reality." He eyed Hama. "This dismal pit is not a grave, but a gateway. And I am the gatekeeper."

Hama said tightly, "You destroy minds on the promise of afterlife—a promise concocted of theory and a scraping of cryptoendolith bacteria."

"Not a theory," Gemo whispered. "I have *seen* it."

Nomi grunted, "We don't have time for this."

But Hama asked, despite himself, "What was it like?"

It was, Gemo said, a vast, spreading landscape, under a towering sky; she had glimpsed a beach, a rising, oily sea, an immense mountain shrouded in mist . . .

Reth stalked back and forth, arms spread wide. "We remain human, Hama Druz. *I* cannot apprehend a multidimensional continuum. So I sought a metaphor. A human interface. A beach of reality dust. A sea of—entropy, chaos. The structures folded into the living things, the shape of the landscape, represent consistency—what we time-bound creatures apprehend as causality."

"And the rising sea—"

"The threat of the Xeelee," he said, smiling thinly. "The destruction to come. The obliteration of possibility. Even there, threats can reach . . . but life, mind can persist.

"Configuration space is real, Hama Druz. This isn't a new idea; *Pleh-toh* saw that, thousands of years ago . . . Ah, but you know nothing of *Pleh-toh*, do you? The higher manifold always existed, you see, long before the coming of mankind, of life itself. All that has changed is that through the patient, blind growth of the Callisto bacteria, I have found a way to reach it. And there, we can truly live forever—"

The ice floor shuddered, causing them to stagger.

Reth peered up the length of the shaft, smiling grimly. "Ah. Our visitors make their presence known. Callisto is a small, hard, static world; it rings like a bell even at the fall of a footstep. And the footsteps of the Xeelee are heavy indeed . . ."

Sarfi pushed forward again, hands twisting, agonized by her inability to touch and be touched. She said to Gemo, "Why do you have to *die*."

Gemo's voice was slow, sleepy; Hama wondered what sedative agents Reth had fed her. "You won't feel anything, Sarfi. It will be as if you never existed at all, as if all this pain never occurred. Won't that be better?"

The ground shuddered again, waves of energy from some remote Xeelee-induced explosion pulsing through Callisto's patient ice, and the walls groaned, stressed.

Hama tried to imagine the black sea, the sharp-grained dust of the beach. Could it be true that Reth was accessing some meta-universe of theory and possibility—a place where every dust grain truly did represent an instant in *this* universe, a frozen slice of time, stars and galaxies and people and Xeelee and unfolding cosmos all embedded within?

But Hama had once visited the ocean—Earth's ocean—to oversee the reclamation of an abandoned Qax sea farm. He remembered the stink of ozone, the taste of salt in the damp air. He had hated it.

Reth seemed to sense his thoughts. "Ah, but I forgot. You are creatures of the Conurbations, of the Extirpation. Of round-walled caverns and a landscape of gray dust. But this is how the Earth used to be, you see, before the Qax unleashed their nanotech plague. No wonder you find the idea strange. But not us." He slipped his hand into his sister's. "For us, you see, it will be like coming home."

On the table, Gemo was convulsing, her mouth open, laced with drool.

Sarfi screamed, a thin wail that echoed from the high walls of the shaft. Once more she reached out to Gemo; once more her fluttering fingers passed through Gemo's face, sparkling.

"Gemo Cana is a collaborator," Nomi said. "Hama, you're letting her escape justice."

Yes, Hama thought, surprised. Nomi, in her blunt way, had once more hit on the essence of the situation here. The pharaohs were the refugees now, and Reth's configuration space—if it existed at all—might prove their ultimate bolthole. Gemo Cana was escaping, leaving behind the consequences of her work, for good or ill.

But did that justify killing her?

The pharaoh turned her head.

Sarfi was crying. "Mother, please. I'll die."

"Hush," said Gemo. "You can't die. You were never alive. Don't you see that? You will always be with me, Sarfi. In a way. In my heart." Her back arched. "*Oh* . . ."

Sarfi straightened and looked at her hands. The illusion of solidity was breaking down, Hama saw; pixels swarmed like fat, cubic insects, grudgingly cooperating to maintain the girl's form. Sarfi looked up at Hama with eyes like pits of darkness, and her voice was a flat, emotionless husk, devoid of intonation and character. "*Help me*."

Again Hama reached out to her; again he dropped his hands, the most basic of human instincts invalidated. "I'm sorry—"

"*It hurts*." Her face swarmed with pixels that erupted and evaporated from the crumbling surface of her skin. Now the pixels fled her body, as if evaporating; she was becoming tenuous, unstable.

Hama forced himself to meet her gaze. "It's all right," he murmured. "It will be over soon . . ." On and on, meaningless endearments; but she gazed into his eyes, as if seeking refuge there.

For a last instant her face congealed, clearly, from the dispersing cloud. "*Oh* . . ." She reached up to him with a hand that was no more than a mass of diffuse light.

And then, with a silent implosion, her face crumbled, eyes closing.

Gemo shuddered once, and was still.

Hama could feel his heart pulse within him, the warm blood course. Nomi placed her strong hand on his shoulder, and he relished its fierce solidity.

Hama faced Reth. "You are monsters."

Reth smiled easily. "Gemo is beyond your mayfly reproach. And as for the Virtual child—you may learn, Hama

Druz, if you pass beyond your current limitations, that the first thing to be eroded by time is sentiment."

Hama flared. "I will never be like you, pharaoh. Sarfi was no toy."

"But you still don't see it," Reth said evenly. "*She is still alive*—but our timebound language can't describe it—she persists, somewhere out there, beyond the walls of our petty realization . . ."

Again the moon shuddered, and primordial ice groaned.

Reth murmured, "Callisto was not designed to take such hammer blows . . . The situation is reduced, you see. Now there is only me."

"And me." Nomi raised the laser pistol.

"Is this what you want?" Reth asked of Hama. "To cut down centuries of endeavor with a bolt of light?"

Hama shook his head. "You really believe you can reach your configuration space—that you can survive there?"

"But I have proof," Reth said. "You saw it."

"All I saw was a woman dying on a slab."

Reth glowered at him. "Hama Druz, make your decision."

Nomi aimed the laser pistol.

"Let him go," Hama said bitterly. "He has only contempt for mayfly justice anyhow."

Reth grinned and stepped back. "You may be a mayfly, but you have the beginnings of wisdom, Hama Druz."

"Yes," Hama said quietly. "Yes, I believe I do. Perhaps there *is* something there, some new realm of logic to be explored. But you, Reth, are blinded by your arrogance and your obsessions. Surely this new reality is nothing like the Earth of your childhood. And it will have little sympathy for your ambitions. Perhaps whatever survives the download will have no resemblance to *you*. Perhaps you won't even remember who you were. What then?"

Reth's mask sparkled; he raised his hand to his face. He made for the pallet, to lie beside the cooling body of his sister. But he stumbled and fell before he got there.

Hama and Nomi watched, neither moving to help him.

Reth, on his hands and knees, turned his masked face to Hama, "You can come with me, Hama Druz. To a better place, a higher place."

"You go alone, pharaoh."

Reth forced a laugh. Then he cried out, his back arching.

He fell forward, and was still.

Nomi raked the body with laser fire. "Good riddance," she growled. "Now can we get out of here?"

There was a mountain.

It rose high above the night-dark sea, proudly challenging the featureless, glowing sky. Rivers flowed from that single great peak, she saw: black and massive, striping its huge conical flanks, merging into great tumbling cascades that poured into the ocean.

The mountain was the center of the world, thrusting from the sea.

She was high above an island, a small scrap of land that defied the dissolving drenching of the featureless sea. Islands were few, small, scattered, threatened everywhere by the black, crowding ocean.

But, not far away, there was another island, she saw, pushing above the sea of mist. It was a heaping of dust on which trees grew thickly, their branches tangled. In fact the branches reached across the neck of sea that separated this island from her own. She thought she could see a way to reach that island, scrambling from tree to tree, following a great highway of branches.

The other island rose higher than her own above the encroaching sea. There, she thought, she—and whoever followed her—would be safe from lapping dissolution. For now, anyhow.

But what did that mean? What would Pharaoh have said of this—that the new island was an unlikely heap of reality dust, further from looming entropic destruction?

She shook her head. The deeper meaning of her journey scarcely mattered—and nor did its connection to any other place. If this world were a symbol, so be it: this was where she lived, and this was where she would, with determination and perseverance, survive.

She looked one last time at the towering mountain. Damaged arm or not, she itched to climb it, to challenge its negentropic heights. But in the future, perhaps. Not now.

Carefully, clinging to her branch with arms and legs and her one good hand, she made her way along the branch to the low-probability island. One by one, the people of the beach followed her.

In the mist, far below, she glimpsed slow, ponderous movement: huge beasts, perhaps giant depraved cousins of Night. But, though they bellowed up at her, they could not reach her.

Once more Hama and Nomi stood on the silver-black surface of Callisto, under a sky littered with stars. just as before, the low, slumped ridges of Valhalla still marched to the silent horizon.

But this was no longer a world of antiquity and stillness. The shudders were coming every few minutes now. In places the ice crust was collapsing, ancient features subsiding, here and there sending up sprays of dust and ice splinters that sparkled briefly before falling back, all in utter silence.

Hama thought back to a time before this assignment, to the convocations he had joined. He had been a foolish boy, he thought, his ideas half-formed. Now, when he looked into his heart, he saw crystal-hard determination.

"No more pharaohs," Hama murmured. "No more immortality. That way lies arrogance and compromise and introversion and surrender. A brief life burns brightly."

Nomi growled, "More theory, Hama? Let's count the ways we might die. The Xeelee starbreaker might cream us. One of these miniature quakes might erupt right under us. Or maybe we'll last long enough to suffocate in our own farts, stuck inside these damn suits. What do you think? I don't know why you let that arrogant pharaoh kill himself."

Hama murmured, "You see death as an escape?"

"If it's easy, if it's under your control—yes."

"Reth did escape," Hama said. "But I don't think it was into death."

"You *believed* all that stuff about theoretical worlds?"

"Yes," Hama said. "Yes, in the end I think I did believe it."

"Why?"

"Because of *them*." He gestured at the sky. "The Xeelee. If our second-hand wisdom has any validity at all, we know that the Xeelee react to *what they fear*. And almost as soon as Reth constructed his interface to his world of logic and data, as soon as the pharaohs began to pass into it, they came here."

"You think the Xeelee fear us?"

"Not us. The bugs in the ice: Reth's cryptoendoliths, dreaming their billion-year dreams . . . The Xeelee seem intent on keeping those dreams from escaping. And that's why I think Reth hit on a truth, you see. Because the Xeelee see it too."

Now, over one horizon, there was a glowing crimson cloud, like dawn approaching—but there could be no dawn on this all-but-airless world.

"Starbreaker light," murmured Nomi. "The glow must be vapor, ice splinters, dust, thrown up from the trench they are digging."

Hama felt a fierce anger burn. "Once again aliens have walked into our System, for their own purposes, and we can do nothing to stop them. This mustn't happen again, Nomi. Let this be an end—and a beginning, a new Day Zero. You know, perhaps the Qax were right to attempt the Extirpation. If we are to survive in this dangerous universe we must remake ourselves, without sentiment, without nostalgia, without pity. History is irrelevant. Only the future is important." He longed to be gone from this place, to bring his hard new ideas to the great debates that were shaping the future of mankind.

"You're starting to frighten me, my friend," Nomi said gently. "But not as much as *that*."

Now the Xeelee nightfighter itself came climbing above the shattered fog of the horizon. It was like an immense, black-winged bird. Hama could see crimson starbreaker light stab down into the passive, defenseless ice of Callisto. The shuddering of the ground was constant now, as that mass of shattered ice and steam rolled relentlessly toward them.

Nomi grabbed onto him; holding each other, they struggled to stay on their feet as ice particles battered their faceplates. A tide of destruction spanned Callisto from horizon to horizon. There was, of course, no escape.

And then the world turned silver, and the stars swam.

Hama cried out, clinging to Nomi, and they fell. They hit the ice hard, despite the low gravity.

Nomi, combat-hardened, was on her feet immediately. An oddly pink light caught her squat outline. But Hama, winded, bewildered, found himself gazing up at the stars.

Different stars? No. Just—moved. The Xeelee ship was gone, vanished.

He struggled to his feet.

The wave of vapor and ice was subsiding, as quickly as it had been created; there was no air here to prevent the parabolic fall of the crystals back to the shattered land, little gravity to prevent the escape of the vapor into Jovian space. The land's shuddering ceased, though he could feel deep slow echoes of huge convulsions washing through the rigid ground . . .

But the stars had moved.

He turned, taking in the changed sky. Surely the shrunken sun was a little further up the dome of sky. And a pink slice of Jupiter now showed above the smoothly curved horizon, where none had shown before on this tide-locked moon.

Nomi touched his arm, and pointed deep into the ice. "*Look.*"

It was like some immense fish, embedded in the ground,

its spread-eagled black wings clearly visible through layers of dusty ice. A red glow shone fitfully at its heart; as Hama watched it sputtered, died, and the buried ship grew dark.

Nomi said, "At first I thought the Xeelee must have lit up some exotic super drive and got out of here. But I was wrong. That thing must be half a kilometer down. How did it get there?"

"I don't think it did," Hama said. He turned away and peered at Jupiter. "*I think Callisto moved*, Nomi."

"What? . . ."

"It didn't have to be far. Just a couple of kilometers. Just enough to swallow up the Xeelee craft."

Nomi was staring at him. "That's insane, Hama, what can move a moon?"

Why, a child could, Hama thought in awe. A child playing on a beach—if every grain on that beach is a slice in time.

I see a line sketched in the dust, a history, smooth and complete. I pick out a grain with Callisto positioned just *here*. And I replace it with a grain in which Callisto is positioned just a little further over *there*. As easy, as willful, as that.

No wonder the Xeelee are afraid.

A new shuddering began, deep and powerful.

"Lethe," said Nomi. "What now?"

Hama shouted, "Not the Xeelee this time. Callisto spent four billion years settling into its slow waltz around Jupiter. Now I think it's going to have to learn those lessons over again."

"Tides," Nomi growled.

"It might be enough to melt the surface. Perhaps those

cryptoendoliths will be wiped out after all. I wonder if the Xeelee *planned* it that way all along . . ."

He saw a slow grin spread across Nomi's face. "We aren't done yet." She pointed.

Hama turned. A new moon was rising over Callisto's tight horizon. It was a moon of flesh and metal, and it bore a sigil, a blue-green tetrahedron, burned into its hide.

"The Spline ship, by Lethe," Nomi said. She punched Hama's arm. "So the story goes on, my friend."

Hama glared down into the ice, at the Xeelee craft buried there. Yes, the story goes on. But we have introduced a virus into the software of the universe. And I wonder what eyes will be here to see, when that ship is finally freed from this tortured ice.

An orifice opened up in the Spline's immense hide. A flitter squirted out and soared over Callisto's ice, seeking a place to land.

Exhausted, disoriented, Callisto and her followers stumbled down the last length of trunk and collapsed to the ground.

She dug her good hand into the loose grains of reality dust. She felt a surge of pride, of achievement. This island, an island of a new possibility, was her island now.

Hers, perhaps, but not empty, she realized slowly. There was a newborn here: lost, bewildered, suddenly arrived. She saw his face smoothing over, working with anguish and doubt, as he *forgot*.

But when his gaze lit on her, he became animated.

He tried to stand, to walk toward her. He stumbled, weak and drained, and fell on his face.

Dredging up the last of her own strength, she went to

him. She dug her hand under him and turned him on his back—as, once, Pharaoh had done for her.

He opened his mouth. Spittle looped between his lips, and his voice was a harsh rasp. "Gemo!" he gasped. "I made you! Help me! Love me!"

Something tugged at her: recognition—and resentment.

She held his head to her chest. "This won't hurt," she said. "Close your eyes."

And she held him, until the last of his unwelcome memories had leaked away, and, forgetting who he was, he lay still.

Making History

Paul J. McAuley

"The drama's done. Why then here does any one step forth?"
Herman Melville, *Moby-Dick*

For the Friday Shut-Ins

One

I believe that I first saw Demi Lacombe at the gala reopening of the theater. She had arrived in Paris, Dione a week before, but I am sure that, had I passed her in one of the gardens or arcades of the diplomatic quarter, or glimpsed her at one of the receptions or *soirées* or cocktail parties or conversations, I would have remembered her, for in an age where beauty could be cheaply bought, hers was a rare and natural wonder, and not easily forgotten.

So I am certain that we first met that night, at the touring company production of *Don Giovanni*. The theater of Paris, Dione, was one of the first buildings in the city's main dome to have been restored after the end of the siege. Although the gala performance which marked its reopening was an overt symbol of the occupation force's power, it was the first time many of the force's executives and officials had ventured outside the diplomatic quarter. It was preceded by speeches made more to the media (represented by a single journalist and a dozen remotes) than to the audience, for it was the kind of event which politicians fondly believe will enhance their status, but which usually wins not so much as a footnote in the pages of history.

The theater was a roofless bowl modelled in miniature on Rome's ruined Colosseum. Tiers of seats and private boxes rose steeply all around the circular stage to the rim, where armored troopers and angular killing machines patrolled, tiny shadows against the artificial night. The colonists, who had fought to the death for freedom from Earth's rule, had kept to the twenty-four hour diurnal cycle of their home planet; the panes of the dome, high above, were polarized against the wan light of Dione's midday, and the suspensor lamps were turned down to mere stars.

On the stage's glowing dish, the cast flitted and swarmed through a web of wires and stays like a flock of gaudy birds, freezing in emblematic tableaux during the great arias. The lackluster production had been foolishly gussied up in modern dress, with the Commendatore a robot, Don Giovanni a dispossessed captain of a Kuiper Belt habitat driven mad by a bioweapon symbiont, his servant Leporello an ambitious neuter who borrowed something of Iago's malevolent glee at the ordinary human weaknesses of its extraordinary master. From the vantage of my fifth tier box, I paid as much attention to the audience as I did to the familiar allegory of the priapic Don's damnation, and two people in a box on the same level as mine quickly caught my eye. One was someone I had come to know well, Cris DeHon, head of the team that was reconstructing the city's information network; DeHon's companion was as breathtaking as she was incongruous. After the statue of the Commendatore had sprung to life and consigned the Don to his doom amidst flares of flame and writhing, red-skinned demons, after the ritual of applause and encore, DeHon found me at the post performance party which, in truth, was more important to most of the audience than the opera's choreographed histrionics.

"Dr. Lacombe has an interest in history," DeHon told me, after it had made the introductions. Like Leporello, the Don's servant, Cris DeHon was a neuter, one of the few people in the room who could not be affected, except in a purely aesthetic sense, by Dr. Lacombe's beauty. And like Leporello, it was consumed by a feverish delight in fomenting intrigue. Perhaps intrigue was to it as sex to most men and women. It was a brilliant and vicious gossip, and a generous source of unreliable information.

"Indeed," I said, helplessly, foolishly smiling at DeHon's companion. I confess that, like most men in the chamber, and not a few women, I could not take my eyes from her. She was so unspeakably lovely, swaying gracefully in the low gravity about the anchor point of her sticky shoes like a Nereid on some sea's floor. When I dared to lift her gloved right hand by the tips of her fingers, and bent over her knuckles, the gorgeous creature actually blushed. She was young, and seemed to have not yet grown into her beauty, for she wore it as carelessly as a child costumed in some fabulously antique robe, and was simultaneously embarrassed and amused by the reactions she provoked. Perhaps even then she had a presentiment that it would be the cause of her death.

She said, so softly I had to lean close to hear her, "I am no more than an amateur of history. But of course I have heard of your work, Professor-Doctor Graves."

Her Portuguese had a soft, husky lilt. A subtle perfume, with a deep note of musk, rose from the cleft between her breasts, which were displayed to their advantage by the blood-red folds of her spidersilk blouson. A wide belt of red leather measured the narrowness of her waist; red silk trousers, cuffed at the ankles, gathered in complex pleats around her long, slim legs. Her hair was silver and frost; her eyes beaten copper flecked with green.

"Demi is too modest," DeHon said. "Her monograph on the conceptual failures in design of early orbital habitats is something of a classic."

I noted that the ghost of a double chin appeared when Demi Lacombe dipped her head in quiet acknowledgment of DeHon's compliment, and that her bare arms were plump and rosy. I thought then that if she ever had children the natural way, she would have to take care not to grow fat, and it was a relief to realize that her beauty was only mortal.

She said, "Cris is probably the only one, apart from myself and my thesis supervisor, who had read all of it."

"I like to keep up with our cultural guests," DeHon said.

"I'm really more of an engineer," Demi Lacombe told me. "What they did here, with the city parklands, that was true artistry."

I learned that she was an environmental engineer, brought to Dione by the Three Powers Occupation Force to survey Paris's damaged ecosystem and to suggest how it could be reconstructed.

When I expressed interest, she deflected it automatically. "I am not here to do anything radical. Simply figure out the best way to make the city habitable again. But for a historian to find himself right at the center of history in the making must be tremendously exciting."

"The war is over. This gala performance was deliberately staged to make the point. I'm merely picking over its ruins."

"Is it true that you go out into the city without any guards?"

"I have a guide. I need to talk to people when they are at

their ease. Bringing them to the diplomatic quarter has unfortunate implications."

"Arrest," DeHon said, with a delicate, refined shudder. "Interrogation."

I said, "I do carry a weapon, but it's as unnecessary as the guards who patrol the perimeter of the theater. The survivors of the siege are by now quite inured to their fate. It's true that many areas of the city are still dangerous, but only because of unrepaired damage and a few undiscovered booby traps."

"Do you believe," Demi Lacombe asked, boldness making her eyes shine, "that he still lives?"

I knew at once whom she meant, of course, as would anyone in Paris. I said, "Of course not."

"Yet I'm told that many of the survivors think that he does."

"It is a frail and foolish hope, but hope is all they have. No, he willed his death from the beginning, when he assassinated the rest of the emergency committee and despoiled the diplomatic quarter, and he sealed his fate when he killed his hostages and the diplomats sent to bargain for peace. He was not the kind of man to run away from the consequences of his actions and so, like most of those he briefly commanded, he would have been killed in the siege. His body has not yet been identified, but the same can be said for more than half of those killed."

"You are very certain."

"I have studied human nature all my life."

"And would you classify him as one of your great men?"

"I'm flattered that you know of my work."

Demi Lacombe said, "I wouldn't lie for the sake of politeness, Professor-Doctor Graves."

"Please, Mademoiselle, I think we might be friends. And my friends call me Fredo."

"And so shall I, because I don't really get on with this false formality. I know it's the fashion in the Pacific Community, but I'm a hick from Europe. So, Fredo, is he a great man?"

The delicate suffusion of her soft cheeks: alabaster in the first light of morning.

I bowed and said, "The corporados think so, or they would not have sponsored my research. However, I have not yet made up my mind."

As we talked, I was aware of the people, mostly men, who were watching Demi Lacombe from near and far. The architects of the cities of the moons of the outer planets, imaginations stimulated by the engineering possibilities of microgravity, made their public spaces as large as possible, to relieve the claustrophobia of their tents and domes and burrows. The theater's auditorium, a great crescent wedged beneath the steep slope of the seats, could easily have held two thousand people, and although almost everyone in the diplomatic quarter had come to the gala opening, we numbered no more than three hundred, scattered sparsely across the vast, black floor, which our shoes gripped tightly in lieu of proper gravity. Diplomats, executives and officials of the *ad hoc* government; *novo abastado* industrialists, sleek as well-fed sharks, trailed by entourages of aides and bodyguards as they lazily cruised the room, hoping to snap up trifles and tidbits of gossip; officers of the Three Powers Occupation Force, in the full dress uniforms of half a dozen different armies; collaborationists in their best formal wear, albeit slightly shabby and out of fashion, mostly *en famille* and mostly gorging themselves at the buffet, for rationing was still in force amongst Paris's defeated population.

There was a stir as, in full costume and make-up, Don Giovanni and Leporello escorted Donna Anna and Donna Elvira into the huge room. The actors half-swam, half-walked through the web of tethers with consummate ease, acknowledging the scattering of applause. At the center of the auditorium's crescent, one man, sleek, dark-haired, in an immaculate pearly uniform, had not turned to watch the actors but was still staring openly at Demi Lacombe. It was Dev Veeder, the dashing colonel in charge of the security force. When Demi Lacombe looked up and saw him watching her I thought I heard the snap of electricity between them.

DeHon nudged me and said loudly, for the benefit of everyone nearby, "Our brave colonel is smitten, don't you think?"

Two

I should not have allowed myself to become involved, of course. But like Cris DeHon (although I was neutered by age and temperament rather than by elective treatment), I had a bystander's fascination with human sexual behavior. And, frankly, my assignment, although lucratively paid, was becoming tiresome.

I had been in Paris, Dione for two months, commissioned by a consortium of half a dozen Greater Brazilian corporados to write an official history of the siege of the city, and in particular to contribute to a psychological model of Marisa Bassi, the leader of the barricades, the amateur soldier who had kept off the forces of the Three Powers Alliance for twenty days after the general surrender which had brought an end of the Quiet War elsewhere in the solar system.

I knew that I had been chosen because of my position as emeritus professor of history at Rio de Janeiro rather than for my ability or even my reputation, tattered as it was by the sniping of jealous younger colleagues. Historians cannot reach an agreement about anything, and most especially they cannot agree on the way history is made. Herodotus and Thucydides believed that the proper subjects of history were war and constitutional history and political personality, times of crisis and change; Plutarch suggested that history was driven by the actions and desires of exemplary characters, of great men. The Christians introduced God into history, a kind of alpha great man presiding over a forced marriage of divine and human realms, and when the notion of an epicurean God was shouldered aside in the Renaissance, the idea that history was shaped by forces beyond the control of ordinary men remained, although these forces were no longer centered on extraordinary individuals but were often considered to be no more than blind chance, the fall of a coin, the want of a nail. Like a maggot in an apple, chance lay at the heart of Gibbon's elegant synthesis of the philosophical studies of Voltaire and the systematic organization of facts by rationalists like Hume and Montesquieu; it was the malignant flaw in Leopold von Ranke's (a distant ancestor of mine) codification of history as a neutral, nonpartisan, scholarly pursuit; and it was made explicit in the twentieth century fragmentation of the history of ideas into a myriad specialties and the leveling of all facts to a common field, so that the frequency of dental caries in soldiers in the trenches of the First World War was considered as important an influence of events as the abilities of generals. Great men or small, all were tossed alike by society's tides.

It was not until the restoration of history as a species of literature, by deployment of virtual theater and probabilistic clades, that the idea of the worth of the individual was restored. Who can say if this view of history caused the collapse of democratic republicanism, or if republicanism's collapse changed our philosophy of history? But it is certain that the rise of nationalism and the restoration of half-forgotten monarchies, aided by supranational corporados which found it convenient to divide their commercial territories into quarreling kingdoms and principalities, paralleled the return of the theory of the great man in history, a theory of which I, in my time, was an important champion.

In my time.

I had hoped that by coming to Paris, Dione, in the midst of reconstruction of a war scarcely ended, I would be able to secure my reputation with a final masterwork and confound my jealous rivals. But I soon discovered that the last days of the free collective of Paris, and of its leader, Marisa Bassi, were a tissue of echoes and conflicting stories supported by too few solid facts.

Those few surviving collectivists who believed that Marisa Bassi was dead could not agree how or where he had died; the majority, who foolishly believed that he had escaped during the hours of madness when special forces of the Three Powers Alliance had finally infiltrated the city, could not agree on how he had escaped, nor where he had escaped to. No ship had left Dione in those last desperate days except the cargo scow which, its navigation system driven mad by viral infection, had ploughed into Saturn's thick atmosphere and had either burned up or now floated, squashed to a two-dimensional profile by crushing atmospheric pressure, near the planet's metallic hydrogen core.

If history is a story told by winners, then the winners have the unconscionable burden of sifting mountains of dross for rare nuggets of pure fact, while the losers are free to fantasize on what could or should have been.

My commission should have been simple, but I found the demands of my employers, who did not trouble to supply me with assistants, were stretching my methodology to its breaking point. The corporados wanted to capture the psyche of great rebel leader in a heuristic model, a laboratory specimen of a troublesome personality they could study and measure and define, as doctors begin to fight a disease by first unraveling the genetic code of the virus, bacterium or faulty gene which is its cause. By knowing what Marisa Bassi had been, they thought that they could prevent another of his kind gaining power in the half-ruined colonies.

After two months, I had a scant handful of facts about Marisa Bassi's life before the Quiet War, and a horrible knot of evasions and half-truths and lies about his role in the siege, a knot which became more complex each day, with no way of cutting through to the truth. I confess, then, that in the days after my first meeting with Demi Lacombe, I was more interested in the rumors and gossip about her and Dev Veeder than in my own work.

It was, you must understand, an interest born of concern for her safety; an almost paternal concern. There was our age difference—almost fifty years—and my devotion to the memory of my dear dead wife. No matter what others may say, I had only pure motives in taking an interest in Dev Veeder's assault on the heart of the young and beautiful environmental engineer.

At first, much of my information came from Cris DeHon, who told me how our head of security personally escorted Demi Lacombe as she surveyed and cataloged the ruined wildernesses and parklands and farms of the city, assiduously transporting her to wherever she desired, arranging picnics in a sealed house or in a bubble habitat laboriously swept clear of booby traps and biowar beasties by squads of troopers. And like everyone else in the claustrophobic shark-pool of Paris's diplomatic quarter, I saw how closely Dev Veeder attended Demi Lacombe at every social gathering, even though she spent most of her time with the science crews while he stood by impotently, unable to participate in their impenetrable, jargon-ridden conversations.

"It's a purely one-sided affair," DeHon told me, when it caught me watching her at a party held by one or another of the corporados, I forget which, on the huge lawn at the center of the diplomatic quarter, part of the parkland that both penetrated and surrounded the built-up area inside the quarter's pyramidal tent. As always, most of us were there, scattered across an oval of brilliant green grass webbed with tethers, the dozens of faint shadows overlapping at our feet cast by brilliant lamps hung from the high ridge of the quarter's roof, Saturn's foggy crescent tilted beyond like a fantastic brooch pinned to a sky as black as jeweler's velvet. In the shade of the efflorescent greenery of a sweet chestnut tree, that sprawled like a banyan in the low gravity, Demi Lacombe was talking earnestly with a couple of techheads; Dev Veeder stood close by in his dress uniform, watching her over the rim of the wine bulb from which, every now and then, he pretended to sip.

Cris DeHon said, "She's such an innocent: she really doesn't see how badly she is humiliating Dev. You've heard how he's increased the number of security sweeps in the general population? I do believe that it is a reliable index of his growing frustration. I think that soon there will be more public executions, unknowing sacrifices on the altar of our gallant police chief's unrequited love."

I said, perhaps a trifle sharply, "What do you know of love?"

"Love or lust," the neuter said, "it's all the same. Love is merely the way by which men fool themselves that they have nobler motives than merely spending their urges, a game sprung from the constant tension between the male's blind need to copulate and the female's desire to win a father who will help provide for her children. Our security chief is parading like a peacock because he knows he is competing against every potential suitor of the delicious Mademoiselle Lacombe. And how many suitors there are!" DeHon bent closer and whispered, "I hear she takes long night walks in the parkland."

Its breath smelt of milk and cinnamon: a baby's breath.

"That's hardly surprising," I said. "She is an environmental engineer. The gardens must fascinate her."

"I've heard she has a particular interest in the gardeners."

I laughed. "That would be obscene if it were not so ridiculous."

Cris DeHon's smile showed small pearl-white teeth. "Perhaps. But perhaps poor beautiful Demi seeks simple relief from the strain of being the focus of a killer's desire."

I suppose the epithet was not an exaggeration, although it shocked me then, as no doubt DeHon hoped it would. Dev Veeder had had a good war, and had risen quickly through the ranks of the Greater Brazilian Army. He was a war hero, although like many heroes of the Quiet War—at least, on the winning side—he had never engaged in combat. His specialty was debriefing; I suppose a more liberal age might say that he was a torturer, although his methods were as much psychological as physical. He once confided to me that showing a prisoner the instruments he proposed to use often had as much effect as application of the instruments themselves—especially if the prisoner had been forced to listen to the screams of others suffering hot questioning. Early in the war, Dev Veeder had interrogated an entire mining community on Europa, some fifty men, women and children; the intelligence he had wrung from them had helped bring a swift and relatively bloodless end to the siege of Minos. This and other exploits had won him his present position of head of security of Paris, which he prosecuted with diligence and vigor.

Dev Veeder was young, the youngest son of a good family with connections in both industry and government. He was fiercely ambitious and highly intelligent. He had a sharp black impatient gaze. His hair was combed back in waves from his high forehead and aquiline nose; his make-up was discretely but skillfully applied. A dandy from the pages of a seventeenth century novel, but no fool. I knew him well from the conversations we had had about history. He was very interested in my theories, and believed, like many middle-ranking military men, that he himself had something of the attributes of a great man. This vanity was his single serious weakness, although it was true that, like all tyrants, he believed himself both benevolent and pragmatic.

"If only I had had the chance to really prove myself," he said to me more than once, showing that he really misunderstood my theory. For great men of history do prove themselves; the will to succeed, not luck or circumstance, is what makes them great. They rise to the occasion; they seize the day; they mold themselves to be all things to all men. Dev Veeder was too proud to realize this, and perhaps too cruel. He could only be what he was, and perhaps that is why I feared for Demi, and why I crossed him.

Three

Each day, I left the safety of the diplomatic quarter for the ruins of the city to interview the survivors of the siege, to try and learn what they knew or claimed to know about Marisa Bassi. In spite of my reputation and the letters of commission I carried, Dev Veeder did not think that I was important enough to warrant a proper escort—an impertinence for which I was grateful, for one cannot properly conduct interviews amongst a defeated population in the presence of troopers of the force which now occupies their territory. And so, each day, armed only with the blazer which I kept holstered at my ankle, I set out to pursue my research in the refugee warrens.

It was my custom to wait for my guide in a small café at the edge of the small plaza just outside the diplomatic quarter. The place had once been the checkpoint for the quarter, with cylinder gates to control access and human guards on duty in case there was a problem the computer was not authorized to handle. On the night of the revolution, a mob had stormed the guardhouse and killed the guards, fried the computer and associated security hardware with an industrial microwave beam, and blown the gates. The diplomatic quarter had already been evacuated, but a small detachment of soldiers and minor executives had been left behind as caretakers; no one had expected the revolutionary committee to violate the diplomatic quarter's sovereign status. The soldiers killed half a hundred of the mob before they were themselves killed, the surviving executives were taken hostage, and the buildings looted.

After the war, the quarter was the first place to be restored, of course, and a memorial had been erected to the murdered soldiers and martyred hostages, virtually the only casualties on our side. But the ruins of the gates still stood to one side of the plaza on which half a dozen pedways and escalators converged, tall hollow columns gutted of their armatures, their bronze facings scorched and ghosted with half-erased slogans.

The guardhouse's airy teepee was slashed and half-collapsed, but an old married couple had set up a tiny kitchen inside it and put a scattering of mismatched chairs and tables outside. Perhaps they hoped to get the custom of those collaborators who had clearance to get past the security things, half dog, half bear, knitted together with cybernetic enhancements and armor, which now guarded the diplomatic quarter. However, I seemed to be their only customer, and I suspected that they were relatives of my assiduous guide; for that reason I never left a tip. That day, two days after the party, I was sitting as usual in a wire frame chair, sipping from a bulb of dark strong coffee and nibbling a meltingly sweet *pain au chocolat,* looking out across the vista of Paris's main dome while I waited for my guide.

Before the Quiet War, Paris, Dione, was one of the loveliest cities in the solar system, and the largest of all the cities on Saturn's moons. Its glassy froth of domes and tunnels and tents straddled a ridge of upthrust brecciated basalt between Romulus and Remus craters. Since the twin craters are close to the equator of the icy moon's sub-Saturnian hemisphere, Saturn stood almost directly overhead, cycling through his phases roughly every three days. The city had been renowned for its microgravity architecture, its wide, tree-lined boulevards and parks—much of its population was involved in the biotech industries—its café culture and opera and theaters, and the interlinked parkland blisters which stepped down the terraces of Remus crater along the waterfall-filled course of what had been renamed the Proudhon River during the revolution and now, after the end of Quiet War and the fall of the barricades, was the Little Amazon—or would be, once the pumps were fixed and the watercourse had been cleared of debris.

The main dome, like many others, had been blown during the bloody end of the siege. It was two kilometers across, bisected by a dry riverbed from east to west and by the Avenue des Étoiles, so-called because of the thousands of lanterns which had hung from the branches of its trees, from north to south, and further divided into segments by boulevards and tramways. Clusters of white buildings stood amongst the sere ruins of parks, while warehouses and offices were packed around its circumference. Although the civic buildings at its center were superficially intact, their windows were shattered and their white walls were pockmarked to the third story by the bullet-holes of the bitter hand-to-hand fighting of the bloody day in which eighty thousand citizens died defending their city from invading troops of the Three Powers Alliance. Every scrap of vegetation in the parks had been killed by exposure to vacuum after the blowout, of course, and now, with the restoration of atmospheric pressure, it was all rotting down to mulch. The air of the plaza where I sat, high above it all, held a touch of that cabbagey stink.

I was woken from my reverie by a light touch on my shoulder, the musk of roses. Demi Lacombe fell, light as a bird, into the wire chair on the other side of the little café table and favored me with her devastating smile. She wore loose white coveralls; I could not help but notice that her breasts were unbound. I scarcely saw Dev Veeder scowling a dozen meters away, or his squad of burly armored troopers.

Demi Lacombe's left wrist was bound by a pressure bandage; when I expressed my concern, she explained that she had fractured it in a silly accident. "I overestimated my ability to jump in this lovely light gravity, and took a bit of a tumble. The clinic injected smart bacteria which will fix up the bone in a couple of days. I've seen this place so many times," she added, "but I didn't know that you were its patron, Professor-Doctor."

"Please, my name is Fredo. Won't you join me in a coffee? And you too, perhaps, Colonel Veeder?"

"There's no time for that," Veeder said brusquely. "You're a fool to patronize these people, Graves."

Inside the guardhouse's half-collapsed shroud, the old couple who ran the makeshift café shrank from his black glare.

I said boldly, "The psychologists tell me that enterprises like this are a healthy sign, Colonel. Even though it is, admittedly, on a microeconomic scale."

"You're being scammed," Veeder said. "I think I ought to re-examine the credentials of your so-called guide."

"History shows us, Colonel, that those defeated benefit

from subsequent cultural and economic fertilization. Besides, my sponsors would be unhappy if you disturbed my work."

Demi Lacombe said, "I think it's a nice thing, Dev. A little sign of reconciliation."

"Whatever. Come on. It's a long way to the tramhead."

"The trams are working again?"

"One or two," Dev Veeder said.

"Dev restored the tram lines which pass through some of the parklands," Demi said. "It really does help my surveys." For a moment, she took my hand in both of hers. "You're a kinder man than you seem, Fredo," she said, and floated up out of her chair and took Dev Veeder's arm.

I watched them cross the plaza to the escalators. Demi had only been in Paris a couple of weeks, but she had already mastered the long loping stride which worked best in Dione's low gravity. Only when they had descended out of sight did I look at the scrap of paper she had thrust into my palm.

I must talk with you.

My guide arrived hardly a minute later; I suspected that he had been watching the whole thing from a safe vantage. I suppose I should tell you something about Lavet Corso. The most important thing was that I never entirely trusted him, an instinctive reaction to which I should have paid more attention. But who does like collaborationists? They are despised by their own people for being traitors, and for the same reason are distrusted by those they are so eager to please.

Lavet Corso had once been something in the lower echelons in the city's government, and was studiedly neutral about Marisa Bassi. Although he had arranged many interviews, I had never tried to interview him. He had been widowed in the war and had to support a young daughter in difficult circumstances. While interviewing survivors of the siege, I had to endure the squalor of the warrens in which they lived. On my first visit, Corso had had the temerity to complain about the noise, lack of privacy, dirt and foul air, and I had told him sharply, "You and your daughter are lucky. Fate saved you from a horrible death. If not for a chance which separated you from your wife, you could have been aboard that scow too. You could have fallen inside a tin can into Saturn's poisonous atmosphere, choking and boiling and flattened in the calorific depths. But you, Mr. Corso, were spared, as was your daughter. Life goes on."

I don't think he took my little homily to heart, but he didn't dare complain again.

Corso was a tremendously tall man, with a pock-marked face, dark eyes and black hair slicked back from his pale face with heavy grease. He was efficient and smarter than he mostly allowed himself to appear; perhaps too smart, for his flattery never seemed sincere, and he was too ready to suggest alternatives to my plans. That day, for instance, after I had told him where I wanted to go, he immediately proposed visiting another sector that was both easier to reach and in a far safer condition.

"It is my life if you are hurt, boss."

"I hardly think so, given the waivers I had to sign in order to do my fieldwork."

"And you have been there already, boss. Several times. Very badly damaged it is, not safe at all. And there are still many booby traps."

"I do remember, Mr. Corso, and I also remember that on each occasion you tried to dissuade me. But I will go again, because it is important to me. If we do get into trouble, the machines of the security force claim to be only five minutes away from any spot in the city."

"It's certainly what we're told," Corso said. "Perhaps it's even true."

"Then lead on, Mr. Corso. I want to see this place today."

A few minutes later, the whole of the main dome was spread beneath us. I sat behind Corso as he labored at the pedals of the airframe, beneath the central joint of its wide, vivid yellow bat wings. I found this mode of travel quite exhilarating, for Corso was an expert pilot, and in Dione's meager gravity we could fall a hundred meters and escape with only bruises and perhaps a broken bone or two.

We swooped out above the cankerous, rotting tangles of parks, above streets dotted with half-cleared barricades, above white buildings and the blackened shells of buildings set afire in the last hours of the siege. One reason for the blowout had been to save Paris from its crazed citizens (riding behind Corso, with cold cabbagey air blowing around me, I could imagine the dome's blister filling with swirling fumes, a smoky pearl that suddenly cleared when its integrity was breached; its huge diamond panes were still smudged with the residue of the suddenly snuffed fires). And then the little flying machine stooped and we bounced once, twice, and were down, taxiing across a wide flat roof above an avenue lined with dead chestnut trees.

I had come here on my second day in Paris. I had insisted, and Dev Veeder had, with ill-grace, provided an escort. I had returned several times since, for here were the ruins of the office building, like a broken tooth in the terraced arcades of this commercial sector, from which Marisa Bassi had run his revolutionary committee. Since I had first visited the place, I had learned much more about those desperate, last days. From one of these terraces, bareheaded and in shirt-sleeves, Bassi had made his crucial speech to the crowds who had packed the stilled pedways and empty tram tracks. It was at an intersection nearby that he had organized the first of the barricades, and inaugurated the block captain system by which the building and defense of each barricade was assigned to platoons of a dozen or so citizens. How proud the survivors still were of their token efforts, singing out the names of the barricades on which they had served like captains recalling the names of their ships.

Place de la Concorde.

The Killing Field.

The Liberty Line.

For a long time, I stood at the remains of that first barricade and tried to imagine how it had been, that day when Bassi had made his speech. To insert myself, by imaginative reconstruction built on plain fact, into the life of another, is the most delicate part of my work. As I stood there, I imagined the plane trees in leaf, the heat and brilliant light of hundreds of suspensor lamps beneath the roof of the dome, like floating stars against the blackness of Dione's night, the restless crowd in the wide avenue, faces turned like flowers towards Marisa Bassi.

An immigrant, he was half the height of most of the population of Paris, but was broad-shouldered and muscular, with a mane of gray hair and a bushy beard woven through with luminescent beads. What had he felt? He was tired, for he had certainly not slept that night. I was certain that he had had a direct hand in the deaths of his former government colleagues, and perhaps he was haunted by the bloody scenes. Murder is a primal event. Did the screams of his murdered colleagues fill him with foreboding, did his hands tremble as he grasped the rail and squared his shoulders and prepared to address the restless crowd? He had showered, and his hair was still wet as he let go of the rail and raised his hands (I had a photograph of his hands which I looked at often: they were square-palmed, the fingers short and stout, with broken nails—a laborer's rather than a murderer's hands) to still the crowd's noise, and began to speak. And in that moment changed history, and condemned most of his audience to a vainglorious death. Had he planned his speech, or did it come unprompted? Several of those I had interviewed had said that he had seemed nervous; several others that he had spoken with flawless confidence; all said that he had spoken without notes, and that he had been cheered to the echo.

I walked about for an hour, every now and then dictating a few words to my notebook, impressions, half-realized ideas. Bassi did not yet stand before me fully-fleshed, but I felt that he was growing closer.

One of the killing machines which patrolled the repressurized parts of the city stalked swiftly across a distant intersection, glittering and angular, like a praying mantis made of steel, there one moment, gone the next. I wondered if it or one of its fellows had caught the man who had painted the silly slogan, *He Lives!*, across the sooty stone of the building's first setback; I would have to ask Dev Veeder.

I told Corso, "I'm pleased to see that our angels of mercy are afoot."

"They might reassure you, boss, but they scare the shit out me. I've seen what those things can do to a man."

"But not to you, my dear Corso. Not while you are under my protection."

"Not while I have the stink of occupation upon me."

"That's putting it crudely," I said.

All of the occupation force and certain of its favored collaborators had been tweaked so that their sweat emitted specific long-chain lipids which placated the primitive brains of the security things and killing machines.

"I'm sorry, boss. This place weirds me out."

"Bad memories, perhaps?"

I was wondering if Corso had been there, that day, but as usual, he did not rise to the bait. He said, "I was on corpse detail, right after they repressurized this part of the city. The bodies had lain in vacuum at minus two hundred degrees Centigrade for more than two months. They were shriveled and very dry. Skin and flesh crisp, like pie crust. It was hard to pick them up without a finger or a hand or a foot breaking off. We all wore masks and gloves, but flakes of dead people got in your skin, and pretty soon all you could smell was death."

"Don't be so gloomy, Corso. When the reconstruction is finished, your city will have regained its former glory."

"Yeah, but it won't be my city any more. So, where do you want to go next?"

"To the sector where he lived, of course."

"Revisiting all your old favorites today, boss?"

"I feel that I'm getting closer to him, Mr. Corso."

We climbed back up to the roof, took off with a sudden stoop, and then, with Corso pedaling furiously, rose high above roofs and avenues and dead parkland.

"I don't understand why you aren't grateful for the reconstruction, Mr. Corso. We could quite easily have demolished your city and started over. Or pulled out entirely, and brought you all back to Earth."

"I was born here. This is where I was designed to live. Earth would kill me."

"And you *will* live here, thanks to the generosity of the Three Powers Occupation Force, but you will live here as part of human mainstream. The high flown nonsense about colonizing the outer limits of the solar system, the comets and the Kuiper Belt, all of that was sheer madness. I have a colleague who has demonstrated that it is economically impossible. There will be a few scientific outposts, perhaps, but the outer system is too cold and dark and energy poor. It's no place to live. Here though, will be the jewel of Earth's reconciliation with her children, Mr. Corso. I believe that the Quiet War will mark the beginning of the first mature epoch of human history, a war to end wars, and an end to childish expansionism. In its place will be as fine a flowering in the sciences and the arts as humanity has ever known. We are lucky to be alive at this time."

"The Chinese might disagree. About an end to war."

"Such disagreements as there are between the Democratic Union of China and the Three Powers Alliance will be settled by diplomacy and the intermingling of trade and culture. Men live for so long now that their lives are too valuable to be wasted in war."

Pedaling hard, Corso said over his shoulder, "Old men have always used that as an excuse to send young men to war."

"You are a cynic, Mr. Corso."

"Maybe. Still, it's funny how the war started because we wouldn't repay our debts, and now you're pouring money into reconstruction."

How do wars start? I suppose you could graph the rise in government debt against public resentment at the colonies funded by Earth's taxes until a trigger point was reached, a crisis which had finally forced the governments of the Three Powers Alliance to act. That crisis was generally agreed to be the refusal by certain colonies to pay increased rates of interest on the corporate and government loans which had funded their expansion, an act of defiance which coincided with the death of the president of Greater Brazil close to an election, and the need by his inexperienced and unpopular vice president to be seen to act decisively. By that view, the Quiet War was no more than an act of debt recovery. Or perhaps one might suggest that the Quiet War was an historical inevitability, the usual reaction of colonies which had chafed under the yoke of an over-stretched and underfunded empire until they could not help but demand independence: there were dozens of precedents for this in Earth's history.

And yet the colonists had lost. The Three Powers Alliance had the technological and economic advantage, and superior access to information; the colonies, fragile bubbles of air and light and heat scattered in the vastness of the outer solar system, were horribly vulnerable. Apart from a few assassinations and acts of sabotage, almost no one had died on Earth during the Quiet War, but hundreds of thousands had died in the colonies on the moons of Jupiter and Saturn, in orbital habitats and in spacecraft.

Sartre wrote that because of technology we can no longer make history; instead, history is something that happens to us. It is an irony, I suppose, that Marisa Bassi's spark of defiance was extinguished because the very technology which sustained his city made it so very vulnerable.

And yet certain important corporados were sufficiently worried about the futile resistance led by that one man, in one city on one of Saturn's small icy moons, to have sent me to profile him, as a police psychologist might profile a mass murderer.

Was Marisa Bassi a great man who had risen from obscurity to fame but had failed? Or was he a fool, or worse than a fool—a psychopath who had hypnotized an emotionally vulnerable population and made them martyrs not for the cause of liberty, but for gratification of his inadequate ego?

I still had too little material to make that judgment, and I confess that on that day, as I returned to places I had already trawled over, my mind was as much on the implications of Demi Lacombe's note as my work, and to Lavet Corso's undisguised relief I brought an early end to my labors.

Four

It was not easy to arrange a private meeting with Demi Lacombe, for the diplomatic quarter was small, and Dev Veeder's already keen eye was sharpened further by jealousy. I took to walking in the parkland after dark, even though I gave little credence to Cris DeHon's gossip, but I met only tame animals and, once, one of the gardeners, who for a moment gazed at me with gentle, mild curiosity before shambling away into the shadows beneath the huge, shaggy puffballs of a stand of cypress trees.

I spent the next few days within the diplomatic quarter, interviewing wretches caught up in Dev Veeder's latest security sweep. They were either sullen and mostly silent, or effusively defiant, and in the latter case their answers to my questions were so full of lies or boasts or blusters that it was almost impossible to find any grain of truth. One wild-eyed man, his face badly bruised, claimed to have seen Bassi shot in the head in the last moments of the resistance, after the invading troops had blown the main dome and stormed the barricades. Several said that he was sleeping deep beneath one of the moon's icefields, and would waken again in Paris's hour of need—something I had heard many times already, unconsciously echoing the Arthurian legend just as the Bassi's revolution had so very consciously echoed the Parisian communes of the 19th century (in our age, all revolutionaries worth their salt must pay fastidious attention to precedent).

All worthless, yet I felt that I was growing near to understanding him. Sometimes he was in my dreams. But suddenly my work no longer mattered, for I contrived my rendezvous with Demi Lacombe.

It was at another of the receptions with which the small community within the diplomatic quarter bolstered its sense of its own worth. It was easily done. By an arrangement I was later to regret, Cris DeHon diverted Dev Veeder into a long and earnest conversation with a visiting journalist about the anti-reconstruction propaganda that was circulating in the general population (in truth no more than a few scruffy leaflets and some motile slogans planted more to irritate the occupying troops than rally the vestigial resistance, but how Dev preened before the journalist's floating camera). I exchanged a glance with Demi Lacombe, and she set her bulb of wheat frappé on a floating tray and set off past the striped tents erected in the airy glade into the woods beyond. I followed a minute later, my heart beating as quickly and lightly as it had when I had set off on romantic assignations half a century ago.

Ferns grew head-high beneath the frothy confections of the trees, but I glimpsed Demi's pale figure flitting through the green shadows and hurried on into the depths of the ravine which split the quarter's parkland. We soon left the safety of the trees behind but still she went on and I had to follow, although my eagerness was becoming tempered with a concern that we would be spotted by one of the security things.

Yet how wonderful it was, to be chasing that gorgeous creature! We flew down a craggy rock face like creatures in a dream, over vertical fields of brilliantly colored tweaked orchids, along great falls of ferns and vines and air-kelp. Birds lazily swam in the air; beyond the brilliant stars of suspensor lamps, beyond the diamond panes of the quarter's tent, Saturn blessed us with his pale, benign gaze.

The chase ended in a triangular meadow of emerald-green moss, starred with the spikes of tiny red flowers and backed by the tall, ferny cliff of black, heat-shocked basalt down which we had swum. There was a steep drop to the dark lake at the bottom of the ravine at one edge, and a dense little wood of roses grown as tall as trees at the other. The wild heady scent of the roses did nothing to quieten my heart; nor did the way Demi pressed her hands over mine. The bandage on her left wrist was gone; those smart bacteria had worked their magic.

"Thank you, Fredo," she said. "Thank you for this. If I couldn't get away from him now and then I swear I would go crazy."

How can I describe what she looked like in that moment? Her silvery hair unbound about her heart-shaped face, which was mere centimeters from my own. Her pale, gauzy trousers and blouson floating about her body. Her scent so much like the scent of the wild roses. The viridescent light of that little meadow, filtered through ferns and roses, gave her pale skin an underwater cast; she might have been a Nereid indeed, clasping a swooning sailor to her bosom.

"Dev Veeder," I said stupidly.

"He's declared his love for me."

"You must be careful how you respond. You may think him foolish, but it will be dangerous to insult his honor."

"It's so fucked up," the gorgeous creature declared. She let go of my hands and strode the width of the meadow in four graceful strides, came back to me in four more. "I can't *work*, the way he follows me around everywhere."

"His devotion is exceptional. I take it that you do not reciprocate his infatuation."

"If you mean do I love him, do I want to marry him, no. No. I thought I liked him, but I knew better than to sleep with him because I know what a big thing it is with you Greater Brazilians."

I thought then that it might have been better if she had slept with him as soon as possible, since it would have instantly devalued her in Dev Veeder's eyes. She would have become his mistress, but never his wife.

Demi said, "I think he's been out here too long. I've heard dreadful stories about him."

"Well, we have been at war."

"That he tortures his prisoners," she said. "That he enjoys it."

"He is a soldier. Sometimes it is necessary to do things in war which would be unforgivable in peacetime."

I did not particularly want to defend Dev Veeder, but I did not yet know what she wanted of me, and I was feeling an old man's caution.

"He enjoys it," she said again.

"Perhaps he enjoys carrying out his duty."

"A Jesuitical distinction if ever I heard one."

"I was educated by them, as a matter of fact."

"So was I! Just outside Dublin. A horrible gray pile of a place that smelled of damp and floor polish and cheap disinfectant. Brr," she said, and shuddered and smiled. "I bet you had to endure that lecture on damnation and eternity. The sparrow flying from one end of the Universe to the other . . ."

"On each circuit carrying away in its beak a grain of rice from a mountain as tall as the Moon's orbit."

"In our lecture the mountain was made of sand. And I guess your priests were men, not women. I still remember the punchline. Even when the sparrow had finished its task not one moment of eternity had passed. They knew how to leave a mark on your soul, the Jesuits. I learned to hate them because they scared me into being good."

"I am sure that you needed little tuition in that direction, Dr. Lacombe."

"Demi, Fredo. Call me Demi. Quit being so formal."

"Demi, then."

"They gave me a strong sense of duty too, the Jesuits. I came here to do a job. An important job."

I began to understand what she wanted. I said, "Dev Veeder's attentions are interfering with your work."

"He's an impossible man. He says that he wants to help me, but he won't listen when I try to tell him that he could best help by letting me get on with my work on my own."

"He is from a good family. Very old-fashioned."

"Right. He insists on going everywhere with me, and insists that I stay locked up in the quarter when he can't spare the time to escort me. So I'm way behind in my survey. I mean, I knew it would be a big job, but Dev is making it impossible. And it's so important that it gets done. This was such a wonderful place, before the war." She made a sweeping gesture that took in the roses, the falls of ferns, the viridescent moss. "It was all like this, then."

"The restoration is an important symbol of political faith."

"Well, there's that. But this city was a biotech showpiece before the war. It had more gene wizards than any other colony, and they exported their expertise to almost everywhere else in the outer system. There's so much we can learn from what's left, and so much more we can learn during the reconstruction."

"And of course you want to play a part in that. It would set the cap on your career."

"It was like a work of art," Demi Lacombe said. "It would be a terrible sin not to try and restore it. There's a man I need to see. Away from Dev."

"One of the survivors."

"Yani Hakaiopulos. He was a gene wizard, once upon a time. As great a talent as Sri Hong-Owen or Avernus. He retired a long time ago, but he helped entrain the basic ecological cycles which underpinned everything else. I can learn so much from him, if I'm given the chance."

"But he won't talk if Dev Veeder is with you."

"The Parisians think that Dev is a war criminal."

"If they had won the war, perhaps that's what he would have become. But they did not."

"Will you help me, Fredo? You go out into the city alone. You interview the people there."

"And you want me to interview this man about the city's ecosystems? I would not know where to begin."

"No," Demi Lacombe said, her gaze bright and bold. "I want you to take me with you."

"Without Dev Veeder's knowledge."

"Under his nose."

"He is the chief of police, Demi. No one can come and go without his knowledge."

"I think I've found a way," Demi Lacombe said. She stepped back and put two fingers between her blood-red lips and whistled, a single shrill note so loud it startled me, and disturbed a flock of small brown birds which had been perching in the ferns overhead. As they tumbled through the air, a man stepped out of the roses on the other side of the little meadow.

My heart gave a little leap, tugged by guilt, and I was suddenly aware of how much like illicit lovers Demi Lacombe and I must have looked. But the man was no man at all, merely one of the gardeners, the tutelary spirits of the parkland.

Before the revolution, before the Quiet War, the government of Paris, Dione was an attempt to revive the quaint notion of technodemocracy, an experiment in citizen participation that on Earth had been dismissed long ago as just another utopian idea that was simply too unwieldy in practice. But it had briefly flourished in the little goldfish bowl of the colony city; every citizen could put a motion to change any aspect of governance providing he could enlist a quorum of supporters, and the motion would be enforced by the appropriate moderating committee if a sufficient majority voted it through.

It was a horrible example of how lazy and misguided rulers, who should have been elevated above the mob by virtue of breeding or ability, devolve their natural obligations to ignorance, prejudice and the leveling force of popular taste. Imagine the time wasted in uniformed debate over trivial issues, the constant babble of prejudices masquerading as opinion or even fact! It had been a society shaped not by taste or intelligence but by a kind of directionless, mindless flailing reminiscent of Darwinian evolution. We have mastered evolution, and we must be masters of the evolution of our civilization, too. Yet Paris's nascent technodemocracy had thrown up one or two interesting ideas, and one of these was its method of capital punishment.

Like all democracies, it mistakenly believed in the essential perfectibility of all men, and so practiced rehabilitation of its criminals rather than punishment. But even it had to admit that there were some criminals who, by genetic inheritance, parental conditioning or choice, were irredeemable. As thrifty as the rest of the energy- and resource-poor colonies of the outer solar system, Paris did not waste material and labor in constructing prisons for these wretches; nor did it waste their potential for labor by executing them. Instead, they were lobotomized and fitted with transducer and control chips, transforming psychopaths into useful servants, meat extensions of the control system which maintained the parklands and wilderness and farms of the city.

The gardener Demi had summoned from his hiding place had obviously been an untweaked immigrant, for he was no taller than me. Like the gardener I had encountered when wandering the parkland like a lorn, lovesick fool, hoping to encounter Demi Lacombe, he was sturdy, barechested and barefoot, his white trousers ragged, his shaven head scarred by the operation which had transformed him, encircled by a coppery headband into which was woven a high-gain broad band antenna. Through this he was linked to both his fellows and the computers which controlled the climate of the parkland, its streams, its hidden machines, and even its animals, which all were fitted with control chips too. Several of the small brown birds which had fallen from the ferns fluttered about his head, calling in high excited voices, unnervingly like those of small children, before flying away over the edge of the meadow. With a rustling and snapping of canes, a pygmy mammoth emerged from the roses, its long russet hair combed straight and gleaming with oils, its trunk flexed at its broad forehead as the sensitive pink tip snuffled the air. Tools and boxes hung on its flanks, attached to a rope harness.

The gardener scarcely glanced at me; his attention was on Demi Lacombe. I thought I saw a look pass between them, crackling with a shared emotion. Desire, I thought, and in that moment unknowingly sealed her fate, for I was suddenly, violently, unreasonably jealous of the poor child of nature she had summoned, believing that Cris DeHon's malicious insinuations may have been right all along.

"He knows me," Demi Lacombe said softly. "I can speak with him."

"Anyone can speak to them," I said. "I understand they are programmed to understand a few simple commands. But mostly they keep away from the people they serve. It's better that way."

Demi Lacombe smiled and touched her left temple with her forefinger. "I mean that I can truly talk with him. I have an implant similar to his, so that I can access the higher functions of the machines which control the habitat. Through them, I can talk with him. Watch, Fredo! I can send him away as easily as I summoned him."

She made no signal, but the gardener turned and parted the canes of the roses and vanished into them. The mammoth turned too and trotted after him. It was unnervingly like magic, and I briefly wondered how else she might have commanded the brute, before crushing the vile image as a man might crush a loathsome worm beneath the heel of his boot.

Demi said, “He showed me a way out of here that Dev and his troopers don’t know about.”

I laughed, a trifle excessively I fear. I was not quite myself. Roses in a wild garden, a woman trapped by her own beauty, a compliant monster. I said, “Really, Demi. A secret passage?”

“A stream was diverted when the layout of the parkland was redesigned twenty years ago. Its sink pipe wasn’t sealed up because it lies at the bottom of the lake, down there.” She stepped gracefully to the edge of the meadow. A light wind blew up the face of the cliff, stirring her long, silvery hair as she pointed downward; she looked like a warrior from some pre-technological myth.

I shuffled carefully to her side, and looked down at the long, narrow sleeve of black water that was wedged at the bottom of the ravine, between the base of the cliff on which we stood and the wall of bare sheetrock which rose in huge bolted slabs toward the foot of one of the tent’s diamond panes, high above us.

Demi said, “The pipe is flooded, but the gardeners can give me one of the air masks they wear when they clean out the bulk storage tanks. There’s a pressure gate which must be opened—it fell closed when the main dome was blown. Then I’ll be outside.”

“It sounds dangerous. More dangerous than Dev Veeder.”

“I’ve tested the pressure gate. I know it works. But I need help getting across the main part of the city.” She had turned to me, her face shining with excitement. How young she was, how lovely! Her scent was very strong at that moment; I could have drowned in it quite happily. She said, "I need your help, Fredo. Will you help me?"

For a moment, I quite forget my loathsome spasm of jealousy. "Of course," I said. "Of course I will, my dear Demi. How could I refuse the plea of a maiden in distress?"

Five

We made our plans as we walked back through the shaggy, exuberances of the cypresses toward the lights and noise of the party. We took care to return to it separately, from different directions, but still my heart gave a little leap when I saw Dev Veeder moving purposefully through knots of chattering people, hauling himself hand over hand along one of the waist-high tethers which webbed the lawn. He was making straight for Demi, and when he reached her she put her hand on his shoulder and her lovely, delicate face close to his and talked quietly into his ear. He nodded and smiled, and she smiled too, my cunning minx.

"Now you can tell me all about it."

I swung around so quickly that I would have floated above the heads of the chattering party-goers if Cris DeHon had not caught my wrist. The neuter's fingers were long and delicate, and fever-hot. It wore a white blouson slashed here and there to show flashes of scarlet lining, as if it were imitating the victim of some primitive and bloody rite. Its hair was dyed a crisp white, and stiffened in little spikes.

"Tell me all about it," DeHon said. "What plot's afoot? Is it love?"

I smiled into the neuter's sharp pale face. "Don't be ridiculous."

"A marriage of summer and winter is not unknown. And if you're half the distinguished scholar you claim to be, you'd be quite a catch for a struggling academic from the most backward and impoverished country of the Alliance."

"She was showing me some of the wonders of our gardens," I said, shaking free of DeHon's hot grasp. "This city is famous for its gene wizards."

DeHon smiled craftily, looking sidelong through the crowd at Demi Lacombe and Dev Veeder. "I don't believe it for a minute, but I won't spoil the fun. The curtain has risen; the play has commenced. For your sake, I hope Dev Veeder will be in a good temper when he discovers your little plot."

The night passed in a daze of half-sleeping, half-waking. I had never slept well in Dione's light gravity, and what sleep I had that night was full of murky dreams colored by fear and desire.

The next morning, I drank an unaccustomed second cup of coffee at the makeshift café and, when Lavet Corso finally arrived, I instructed him to fly us to the coordinates which Demi Lacombe had given me.

He stared at me insolently, the seams in his face tightening around his mouth. "That's nothing but a park, boss."

"Nevertheless, that is where we will go."

And so we did, after a brief argument which I quite enjoyed, and which did more to wake me than the coffee did. I was beginning to suspect that Corso's protests were ritual, like the bargaining one must do in a souk when making a purchase. Now that the game was afoot, I was in a careless mood of anticipation, and did not complain at the pitch and yaw of the airframe as Corso slipped it through updraughts, spiraling down to the brown and black wreckage of the park.

We swooped in low over the tops of skeletal trees which raised their white arms high above a wasteland of deliquescing vegetation. The stink was horrible. An eye of water gleamed in the shadow of a low cliff of raw basalt, and a small figure stepped from a cleft at the foot of the cliff and semaphored its arms. A flood of relief and renewed desire turned my poor foolish heart quite over. I tapped Corso's shoulder, but he had already seen her. The wings of the airframe boomed as they shed air, and we skidded across a black carpet of mulch.

Demi Lacombe floated down from the cleft, from which a little water still trickled into what had once been a lake, and ran to us with huge loping strides, sleek in silvery skinthins which hugged every contour of her slim body. An airmask and a small tank dangled from one hand. Her wet hair was snarled around her beautiful face, made yet more beautiful by the brilliant smile she turned on me.

Corso gave a low whistle, and I said sharply, "Enough of that. Remember your poor dead wife."

"You're late," Demi said breathlessly.

"My guide has a bad sense of time."

"It doesn't matter. Well, I'm ready. Let's go!"

"You have not brought . . . more suitable attire?"

Demi laughed, and cocked her hip. The silvery material was molded tightly to every centimeter of her body. "What's wrong? You don't like this?"

I liked it very much indeed, of course, and it was obvious that Corso did too. He was cranking up the prop, to give enough kinetic energy to assist takeoff. When I told him sharply to hurry up, he mumbled something about overloading.

"Nonsense. You hardly expect my passenger to walk. Look lively! Every moment we stay here risks discovery."

"I didn't sign up for adventure," Corso said. He straightened, with one hand to the small of his back. "Maybe you better tell me what this is all about, boss."

"You just get us to the warrens," I said.

"No," Demi said, "he's right." She stepped up to Corso and touched his arm and said, "You're Lavet Corso, aren't you? Professor-Doctor Graves has told me so much about the help you've given him."

"And who are you?"

"Dr. Demi Lacombe. I'm here to help reconstruct your wonderful ecosystem, and I want to talk to Yani Hakaiopulos."

"Really," Corso said, but I could see that he was weakening. "Why not have your boyfriend haul him in?"

"My boyfriend?"

"Colonel Veeder. You are the woman he's been escorting everywhere."

"Well, that's true, but he isn't my boyfriend, and that's why I need your help."

Corso locked the prop's winding mechanism and said, "You can try and talk to Yani if you like, but you'll find he's immune to your charms. Climb on board now, both of you. Let's see if I can get this higher than the trees."

Demi looked at the flimsy airframe and said, "I thought it would be safer to walk."

"Not at all," I said. "It would take several hours, and we would be bound to encounter more than one of the killing machines, and they would report straight back to the security forces. But no one bothers to watch where we go."

"You had better be right, boss."

The airframe jinked across the rotten black carpet and bounded into the air. Demi, seated behind me, screamed loudly and happily. She had put her arms around my waist; the pressure of her body against my back, and her musky scent, almost as strong as the cabbage-stink of the rotten vegetation, awakened a part of me that had been sleeping for quite some time.

Although Corso was pedaling hard, the airframe clambered through the middle air of the dome with the grace of a pregnant dragonfly. I leaned back and pointed out to Demi the remains of barricades across the avenues, the ruined hulk of the Bourse, like a shattered wedding cake, where the last of those citizens who had been in or near to pressure suits when the dome had been blown open had made their final stand. Once, I saw the silver twinkle of a killing machine stalking down the middle of the Avenue des Étoiles; Corso must have seen it too, for he veered the airframe away, scudding in toward one of the flat rooftops clustered around the edge of the dome.

The place was an automated distribution warehouse of some kind, and although it would have been cleared of any bodies, the red-lit echoing emptiness of its storage areas and ramps was eerie. Demi kept close to me as Corso led us down a narrow street. I told her about Marisa Bassi's early days in Paris, Dione, when as an immigrant he had worked in one of these warehouses, rising quickly to become its supervisor, then moving on to become a partner in an import-export business of dubious legality, where he had made enough money to buy his citizenship.

"And two years after that he became a councillor, and then the war came. The rest will be history, once I have written it."

"Your history, maybe," Corso said.

"All history belongs to the winners," I said, "so it will be your history too. If you know anything about Bassi, now's the time to tell me."

"Nothing you need to know, boss," Corso said, with his maddening disingenuousness.

Marisa Bassi had been living in this semi-industrial sector when the war began. Imagine his small, sparsely furnished room that evening, the sounds of the street drifting up through a window open to catch any stray breeze: a tram rattling through a nearby intersection; the conversation of people strolling about as the suspensor lights dimmed overhead; the smell of food from the cafés and restaurants. Bassi was sitting in a chair, flicking through page after page on his slate—he hated the paperwork which went with his job, and was especially impatient with it now that the first move toward independence had been made—when he heard a distant thump, like a huge door closing. At the same moment the suspensor lights flickered, came back on. Bassi looked out of the window and saw people running, all in one direction, running with huge loping strides like gazelles fleeing a lion's rush. His heart felt hollow for a moment, then filled with a rush of adrenaline. He called out to someone he recognized, and the man stopped and shouted up that it was the parliament building, someone had blown it up.

"It's war!" the man added, holding up a little scrap of TV film. Let's say that he was a Sicilian too, Bep Martino or some such rough hewn name, a construction worker. He and

Bassi played chess and drank rough red wine under the chestnut trees in the little park at the end of the street.

"Wait there!" Bassi said. "I'm coming with you!"

It seemed that most of the population of Paris had converged on the ruins of the parliament building. It had neatly collapsed on itself, its flat roof draped broken-backed across the pancaked remains of its three stories. People had organized themselves into teams and were carefully picking through the wreckage, chains of men and women passing chunks of fractured concrete from top to bottom, stopping every now and again while someone listened for the calls of those who had been buried. Living casualties were carried off to hospital; the dead lay in a neat row under orange blankets on the trampled lawns.

Followed by his friend, Marisa Bassi restlessly stalked all the way around the perimeter of the building. Five killed, eighteen injured, a doctor told him, and probably more still to be found in the rubble.

Bep Martino appraised the ruins with a critical eye and said that it was a professional job. "Charges placed just so, the walls went out and the floors fell straight down. Boom!" Every so often, he flattened out the TV on his palm and gave a report on what it was saying. Earth's three major powers had made good their threat, and were sending out what they called an expeditionary force to quell revolutionary elements in their outer colonies.

"Note the possessive," Bassi said.

"Well, we voted to suspend payments," Martino said, "so I guess we're all revolutionaries now."

"This is our moment," Bassi said.

He stopped to talk with another councillor, a third generation tweak, very tall, and thin as a rail. Stooping, he told

Bassi that the air conditioning had failed because of a virus, and software faults had shut down the fusion reactors; the city was running on battery power.

"We expected all this," Bassi said impatiently. "It is only a warning. We will get the systems back on line, we will clear this up. We will bury our dead and swear on their graves that they will not have died in vain."

He said this last loudly, for the benefit of the people who were gathering around the two councillors, felt a gleeful kick of adrenaline, and added, because he liked the phrase, "This is our moment."

"We did not expect them to send soldiers," the tall councillor said gloomily.

"We'll fight if we have to," Bassi said, his face burning with a sudden self-righteous anger. "We built this city; no soldiers can take it from us."

People were clapping and shouting all around him now. The councillor took his elbow and said quietly, "Be careful of the mob, Bassi. It'll eat you up, if you let it."

Surely someone would have told him something like that, but with the taste of concrete dust in his throat and his blood up, Marisa Bassi would have shrugged off any advice. It was not a time for moderation or conciliation. That was what he told the city's prime committee a day later, as they debated their response to the threats made by the Three Powers Alliance, and on that day at least, the council was with him, for it agreed to declare a state of war.

The stage was set. Soon, Marisa Bassi would dominate it.

The sector where he had lived was dead now; his entire city was dead. Corso, Demi Lacombe and I crept like mice in a deserted house along a walkway which plunged through the dome's rocky skirt (its diamond panes arching high above us as if we were microbes trapped in a fly's eye). It was one of the many ways into the warrens where the survivors of the city's siege had hidden, walkways and passages and shafts linking insulated dormitories or hydroponic tunnels. One of the walkways actually ran a little way across the naked face of the ridge, and gave views to the northwest of the dark, rumpled floor of the Romulus crater. The moon was so small that the far side of crater was well below the horizon, and we seemed to be standing on a high, curved cliff looking out across a sea frozen in the midst of a violent tempest. Saturn's banded disc of salmon and saffron was tipped high in the black sky, the narrow arc of his rings shining like polished steel.

There was the landing platform, two shuttles standing on top of it like toys on a cakestand. There were the orange slashes and dashes and squiggles, like ribbons of cuneiform code, of the vacuum organism fields. As I pointed these out to Demi, a huge trembling and translucent jellyfish rose up from the sharply drawn line of the close horizon, its skirts glittering in the harsh sunlight even as it began to lose shape and fall back toward the plain. It was where many of the surviving population of Paris had been put to work, excavating fragments of the iron-rich bolide whose impact had formed the twin craters. I had not finished explaining this when another jellyfish rose, writhing, into the sunlight, and a moment later the tremor of the first explosion passed through the walkway.

I told Demi, "It is an open-cast mine. They must be making it wider or deeper. The ice is so cold it is hard as rock, and that's why they must use explosives."

"Means two or three more people will die out there today," Corso said. "Or get badly hurt."

"Don't be impertinent," I told him. "It's important work, necessary work. The metals will aid in the reconstruction of your city."

"I only mean that Yani might suddenly be too busy to have time to talk to the young lady, boss," Corso said.

"Keep a civil tongue in your head, Mr. Corso, or you might find yourself working in the mines. Or back on corpse detail."

"It would most likely be the mines," Corso said, "seeing as they've mostly cleared away the dead."

We passed through an antiquated airlock, a sequence of diamond slabs which had to be cranked open and shut by hand, into the noise and squalor and stink of refugee town. It had once been part of the city's farm system, first growing raw organics in the form of unicellular algae, and then, after vacuum organisms had been developed, cultivating fruits and vegetables for the luxury market.

Now, the wide, low-roofed tunnels, mercilessly lit by piped sunlight, divided by panels of extruded plant waste or pressed rock-dust, by blankets or sheets hung from wires and plastic string, were the rude dormitory quarters of the thousand or so surviving Parisians. Although many were off working two- or three-day shifts at the mines or helping to restore the vacuum farms (the city's vacuum organisms had been killed by prions which had catalyzed a debilitating change in their photosynthetic pigments, and were slowly being stripped out and replaced), the wretched place seemed noisy and crowded. Everything was damp, and the hot, heavy air was ripe with the smell of sewage and body odor. A dubious brown liquid trickled under the raised slats of the walkway down which Corso led Demi and me. He walked several paces ahead of us, with a self-consciousness I'd not seen before, as he led us to the hospital where Yani Hakaiopulos worked.

People were sitting at the openings of their crudely partitioned spaces. A few looked up and, with dull eyes, watched us go by. Old men and women mostly; one crone dandled a fretting baby whose face was encrusted with bloody mucus.

"Poor thing," Demi whispered to me.

War is cruel, I almost said, but her look of compassion was genuine and my sentiment was not. I had been here many times before to interview the unfortunate survivors about Marisa Bassi, and I confess that my heart had been hardened to the squalor to which their reckless actions had consigned them.

The hospital was another converted agricultural tunnel, beyond yet another set of tiresome mechanically operated doors. The reception area, where a dozen patients waited on stretchers or a medley of plastic chairs, was walled off by scratched and battered transparent plastic scarred with the lumpy seams of hasty welds. Corso talked with a weary woman in a traditional white smock, and was allowed through into the main part of the hospital, where beds stood in neat rows in merciful dimness—in there, the piped sunlight was filtered through beta cloth tacked over the openings in the low ceiling.

Most of the medical orderlies were missionary Redeemers, gray-skinned, tall and skinny, wrapped in bandages like so many of their patients, or Egyptian mummies come to life. They all had the same face. There were many badly burned patients, immobilized inside molded plastic casings while damaged skin and muscles were reconstructed. A few people shuffled about, often on crutches; many were missing limbs. Corso passed between the beds into the obscure dimness at the far end of the hospital, and within a minute returned, leading a stooped old man in a white smock spattered with blood stains. As they came into the reception area, I understood what Corso had meant when, he had said that Demi's charms might not work, for Yani Hakaiopulos was blind.

The old gene wizard was congenitally sightless, in fact, having been born with an undeveloped optic chiasma, but he could see, after a fashion. Corso commandeered the hospital's single office, and stuck three tiny cameras to its walls; Yani Hakaiopulos had an implant which transmitted the camera pictures as the sensation of needles on his skin, and so gave him a crude analog of vision. All this Yani Hakaiopulos explained while Corso set up the cameras.

"It hurts to see," he said, smiling at us one by one when the system had been switched on, "which is why I do not use it most of the time. Also, I see little more than shapes and movement, and so for my work it is more convenient to use my other senses."

"A blind doctor!" I exclaimed. "Now I have seen everything."

"I am not a qualified doctor, sir," Yani Hakaiopulos said, "but in these terrible times even I may be of some help." He turned his face in Demi's direction. "I understand that you have come to talk with me, my dear. I'm flattered, of course."

"I'm honored that you would interrupt your work to talk with me," Demi said.

"There's not much to be done now, except try and keep those well enough to recover from dying of an opportune infection, and to nurse those who are too ill to recover through their last days. And the Redeemers are far better at that than

I am. You," he said, turning his face approximately in my direction, "I believe that you are the historian. The one who goes around asking people about Marisa Bassi."

"Did you know him?"

"No, not really. I had been long retired and out of the public eye when the war began, and I could hardly help in the defense of the city. I did meet him once, after his escape from the invaders, in the last hours of our poor city. He came to the hospital—not this one, but the one which lies in ruins in the main dome—to be treated for the gunshot wound he had received, but he was only there for a handful of minutes. A good voice he had. Warm and quiet, but it could fill a room if he let it."

"He was wounded in the side," I said.

"Yes," the old man, Yani Hakaiopulos said, and touched the left side of his stained white smock, just under his ribs. The dark, mottled skin of his face was tight on the skull beneath, his teeth large and square and yellow, his white hair combed sideways across a bald pate. He had an abstracted yet serene air, as if he was happy with the world just as he found it.

I said, "Some claim that he later died of his wound."

"I would not know, Professor-Doctor Graves, for I did not treat him." He turned his smile to Demi and added, "But I believe you have come here to talk of the future, not the past. I am afraid that I do not give much thought to the future—there's very little of it left for me."

"I am here to learn," Demi said, and suddenly knelt down in front of him like a supplicant, and took his hands in hers. She said, in a small, quiet voice, "I do want to learn. That is, if you will allow it."

The old man allowed her to bring his fingers to her face.

He traced her lips, the bridge of her noise, the downy curve of her cheek. He smiled and said, "I haven't had a pupil for many years, and besides, I am long out of practice. My small contribution to the greening of the city was made long ago."

"Knowledge of the past can help remake the future," Demi said, with fierce ardor.

"Many of my people would say that the city should be destroyed," Yani Hakaiopulos said.

"They certainly did their best," I said.

"Yes, indeed. At the end, many were possessed by the idea that they should destroy their city rather than let it fall into the hands of their enemies. They knew that the war was lost, and that if the city survived it would no longer be their city."

"But it will be," Demi insisted, "once it has been rebuilt."

"No, my dear. It will be like a doppelganger of a dear dead friend, living in that dead friend's house, wearing their clothes."

Demi sat back, and I was aware once more of the way her slim, full-breasted body moved inside the tight fabric of her silvery skinthins. She said, "Do you believe that?"

"I do not believe that the great, delicate systems we engineered, the animals and plants we made, can be brought back as they once were. Perhaps something equally wonderful might rise in its place, but I wouldn't know. I'm an old man, the last of gene wizards. All of my colleagues are dead, from old age, from the war . . ."

"I have studied the parkland in the diplomatic quarter," Demi said. "I have talked with its gardeners, walked its paths . . . I think I understand a small part of what this city once possessed."

Yani Hakaiopulos breathed deeply, then reached out and

briefly caressed the side of her face. He said, "You truly want to do this thing?"

"I want to learn," Demi said.

"Well, if you can endure an old man's ramblings, I will do my best to tell something of how it was done."

They talked a long time. An hour, two. I sat outside the office while they talked, and drank weak, lukewarm green tea, with Corso fretting beside me. He was worried that Dev Veeder would learn about our little escapade.

"Go and see your daughter," I suggested at last, tired of his complaints.

"She's in school, and her teacher is this fierce old woman who does not like her classes disturbed. It's okay for you, boss. Veeder can't touch you. But if he finds that I brought his girlfriend here—"

"She isn't his girlfriend."

"*He* thinks she is."

"Well, that is true. She is cursed by her beauty, I think."

"She's dangerous. You be careful, boss."

"What nonsense, Mr. Corso. I'm nearly as old as your friend Yani Hakaiopulos."

"He's a great man, boss. And she got him telling her his secrets almost straight away. It's spooky."

"Unlike most of you, I think he wants the city rebuilt."

"Spooky," Corso said again. "And she said she was talking with the gardeners."

"Oh, that. She has had transducers or the like implanted in her brain." I touched my temples. The knife-blade of a headache had inserted itself in the socket of my left eye. The air in the warrens was bad, heavy with carbon dioxide and no doubt laced with a vile mixture of pollutants, and the brightly lit reception area was very noisy. I said, "She told me that she can interface with the computers which control the climate of the parklands and so on. And through them, she can, in a fashion, communicate with the gardeners. There is no magic about it, nothing sinister."

"If you say so, boss," Corso said. He fell into a kind of sulk, and barely spoke as he led us back through the warrens to the main part of the city, and the rooftop where he had left the airframe.

Six

Dev Veeder found me the next morning at the café, where I was waiting for Lavet Corso to make an appearance. The colonel came alone, sat opposite me and waved off the old man who came out of the half-collapsed guardhouse to ask what he wanted. He seemed amiable enough, and asked me several innocuous questions about the progress of my work.

"I find this Bassi intriguing," he said. "A shame he's dead."

"I hope I might bring his memories to life."

"Hardly the same thing, Professor-Doctor Graves, if you don't mind my saying so."

"Not at all. I am quite aware of the limitations of my technique, but alas, there is no better way."

"It's interesting. He was a fool, an amateur soldier who chose to stand and fight in a hopeless situation, yet he was able to rally the entire population of the city to his cause. But perhaps he was not really their leader at all. Perhaps he was merely a figurehead raised up by the mob."

"He was certainly no figurehead," I said. "The assassination of his fellow members of the government shows that he was capable of swift and ruthless action. He was tireless in rallying the morale of those who manned the barricades—

indeed, when the invasion of Paris began, he was captured at an outlying barricade."

"The sole survivor amongst a rabble of women and old men. They were fighting against fully armored troopers with hand weapons, industrial lasers and crude bombs."

"And he escaped, and went back to fight."

Dev Veeder thought about that, and admitted, "I suppose I do like him for that."

"You do?"

Dev Veeder was staring at me thoughtfully. His dark, almost black eyes were hooded and intense. I had the uncomfortable feeling that he was seeing through my skin. He said, "Marisa Bassi didn't have to escape. He didn't have to fight on."

"He would have been executed."

"Not at all, Professor-Doctor. Once captured, he could have sued for peace. If he truly was the leader of the mob, they would have obeyed him. He would have saved many lives; some might have even been grateful. The Three Powers Alliance wouldn't have been able to install him as head of a puppet government, of course, but they could have pensioned him off, returned him to wherever it was on Earth he was born."

"Sicily."

"There you are. He could have opened a pizza parlor, become mayor of some small town, made a woman fat and happy with a pack of bambinos."

"The last is unlikely, Colonel."

"But he stuck to the cause he had adopted. He went back. He finished the job. He may have been an amateur and a fool, Professor-Doctor Graves, but he had a soldier's backbone."

"And caused, as you said, many unnecessary deaths, and much unnecessary destruction."

I gestured at the devastation spread beyond the foot of the plaza's escalators: the rotting parks; the streets still choked with rubble; the shattered buildings. Dev Veeder did not look at it, but continued to stare at me with a dark, unfathomable intensity.

I made a show of peering at the empty air above the rooftops of the city and said, "My wretched guide is late."

"He'll come. He has no choice. This talk interests me, Professor-Doctor. We haven't talked like this for a while."

"Well, you've been busy."

"I have?"

"With your new prisoners. And of course, escorting Demi."

"Dr. Lacombe?"

I felt heat rise in my face. "Yes, of course. Dr. Lacombe."

"Tell me, Professor-Doctor Graves, do you think that Marisa Bassi was one of your great men?"

"His people—those who survive—think that he was."

"His people. Yes. Do you know, many of them cry out his name in the heat of questioning?"

"I don't see—"

"Usually, those subjected to hot questioning scream for their mothers at the end. When they're emptied, when they've given up everything. Huge bloodied babies shitting and pissing themselves, unable to move because we've broken every major bone, bawling for the only unfailing comfort in all the world. But these people, they cry out for Bassi." Dev Veeder's right hand made a fist and softly struck the cradle of his left. He wore black gloves of fine, soft leather. One rumor was that they were vat-grown human skin. Another that they were not vat-grown. He said, "Can you imagine it, Professor-Doctor? You've been broken so badly you know you're going to die. You're flayed open. You've given up everything you've ever loved. Except for this one thing. Your love of the man who led you in your finest hour. You don't give him up. No, in your last wretched moment, you call out to him. You think he'll come and *help* you."

"That's . . . remarkable."

"Oh yes. Remarkable. Astonishing. Amazing. What do you think you would call out, if you were put to the question, Professor-Doctor Graves?"

"I'm sure I don't—"

"Nobody knows," Dev Veeder said, "until the moment. But I'm sure you'd call for your mother, eh?" His smile was a thing of muscles and teeth, with only cold calculation behind it, "Was Marisa Bassi a great man? His people think so, and perhaps that's enough."

I said, eager to grasp this thread, "He lost his war. Great men are usually remembered because they won."

"It goes deeper than winning or losing," Dev Veeder said. "The important thing is that Bassi took responsibility for his actions. He was captured; he escaped and returned at once to the fight. Technology makes most men remote from the war they create. At the end of the Second World War, which was, as you know, the first truly modern war, neither the crew of the American aircraft *Enola Gay* nor most of the technicians and scientists who built the atomic bomb, nor even the politicians who ordered its use, none of them felt any guilt over what they did. Why not? The answer is simple: the destruction was remote from them. In the Quiet War, most people were killed by technicians millions of kilometers away.

Technicians who fought the war in eight-hour shifts and then went home to their spouses and children. Remoteness and division of labor induces both a diminished sense of responsibility and moral tunnel vision, so that men see the task of killing only in terms of efficiency and meeting operation parameters. In my line of work it is different, of course. That is why I am despised by so many, but I believe that I am a more moral man than they for at least I know exactly what I do. I see the fear in my victims' eyes; I smell their sweat and their voided bladders and guts; I get blood on my hands. And I am often the last person they see, so I do not stint my sympathy for their plight."

I said, "It must make breaking their bones difficult."

"Not at all. I do it with a clear conscience because they are the enemy, because it is necessary. But at no time do I reduce them to ciphers or quotients or statistics. They are not targets or casualties or collateral damage. They are men and women in the glory of their final agony. People hate me, yes. But while they think they hate me because of what I do, in fact they hate me because they see in me what they know is lacking in them. Nietzsche had it right: the weak mass always despises the strong individual."

I was sure that Nietzsche had said no such thing, and told Dev Veeder, "Nietzsche tried to erase moral responsibility and went mad doing it. On the morning when they finally had to haul him off to the asylum, he rushed out of his lodgings, still wearing his landlord's nightcap, and tearfully embraced a carthorse. The amoral philosophy which the Nazis would adopt as their own in the Second World War, the creed which would shatter Europe, had already shattered his mind."

"Do you fear me, Professor-Doctor?"

"Fear? What a question!"

"Because, you know, you should. This place, where you play-act the role of conqueror of the world, it will have to go. It endangers security. I will see to it," Dev Veeder said, and stood up and bowed and loped away.

I knew that Cris DeHon had betrayed me, but when I returned from my research in the ruins of the city and confronted him, the neuter denied it with an uncomfortable laugh.

"Why should I spoil all the fun?"

"Fun?"

"The plot. The play. The unfolding mysteries of the human heart."

"You have no right to talk of such things, DeHon. You opted out of all that."

DeHon clutched its breast dramatically. "A cruel cut, Graves. I might be desexed, but I'm still human, and part of life's great comedy. If nothing else, I can still watch. And I do like to watch."

"Nevertheless, you told him."

"I won't deny that our gallant love-struck colonel asked me if I knew where his sweetheart had been while I was talking with him at that party. You still owe me for that, by the way."

"Not if you told him."

"Perhaps I did let a little something slip. Please, don't look at me that way! I didn't mean to, but our colonel is very persistent. It is his job, after all."

The small, bright-eyed smile with which this admission was delivered let me know that DeHon had deliberately revealed something about the assignation to Dev Veeder. I said, "It was innocent. Quite innocent."

"I do not believe," DeHon said, "that Demi Lacombe is as innocent as she likes people to think she is."

This was at a reception held by the Pacific Community's trade association. Several of its companies had just won the contract to rebuild Dione's organic refineries. Most of us were there. Dev Veeder was standing to one side of a group of biochemists who were talking to Demi Lacombe. He saw me looking at him, and raised his bulb of wine in an ironic salute.

When I had returned to the plaza that afternoon, I had found that Dev Veeder had been true to his word. The café was gone, its mismatched chairs and tables and the shell of the half-ruined guardshouse cleared away. Later, I discovered that the old man and woman who had run it had been sent to work in the vacuum organism fields, a virtual death sentence for people their age, but I did not need to know that to understand that Dev Veeder had made his point, and I managed to have a brief word with Demi at the buffet of sushi, seaweed, and twenty varieties of bananas stewed and fried and stuffed—exotic food shipped from Earth at God knows what expense for our delectation.

As I transferred morsels I would not eat from the prongs of their serving plates to the prongs of my bowl, I told Demi, "He knows."

"He doesn't know. If he did, he would have done something."

"He *has* done something," I said, and told her about the café. Had I known then about the fate of its proprietors I would not have dared to even speak with her.

She said, "I'm going again tomorrow. If you are too scared to help me, Professor-Doctor Graves, I will find my own way across the city."

With a pang of jealousy, I thought of the way that Yani Hakaiopulos's fingers had caressed her face. The two of them sharing secrets while I waited outside like a court eunuch. I said, "Colonel Veeder will be watching you."

"He has to make a presentation about security to company representatives, and I've told him that I will be working in diplomatic quarter's parkland." She touched her temple. "If his men do try to follow me in there, and so far they have not, I'll see them long before they see me. And I know you won't tell him, Fredo. But we shouldn't talk any more, at least, not here. I think Dev is getting suspicious."

"He is more than suspicious," I said. My cheeks were burning like those of a foolish adolescent. "And that is why, I am afraid, I can no longer help you."

I did not go into the city the next day, for if I did I knew that I would have to go back to that ruined park and wait for Demi to emerge from the cliff, like Athena stepping newborn from the brow of Zeus. If nothing else, I still had my pride. She will need my help, I thought, and I was wounded when, of course, she did not seek me out.

The day passed, and the next, and still she did not come. I discounted the third day because she was taken out into the city by Dev Veeder; but on the morning of fourth, hollow, anxious, defeated, I summoned Lavet Corso and ordered him to fly me straight to the ruined park.

He knew what I was about, of course; I made no pretense about it. We landed on the black slime of the lawn, and I saw a rill of water falling from the cleft in the black basalt cliff and felt my heart harden.

"Take me back," I told Corso.

"Sure, boss, but I'll have to wind the prop first."

While he worked, I said, "You knew all along, didn't you?"

"A woman like that coming down to the warrens, well, she's hard to miss, boss."

"I suppose that she is talking with that gene wizard. With Yani Hakaiopulos.

"I don't like it either, boss."

"You were right about her, Mr. Corso. She uses men. Even old fools like me and your Mr. Hakaiopulos. There was a school of thought in the late twentieth century that men—even great men—were ruled by their genitals. They couldn't help themselves, and as a result they either treated all women like prostitutes, or the women who were involved in their lives had an undue influence on them. It's long been discredited, but I wonder if there isn't some truth to it. We can never really know what is in the hearts of men, for after all, most refuse to admit it to themselves. At least your own great man, Marisa Bassi, was not troubled by women. The sector where he went looking for sex . . ."

"The Battery?"

"Yes, you took me there. One must admire, I suppose, the meticulousness of city planners who would design a neighborhood where men can go to find other men, free of class, driven only by desire."

"It wasn't really designed, boss. It sort of grew up. And it wasn't just gay men who went there."

"Do you think he went there while he was organizing the resistance to the siege?"

"I wouldn't know, boss."

"No, of course not. You did not know him, as you keep reminding me, and you are a family man. But I expect that he did. Leaders of men are almost always highly sexed. We can't condemn such impulses."

Corso locked the crank of the prop and stood back, dusting his hands. "You're not just talking about Marisa Bassi now, are you?"

"No. No, I suppose not. It's all part of the human comedy . . . or tragedy."

"We can go now, boss. It's all wound up and waiting."

"Of course. Then take me back to the quarter, Mr. Corso. I think I must tell Colonel Veeder about this security problem."

Corso paused, halfway through swinging into the pilot's sling. One hand was raised, grasping a support strut of the airframe's wide canary yellow wings, and half his face was in shadow. He gave me a level, appraising look and said, "Are you sure you want to do that?"

"The security of the diplomatic quarter is at risk. It's not only Demi Lacombe who could be using that way in and out of the parklands." When Corso did not reply, I bent and touched the bulge of the blazer, holstered at my calf. "Get me back, Mr. Corso. I insist."

"You will get more people than her into trouble, boss."

"I will tell Colonel Veeder that your part in this was blameless. That you were under my orders."

"I'm not just thinking of myself."

"Yani Hakaiopulos will have to take his chance. I shudder to think what Demi must have done, to gain his secrets."

"I think it's more a question of what she did to him," Corso said.

"I have had enough of your impertinence, Mr. Corso. Look sharp, now. I want to get this whole unfortunate business over with."

"I don't think so, boss."

"What?"

He let go of the strut and stepped back and said flatly, "It won't take you long to walk back, even if you have to use the stairs to climb up to the quarter. And as you always like to remind me, you have your blazer to protect you."

"Corso! Damn you Corso, come back here!"

But he did not look back as he walked away across the blackened ruins of the lawn, even when I drew the blazer and blew a dead tree to splinters. I hoped that the shot might attract one of the killing machines which patrolled the city, but although I waited a full ten minutes, nothing stirred. At last, I climbed out of the airframe and began the long walk home.

Seven

Dev Veeder took my revelation more calmly than I had thought he would, even though I had taken the precaution of having arranged to meet with him in the presence of Colm Wardsmead, the nominal director of the diplomatic quarter and, therefore, of the entire city. Wardsmead was a shifty, self-satisfied man; although he liked to think of himself as a Medici prince, the effectiveness of his native cunning was limited by his laziness and contempt for others. I knew that Dev Veeder despised Wardsmead, but also knew that he would not dare lose control of his temper in the director's presence.

"This is all very awkward," Wardsmead said, when I was done. "Perhaps you would care to make a recommendation, Colonel Veeder. I am sure that you would want this matter handled discreetly."

During my exposition, Dev Veeder had stood with his back to the eggshaped room, looking out of the huge window toward the shaggy treetops of the parkland. Without turning around, he said, "She's supposed to be doing research out there. It would be the best place for an arrest."

"Away from the excitable gaze of the diplomatic community," Wardsmead said. "I quite understand, Colonel."

He was unable to hide his satisfaction at Dev Veeder's discomfort. Veeder was a war hero and so difficult to discipline, but now Wardsmead believed that he had a stick with which to beat him.

Perhaps Veeder heard something he did not like in Wardsmead's tone. He turned and gave the man a hard stare and said, "I always do what is best, Mr. Wardsmead, not what is convenient. My men are tracking her as she makes her way back across the main dome. They will allow her to enter the back door to the quarter's parkland, and I will arrest her when she arrives."

Wardsmead swung to and fro in the cradle of his chair, hands folded across his ample stomach, and said, "I suppose the question is, once you have arrested her, has she done anything wrong?"

"Consorting with the enemy without permission is a crime," Dev Veeder said promptly. "Failing to reveal a weakness in the security of the diplomatic quarter is also a crime. Both are betrayals of trust."

"Well, there we have it," Wardsmead said.

"There will have to be a trial," Dev Veeder told him.

"Oh, now, that would be an unnecessary embarrassment, don't you think? One of the shuttles is due to leave in a couple of days. We can ship her off—"

"There will be a trial," Dev Veeder said. "It is a security matter, and the crime was committed outside the diplomatic quarter, so it falls under martial law. She will be tried, and so will the old man."

I said, "You have arrested Yani Hakaiopulos?"

For the first time, Dev Veeder looked directly at me. I confess that I flinched. He said, "The old man was not at the hospital, but there are only so many places he can hide. Your guide, the man Corso, has also vanished. I must assume that he is also part of the plot."

I said, "Yani Hakaiopulos was simply helping Demi understand how the parklands and wilderness had been put together. Surely that's not a crime?"

Using her first name was a mistake. Dev Veeder said coldly, "You have admitted, Professor-Doctor Graves, that you did not know what they talked about. I have not arrested you only because stupidity is not a crime under either civil or martial law."

Wardsmead said, "I don't much care what happens to the two tweaks, but even if I allow you your trial, Colonel Veeder, I want an assurance that Dr. Lacombe will be deported at the end of it."

Despite his amiable tone, his forehead was greasy with sweat. He scented a scandal, and did not want its taint to sully his career.

Dev Veeder said, "That depends on what I discover during my interrogation. And I can assure you, gentlemen, that it will be a very thorough interrogation. You will come with me, Professor-Doctor Graves."

"I have already told you—"

"You will come with me," Dev Veeder said again.

He wanted his revenge to be complete.

Eight

Camelot, Mimas fell; Baghdad, Enceladus fell; Athens and Spartica on Tethys surrendered within days of each other, blasted into submission by singleship attacks; the vacuum organism farms of Iapetus's carbonaceous plains were destroyed by viral infection; Phoebe, settled by the Redeemers, and the habitats which had remained in orbit around Titan, had all declared neutrality at the beginning of the war, and were under martial law.

Within two months of the arrival of the expeditionary force from Earth, the war was almost over. Only Paris, Dione remained defiant to the end. Singleships had taken out most of the city's peripheral installations. Its vacuum organism farms were dying. And now new stars flared in its sky as troop ships took up their eccentric orbits. The emergency committee of Paris voted to surrender, and the same night were assassinated by Marisa Bassi's followers. Bassi rallied the citizens, organized the barricades and the block captains, killed a party of negotiators in a fit of fury and killed his hostages too.

It was an unforgivable act, a terrible war crime, yet for Marisa Bassi and the citizens of Paris it was deeply necessary. It was an affirmation of their isolation and their outlaw status. It united them against the rest of humanity.

I believe that Bassi was tired of waiting, tired of the slow attrition of the blockade. He was bringing the war to the heart right into his city and, like the people he led, was eager to embrace it.

Imagine that last day, as lights streaked across the sky as the troop ships launched their drop capsules. A battery of industrial X-ray lasers tried and failed to target them; a troop ship came over the horizon, pinpointed the battery, and destroyed it with a single low-yield fission missile, stamping a new crater a kilometer wide on Remus crater's floor.

Marisa Bassi felt the shock wave of that strike as a low rumbling that seemed to pass far beneath the ground, like a subway train. He was in the street, organizing the people who manned one of the barricades. It was mid-morning. He had been awake for more than forty-eight hours. His throat was sore and his lips were cracked. His eyes ached in their dry sockets and there was a low burning in his belly; he had drunk far too much coffee.

The scow had gone, and those citizens too old or too young to fight had been moved into the tunnels of the original colony. There was nothing left to do now but fight. The people knew this and seemed to be in good heart. They still believed that the Three Powers Alliance would not dare to destroy their beautiful city, the jewel of the outer system, and perhaps Marisa Bassi believed it too. He felt that he carried the whole city in his heart, its chestnut trees and cafés, trams and parklands, the theater and the Bourse and the lovely glass cathedral, and he had never loved his adopted home as fiercely as he loved it now, in its last hours.

The barricade was in one of the service sectors near the

perimeter of the dome, with diamond panes arching just above the rooftops of the offices and warehouses. It commanded a good view of a wide traffic circle, and on Bassi's orders men and women were cutting down stands of slim aspens to improve the fire lanes. Bassi was working with them, getting up a good sweat, when the tremor passed underneath. One of his young aides came running up, waving a TV strip like a handkerchief.

"They got the lasers," she said breathlessly. She was fifteen or sixteen, almost twice Bassi's height, and trembled like a racehorse at the off. Like everyone else, she was wearing a pressure suit. The bowl of its helmet was hooked to her utility belt.

"We expected that," Bassi said, staring up at her. He had shaved off his beard, cut his hair to within a millimeter of his scalp. His hands, grasping the shaft of his diamond-edged axe, tingled. He said, "What else?"

"They're down," the girl said, "and coming along both ends of the ridge."

"Any message from their command ship?"

"No sir."

"And we won't send one. Get back to headquarters. Tell them I'll be back in twenty minutes."

"Sir, shouldn't you—"

Bassi lifted the axe. "I've a job to finish here. Go!"

They were mostly old men and women on that barricade, and knew that they would be among the first to engage the invaders. Why did Bassi stay with them? Perhaps he was exhausted. He had brought the whole city to this point by sheer force of will, and perhaps he saw nothing beyond the moment when the fighting started. Perhaps he knew then that defeat was inevitable, and wanted to make a last heroic gesture rather than face the ignominy of surrender.

In any case, he stayed. Once the aspens had been cleared, he went back with the others to the barricade. It was no more than a ridge of roadway which had been turned up by a bulldozer and topped with tangles of razor wire. They closed up the wire and started checking their weapons—machine pistols and blazers stamped out by a rejigged factory, an ungainly machine which used compressed air to fire concrete-filled cans.

Someone had a flask of brandy and they all took a sip, even Bassi's remaining aide. The flask was going around the second time when there was a brisk series of bangs in the distance, and a wind got up, swirling foliage broken from the aspens high into the air.

The invaders broke into the main dome of the city at nine points, breaching the basalt skirt with shaped charges, driving their transports straight through, and then spraying sealant to close the holes. At that point, they thought they could take the city without inflicting much damage.

While some of the people at the barricade latched up their helmets and checked their weapons, others were still looking at TV strips. Bassi ripped the TVs from their hands, told them roughly to watch the street. The motor of the compressor gun started up with a tremendous roar and at the same moment sleek shining man-sized machines appeared on the far side of the traffic circle.

The killing things moved very quickly. It is doubtful that anyone got off a shot before the machines had crossed the traffic circle and leaped the razor wire. Bassi's aide ran, and a killing thing was on him in two strides, slicing and jabbing, throwing the corpse aside. The others were dispatched with the same quick ruthlessness, and then only Bassi was left, drenched in the blood of the men and women who had died around him, his arms and legs pinned by one of the killing things.

Once the barricade had been cleared, a squad of human troopers in sealed pressure suits came forward. Their sergeant photographed Bassi, cuffed him, and ordered one of his men to take him back for what he called a debriefing. Bassi knew then that he had been selected by chance, not because he had been recognized; shaving off his trademark beard had saved him. He smiled and spat on the sergeant's visor. The squad and the killing things moved on; the trooper marched Bassi at gunpoint across the traffic circle toward the command post at the breached perimeter.

No one knows how Bassi got free, only that he was captured at a barricade in the first minutes of fighting and then escaped. Certainly, he never reached the command post. Perhaps the trooper was killed by one of the snipers which infested the city, or perhaps Bassi got free on his own; after all, he was a very resourceful man. In any case, it is known that he reached the Bourse two hours after the barricade fell, because he made a brief, defiant television transmission there.

I have watched this speech many times. It is the last sighting of him. He was wounded when he escaped, and the wound had been patched but the bullet was still inside him; he must have felt it, and felt the blood heavy and loose inside his belly as he spoke, but he showed no sign that he was in pain. He spoke for five minutes. He spoke clearly and defiantly, but it was a poor, rambling speech, full of allusions to freedom and idealism and martyrdom, and his steady gaze had a crazed, glittering quality.

By then, most of the outlying tents and domes of the city had been captured by the invaders; even Bassi's headquarters had been taken. The citizens of Paris had fallen back to the central part of the main dome. Most of the barricades had been overrun by killing things. Thousands of citizens lay dead at their posts, while the invaders had incurred only half a dozen casualties, mostly from snipers. The battle for Paris was clearly over, but still its citizens fought on.

"I warn the commander of the invaders," Marisa Bassi said, "that we will fight to the end. We will not let you take what we have built with our sweat and our blood. Paris will die, but Paris lives on. The war is not over."

A few minutes later, the main buildings of the city were set on fire, filling the dome with smoke. A few minutes after that, the commander of the invasion force gave the order to breach the integrity of the main dome.

By then, no doubt, Bassi was already at one of the last barricades, armed with the carbine he had taken from the dead trooper, his pressure suit sealed. A great wind sucked fire and smoke from the burning, broken wedding cake of the Bourse; smoke rushed along the ground in great billows which thinned and vanished, leaving the eerie clarity and silence of vacuum. And then a shout over the radio, doubling and redoubling. Killing things were running swiftly across the wide lawns toward the last barricades, puffs of earth jumping around them as people started to fire.

Bassi drew himself up to face his enemy, no longer the leader of the free government of Paris, his fate no more significant now than any of the last of its citizens. He thought that he was only moments from death. He was wrong.

Nine

Demi Lacombe had stapled a nylon rope to a basalt outcrop at the edge of the mossy, emerald-green meadow; its blue thread fell away to the trough of black water a hundred meters below. Dev Veeder squatted on his heels and ran a gloved finger around the knot doubled around the eye of the staple, then looked up at me and said, "I could loosen this so that she would fall as she climbed back up. Do you think the fall would kill her?"

"I think not. Not in this low gravity."

He stood. "No. I don't think so either. Well, she'll be here soon. We'd better keep out of sight."

I dabbed sweat from my brow with the cuff of my shirt. I had been marched quickly through the parkland by Veeder's squad of troopers, as if I had been under arrest, with no chance until now of talking with him, of trying to change his mind. I said, "Are you enjoying yourself, Colonel?"

"You want revenge too. Don't deny it. She used us both, Graves."

"This seems so . . . melodramatic."

"History is made with bold gestures. I want her arrested in the act of returning through a passageway which presents a clear and present danger to the security of the diplomatic community. I want you to be a witness."

"No bold gesture can be based on so petty a motive as revenge."

Dev Veeder moved closer to me, so close that when he spoke a spray of saliva fell on my cheek. "We're in this together, Graves. Don't pretend that you're just an observer like that thing, DeHon. Be a man. Face up to the consequences of your actions."

"She was only trying to do her work, Colonel. Your crazy jealousy got in the way—"

"We are both jealous men, Graves. But at least I did not betray her."

Veeder shoved me away from him then, and I went sprawling on the soft, wet moss. By the time I had regained my feet, he was on the other side of the little meadow, showing the four troopers where to take cover. As they concealed themselves amongst the exuberant rose briars, the sergeant of the squad took me by the arm and pulled me into the shade of the ferns which cascaded down the basalt cliff.

It was hot and close inside the curtain of fern fronds. Sweat dripped from my nose, my chin, ran down my flanks inside my shirt. Tiny black flies danced about my face with dumb persistence. In the meadow, huge, sulfur-yellow butterflies circled each other above the bright green moss, their hand-sized wings flapping once a minute. The sergeant, a muscular, dark-eyed woman, hummed softly to herself, watching the screen she had spread on her knee. It showed a view of the lake below the meadow, transmitted from one of the tiny cameras the troopers had spiked here and there. Time passed. At last, the sergeant nudged me and pointed.

Centered in the screen, Demi Lacombe's silvery figure

suddenly stood up, waist-deep, in black water. She stripped off her airmask and hooked it to her belt, waded to the gravelly shore and grasped the rope and swarmed up it, moving so quickly, hand over hand, that it seemed she was swimming through the air.

I looked up from the screen as she pulled herself over the edge of the meadow and rolled onto the vivid green moss. As she got to her feet, Dev Veeder stepped out of his hiding place, followed by his troopers; the sergeant shoved me roughly and I tumbled forward, landing on my hands and knees.

Demi looked at Dev Veeder, at me. For a moment I thought she might jump into the chasm, but then Dev Veeder crossed the meadow in two bounds and caught her by the left wrist, the one she had broken soon after arriving in Paris. She turned pale, and would have dropped to her knees if Dev Veeder had not held her up.

"All right," he growled. "All right."

The brilliant light of the suspensor lamps hung high above dimmed. I felt a few fat raindrops on my face and hands, congealing rather than falling from the humid air. The pathetic fallacy made real by Demi Lacombe's implants, I thought, and Dev Veeder must have had the same idea, because he said, "Stop that, you bitch," and delivered a back-handed slap to her face while still holding on to her wrist.

Demi's cry of pain was cut off by a roll of thunder; I think I must have shouted out then, too, for the sergeant grasped my arm and shook me and told me to shut the fuck up. Those were her words. A sheet of sickly light rippled overhead and the air darkened further as a wind got up, blowing clouds of raindrops as big as marbles. They hissed against the curtain of ferns above, and drenched me to the skin in an instant.

Someone was standing at the edge of the rose thicket.

It was one of the gardeners. I was sure that it was the one that Demi had summoned before—their shaven heads and blank expression effaced individuality, but he had the same stocky immigrant build and wary manner. At his side was a pair of tawny panthers; a huge bird perched on his upraised arms, its gripping claws digging rivulets of bright blood from his flesh.

With a sudden snap, like playing cards dealt by a conjurer, the four troopers formed a half circle in front of Dev Veeder and Demi Lacombe. Their carbines were raised. The rain was very thick now, blown up and down and sideways by the gusting wind; water sheeted down the closed visors of the troopers' helmets, the slick resin of their chestplates.

The gardener made no move, but the panthers and huge bird suddenly launched themselves across the meadow. Two wild shots turned every drop of rain blood red; the scream of air broken by their energy echoed off the ferny cliff. Dev Veeder was struggling with Demi Lacombe, a horrible, desperate waltz right at the edge of the cliff. One trooper was down, beating at the bird whose wings beat about his head; one of the panthers had bowled over two more troopers and the second took down a trooper as he fled. The trooper struggling with the bird took a step backward, and fell from the edge of the meadow; a moment later, the bird rose up alone, wings spread wide as it rode the gust of wind that for a moment blew the rain clear of the meadow.

The sergeant raised her carbine. I saw that she had the presence of mind to aim at the gardener, and threw myself at her legs. The shot went wild. She kicked me hard and in the light gravity her legs flew from beneath her and she sat down. I fell flat on sodden moss, and was trying to unholster my blazer, although I do not know who I would have shot at, when the sergeant hauled me half-around by one of my arms—fracturing a small bone in my wrist, I later discovered—and struck my head with the stock of her carbine.

Then the bird fell upon her.

Ten

I was dazed and bloodied and far from the meadow when Lavet Corso found me. I did not remember how I had gotten away from the troopers—perhaps the gardener had led me to my former guide—nor did I remember seeing Dev Veeder and Demi Lacombe fall, but their drowned bodies were found a day later, lying together on a spit of gravel at the far end of the dark little lake, like lovers at the end of a tale of doomed romance. Although, of course, they were never lovers. Of that, at least, I am certain.

Corso told me that Demi Lacombe had been in the habit of using a pheromone-rich perfume to befuddle men from whom she wanted some favor or other. "A kind of hypnotic, Yani Hakaiopulos said. It does exactly what other perfumes only claim to do. He recognized it at once, and confirmed his suspicion using the hospital's equipment. He was amused at her presumption, and rather admired her ambition."

We were crouched under the billowing skirts of a cypress, while the gale blew itself out around us. The gardener sat on his haunches a little way off, staring out into the rainy dark.

"Hakaiopulos only wanted his gardens rebuilt," I said

dully. My head and wrist ached abominably, and I felt very cold.

Corso said, "He'll get his chance, but not here. You know, you're a lucky man. Lucky that Veeder didn't kill you when he had the chance; lucky that I don't kill you now."

"You should get away, Mr. Corso. Go on: leave me. If Colonel Veeder finds you here —"

I did not know then that he was dead.

"I'm leaving Paris," Corso said. "I'm going to join my wife."

For a moment, I thought he meant that he was going to kill himself. Perhaps he saw it in my face, because he added, "She's not dead. None of the people who left on the scow are dead."

"It fell into Saturn."

"The scow did, yes. But before it took its dive, it traveled most of the way around the planet within the ring system, long enough to drop off its passengers and cargo in escape pods. There are millions of ice and rock bolides in the rings. Sure, most of them have been ground down to gravel and dust, but there's a sizable percentage of bodies more than a couple of kilometers across—something like half a million."

"This is fantasy, Mr. Corso."

"My wife and the other people who escaped have made their home on one of them; that's where I'm taking my daughter and a couple of other people. I would have gone sooner, but I had work to do here, and I couldn't justify the risk of stealing a shuttle until now."

"You're saving Yani Hakaiopulos."

"Him too. We can always use a gene wizard. But there's someone else, someone more important to us than anyone else."

I said, "It was you who painted those slogans, wasn't it? You could move freely about the city because you smell right to the killing machines. *He lives*. Another silly fantasy, Mr. Corso. He died with the fools he was leading."

Corso shook his head. "After he escaped, he made his way back to the main dome and rallied the last of the barricades. We still thought then that if enough soldiers died while attempting to take Paris, we might carry the day. We were giving our lives for the city, after all, but the soldiers were dying for no more than the redemption of a loan. But you sent in killing machines, and then you blew the dome. Like most of the people at the barricades, Marisa Bassi was wearing a pressure suit, and he continued to fight until he ran out of air. In his last moments of consciousness he hid amongst the dead who lay all around him. The suit saved his life by chilling him down, but lack of oxygen had already caused brain damage. After one of the corpse details found him, he was carefully resuscitated, but his frontal lobes were badly damaged. The implants keep him functioning, and one day we'll be able to reconstruct him."

You have to understand that although this was the most fantastic part of Corso's story, it is the part I believe without question, for I insisted on examining the gardener myself. His hands were strong and square, with blunt fingers, yes, but so are the hands of most laborers. But I also saw the wound in his side, just under his ribs, the wound he suffered when he escaped, a wound into which I could insert my smallest finger.

Corso took me as far as the edge of the parkland, and I do not know what became of him—or of his daughter, or Yani Hakaiopulos, or the gardener, Marisa Bassi. A shuttle was stolen during the confusion after Colonel Veeder's death, and was later found, abandoned and gutted, in an eccentric orbit that intersected the ring system.

As for myself, I have decided not to return to Earth. There are several colonies which managed to remain neutral during the Quiet War, and I hope to find a place in one of them. The advance of my fee should be sufficient to buy citizenship. I once planned to endow a chair of history in my name, as a snub to my rivals, but using the credit to win a new life, if only for a few years, now seems a better use for it.

I hope that they will be peaceful years. But before he left me to my grief and to my dead, Lavet Corso told me that his was not the only clandestine colony hidden within the ring system's myriad shifting orbits, and his last words still make me shiver.

"The war's not over."

and was later [illegible] questioned and [illegible] [illegible]

[illegible]

As for myself, I [illegible]

[illegible]

[illegible]

Tendeléo's Story

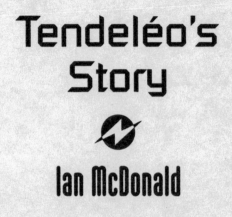

Ian McDonald

I shall start my story with my name. I am Tendeléo. I was born here, in Gichichi. Does that surprise you? The village has changed so much that no one born then could recognize it now, but the name is still the same. That is why names are important. They remain.

I was born in 1995, shortly after the evening meal and before dusk. That is what Tendeléo means in my language, Kalenjin: early-evening-shortly-after-dinner. I am the oldest daughter of the pastor of St. John's Church. My younger sister was born in 1998, after my mother had two miscarriages, and my father asked the congregation to lay hands on her. We called her Little Egg, That is all there are of us, two. My father felt that a pastor should be an example to his people, and at that time the government was calling for smaller families.

My father had cure of five churches. He visited them on a red scrambler bike the bishop at Nukuru had given him. It was a good motorbike, a Yamaha. Japanese. My father loved riding it. He practiced skids and jumps on the back roads because he thought a clergyman should not be seen stunt-riding. Of course, people did, but they never said to him. My father built St. John's. Before him, people sat on benches under trees. The church he made was sturdy and rendered in white concrete. The roof was red tin, trumpet vine climbed over it. In the season flowers would hang down outside the window. It was like being inside a garden. When I hear the story of Adam and Eve, that is how I think of Eden, a place among the flowers. Inside there were benches for the people, a lectern for the sermon and a high chair for when the bishop came to confirm children. Behind the altar rail was the holy table covered with a white cloth and an alcove in the wall for the cup and holy communion plate. We didn't have a font. We took people to the river and put them under. I and my mother sang in the choir. The services were long and, as I see them now, quite boring, but the music was wonderful. The women sang, the men played instruments. The best was played by a tall Luo, a teacher in the village school we called, rather blasphemously, Most High. It was a simple instrument: a piston ring from an old Peugeot engine which he hit with a heavy steel bolt. It made a great, ringing rhythm.

What was left over from the church went into the pastor's house. It had poured concrete floors and louver windows, a separate kitchen and a good charcoal stove a parishioner who could weld hand made from a diesel drum. We had electric light, two power sockets and a radio/cassette player, but no television. It was inviting the devil to dinner, my father told us. Kitchen, living room, our bedroom, my mother's bedroom, and my father's study. Five rooms. We were people of some distinction in Gichichi; for Kalenjin.

Gichichi was a thin, straggly sort of village; shops, school, post office, matatu office, petrol station and mandazi shop up on the main road, with most of the houses set off the footpaths that followed the valley terraces. On one of them was our shamba, half a kilometer down the valley. The path to it went past the front door of the Ukerewe family. They had seven children who hated us. They threw dung or stones and called us see-what-we-thought-of-ourselves-Kalenjin and hated-of-God-Episcopalians. They were African Inland Church Kikuyu, and they had no respect for the discipline of the bishop.

If the church was my father's Eden, the shamba was my mother's. The air was cool in the valley and you could hear the river over the stones down below. We grew maize and gourds and some sugar cane, which the local rummers bought from my father and he pretended not to know. Beans and chillis. Onions and potatoes. Two trees of finger bananas, though M'zee Kipchobe maintained that they sucked the life out of the soil. The maize grew right over my head, and I would run into the sugar cane and pretend that two steps had taken me out of this world into another. There was always music there; the solar radio, or the women singing together when they helped each other turn the soil or hoe the weeds. I would sing with them, for I was considered good at harmonies. The shamba too had a place where the holy things were kept. Among the thick, winding tendrils of an old tree killed by strangling fig the women left little wooden figures, gifts of money, Indian-trader jewelry and beer.

You are wondering, what about the Chaga? You've worked out from the dates that I was nine when the first package came down on Kilimanjaro. How could such tremendous events, a thing like another world taking over our own, have made so little impression on my life? It is easy, when it is no nearer to you than another world. We were not ignorant in Gichichi. We had seen the pictures from

Kilimanjaro on the television, read the articles in the Nation about the thing that is like a coral reef and a rainforest that came out of the object from the sky. We had heard the discussions on the radio about how fast it was growing—fifty meters every day, it was ingrained on our minds—and what it might be and where it might come from. Every morning the vapor trails of the big UN jets scored our sky as they brought more men and machines to study it, but it was another world. It was not our world. Our world was church, home, shamba, school. Service on Sunday, Bible Study on Monday, singing lessons, homework club. Sewing, weeding, stirring the ugali. Shooing the goats out of the maize. Playing with Little Egg and Grace and Reth from next door in the compound: not too loud, Father's working. Once a week, the mobile bank. Once a fortnight, the mobile library. Mad little matatus dashing down, overtaking everything they could see, people hanging off every door and window. Big dirty country buses winding up the steep road like oxen. Gikombe, the town fool, if we could have afforded one, wrapped in dung-colored cloth sitting down in front of the country buses to stop them moving. Rains and hot seasons and cold fogs. People being born, people getting married, people running out on each other, or getting sick, or dying in accidents. Kilimanjaro, the Chaga? Another picture in a world where all pictures come from the same distance.

I was thirteen and just a woman when the Chaga came to my world and destroyed it. That night I was at Grace Muthiga's where she and I had a homework club. It was an excuse to listen to the radio. One of the great things about the United Nations taking over your country is the radio is very good. I would sing with it. They played the kind of music that wasn't approved of in our house.

We were listening to trip hop. Suddenly the record started to go all phasey, like the radio was tuning itself on and off the station. At first we thought the disc was slipping or something, then Grace got up to fiddle with the tuning button. That only made it worse. Grace's mother came in from the next room and said she couldn't get a picture on the battery television. It was full of wavy lines. Then we heard the first boom. It was far away and hollow and it rolled like thunder. Most nights up in the Highlands we get thunder. We know very well what it sounds like. This was something else. Boom! Again. Closer now. Voices outside, and lights. We took torches and went out to the voices. The road was full of people; men, women, children. There were torch beams weaving all over the place. Boom! Close now, loud enough to rattle the windows. All the people shone their torches straight up into the sky, like spears of light. Now the children were crying and I was afraid. Most High had the answer: "Sonic booms! There's something up there!" As he said those words, we saw it. It was so slow. That was the amazing thing about it. It was like a child drawing a chalk line across a board. It came in from the south east, across the hills east of Kiriani, straight as an arrow, a little to the south of us. The night was such as we often get in late May, clear after evening rains, and very full of stars. We all saw a glowing dot cut across the face of the stars. It seemed to float and dance, like illusions in the eye if you look into the sun. It left a line behind it like the trails of the big UN jets, only pure, glowing blue, drawn on the night. Double-boom now, so close and loud it hurt my ears. At that, one of the old women began wailing. The fear caught, and soon whole families were looking at the line of light in the sky with tears running down their faces, men as well as women. Many sat down and put their torches in their laps, not knowing what they should do. Some of the old people covered their heads with jackets, shawls, newspapers. Others saw what they were doing, and soon everyone was sitting on the ground with their heads covered. Not Most High. He stood looking up at the line of light as it cut his night in half. "Beautiful!" he said. "That I should see such things, with these own eyes!"

He stood watching until the object vanished in the dark of the mountains to the west. I saw its light reflected in his eyes. It took a long time to fade.

For a few moments after the thing went over, no one knew what to do. Everyone was scared, but they were relieved at the same time because, like the angel of death, it had passed over Gichichi. People were still crying, but tears of relief have a different sound. Someone got a radio from a house. Others fetched theirs, and soon we were all sitting in the middle of the road in the dark, grouped around our radios. An announcer interrupted the evening music show to bring a news flash. At twenty-twenty-eight a new biological package had struck in Central Province. At those words, a low keen went up from each group.

"Be quiet!" someone shouted, and there was quiet. Though the words would be terrible, they were better than the voices coming out of the dark.

The announcer said that the biological package had come down on the eastern slopes of the Nyandarua near to Tusha, a small Kikuyu village. Tusha was a name we knew. Some of us had relatives in Tusha. The country bus to Nyeri went through Tusha. From Gichichi to Tusha was twenty kilometers. There were cries. There were prayers. Most said nothing. But we all knew time had run out. In four years the Chaga had swallowed up Kilimanjaro, and Amboseli, and the border country of Namanga and was advancing up the A104 on Kijiado and Nairobi. We had ignored it and gone on with our lives, believing that when it finally came, we would know what to do. Now it had dropped out of the sky twenty kilometers north of us and said, Twenty kilometers, four hundred days: that's how long you've got to decide what you're going to do.

Then Jackson who ran the Peugeot Service Office stood up. He cocked his head to one side. He held up a finger. Everyone fell silent. He looked to the sky. "Listen!" I could hear nothing. He pointed to the south, and we all heard it: aircraft engines. Flashing lights lifted out of the dark tree-line on the far side of the valley. Behind it came others, then others, then ten, twenty, thirty more helicopters swarmed over Gichichi like locusts. The sound of their engines filled the whole world. I wrapped my school shawl around my head and put my hands over my ears and yelled over the noise but it still felt like it would shatter my skull like a clay pot. Thirty-five helicopters. They flew so low their down-wash rattled our tin roofs and sent dust swirling up around our faces. Some of the teenagers cheered and waved their torches and white school shirts to the pilots. They cheered the helicopters on, right over the ridge. They cheered until the noise of their engines was lost among the night-insects. Where the Chaga goes, the United Nations comes close behind, like a dog after a bitch.

A few hours later the trucks came through. The grinding of engines as they toiled up the winding road woke all Gichichi. "It's three o'clock in the morning!" Mrs. Kuria shouted at the dusty white trucks with the blue symbol of UNECTA on the doors, but no one would sleep again. We lined the main road to watch them go through our village. I wonder what the drivers thought of all those faces and eyes suddenly appearing in their headlights as they rounded the bend. Some waved. The children waved back. They were still coming through as we went down to the shamba at dawn to milk the goats. They were a white snake coiling up and down the valley road as far as I could see. As they reached the top of the pass the low light from the east caught them and burned them to gold.

The trucks went up the road for two days. Then they stopped and the refugees started to come the other way, down the road. First the ones with the vehicles: matatus piled high with bedding and tools and animals, trucks with the family balanced in the back on top of all the things they had saved. A Toyota microbus, bursting with what looked like bolts of colored cloth but which were women, jammed in next to each other. Ancient cars, motorbikes and mopeds vanishing beneath sagging bales of possessions. It was a race of poverty; the rich ones with machines took the lead. After motors came animals; donkey carts and ox-wagons, pedal-rickshaws. Most came in the last wave, the ones on foot. They pushed handcarts laden with pots and bedding rolls and boxes lashed with twine, or dragged trolleys on rope or shoved frightened-faced old women in wheelbarrows. They struggled their burdens down the steep valley road. Some broke free and bounced over the edge down across the terraces, strewing clothes and tools and cooking things over the fields. Last of all came hands and heads. These people carried their possessions on their heads and backs and children's shoulders.

My father opened the church to the refugees. There they could have rest, warm chai, some ugali, some beans. I helped stir the great pots of ugali over the open fire. The village doctor set up a treatment center. Most of the cases were for damaged feet and hands, and dehydrated children. Not everyone in Gichichi agreed with my father's charity. Some thought it would encourage the refugees to stay and take food from our mouths. The shopkeepers said he was ruining their trade by giving away what they should be selling. My father told them he was just trying to do what he thought Jesus would have done. They could not answer that, but I know he had another reason. He wanted to hear the refugee's stories. They would be his story, soon enough.

What about Tusha?

The package missed us by a couple of kilometers. It hit a place called Kombé; two Kiluyu farms and some shit-caked cows. There was a big bang. Some of us from Tusha took a matatu to see what had happened to Kombé. They tell us there is nothing left. There they are, go, ask them.

This nothing, my brothers, what was it like? A hole?

No, it was something, but nothing we could recognize. The photographs? They only show the thing. They do not show how it happens. The houses, the fields, the fields and the track, they run like fat in a pan. We saw the soil itself melt and new things reach out of it like drowning men's fingers.

What kind of things?

We do not have the words to describe them. Things like you see in the television programs about the reefs on the coast, only the size of houses, and striped like zebras. Things like fists punching out of the ground, reaching up to the sky and opening like fingers. Things like fans, and springs, and balloons, and footballs.

So fast?

Oh yes. So fast that even as we watched, it took our matatu. It came up the tires and over the bumper and across the paintwork like a lizard up a wall and the whole thing came out in thousands of tiny yellow buds.

What did you do?

What do you think we did? We ran for our lives.

The people of Kombé?

When we brought back help from Tusha, we were stopped by helicopters. Soldiers, everywhere. Everyone must leave, this is a quarantine area. You have twenty-four hours.

Twenty-four hours!

Yes, they order you to pack up a life in twenty-four hours. The Blue Berets brought in all these engineers who started building some great construction, all tracks and engines. The night was like day with welding torches. They ploughed Kiyamba under with bulldozers to make a new airstrip. They were going to bring in jets there. And before they let us go they made everyone take medical tests. We lined up and went past these men in white coats and masks at tables.

Why?

I think they were testing to see if the Chaga-stuff had got into us.

What did they do, that you think that?

Pastor, some they would tap on the shoulder, just like this. Like Judas and the Lord, so gentle. Then a soldier would take them to the side.

What then?

I do not know, pastor. I have not seen them since. No one has.

These stories troubled my father greatly. They troubled the people he told them to, even Most High, who had been so thrilled by the coming of the alien to our land. They especially troubled the United Nations. Two days later a team came up from Nairobi in five army hummers. The first thing they did was tell my father and the doctor to close down their aid station. The official UNHCR refugee center was Muranga. No one could stay here in Gichichi, everyone must go.

In private they told my father that a man of his standing should not be sowing rumors and half truths in vulnerable communities. To make sure that we knew the real truth, UNECTA called a meeting in the church. Everyone packed on to the benches, even the Muslims. People stood all the way around the walls; others outside, lifted out the louvers to listen in at the windows. My father sat with the doctor and our local chief at a table. With them was a government man, a white soldier and an Asian woman in civilian dress who looked scared. She was a scientist, a xenologist. She did most of the talking; the government man from Nairobi twirled his pencil between his fingers and tapped it on the table until he broke the point. The soldier, a French general with experience of humanitarian crises, sat motionless.

The xenologist told us that the Chaga was humanity's first contact with life from beyond the Earth. The nature of this contact was unclear; it did not follow any of the communication programs we had predicted. This contact was the physical transformation of our native landscape and vegetation. But what was in the package was not seeds and spores. The things that had consumed Kombé and were now consuming Tusha were more like tiny machines, breaking down the things of this world to pieces and rebuilding them in strange new forms. The Chaga responded to stimuli and adapted to counterattacks on itself. UNECTA had tried fire, poison, radioactive dusting, genetically modified diseases. Each had been quickly routed by the Chaga. However, it was not apparent if it was intelligent, or the tool of an as yet unseen intelligence.

"And Gichichi?" Ismail the barber asked.

The French general spoke now.

"You will all be evacuated in plenty of time."

"But what if we do not want to be evacuated?" Most High asked. "What if we decide we want to stay here and take our chances with the Chaga?"

"You will all be evacuated," the general said again.

"This is our village, this is our country. Who are you to tell us what we must do in our own country?" Most High was indignant now. We all applauded, even my father up there with the UNECTA people. The Nairobi political looked vexed.

"UNECTA, UNHCR and the UN East Africa Protection Force operate with the informed consent of the Kenyan government. The Chaga has been deemed a threat to human life. We're doing this for your own good."

Most High drove on. "A threat? Who 'deems' it so? UNECTA? An organization that is eighty percent funded by the United States of America? I have heard different, that it doesn't harm people or animals. There are people living inside the Chaga; it's true, isn't it?"

The politician looked at the French general, who shrugged. The Asian scientist answered.

"Officially, we have no data."

Then my father stood up and cut her short.

"What about the people who are being taken away?"

"I don't know anything . . ." the UNECTA scientist began but my father would not be stopped.

"What about the people from Kombé? What are these tests you are carrying out?"

The woman scientist looked flustered. The French general spoke.

"I'm a soldier, not a scientist. I've served in Kosovo and Iraq and East Timor. I can only answer your questions as a soldier. On the fourteenth of June next year, it will come down that road. At about seven thirty in the evening, it will come through this church. By Tuesday night, there will be no sign that a place called Gichichi ever existed."

And that was the end of the meeting. As the UNECTA people left the church, the Christians of Gichichi crowded around my father. What should they believe? Was Jesus come again, or was it anti-Christ? These aliens, were they angels, or fallen creatures like ourselves? Did they know Jesus? What was God's plan in this? Question after question after question.

My father's voice was tired and thin and driven, like a leopard harried by beaters toward guns. Like that leopard, he turned on his hunters.

"I don't know!" he shouted. "You think I have answers to all these things? No. I have no answers. I have no authority to speak on these things. No one does. Why are you asking these silly silly questions? Do you think a country pastor has the answers that will stop the Chaga in its tracks and drive it back where it came from? No. I am making them up as I go along, like everyone else."

For a moment the whole congregation was silent. I remember feeling that I must die from embarrassment. My mother touched my father's arm. He had been shaking. He excused himself to his people. They stood back to let us out of the church. We stopped on the lintel, amazed. A rapture had indeed come. All the refugees were gone from the church compound. Their goods, their bundles, their carts and animals. Even their excrement had been swept away.

As we walked back to the house, I saw the woman scientist brush past Most High as she went to the UNECTA hummer. I heard her whisper, "About the people. It's true. But they're changed."

"How?" Most High asked but the door was closed. Two blue berets lifted mad Gikombe from in front of the hummer and it drove off slowly through the throng of people. I remembered that the UNECTA woman looked frightened.

That afternoon my father rode off on the red Yamaha and did not come back for almost a week.

I learned something about my father's faith that day. It was that it was strong in the small, local questions because it was weak in the great ones. It believed in singing and teaching the people and the disciplines of personal prayer and meditation, because you could see them in the lives of others. In the big beliefs, the ones you could not see, it fell.

That meeting was the wound through which Gichichi slowly bled to death. "This is our village, this is our country," Most High had declared, but before the end of the week the first family had tied their things on to the back of their pickup and joined the flow of refugees down the road to the south. After that a week did not pass that someone from our village would not close their doors a last time and leave Gichichi. The abandoned homes soon went to ruin. Water got in, roofs collapsed, then rude boys set fire to them. The dead houses were like empty skulls. Dogs fell into toilet pits and drowned. One day when we went down to the shamba there were no names and stones from the Ukerewe house. Within a month its windows were empty, smoke-stained sockets.

With no one to tend them, the shambas went to wild and weeds. Goats and crows grazed where they would, the terrace walls crumbled, the rains washed the soil down the valley in great red tears. Fields that had fed families for generations vanished in a night. No one cared for the women's tree any more, to give the images their cups of beer. Hope stopped working in Gichichi. Always in the minds of the ones who remained was the day when we would look up the road and see the spines and fans and twisted spires of the Chaga standing along the ridge-line like warriors.

I remember the morning I was woken by the sound of voices from the Muthiga house. Men's voices, speaking softly so as not to waken anyone, for it was still dark, but they woke me. I put on my things and went out into the compound. Grace and Reth were carrying cardboard boxes from the house, their father and a couple of the other men from the village were loading them on to a Nissan pickup. They had started early, and the pickup was well laden. The children were gathering up the last few things.

"Ah, Tendeléo," Mr. Muthiga said sadly. "We had hoped to get away before anyone was around."

"Can I talk to Grace?" I asked.

I did not talk to her. I shouted at her. I would be all alone when she went. I would be abandoned. She asked me a question. She said, "You say we must not go. Tell me, Tendeléo, why must you stay?"

I did not have an answer to that. I had always presumed that it was because a pastor must stay with his people, but the bishop had made several offers to my father to relocate us to a new parish in Eldoret.

Grace and her family left as it was getting light. Their red taillights swung into the slow stream of refugees. I heard the horn hooting to warn stragglers and animals all the way down the valley. I tried to keep the house good and safe but two weeks later a gang of rude boys from another village broke in, took what they could and burned the rest. They were a new thing in what the radio called the "sub-terminum," gangs of raiders and looters stripping the corpses of the dead towns.

"Vultures, is what they are," my mother said.

Grace's question was a dark parting gift to me. The more I thought about it, the more I became convinced that I must see this thing that had forced such decisions on us. The television and newspaper pictures were not enough. I had to see it with my own eyes. I had to look at its face and ask it its reasons. Little Egg became my lieutenant. We slipped money from the collection plate, and we gathered up secret bundles of food. A schoolday was the best to go. We did not go straight up the road, where we would have been noticed. We caught a matatu to Kinangop in the Nyandarua valley where nobody knew us. There was still a lively traffic; the matatu was full of country people with goods to sell and chickens tied together by the feet stowed under the bench. We sat in the back and ate nuts from a paper cone folded from a page of the Bible. Everywhere were dirty white United Nations vehicles. One by one the people got out and were not replaced. By Ndunyu there was only me and Little Egg, jolting around in the back of the car.

The driver's mate turned around and said, "So, where for, girls?"

I said, "We want to look at the Chaga."

"Sure, won't the Chaga be coming to look at you soon enough?"

"Can you take us there?" I showed him Church shillings.

"It would take a lot more than that." He talked to the driver a moment. "We can drop you at Njeru. You can walk from there, it's under seven kilometers."

Njeru was what awaited Gichichi, when only the weak and poor and mad remained. I was glad to leave it. The road to the Chaga was easy to find, it was the direction no one else was going in. We set off up the red dirt road toward the mountains. We must have looked very strange, two girls walking through a ruined land with their lunches wrapped in kangas. If anyone had been there to watch.

The soldiers caught us within two kilometers of Njeru. I had heard the sound of their engine for some minutes, behind us. It was a big eight-wheeled troop carrier of the South African army.

The officer was angry, but I think a little impressed. What did we think we were doing? There were vultures everywhere. Only last week an entire bus had been massacred, five kilometers from here. Not one escaped alive. Two girls alone, they would rob us and rape us, hang us up by our heels and cut our throats like pigs. All the time he was preaching, a soldier in the turret swept the countryside with a big heavy machine gun.

"So, what the hell are you doing here?"

I told him. He went to talk on the radio. When he came back, he said, "In the back."

The carrier was horribly hot and smelled of men and guns and diesel. When the door clanged shut on us I thought we were going to suffocate.

"Where are you taking us?" I asked, afraid.

"You came to see the Chaga," the commander said. We ate our lunch meekly and tried not to stare at the soldiers. They gave us water from their canteens and tried to make us laugh. The ride was short but uncomfortable. The door clanged open. The officer helped me out and I almost fell over with shock.

I stood in a hillside clearing. Around me were tree stumps, fresh cut, sticky with sap. From behind came the noise of chain saws. The clearing was full of military vehicles and tents. People hurried every way. Most of them were white. At the center of this activity was what I can only call a city on wheels. I had not yet been to Nairobi, but I knew it from photographs, a forest of beautiful towers rising out of a circle of townships. That was how the base seemed to me when I first saw it. Looking closer, I saw that the buildings were portable cabins stacked up on big tracked flatbeds, like the heavy log-carriers up in Eldoret. The tractors and towers were joined together with walkways and loops of cable. I saw people running along the high walkways. I would not have done that, not for a million shillings.

I tell you my first impressions, of a beautiful white city—and you may laugh because you know it was only a UN-ECTA mobile base—that they had put together as fast and cheap as they could. But there is a truth here; seeing is magical. Looking kills. The longer I looked, the more the magic faded.

The air in the clearing smelled as badly of diesel smoke as it had in the troop carrier. Everywhere was engine-noise. A path had been slashed through the forest, as if the base had come down it. I looked at the tracks. The big cog wheels were turning. The base was moving, slowly and heavily, like the hands of a clock, creaking backwards on its tracks in pace with the advance of the Chaga. Little Egg took my hand. I think my mouth must have been open in wonder for some time.

"Come on then," said the officer. He was smiling now. "You wanted to see the Chaga."

He gave us over to a tall American man with red hair and a red beard and blue eyes. His name was Byron and he spoke such bad Swahili that he did not understand when Little Egg said to me, "He looks like a vampire."

"I speak English," I told him and he looked relieved.

He took us through the tractors to the tower in the middle, the tallest. It was painted white, with the word UNECTA big in blue on the side and beneath it, the name, Nyandarua Station. We got into a small metal cage. Byron closed the door and pressed a button. The cage went straight up the side of the building. I tell you this, that freight elevator was more frightening than any stories about murdering gangs of vultures. I gripped the handrail and closed my eyes. I could feel the whole base swaying below me.

"Open your eyes," Byron said. "You wouldn't want to come all this way and miss it."

As we rose over the tops of the trees the land opened before me. Nyandarua Station was moving down the eastern slopes of the Aberdare range: the Chaga was spread before me like a wedding kanga laid out on a bed.

It was as though someone had cut a series of circles of colored paper and let them fall on the side of the mountains. The Chaga followed the ridges and the valleys, but that was all it had to do with our geography. It was completely something else. The colors were so bright and silly I almost laughed: purples, oranges, lots of pink and deep red. Veins of bright yellow. Real things, living things were not these colors. This was a Hollywood trick, done with computers for a film. I guessed we were a kilometer from the edge. It was not a very big Chaga, not like the Kilimanjaro Chaga that had swallowed Moshi and Arusha and all the big Tanzanian towns at the foot of the mountain and was now half-way to Nairobi. Byron said this Chaga was about five kilometers across and beginning to show the classic form, a series of circles. I tried to make out the details. I thought details would make it real to me. I saw jumbles of reef-stuff the color of wiring. I saw a wall of dark crimson trees rise straight for a tremendous height. The trunks were as straight and smooth as spears. The leaves were joined together like umbrellas. Beyond them, I saw things like icebergs tilted at an angle, things like open hands, praying to the sky, things like oil refineries made out of fungus, things like brains and fans and domes and footballs. Things like other things. Nothing that seemed a thing in itself. And all this was reaching toward me. But, I realized, it would never catch me. Not while I remained here, on this building that was retreating from it down the foothills of the Aberdares, fifty meters every day.

We were close to the top of the building. The cage swayed in the wind. I felt sick and scared and grabbed the rail and that was when it became real for me. I caught the scent of the Chaga on the wind. False things have no scent. The Chaga smelled of cinnamon and sweat and soil new turned up. It smelled of rotting fruit and diesel and concrete after rain. It smelled like my mother when she had The Visit. It smelled like the milk that babies spit out of their mouths. It smelled like televisions and the stuff the Barber Under the Tree put on my father's hair and the women's holy place in the shamba. With each of these came a memory of Gichichi and my life and people. The scent stirred the things I had recently learned as a woman. The Chaga became real for me there, and I understood that it would eat my world.

While I was standing, putting all these things that were and would be into circles within circles inside my head, a white man in faded jeans and Timberland boots rushed out of a sliding door on to the elevator.

"Byron," he said, then noticed that there were two little Kenyan girls there with him. "Who're these?"

"I'm Tendeléo and this is my sister," I said. "We call her Little Egg. We've come to see the Chaga."

This answer seemed to please him.

"I'm called Shepard." He shook our hands. He also was American. "I'm a Peripatetic Executive Director. That means I rush around the world finding solutions to the Chaga."

"And have you?"

For a moment he was taken aback, and I felt bold and rude. Then he said, "Come on, let's see."

"Shepard," Byron the vampire said. "It'll wait."

He took us in to the base. In one room were more white people than I had seen in the whole of my life. Each desk had a computer but the people—most of them were men dressed very badly in shorts, with beards—did not use them. They preferred to sit on each other's desks and talk very fast with much gesturing.

"Are African people not allowed in here?" I asked.

The man Shepard laughed. Everything I said that tour he treated as if it had come from the lips of a wise old m'zee. He took us down into the Projection Room where computers drew huge plans on circular tables: of the Chaga now, the

Chaga in five years time and the Chaga when it met with its brother from the south and both of them swallowed Nairobi like two old men arguing over a stick of sugar cane.

"And after Nairobi is gone?" I asked. The maps showed the names of all the old towns and villages, under the Chaga. Of course. The names do not change. I reached out to touch the place that Gichichi would become.

"We can't project that far," he said. But I was thinking of an entire city, vanished beneath the bright colors of the Chaga like dirt trodden into carpet. All those lives and histories and stories. I realized that some names can be lost, the names of big things, like cities, and nations, and histories.

Next we went down several flights of steep steel stairs to the "tab levels." Here samples taken from the Chaga were stored inside sealed environments. A test tube might hold a bouquet of delicate fungi, a cylindrical jar a fistful of blue spongy fingers, a tank a square meter of Chaga, growing up the walls and across the ceiling. Some of the containers were so big people could walk around inside. They were dressed in bulky white suits that covered every part of them and were connected to the wall with pipes and tubes so that it was hard to tell where they ended and alien Chaga began. The weird striped and patterned leaves looked more natural than the UNECTA people in their white suits. The alien growing things were at least in their right world.

"Everything has to be isolated," Mr. Shepard said.

"Is that because even out here, it will start to attack and grow?" I asked.

"You got it."

"But I heard it doesn't attack people or animals," I said.

"Where did you hear that?" this man Shepard asked.

"My father told me," I said mildly.

We went on down to Terrestrial Cartography, which was video-pictures the size of a wall of the world seen looking down from satellites. It is a view that is familiar to everyone of our years, though there were people of my parents' generation who laughed when they heard that the world is a ball, with no string to hold it up. I looked for a long time—it is the one thing that does not pale for looking—before I saw that the face of the world was scarred, like a Giriama woman's. Beneath the clouds, South America and South Asia and mother Africa were spotted with dots of lighter color than the brown-green land. Some were large, some were specks, all were precise circles. One, on the eastern side of Africa, identified this disease of continents to me. Chagas. For the first time I understood that this was not a Kenyan thing, not even an African thing, but a whole world thing.

"They are all in the south," I said. "There is not one in the north."

"None of the biological packages have seeded in the northern hemisphere. This is what makes us believe that there are limits to the Chaga. That it won't cover our whole world, pole to pole. That it might confine itself only to the southern hemisphere."

"Why do you think that?"

"No reason at all."

"You just hope."

"Yeah. We hope."

"Mr. Shepard," I said. "Why should the Chaga take away our lands here in the south and leave you rich people in the north untouched? It does not seem fair."

"The universe is not fair, kid. Which you probably know better than me."

We went down then to Stellar Cartography, another dark room, with walls full of stars. They formed a belt around the middle of the room, in places so dense that individual stars blurred into masses of solid white.

"This is the Silver River," I said. I had seen this on Grace's family's television, which they had taken with them.

"Silver River. It is that. Good name."

"Where are we?" I asked.

Shepard went over to the wall near the door and touched a small star down near his waist. It had a red circle around it. Otherwise I do not think even he could have picked it out of all the other small white stars. I did not like it that our sun was so small and common. I asked, "And where are they from?"

The UNECTA man drew a line with his finger along the wall. He walked down one side of the room, half way along the other, before he stopped. His finger stopped in a swirl of rainbow colors, like a flame.

"Rho Ophiuchi. It's just a name, it doesn't matter. What's important is that it's a long long way from us . . . so far it takes light—and that's as fast as anything can go—eight hundred years to get there, and it's not a planet, or even a star. It's what we call a nebula, a huge cloud of glowing gas."

"How can people live in a cloud?" I asked. "Are they angels?"

The man laughed at that.

"Not people," he said. "Not angels either. Machines. But not like you or I think of machines. Machines more like living things, and very very much smaller. Smaller even than the smallest cell in your body. Machines the size of chains of atoms, that can move other atoms around and so build copies of themselves, or copies of anything else they want. And we think those gas clouds are trillions upon trillions of those tiny, living machines."

"Not plants and animals," I said.

"Not plants and animals, no."

"I have not heard this theory before." It was huge and thrilling, but like the sun, it hurt if you looked at it too closely. I looked again at the swirl of color, colored like the Chaga scars on Earth's face, and back at the little dot by the door that was my light and heat. Compared to the rest of the room, they both looked very small. "Why should things like this, from so far away, want to come to my Kenya?"

"That's indeed the question."

That was all of the science that the UNECTA man was allowed to show us, so he took us down through the areas where people lived and ate and slept, where they watched television and films and drank alcohol and coffee, the places where they exercised, which they liked to do a lot, in immodest costumes. The corridors were full of them, immature and loosely put together, like leggy puppies.

"This place stinks of wazungu," Little Egg said, not thinking that maybe this m'zungu knew more Swahili than the other one. Mr. Shepard smiled.

"Mr. Shepard," I said. "You still haven't answered my question."

He looked puzzled a moment, then remembered.

"Solutions. Oh yes. Well, what do you think?"

Several questions came into my head but none as good, or important to me, as the one I did ask.

"I suppose the only question that matters, really, is can people live in the Chaga?"

Shepard pushed open a door and we were on a metal platform just above one of the big track sets.

"That, my friend, is the one question we aren't even allowed to consider," Shepard said as he escorted us on to a staircase.

The tour was over. We had seen the Chaga. We had seen our world and our future and our place amongst the stars; things too big for country church children, but which even they must consider, for unlike most of the wazungu here, they would have to find answers.

Down on the red dirt with the diesel stink and roar of chain saws, we thanked Dr. Shepard. He seemed touched. He was clearly a person of power in this place. A word, and there was a UNECTA Landcruiser to take us home. We were so filled up with what we had seen that we did not think to tell the driver to let us off at the next village down so we could walk. Instead we went landcruising right up the main road, past Haran's shop and the Peugeot Service Station and all the Men Who Read Newspapers under the trees.

Then we faced my mother and father. It was bad. My father took me into his study. I stood. He sat. He took his Kalenjin Bible, that the Bishop gave him on his ordination so that he might always have God's word in his own tongue, and set it on the desk between himself and me. He told me that I had deceived my mother and him, that I had led Little Egg astray, that I had lied, that I had stolen, not God's money, for God had no need of money, but the money that people I saw every day, people I sang and prayed next to every Sunday, gave in their faith. He said all this in a very straightforward, very calm way, without ever raising his voice. I wanted to tell him all the things I had seen, offer them in trade, yes, I have cheated, I have lied, I have stolen from the Christians of Gichichi, but I have learned. I have seen. I have seen our sun lost among a million other suns. I have seen this world that God is supposed to have made most special of all worlds, so small it cannot even be seen. I have seen men, that God is supposed to have loved so much that he died for their evils, try to understand living machines, each smaller than the smallest living thing, but together, so huge it takes light years to cross their community. I know how different things are from what we believe, I wanted to say, but I said nothing, for my father did an unbelievable thing. He stood up. Without sign or word or any display of strength, he hit me across the face. I fell to the ground, more from the unexpectedness than the hurt. Then he did another unbelievable thing. He sat down. He put his head in his hand. He began to cry. Now I was very scared, and I ran to my mother.

"He is a frightened man," she said. "Frightened men often strike out at the thing they fear."

"He has his church, he has his collar, he has his Bible, what can frighten him?"

"You," she said. This answer was as stunning as my father hitting me. My mother asked me if I remembered the time, after the argument outside the church, when my father had disappeared on the red Yamaha for a week. I said I did, yes.

"He went down south, to Nairobi, and beyond. He went to look at the thing he feared, and he saw that, with all his faith, he could not beat the Chaga."

My father stayed in his study a long time. Then he came to me and went down on his knees and asked me to forgive him. It was a Biblical principle, he said. Do not let the sun go down on your anger. But though Bible principles lived, my father died a little to me that day. This is life: a series of dyings and being born into new things and understandings.

Life by life, Gichichi died too. There were only twenty families left on the morning when the spines of the alien coral finally reached over the tree tops up on the pass. Soon after dawn the UNECTA trucks arrived. They were dirty old Sudanese Army things, third hand Russian, badly painted and billowing black smoke. When we saw the black soldiers get out we were alarmed because we had heard bad things about Africans at the hands of other Africans. I did not trust their officer; he was too thin and had an odd hollow on the side of his shaved head, like a crater on the moon. We gathered in the open space in front of the church with our things piled around us. Ours came to twelve bundles wrapped up in kangas. I took the radio and a clatter of pots. My father's books were tied with string and balanced on the petrol tank of his red scrambler.

The moon-headed officer waved and the first truck backed up and let down its tail. A soldier jumped out, set up a folding beach chair by the tailgate and sat with a clipboard and a pencil. First went the Kurias, who had been strong in the church. They threw their children up into the truck, then passed up their bundles of belongings. The soldier in the beach chair watched for a time, then shook his head.

"Too much, too much," he said in bad Swahili. "You must leave something."

Mr. Kuria frowned, measuring all the space in the back of the truck with his eyes. He lifted off a bundle of clothes.

"No no no," the soldier said, and stood up and tapped their television with his pencil. Another soldier came and took it out of Mr. Kuria's arms to a truck at the side of the road, the tithe truck.

"Now you get on," the soldier said, and made a check on his clipboard.

It was as bold as that. Wide-open crime under the blue sky. No one to see. No one to care. No one to say a word.

Our family's tax was the motorbike. My father's face had gone tight with anger and offense to God's laws, but he gave it up without a whisper. The officer wheeled it away to a group of soldiers squatting on their heels by a smudge-fire. They were very pleased with it, poking and teasing its engine with their long fingers. Every time since that I have heard a Yamaha engine I have looked to see if it is a red scrambler, and what thief is riding it.

"Oh, on," said the tithe-collector.

"My church," my father said and jumped off the truck. Immediately there were a dozen Kalashnikovs pointing at him. He raised his hands, then looked back at us.

"Tendeléo, you should see this."

The officer nodded. The guns were put down and I jumped to the ground. I walked with my father to the church. We proceeded up the aisle. The prayer books were on the bench seats, the woven kneelers set square in front of the pews. We went into the little vestry, where I had stolen the money from the collection. There were other dark secrets here. My father took a battered red petrol can from his robing cupboard and carried it to the communion table. He took the chalice, offered it to God, then filled it with petrol from the can. He turned to face the holy table.

"The blood of Christ keep you in eternal life," he said, raising the cup high. Then he poured it out on to the white altar cloth. A gesture too fast for me to see; he struck fire.

There was an explosion of yellow flame. I cried out. I thought my father had gone up in the gush of fire. He turned to me. Flames billowed behind him.

"Now do you understand?" he said.

I did. Sometimes it is better to destroy a thing you love than have it taken from you and made alien. Smoke was pouring from under the roof by the time we climbed back on to the truck. The Sudanese soldiers were only interested in that it was fire, and destruction excites soldiers. Ours was the church of an alien god.

Old Gikombe, too old and stupid to run away, did his "sitting in front of the trucks" trick. Every time the soldiers moved him, he scuttled back to his place. He did it once too often. The truck behind us had started to roll, and the driver did not see the dirty, rag-wrapped thing dart under his wing. With a cry, Gikombe fell under the wheels and was crushed.

A wind from off the Chaga carried the smoke from the burning church over us as we went down the valley road. The communion at Gichichi was broken.

I think time changes everything into its opposite. Youth into age, innocence into experience, certainty into uncertainty. Life into death. Long before the end, time was changing Nairobi into the Chaga. Ten million people were crowded into the shanties that ringed the towers of downtown. Every hour of every day, more came. They came from north and south, from Rift Valley and Central Province, from Ilbisil and Naivasha, from Makindu and Gichichi.

Once Nairobi was a fine city. Now it was a refugee camp. Once it had great green parks. Now they were trampled dust between packing-case homes. The trees had all been hacked down for firewood. Villages grew up on road roundabouts, like castaways on coral islands, and in the football stadiums and sports grounds. Armed patrols daily cleared squatters from the two airport runways. The railway had been abandoned, cut south and north. Ten thousand people now lived in abandoned carriages and train sheds and between the tracks. The National Park was a dust bowl, ravaged for fuel and building material, its wildlife fled or slaughtered for food. Nairobi air was a smog of wood smoke, diesel and sewage. The slums spread for twenty kilometers on every side. It was an hour's walk to fetch water, and that was stinking and filthy. Like the Chaga, the shanties grew, hour by hour, family by family. String up a few plastic sheets here, shove together some cardboard boxes there, set up home where a matatu dies, pile some stolen bricks and sacking and tin. City and Chaga reached out to each other, and came to resemble each other.

I remember very little of those first days in Nairobi. It was too much, too fast—it numbed my sense of reality. The men who took our names, the squatting people watching us as we walked up the rows of white tents looking for our number, were things done to us that we went along with without thinking. Most of the time I had that high-pitched sound in my ear when you want to cry but cannot.

Here is an irony: we came from St. John's, we went to St. John's. It was a new camp, in the south close by the main airport. One eight three two. One number, one tent, one oil lamp, one plastic water bucket, one rice scoop. Every hundred tents there was a water pipe. Every hundred tents there was a shit pit. A river of sewage ran past our door. The stench would have stopped us sleeping, had the cold not done that first. The tent was thin and cheap and gave no protection from the night. We huddled together under blankets. No one wanted to be the first to cry, so no one did. Between the big aircraft and people crying and fighting, there was no quiet, ever. The first night, I heard shots. I had never heard them before but I knew exactly what they were.

In this St. John's we were no longer people of consequence. We were no longer anything. We were one eight three two. My father's collar earned no respect. The first day he went to the pipe for water he was beaten by young men, who stole his plastic water pail. The collar was a symbol of God's treachery. My father stopped wearing his collar; soon after, he stopped going out at all. He sat in the back room listening to the radio and looking at his books, which were still in their tied-up bundles. St. John's destroyed the rest of the things that had bound his life together. I think that if we had not been rescued, he would have gone under. In a place like St. John's, that means you die. When you went to the food truck you saw the ones on the way to death, sitting in front of their tents, holding their toes, rocking, looking at the soil.

We had been fifteen days in the camp—I kept a tally on the tent wall with a burned-out match—when we heard the vehicle pull up and the voice call out, "Jonathan Bi. Does anyone know Pastor Jonathan Bi?" I do not think my father could have looked any more surprised if Jesus had called his name. Our savior was the Pastor Stephen Elezeke, who ran the Church Army Center on Jogoo Road. He and my father had been in theological college together; they had been great footballing friends. My father was godfather to Pastor Elezeke's children; Pastor Elezeke, it seemed, was my godfather. He piled us all in the back of a white Nissan minibus with Praise Him on the Trumpet written on one side and Praise Him with the Psaltery and Harp, rather squashed up, on the other. He drove off hooting at the crowds of young men, who looked angrily at church men in a church van. He explained that he had found us through the net. The big churches were flagging certain clergy names. Bi was one of them.

So we came to Jogoo Road. Church Army had once been an old, pre-Independence teaching center with a modern, two-level accommodation block. These had overflowed long ago; now every open space was crowded with tents and wooden shanties. We had two rooms beside the metal working shop. They were comfortable but cramped, and when the metal workers started, noisy. There was no privacy.

The heart of Church Army was a little white chapel, shaped like a drum, with a thatched roof. The tents and lean-tos crowded close to the chapel but left a respectful distance. It was sacred. Many went there to pray. Many went to cry away from others, where it would not infect them like dirty water. I often saw my father go into the chapel. I thought about listening at the door to hear if he was praying or crying, but I did not. Whatever he looked for there, it did not seem to make him a whole man again.

My mother tried to make Jogoo Road Gichichi. Behind the accommodation block was a field of dry grass with an open drain running down the far side. Beyond the drain was a fence and a road, then the Jogoo Road market with its name painted on its rusting tin roof, then the shanties began again. But this field was untouched and open. My mother joined a group of women who wanted to turn the field into shambas. Pastor Elezeke agreed and they made mattocks in the workshops from bits of old car, broke up the soil and planted maize and cane. That summer we watched the crops grow as the shanties crowded in around the Jogoo Road market, and stifled it, and took it apart for roofs and walls. But they never touched the shambas. It was as if they were protected. The women hoed and sang to the radio and laughed and talked women-talk, and Little Egg and the Chole girls chased enormous sewer rats with sticks. One day I saw little cups of beer and dishes of maize and salt in a corner of the field and understood how it was protected.

My mother pretended it was Gichichi but I could see it was not. In Gichichi, the men did not stand by the fence wire and stare so nakedly. In Gichichi the helicopter gunships did not wheel overhead like vultures. In Gichichi the brightly painted matatus that roared up and down did not have heavy machine-guns bolted to the roof and boys in sports fashion in the back looking at everything as if they owned it. They were a new thing in Nairobi, these gun-gangs; the Tacticals. Men, usually young, organized into gangs, with vehicles and guns, dressed in anything they could make a uniform. Some were as young as twelve. They gave themselves names like the Black Simbas and the Black Rhinos and the Ebonettes and the United Christian Front and the Black Taliban. They liked the word black. They thought it sounded threatening. These Tacticals had as many philosophies and beliefs as names, but they all owned territory, patrolled their streets and told their people they were the law. They enforced their law with kneecappings and burning car tires, they defended their streets with AK47s. We all knew that when the Chaga came, they would fight like hyenas over the corpse of Nairobi. The Soca Boys was our local army. They wore sports fashion and knee-length Manager's coats and had football team logos painted in the sides of their picknis, as the armed matatus were called. On their banners they had a black-and-white patterned ball on a green field. Despite their name, it was not a football. It was a buckyball, a carbon fullerene molecule, the half-living, half-machine building-brick of the Chaga. Their leader, a rat-faced boy in a Manchester United Coat and shades that kept sliding down his nose, did not like Christians, so on Sundays he would send his picknis up and down Jogoo Road, roaring their engines and shooting into the air, because they could.

The Church Army had its own plans for the coming time of changes. A few nights later, as I went to the choo, I overheard Pastor Elezeke and my father talking in the Pastor's study. I put my torch out and listened at the louvers.

"We need people like you, Jonathan," Elezeke was saying. "It is a work of God, I think. We have a chance to build a true Christian society."

"You cannot be certain."

"There are Tacticals . . ."

"They are filth. They are vultures."

"Hear me out, Jonathan. Some of them go into the Chaga. They bring things out—for all their quarantine, there are things the Americans want very much from the Chaga. It is different from what we are told is in there. Very very different. Plants that are like machines, that generate electricity, clean water, fabric, shelter, medicines. Knowledge. There are devices, the size of this thumb, that transmit information directly into the brain. And more; there are people living in there, not like primitives, not, forgive me, like refugees. It shapes itself to them, they have learned to make it work for them. There are whole towns—towns, I tell you—down there under Kilimanjaro. A great society is rising."

"It shapes itself to them," my father said. "And it shapes them to itself."

There was a pause.

"Yes. That is true. Different ways of being human."

"I cannot help you with this, my brother."

"Will you tell me why?"

"I will," my father said, so softly I had to press close to the window to hear. "Because I am afraid, Stephen. The Chaga has taken everything from me, but that is still not enough for it. It will only be satisfied when it has taken me, and changed me, and made me alien to myself."

"Your faith, Jonathan. What about your faith?"

"It took that first of all."

"Ah," Pastor Elezeke sighed. Then, after a time, "You understand you are always welcome here?"

"Yes, I do. Thank you, but I cannot help you."

That same night I went to the white chapel—my first and last time—to force issues with God. It was a very beautiful building, with a curving inner wall that made you walk half way around the inside before you could enter. I suppose you could say it was spiritual, but the cross above the table angered me. It was straight and true and did not care for anyone or anything. I sat glaring at it some time before I found the courage to say, "You say you are the answer."

I am the answer, said the cross.

"My father is destroyed by fear. Fear of the Chaga, fear of the future, fear of death, fear of living. What is your answer?"

I am the answer.

"We are refugees, we live on wazungu's charity, my mother hoes corn, my sister roasts it at the roadside; tell me your answer."

I am the answer.

"An alien life has taken everything we ever owned. Even

now, it wants more, and nothing can stop it. Tell me, what is your answer?"

I am the answer.

"You tell me you are the answer to every human need and question, but what does that mean? What is the answer to your answer?"

I am the answer, the silent, hanging cross said.

"That is no answer!" I screamed at the cross. "You do not even understand the questions, how can you be the answer? What power do you have? None. You can do nothing! They need me, not you. I am going to do what you can't."

I did not run from the chapel. You do not run from gods you no longer believe in. I walked, and took no notice of the people who stared at me.

The next morning, I went into Nairobi to get a job. To save money I went on foot. There were men everywhere, walking with friends, sitting by the roadside selling sheet metal charcoal burners or battery lamps, or making things from scrap metal and old tires, squatting together outside their huts with their hands draped over their knees. There must have been women, but they kept themselves hidden. I did not like the way the men worked me over with their eyes. They had shanty-town eyes, that see only what they can use in a thing. I must have appeared too poor to rob and too hungry to sexually harass, but I did not feel safe until the downtown towers rose around me and the vehicles on the streets were diesel-stained green and yellow buses and quick white UN cars.

I went first to the back door of one of the big tourist hotels.

"I can peel and clean and serve people," I said to an undercook in dirty wellies. "I work hard and I am honest. My father is a pastor."

"You and ten million others," the cook said. "Get out of here."

Then I went to the CNN building. It was a big, bold idea. I slipped in behind a motorbike courier and went up to a good-looking Luo on the desk.

"I'm looking for work," I said. "Any work. I can do anything. I can make chai, I can photocopy, I can do basic accounts. I speak good English and a little French. I'm a fast learner."

"No work here today," the Luo on the desk said. "Or any other day. Learn that, fast."

I went to the Asian shops along Moi Avenue.

"Work?" the shopkeepers said. "We can't even sell enough to keep ourselves, let alone some up-country refugee."

I went to the wholesalers on Kimathi Street and the City Market and the stall traders and I got the same answer from each of them: no economy, no market, no work. I tried the street hawkers, selling liquidated stock from tarpaulins on the pavement, but their bad mouths and lewdness sickened me. I walked the five kilometers along Uhuru Highway to the UN East Africa Headquarters on Chiromo Road. The soldier on the gate would not even look at me. Cars and hummers he could see. His own people, he could not. After an hour I went away.

I took a wrong turn on the way back and ended up in a district I did not know, of dirty-looking two-story buildings that once held shops, now burned out or shuttered with heavy steel. Cables dipped across the street, loop upon loop upon loop sagging and heavy. I could hear voices but see no one around. The voices came from an alley behind a row of shops. An entire district was crammed into this alley. Not even in St. John's camp have I seen so many people in one place. The alley was solid with bodies, jammed together, moving like one thing, like a rain cloud. The noise was incredible. At the end of the alley I glimpsed a big black foreign car, very shiny, and a man standing on the roof. He was surrounded by reaching hands, as if they were worshipping him.

"What's going on?" I shouted to whoever would hear. The crowd surged. I stood firm.

"Hiring," a shaved-headed boy as thin as famine shouted back. He saw I was puzzled. "Watekni. Day jobs in data processing. The UN treats us like shit in our own country, but we're good enough to do their tax returns."

"Good money?"

"Money." The crowd surged again, and made me part of it. A new car arrived behind me. The crowd turned like a flock of birds on the wing and pushed me toward the open doors. Big men with dark glasses got out and made a space around the watekni broker. He was a small Luhya in a long white jellaba and the uniform shades. He had a mean mouth. He fanned a fistful of paper slips. My hand went out by instinct and I found a slip in it. A single word was printed on it: Nimepata.

"Password of the day," my thin friend said. "Gets you into the system."

"Over there, over there," one of the big men said, pointing to an old bus at the end of the alley. I ran to the bus. I could feel a hundred people on my heels. There was another big man at the bus door.

"What're your languages?" the big man demanded.

"English and a bit of French," I told him.

"You waste my fucking time, kid," the man shouted. He tore the password slip from my hand, pushed me so hard, with two hands, I fell. I saw feet, crushing feet, and I rolled underneath the bus and out the other side. I did not stop running until I was out of the district of the watekni and into streets with people on them. I did not see if the famine-boy got a slip. I hope he did.

Singers wanted, said the sign by the flight of street stairs to an upper floor. So, my skills had no value in the information technology market. There were other markets. I climbed the stairs. They led to a room so dark I could not at first make out its dimensions. It smelled of beer, cigarettes and poppers. I sensed a number of men.

"Your sign says you want singers," I called into the dark.

"Come in then." The man's voice was low and dark, smoky, like an old hut. I ventured in. As my eyes grew used to the dark, I saw tables, chairs upturned on them, a bar, a raised stage area. I saw a number of dark figures at a table, and the glow of cigarettes.

"Let's have you."

"Where?"

"There."

I got up on the stage. A light stabbed me and blinded me.

"Take your top off."

I hesitated, then unbuttoned my blouse. I slipped it off, stood with my arms loosely folded over my breasts. I could not see the men, but I felt the shanty-eyes.

"You stand like a Christian child," a smoky voice said. "Let's see the goods."

I unfolded my arms. I stood in the silver light for what seemed like hours.

“Don’t you want to hear me sing?”

“Girl, you could sing like an angel, but if you don’t have the architecture . . .”

I picked up my blouse and rebuttoned it. It was much more shaming putting it on than taking it off. I climbed down off the stage. The men began to talk and laugh. As I reached the door, the dark voice called me.

“Can you do a message?”

“What do you want?”

“Run this down the street for me right quick.”

I saw fingers hold up a small glass vial. It glittered in the light from the open door.

“Down the street.”

“To the American Embassy.”

“I can find that.”

“That’s good. You give it to a man.”

“What man?”

“You tell the guard on the gate. He’ll know.”

“How will he know me?”

“Say you’re from Brother Dust.”

“And how much will Brother Dust pay me?”

The men laughed.

“Enough.”

“In my hand?”

“Only way to do business.”

“We have a deal.”

“Good girl. Hey.”

“What?”

“Don’t you want to know what it is?”

“Do you want to tell me?”

“They’re fullerenes. They’re from the Chaga. Do you understand that? They are alien spores. The Americans want them. They can use them to build things, from nothing up. Do you understand any of this?"

"A little."

"So be it. One last thing."

"What?"

"You don't carry it in your hand. You don't carry it anywhere on you. You get my meaning?"

"I think I do."

"There are changing rooms for the girls back of the stage. You can use one of them."

"Okay. Can I ask a question?"

"You can ask anything you like."

"These . . . fullerenes. These Chaga things . . . What if they go off, inside?"

"You trust the stories that they never touch human flesh. Here. You may need this." An object flipped through the air toward me. I caught it . . . a tube of KY jelly. "A little lubrication."

I had one more question before I went backstage area."

"Can I ask, why me?"

"For a Christian child, you've had a decent amount of dark," the voice said. "So, you've a name?"

"Tendeléo."

Ten minutes later I was walking across the town, past all the UN checkpoints and security points, with a vial of Chaga fullerenes slid into my vagina. I walked up to the gate of the American Embassy. There were two guards with white helmets and white gaiters. I picked the big black one with the very good teeth.

"I'm from Brother Dust," I said.

"One moment please," the marine said. He made a call on

his PDU. One minute later the gates swung open and a small white man with sticking-up hair came out.

"Come with me," he said, and took me to the guard unit toilets, where I extracted the consignment. In exchange he gave me a playing card with a portrait of a President of the United States on the back. The President was Nixon.

"You ever go back without one of these, you die," he told me. I gave the Nixon card to the man who called himself Brother Dust. He gave me a roll of two shillings and told me to come back on Tuesday.

I gave two thirds of the roll to my mother.

"Where did you get this?" she asked, holding the notes in her hands like blessings.

"I have a job," I said, challenging her to ask. She never did ask. She bought clothes for Little Egg and fruit from the market. On the Tuesday, I went back to the upstairs club that smelled of beer and smoke and come and took another load inside me to the spikey-haired man at the Embassy.

So I became a runner. I became a link in a chain that ran from legendary cities under the clouds of Kilimanjaro across terminum, past the UN Interdiction Force, to an upstairs club in Nairobi, into my body, to the US Embassy. No, I do not have that right. I was a link in a chain that started eight hundred years ago, as light flies, in a gas cloud called Rho Ophiuchi, that ran from US Embassy to US Government, and on to a man whose face was on the back of one of my safe-conduct cards and from him into a future no one could guess.

"It scares them, that's why they want it," Brother Dust told me. "Americans are always drawn to things that terrify them. They think these fullerenes will give the edge to their industries, make the economy indestructible. Truth is, they'll destroy their industries, wreck their economy. With these, anyone can make anything they want. Their free market can't stand up to that."

I did not stay a runner long. Brother Dust liked my refusal to be impressed by what the world said should impress me. I became his personal assistant. I made appointments, kept records. I accompanied him when he called on brother Sheriffs. The Chaga was coming closer, the Tacticals were on the streets; old enemies were needed as allies now.

One such day, Brother Dust gave me a present wrapped in a piece of silk. I unwrapped it, inside was a gun. My first reaction was fear; that a sixteen-year-old girl should have the gift of life or death in her hand. Would I, could I, ever use it on living flesh? Then a sense of power crept through me. For the first time in my life, I had authority.

"Don't love it too much," Brother Dust warned. "Guns don't make you safe. Nowhere in this world is safe, not for you, not for anyone."

It felt like a sin, like a burn on my body as I carried it next to my skin back to Jogoo Road. It was impossible to keep it in our rooms, but Simeon in the metal shop had been stashing my roll for some time now and he was happy to hide the gun behind the loose block. He wanted to handle it. I would not let him, though I think he did when I was not around. Every morning I took it out, some cash for lunch and bribes, and went to work.

With a gun and money in my pocket, Brother Dust's warning seemed old and full of fear. I was young and fast and clever. I could make the world as safe or as dangerous as I liked. Two days after my seventeenth birthday, the truth of what he said arrived at my door.

It was late, it was dark and I was coming off the matatu

outside Church Army. It was a sign of how far things had gone with my mother and father that they no longer asked where I was until so late, or how the money kept coming. At once I could tell something was wrong; a sense you develop when you work on the street. People were milling around in the compound, needing to do something, not knowing what they could do. Elsewhere, women's voices were shouting. I found Simeon.

"What's happening, where is my mother?"

"The shambas. They have broken through into the shambas."

I pushed my way through the silly, mobbing Christians. The season was late, the corn over my head, the cane dark and whispering. I strayed off the shamba paths in moments. The moon ghosted behind clouds, the air-glow of the city surrounded me but cast no light. The voices steered me until I saw lights gleaming through the stalks: torches and yellow naphtha flares. The voices were loud now, close. There were now men, loud men. Loud men have always frightened me. Not caring for the crop, I charged through the maize, felling rich, ripe heads.

The women of Church Army stood at the edge of the crushed crop. Maize, potatoes, cane, beans had been trodden down, ripped out, torn up. Facing them was a mob of shanty-town people. The men had torches and cutting tools. The women's kangas bulged with stolen food. The children's baskets and sacks were stuffed with bean pods and maize cobs. They faced us shamelessly. Beyond the flattened wire fence, a larger crowd was waiting in front of the market; the hyenas, who if the mob won, would go with them, and if it lost, would sneak back to their homes. They outnumbered the women twenty to one. But I was bold. I had the authority of a gun.

"Get out of here," I shouted at them. "This is not your land."

"And neither is it yours," their leader said, a man thin as a skeleton, barefoot, dressed in cut-off jeans and a rag of a fertilizer company T-shirt. He held a tin-can oil lamp in his left hand, in his right a machete. "It is all borrowed from the Chaga. It will take it away, and none of us will have it. We want what we can take, before it is lost to all of us."

"Go to the United Nations," I shouted.

The leader shook his head. The men stepped forward. The women murmured, gripping their mattocks and hoes firmly.

"The United Nations? Have you not heard? They are scaling down the relief effort. We are to be left to the mercy of the Chaga."

"This is our food. We grew it, we need it. Get off our land!"

"Who are you?" the leader laughed. The men hefted their pangas and stepped forward. The laughter lit the dark inside me that Brother Dust had recognized, that made me a warrior. Light-headed with rage and power, I pulled out my gun. I held it over my head. One, two, three shots cracked the night. The silence after was more shocking than the shots.

"So. The child has a gun," the hungry man said.

"The child can use it too. And you will be first to die."

"Perhaps," the leader said. "But you have three bullets. We have three hundred hands."

My mother pulled me to one side as the shanty men came through. Their pangas caught the yellow light as they cut their way through our maize and cane. After them came the women and the children, picking, sifting, gleaning. The three hundred hands stripped our fields like locusts. The gun pulled my arm down like an iron weight. I remember I cried with frustration and shame. There were too many of them. My power, my resolve, my weapon, were nothing. False bravery. Boasting. Show.

By morning the field was a trampled mess of stalks, stems and shredded leaves. Not a grain worth eating remained. By morning I was waiting on the Jogoo Road, my thumb held out for a matatu, my possessions in a sports bag on my back. A refugee again. The fight had been brief and muted.

"What is this thing?" My mother could not touch the gun. She pointed at it on the bed. My father could not even look. He sat hunched up in a deep, old armchair, staring at his knees. "Where did you get such a thing?"

The dark thing was still strong in me. It had failed against the mob, but it was more than enough for my parents.

"From a Sheriff," I said. "You know what a sheriff is? He is a big man. For him I stick Chaga-spores up my crack. I give them to Americans, Europeans, Chinese, anyone who will pay."

"Do not speak to us like that!"

"Why shouldn't I? What have you done, but sit here and wait for something to happen? I'll tell you the only thing that is going to happen. The Chaga is going to come and destroy everything. At least I have taken some responsibility for this family, at least I have kept us out of the sewer! At least we have not had to steal other people's food!"

"Filth money! Dirt money, sin money!"

"You took that money readily enough."

"If we had known . . ."

"Did you ever ask?"

"You should have told us."

"You were afraid to know."

My mother could not answer that. She pointed at the gun again, as if it were the proof of all depravity.

"Have you ever used it?"

"No," I said, challenging her to call me a liar.

"Would you have used it, tonight?"

"Yes," I said. "I would, if I thought it would have worked."

"What has happened to you?" my mother said. "What have we done?"

"You have done nothing," I said. "That's what's wrong with you. You give up. You sit there, like him." My father had not yet said a word. "You sit there, and you do nothing. God will not help you. If God could, would he have sent the Chaga? God has made you beggars."

Now my father got up out of his deep chair.

"Leave this house," he said in a very quiet voice. I stared. "Take your things. Go on. Go now. You are no longer of this family. You will not come here again."

So I walked out with my things in my bag and my gun in my pants and my roll in my shoe and I felt the eyes in every room and lean-to and shack and I learned Christians can have shanty-eyes too. Brother Dust found me a room in the back of the club. I think he hoped it would give him a chance to have sex with me. It smelled and it was noisy at night and I often had to quit it to let the prostitutes do their business, but it was mine, and I believed I was free and happy. But his words were a curse on me. Like Evil Eye, I knew no peace. You do nothing. I had accused my parents but what had I done? What was my plan for when the Chaga came? As the months passed and the terminum was now at Muranga, now at Ghania Falls, now at Thika, Brother Dust's curse accused me. I watched the Government pull out of Mombasa in a convoy of trucks and cars that took an hour and a half to go past the Haile Selassie Avenue café where I bought my runners morning coffee. I saw the gangs of pick-nis race through the avenues, loosing off tracer like fire-crackers, until the big UN troop carriers drove them before them like beggars. I crouched in roadside ditches from terrible firefights over hijacked oil tankers. I went up to the observation deck of the Moi Telecom Tower and saw the smoke from battles out in the suburbs, and beyond, on the edge of the heat-haze, to south and north, beyond the mottled duns and dusts of the squatter towns, the patterned colors of the Chaga. I saw the newspapers announce that on July 18th, 2013, the walls of the Chaga would meet and Nairobi cease to exist. Where is safe? Brother Dust said in my spirit. What are you going to do?

A man dies, and it is easy to say when the dying ends. The breath goes out and does not come in again. The heart stills. The blood cools and congeals. The last thought fades from the brain. It is not so easy to say when a dying begins. Is it, for example, when the body goes into the terminal decline? When the first cell turns black and cancerous? When we pass our DNA to a new human generation, and become genetically redundant? When we are born? A civil servant once told me that when they make out your birth certificate, they also prepare your death certificate.

It was the same for the big death of Nairobi. The world saw the end of the end from spy satellites and camera-blimps. When the end for a city begins is less clear. Some say it was when the United Nations pulled out and left Nairobi open. Others, when the power plants at Embakasi went down and the fuel and telephone lines to the coast were cut. Some trace it to the first Hatching Tower appearing over the avenues of Westlands; some to the pictures on the television news of the hexagon pattern of Chaga-moss slowly obliterating a "Welcome to Nairobi" road sign. For me it was when I slept with Brother Dust in the back room of the upstairs club.

I told him I was a virgin.

"I always pegged you for a Christian child," he said, and though my virginity excited him, he did not try and take it from me forcefully or disrespectfully. I was fumbling and dry and did not know what to do and pretended to enjoy it more than I did. The truth was that I did not see what all the fuss was about. Why did I do it? It was the seal that I had become a fine young criminal, and tied my life to my city.

Though he was kind and gentle, we did not sleep together again.

They were bad times, those last months in Nairobi. Some times, I think, are so bad that we can only deal with them by remembering what is good, or bright. I will try and look at the end days straight and honestly. I was now eighteen, it was over a year since I left Jogoo Road and I had not seen my parents or Little Egg since. I was proud and angry and afraid. But a day had not passed that I had not thought about them and the duty I owed them. The Chaga was advancing on two fronts, marching up from the south and sweeping down from the north through the once-wealthy suburbs of Westlands and Garden Grove. The Kenyan Army was up there, firing mortars into the cliff of vegetation called the

Great Wall, taking out the Hatching Towers with artillery. As futile as shelling the sea. In the south the United Nations was holding the international airport open at every cost. Between them, the Tacticals tore at each other like street dogs. Alliances were formed and were broken in the same day. Neighbor turned on neighbor, brother killed brother. The boulevards of downtown Nairobi were littered with bullet casings and burned out picknis. There was not one pane of glass whole on all of Moi Avenue, nor one shop that was not looted. Between them were twelve million civilians, and the posses.

We too made and dissolved our alliances. We had an arrangement with Mombi, who had just bloodily ended an agreement with Haran, one of the big sheriffs, to make a secret deal with the Black Simbas, who intended to be a power in the new order after the Chaga. The silly, vain Soca Boys had been swept away in one night by the Simbas East Starehe Division. Custom matatus and football managers' coats were no match for Russian APCs and light-scatter combat-suits. Brother Dust's associations were precarious; the posses had wealth and influence but no power. Despite our AK47s and street cool uniforms—in the last days, everyone had a uniform—even the Soca Boys could have taken us out. We were criminals, not warriors.

Limuru, Tigani, Kiambu, in the north. Athi River, Matathia, Embakasi to the south. The Chaga advanced a house here, a school there, half a church, a quarter of a street. Fifty meters every day. Never slower, never faster. When the Supreme Commander East African Protection Force announced terminum at Ngara, I made my move. In my Dust Girl uniform of street-length, zebra stripe PVC coat over short-shorts, I took a taxi to the Embassy of the United States of America. The driver detoured through Riverside.

"Glider come down on Limuru Road," the driver explained. The gliders scared me, hanging like great plastic bats from the hatching towers, waiting to drop, spread their wings and sail across the city sowing Chaga spores. To me they were dark death on wings. I have too many Old Testament images still in me. The army took out many on the towers, the helicopters the ones in the air, but some always made it down. Nairobi was being eaten away from within.

Riverside had been rich once. I saw a tank up-ended in a swimming pool, a tennis court strewn with swollen bodies in purple combats. Chaga camouflage. Beyond the trees I saw fans of lilac land-coral.

I told the driver to wait outside the Embassy. The grounds were jammed with trucks. Chains of soldiers and staff were loading them with crates and machinery. The black marine knew me by now.

"You're going?" I asked.

"Certainly are, ma'am," the marine said. I handed him my gun. He nodded me through. People pushed through the corridors under piles of paper and boxes marked Property of the United States Government. Everywhere I heard shredders. I found the right office. The spikey-haired man, whose name was Knutson, was piling cardboard boxes on his desk.

"We're not open for business."

"I'm not here to trade," I said. I told him what I was here for. He looked at me as if I had said that the world was made of wool, or the Chaga had reversed direction. So I cleared a space on his desk and laid out the photographs I had brought.

"Please tell me, because I don't understand this attraction," I said. "Is it that, when they are that young, you cannot tell the boys from the girls? Or is it the tightness?"

"Fuck you. You'll never get these public."

"They already are. If the Diplomatic Corps Personnel Section does not receive a password every week, the file will download."

If there had been a weapon to hand, I think Knutson would have killed me where I stood.

"I shouldn't have expected any more from a woman who sells her cunt to aliens."

"We are all prostitutes, Mr. Knutson. So?"

"Wait there. To get out you need to be chipped." In the few moments he was out of the room I studied the face of the President on the wall. I was familiar with Presidential features; is it something in the nature of the office, I wondered, that gives them all the same look? Knutson returned with a metal and plastic device like a large hypodermic. "Name, address, Social Security Number." I gave them to him. He tapped tiny keys on the side of the device, then he seized my wrist, pressed the nozzle against forearm. There was a click, I felt a sharp pain but I did not cry out.

"Congratulations, you're an employee of US Military Intelligence. I hope that fucking hurt."

"Yes it did." Blood oozed down my wrist. "I need three more. These are the names."

Beside the grainy snaps of Knutson on the bed with the naked children, I laid out my family. Knutson thrust the chip gun at me.

"Here. Take it. Take the fucking thing. They'll never miss it, not in all this. It's easy to use, just dial it in there. And those."

I scooped up the photographs and slid them with the chip

gun into my inside pocket. The freedom chip throbbed under my skin as I walked through the corridors full of people and paper into the light.

Back at the club I paid the driver in gold. It and cocaine were the only universally acceptable street currencies. I had been converting my roll to Krugerrands for some months now. The rate was not good. I jogged up the stairs to the club, and into slaughter.

Bullets had been poured into the dark room. The bar was shattered glass, stinking of alcohol. The tables were spilled and splintered. The chairs were overturned, smashed. Bodies lay among them, the club men, sprawled inelegantly. The carpet was sticky with blood. Flies buzzed over the dead. I saw the Dust Girls, my sisters, scattered across the floor, hair and bare skin and animal prints drenched with blood. I moved among them. I thought of zebras on the high plains, hunted down by lions, limbs and muscle and skin torn apart. The stench of blood is an awful thing. You never get it out of you. I saw Brother Dust on his back against the stage. Someone had emptied a clip of automatic fire into his face.

Our alliances were ended.

A noise; I turned. I drew my gun. I saw it in my hand, and the dead lying with their guns in their hands. I ran from the club. I ran down the stairs onto the street. I was a mad thing, screaming at the people in the street, my gun in hand, my coat flying out behind me. I ran as fast as I could. I ran for home, I ran for Jogoo Road. I ran for the people I had left there. Nothing could stop me. Nothing dared, with my gun in my hand. I would go home and I would take them away from this insanity. The last thing the United Nations will ever do for us is fly us out of here, I would tell them. We will fly somewhere we do not need guns or camps or charity, where we will again be what we were. In my coat and stupid boots, I ran, past the plastic city at the old country bus terminal, around the metal barricades on Landhies Road, across the waste ground past the Lusaka Road roundabout where two buses were burning. I ran out into Jogoo Road.

There were people right across the road. Many many people, with vehicles, white UN vehicles. And soldiers, a lot of soldiers. I could not see Church Army. I slammed into the back of the crowd, I threw people out of my way, hammered at them with the side of my gun.

"Get out of my way, I have to get to my family!"

Hands seized me, spun me around. A Kenyan Army soldier held me by the shoulders.

"You cannot get through."

"My family lives there. The Church Army Center, I need to see them."

"No one goes through. There is no Church Army."

"What do you mean? What are you saying?"

"A glider came down."

I tore away from him, fought my way through the crowd until I came to the cordon of soldiers. A hundred meters down the road was a line of hummers and APCs. A hundred yards beyond them, the alien infection. The glider had crashed into the accommodation block. I could still make out the vile batshape among the crust of fungus and sponge spreading across the white plaster. Ribs of Chaga-coral had burst the tin roof of the teaching hall, the shacks were a stew of dissolving plastic and translucent bubbles that burst in a cloud of brown dust. Where the dust touched, fresh bubbles grew. The chapel had vanished under a web of red veins. Even Jogoo Road was blistered by yellow flowers and blue barrel-like objects. Fingers of the hexagonal Chaga moss were reaching toward the roadblock. As I watched, one of the thorn trees outside the center collapsed into the sewer and sent up a cloud of buzzing silver mites.

"Where are the people?" I asked a soldier.

"Decontamination," he said.

"My family was in there!" I screamed at him. He looked away. I shouted at the crowd. I shouted my father's name, my mother's name, Little Egg's, my own name. I pushed through the people, trying to look at the faces. Too many people, too many faces. The soldiers were looking at me. They were talking on radios, I was disturbing them. At any moment they might arrest me. More likely, they would take me to a quiet place and put a bullet in the back of my skull. Too many people, too many faces. I put the gun away, ducked down, slipped between the legs to the back of the crowd. Decontamination. A UD word, that. Headquarters would have records of the contaminated. Chiromo Road. I would need transport. I came out of the crowd and started to run again. I ran up Jogoo Road, past the sports stadium, around the roundabout on to Landhies Road. There were still a few civilian cars on the street. I ran up the middle of the road, pointing my gun at every car that came toward me.

"Take me to Chiromo Road!" I shouted. The drivers would veer away, or hoot and swear. Some even aimed at me. I sidestepped them, I was too fast for them. "Chiromo Road, or I will kill you!" Tacticals laughed and yelled as they swept past in their picknis. Not one stopped. Everyone had seen too many guns.

There was a Kenyan Army convoy on Pumwani Road, so I cut up through the cardboard cities into Kariokor. As long as I kept the Nairobi River, a swamp of refuse and sewage, to my left, I would eventually come out on to Ngara Road. The shanty people fled from the striped demon with the big gun.

"Get out of my way!" I shouted. And then, all at once, the alley people disobeyed me. They stood stock still. They looked up.

I felt it before I saw it. Its shadow was cold on my skin. I stopped running. I too looked up and it swooped down on me. That is what I thought, how I felt—this thing had been sent from the heart of the Chaga to me alone. The glider was bigger than I had imagined, and much much darker. It swept over me. I was paralyzed with dread, then I remembered what I held in my hand. I lifted my gun and fired at the dark bat-thing. I fired and fired and fired until all I heard was a stiff click. I stood, shaking, as the glider vanished behind the plastic shanty roofs. I stood, staring at my hand holding the gun. Then the tiniest yellow buds appeared around the edge of the cylinder. The buds unfolded into crystals, and the crystals spread across the black, oiled metal like scale. More buds came out of the muzzle and grew back down the barrel. Crystals swelled up and choked the cocked hammer.

I dropped my gun like a snake. I tore at my hair, my clothes, I scrubbed at my skin. My clothes were already beginning to change. My zebra-striped coat was blistering. I pulled out the chip injector. It was a mess of yellow crystals and flowers. I could not hope to save them now. I threw it away from me. The photographs of Knutson with the children fell to the earth. They bubbled up and went to dust. I tore at my coat; it came apart in my fingers into tatters of plastic and spores. I ran. The heel of one knee-boot gave way. I fell, rolled, recovered, and stripped the foolish things off me. All around me, the people of Kariokor were running, ripping at their skin and their clothes with their fingers. I ran with them, crying with fear. I let them lead me. My finery came apart around me. I ran naked, I did not care. I had nothing now. Everything had been taken from me, everything but the chip in my arm. On every side the plastic and wood shanties sent up shoots and stalks of Chaga.

We crashed up against the UN emergency cordon at Kariokor Market. Wicker shields pushed us back; rungu clubs went up, came down. People fell, clutching smashed skulls. I threw myself at the army line.

"Let me through!"

I thrust my arm between the riot shields.

"I'm chipped! I'm chipped!"

Rungus rose before my face.

"UN pass! I'm chipped!"

The rungus came down, and something whirled them away. A white man's voice shouted.

"Jesus fuck, she is! Get her out of there! Quick!"

The shield wall parted, hands seized me, pulled me through.

"Get something on her."

A combat jacket fell on my shoulders. I was taken away very fast through the lines of soldiers to a white hummer with a red cross on the side. A white man with a red cross vest sat me on the back step and ran a scanner over my forearm. The wound was livid now, throbbing.

"Tendeléo Bi. US Embassy Intelligence Liaison. Okay Tendeléo Bi, I've no idea what you were doing in there, but it's decontam for you."

A second soldier—an officer, I guessed—had come back to the hummer.

"No time. Civs have to be out by twenty-three hundred."

The medic puffed his cheeks.

"This is not procedure . . ."

"Procedure?" the officer said. "With a whole fucking city coming apart around us? But I guarantee you this, the Americans will go fucking ballistic if we fuck with one of their spooks. A surface scrub'll do . . ."

They took me over to a big boxy truck with a biohazard symbol on the side. It was parked well away from the other vehicles. I was shivering from shock, I made no complaint as they shaved all hair from my body. Someone gently took away the army jacket and showed me where to stand. Three men unrolled high-pressure hoses from the side of the truck and worked me from top to bottom. The water was cold, and hard enough to be painful. My skin burned. I twisted and turned to try to keep it away from my nipples and the tender parts of my body. On the third scrub, I realized what they were doing, and remembered.

"Take me to decontam!" I shouted. "I want to go to decontam! My family's there, don't you realize?" The men would not listen to me. I do not think they even knew it was a young woman's body they were hosing down. No one listened to me. I was dried with hot air guns, given some loose fatigues to wear, then put in the back of a diplomatic hummer that drove very fast through the streets to the airport. We did not go to the terminal building. There, I might have broken and run. We went through the wire gates, and straight to the open back of a big Russian transport plane. A line of people was going up the ramp into the cavern of its belly. Most of them were white, many had children, and all were laden with bags and goods. All were refugees, too . . . like me.

"My family is back there. I have to get them," I told the man with the security scanner at the foot of the ramp.

"We'll find them," he said as he checked off my Judas chip against the official database. "That's you. Good luck." I went up the metal ramp into the plane. A Russian woman in uniform found me a seat in the middle block, far from any window. Once I was belted in I sat trembling until I heard the ramp close and the engines start up. Then I knew I could change nothing, and the shaking stopped. I felt the plane bounce over the concrete and turn on to the runway. I hoped a terrible hope: that something would go wrong and the plane would crash and I would die. Because I needed to die. I had destroyed the thing I meant to save and saved the thing that was worthless. Then the engines powered up and we made our run and though I could see only the backs of seats and the gray metal curve of the big cabin, I knew when we left the ground because I felt my bond with Kenya break and my home fall away beneath me as the plane took me into exile.

I pause now in my story, for where it goes now is best told by another voice.

My name is Sean. It's an Irish name. I'm not Irish. No bit of Irish in me, as you can probably see. My mom liked the name. Irish stuff was fashionable, thirty years ago. My telling probably won't do justice to Tendeléo's story; I apologize. My gift's numbers. Allegedly. I'm a reluctant accountant. I do what I do well, I just don't have a gut feel for it. That's why my company gave me all the odd jobs. One of them was this African-Caribbean-World restaurant just off Canal Street. It was called I-Nation—the menu changed every week, the ambiance was great and the music was mighty. The first time I wore a suit there, Wynton the owner took the piss so much I never dressed up for them again. I'd sit at a table and poke at his VAT returns and find myself nodding to the drum and bass, Wynton would try out new grooves on me and I'd give them thumbs up or thumbs down. Then he'd fix me coffee with this liqueur he imported from Jamaica and that was the afternoon gone. It seemed a shame to invoice him.

One day Wynton said to me, "You should come to our evening sessions. Good music. Not this fucking bang bang bang. Not fucking deejays. Real music. Live music."

However, my mates liked fucking deejays and bang bang bang so I went to I-Nation on my own. There was a queue but the door staff nodded me right in. I got a seat at the bar and a Special Coffee, compliments of the house. The set had already begun, the floor was heaving. That band knew how to get a place moving. After the dance set ended, the lead guitarist gestured offstage. A girl got up behind the mic. I recognized her—she waitressed in the afternoons. She was a small, quiet girl, kind of unnoticeable, apart from her hair which stuck out in spikes like it was growing back after a Number Nought cut with the razor.

She got up behind that mic and smiled apologetically. Then she began to sing, and I wondered how I had ever thought her unnoticeable. It was a slow, quiet song. I couldn't understand the language. I didn't need to, her voice said it all: loss and hurt and lost love. Bass and rhythm felt out the depth and damage in every syllable. She was five foot nothing and looked like she would break in half if you blew on her, but her voice had a stone edge that said, I've been where I'm singing about. Time stopped, she held a note then gently let it go. I-Nation was silent for a moment. Then it exploded. The girl bobbed shyly and went down through the cheering and whistling. Two minutes later she was back at work, clearing glasses. I could not take my eyes off her. You can fall in love in five minutes. It's not hard at all.

When she came to take my glass, all I could say was, "That was . . . great."

"Thank you."

And that was it. How I met Ten, said three shit words to her, and fell in love.

I never could pronounce her name. On the afternoons

when the bar was quiet and we talked over my table she would shake her head at my mangling the vowel sounds.

"Eh-yo."

"Ay-oh?"

The soft spikes of hair would shake again. Then, she never could pronounce my name either. Shan, she would say.

"No, Shawn."

"Shone . . . "

So I called her Ten, which for me meant Il Primo, Top of the Heap, King of the Hill, A-Number-One. And she called me Shone. Like the sun. One afternoon when she was off shift, I asked Boss Wynton what kind of name Tendeléo was.

"I mean, I know it's African, I can tell by the accent, but it's a big continent."

"It is that. She not told you?"

"Not yet."

"She will when she's ready. And Mr. Accountant, you fucking respect her."

Two weeks later she came to my table and laid a series of forms before me like tarot cards. They were Social Security applications, Income Support, Housing Benefit.

"They say you're good with numbers."

"This isn't really my thing, but I'll take a look." I flipped through the forms. "You're working too many hours . . . they're trying to cut your benefits. It's the classic welfare trap. It doesn't pay you to work."

"I need to work," Ten said.

Last in line was a Home Office Asylum Seeker's form. She watched me pick it up and open it. She must have seen my eyes widen.

"Gichichi, in Kenya."

"Yes."

I read more.

"God. You got out of Nairobi."

"I got out of Nairobi, yes."

I hesitated before asking, "Was it bad?"

"Yes," she said. "I was very bad."

"I?" I said.

"What?"

"You said 'I.' I was very bad."

"I meant, it was very bad."

The silence could have been uncomfortable, fatal even. The thing I had wanted to say for weeks rushed into the vacuum.

"Can I take you somewhere? Now? Today? When you finish? Would you like to eat?"

"I'd like that very much," she said.

Wynton sent her off early. I took her to a great restaurant in Chinatown where the waiters ask you before you go in how much you'd like to spend.

"I don't know what this is," she said as the first of the courses arrived.

"Eat it. You'll like it."

She toyed with her wontons and chopsticks.

"Is something wrong with it?"

"I will tell you about Nairobi now," she said. The food was expensive and lavish and exquisitely presented and we hardly touched it. Course after course went back to the kitchen barely picked over as Ten told me the story of her life, the church in Gichichi, the camps in Nairobi, the career as a posse girl, and of the Chaga that destroyed her family, her career, her hopes, her home, and almost her life. I had seen the coming of the Chaga on the television. Like most people, I had tuned it down to background muzak in my life; oh, wow, there's an alien life-form taking over the southern hemisphere. Well, it's bad for the safari holidays and carnival in Rio is fucked and you won't be getting the Brazilians in the next World Cup, but the Cooperage account's due next week and we're pitching for the Maine Road job and interest rates have gone up again. Aliens schmaliens. Another humanitarian crisis. I had followed the fall of Nairobi, the first of the really big cities to go, trying to make myself believe that this was not Hollywood, this was not Bruce Willis versus the CGI. This was twelve million people being swallowed by the dark. Unlike most of my friends and work mates, I had felt something move painfully inside me when I saw the walls of the Chaga close on the towers of downtown Nairobi. It was like a kick in my heart. For a moment I had gone behind the pictures that are all we are allowed to know of our world, to the true lives. And now the dark had spat one of these true lives up on to the streets of Manchester. We were on the last candle at the last table by the time Ten got round to telling me how she had been dumped out with the other Kenyans at Charles de Gaulle and shuffled for months through EU refugee quotas until she arrived, jet-lagged, culture-shocked and poor as shit, in the gray and damp of an English summer.

Afterwards, I was quiet for some time. Nothing I could have said was adequate to what I had heard. Then I said, "would you like to come home with me for a drink, or a coffee, or something?"

"Yes," she said. Her voice was husky from much talking, and low, and unbearably attractive. "I would, very much."

I left the staff a big tip for above-and-beyondness.

Ten loved my house. The space astonished her. I left her curled up on my sofa savoring the space as I went to open wine.

"This is nice," she said. "Warm. Big. Nice. Yours."

"Yes," I said and leaned forward and kissed her. Then, before I could think about what I had done, I took her arm and kissed the round red blemish of her chip. Ten slept with me that night, but we did not make love. She lay, curled and chaste, in the hollow of my belly until morning. She cried out in her sleep often. Her skin smelled of Africa.

The bastards cut her housing benefit. Ten was distraught. Home was everything to her. Her life had been one long search for a place of her own; safe, secure, stable.

"You have two options," I said. "One, give up working here."

"Never," she said. "I work. I like to work." I saw Wynton smile, polishing the glasses behind the bar.

"Option two, then."

"What's that?"

"Move in with me."

It took her a week to decide. I understood her hesitation. It was a place, safe, secure, stable, but not her own. On the Saturday I got a phone call from her. Could I help her move? I went round to her flat in Salford. The rooms were tatty and cold, the furniture charity-shop fare, and the decor ugly. The place stank of dope. The television blared, unwatched; three different boomboxes competed with each other. While Ten fetched her stuff, her flatmates stared at me as if I were something come out of the Chaga. She had two bags—one of clothes, one of music and books. They went in the back of the car and she came home with me.

Life with Ten. She put her books on a shelf and her

clothes in a drawer. She improvised harmonies to my music. She would light candles on any excuse. She spent hours in the bathroom and used toilet paper by the roll. She was meticulously tidy. She took great care of her little money. She would not borrow from me. She kept working at I-Nation, she sang every Friday. She still killed me every time she got up on that stage.

She said little, but it told. She was dark and intensely beautiful to me. She didn't smile much. When she did it was a knife through the heart of me. It was a sharp joy. Sex was a sharpness of a different kind—it always seemed difficult for her. She didn't lose herself in sex. I think she took a great pleasure from it, but it was controlled . . . it was owned, it was hers. She never let herself make any sound. She was a little afraid of the animal inside. She seemed much older than she was; on the times we went dancing, that same energy that lit her up in singing and sex burned out of her. It was then that she surprised me by being a bright, energetic, sociable eighteen-year-old. She loved me. I loved her so hard it felt like sickness. I would watch her unaware I was doing it . . . watch the way she moved her hands when she talked on the phone, how she curled her legs under her when she watched television, how she brushed her teeth in the morning. I would wake up in the night just to watch her sleep. I would check she was still breathing. I dreaded something insane, something out of nowhere, taking her away.

She stuck a satellite photograph of Africa on the fridge. She showed me how to trace the circles of the Chaga through the clouds. Every week she updated it. Week by week, the circles merging. That was how I measured our life together, by the circles, merging. Week by week, her home was taken away. Her parents and sister were down there, under those blue and white bars of cloud; week by week the circles were running them out of choices.

She never let herself forget she had failed them. She never let herself forget she was a refugee. That was what made her older, in ways, than me. That was what all her tidiness and orderliness around the house were about. She was only here for a little time. It could all be lifted at a moment's notice.

She looked to cook for me on Sundays, though the kitchen smelled of it for a week afterwards. I never told her her cooking gave me the shits. She was chopping something she had got from the Caribbean stores and singing to herself. I was watching from the hall, as I loved to watch her without being watched. I saw her bring the knife down, heard a Kalenjin curse, saw her lift her hand to her mouth. I was in like a shot.

"Shit shit shit shit," she swore. It was a deep cut, and blood ran freely down her forefinger. I rushed her to the tap, stuck it under the cold, then went for the medical bag. I returned with gauze, plasters and a heal-the-world attitude.

"It's okay," she said, holding the finger up. "It's better."

The cut had vanished. No blood, no scab. All that remained was a slightly raised red weal. As I watched, even that faded.

"How?"

"I don't know," Ten said. "But it's better."

I didn't ask. I didn't want to ask. I didn't want there to be anything more difficult or complex in Ten's life. I wanted what she had from her past to be enough, to be all. I knew this was something alien; no one healed like that. I thought that if I let it go, it would never trouble us again. I had not calculated on the bomb.

Some fucking Nazis or other had been blast-bombing gay bars. London, Edinburgh, Dublin so far, always a Friday afternoon, work over, weekend starting. Manchester was on the alert. So were the bombers. Tuesday, lunch time, half a kilo of semtex with nails and razor blades packed round it went off under a table outside a Canal Street bar. No one died, but a woman at the next table lost both legs from the knees down and there were over fifty casualties. Ten had been going in for the afternoon shift. She was twenty meters away when the bomb went off. I got the call from the hospital same time as the news broke on the radio.

"Get the fuck over there," Willy the boss ordered. I didn't need ordering. Manchester Royal Infirmary casualty was bedlam. I saw the doctors going around in a slow rush and the people looking up at everyone who came in, very very afraid and the police taking statements and the trolleys in the aisles and I thought, It must have been something like this in Nairobi, at the end. The receptionist showed me to a room where I was to wait for a doctor. I met her in the corridor, a small, harassed-looking Chinese girl.

"Ah, Mr. Giddens. You're with Ms. Bi, that's right?"

"That's right, how is she?"

"Well, she was brought in with multiple lacerations, upper body, left side of face, left upper arm and shoulder . . ."

"Oh Jesus God. And now?"

"See for yourself."

Ten walked down the corridor. If she had not been wearing a hospital robe, I would have sworn she was unchanged from how I had left her that morning.

"Shone."

The weals were already fading from her face and hands. A terrible prescience came over me, so strong and cold I almost threw up.

"We want to keep her in for further tests, Mr. Giddings,"

the doctor said. "As you can imagine, we've never seen anything quite like this before."

"Shone, I'm fine. I want to go home."

"Just to be sure, Mr. Giddens."

When I brought Ten back a bag of stuff, the receptionist directed me to Intensive Care. I ran the six flights of stairs to ICU, burning with dread. Ten was in a sealed room full of white equipment. When she saw me, she ran from her bed to the window, pressed her hands against it.

"Shone!" Her words came through a speaker grille. "They won't let me out!"

Another doctor led me to a side room. There were two policemen there, and a man in a suit.

"What the hell is this?"

"Mr. Giddens. Ms. Bi, she is a Kenyan refugee?"

"You fucking know that."

"Easy, Mr. Giddens. We've been running some tests on Ms. Bi, and we've discovered the presence in her bloodstream of fullerene nanoprocessors."

"Nanowhat?"

"What are commonly known as Chaga spores."

Ten, Dust Girl, firing and firing and firing at the glider, the gun blossoming in her hand, the shanty town melting behind her as her clothes fell apart, her arm sticking through the shield wall as she shouted, I'm chipped, I'm chipped! The soldiers shaving her head, hosing her down. Those things she had carried inside her. All those runs for the Americans.

"Oh my God."

There was a window in the little room. Through it I saw Ten sitting on a plastic chair by the bed, hands on her thighs, head bowed.

"Mr. Giddens." The man in the suit flashed a little plastic

wallet. "Robert McGlennon, Home Office Immigration. Your, ah . . ." He nodded at the window.

"Partner."

"Partner. Mr. Giddens, I have to tell you, we cannot be certain that Ms. Bi's continued presence is not a public health risk. Her refugee status is dependent on a number of conditions, one of which is that . . ."

"You're fucking deporting her . . ."

The two policemen stirred. I realized then that they were not there for Ten. They were there for me.

"It's a public health issue, Mr. Giddens. She should never have been allowed in in the first place. We have no idea of the possible environmental impact. You, of all people, should be aware what these things can do. Have done. Are still doing. I have to think of public safety."

"Public safety, fuck!"

"Mr. Giddens . . ."

I went to the window. I beat my fists on the wired glass.

"Ten! Ten! They're trying to deport you! They want to send you back!"

The policemen prised me away from the window. On the far side, Ten yelled silently.

"Look, I don't like having to do this," the man in the suit said.

"When?"

"Mr. Giddens."

"When? Tell me, how long has she got?"

"Usually there'd be a detention period, with limited rights of appeal. But as this is a public health issue . . ."

"You're going to do it right now."

"The order is effective immediately, Mr. Giddens. I'm

sorry. These officers will go with you back to your home. If you could gather up the rest of her things . . ."

"At least let me say goodbye. Jesus, you owe me that!"

"I can't allow that, Mr. Giddens. There's a contamination risk."

"Contamination? I've only been fucking her for the past six months."

As the cops marched me out, the doctor came up for a word.

"Mr. Giddens, these nanoprocessors in her bloodstream . . ."

"That are fucking getting her thrown out of the country."

"The fullerenes . . ."

"She heals quick. I saw it."

"They do much more than that, Mr. Giddens. She'll probably never get sick again. And there's some evidence that they prevent telomere depletion in cell division."

"What does that mean?"

"It means, she ages very much more slowly than we do. Her life expectancy may be, I don't know, two, three hundred years."

I stared. The policemen stared.

"There's more. We observed unfamiliar structures in her brain; the best I can describe them is, the nanoprocessors seem to be re-engineering dead neurons into a complementary neural network."

"A spare brain?"

"An auxiliary brain."

"What would you do with that?"

"What wouldn't you do with that, Mr. Giddens." He wiped his hand across his mouth. "This bit is pure speculation, but . . ."

"But."

"But in some way, she's in control of it all. I think—this is just a theory—that through this auxiliary brain she's able to interact with the nanoprocessors. She might be able to make them do what she wants. Program them."

"Thank you for telling me that," I said bitterly. "That makes it all so much easier."

I took the policemen back to my house. I told them to make themselves tea. I took Ten's neatly arranged books and CDs off my shelves and her neatly folded clothes out of my drawers and her toilet things out of my bathroom and put them back in the two bags in which she had brought them. I gave the bags to the policemen, they took them away in their car. I never got to say goodbye. I never learned what flight she was on, where she flew from, when she left this country. A face behind glass. That was my last memory. The thing I feared—insane, out of nowhere—had taken her away.

After Ten went, I was sick for a long time. There was no sunshine, no rain, no wind. No days or time, just a constant, high-pitched, quiet whine in my head. People at work played out a slightly amplified normality for my benefit. Alone, they would ask, very gently, How do you feel?

"How do I feel?" I told them. "Like I've been shot with a single, high velocity round, and I'm dead, and I don't know it."

I asked for someone else to take over the I-Nation account. Wynton called me but I could not speak with him. He sent round a bottle of that good Jamaican import liqueur, and a note, "Come and see us, any time." Willy arranged me a career break and a therapist.

His name was Greg, he was a client-centered therapist, which meant I could talk for as long as I liked about whatever I liked and he had to listen. I talked very little, those first few sessions. Partly I felt stupid, partly I didn't want to talk, even to a stranger. But it worked, little by little, without my knowing. I think I only began to be aware of that the day I realized that Ten was gone, but not dead. Her last photo of Africa was still on the fridge and I looked at it and saw something new: down there, in there, somewhere, was Ten. The realization was vast and subtle at the same time. I think of it like a man who finds himself in darkness. He imagines he's in a room, no doors, no windows, and that he'll never find the way out. But then he hears noises, feels a touch on his face, smells a subtle smell, and he realizes that he is not in a room at all—he is outside: the touch on his face is the wind, the noises are night birds, the smell is from night-blooming flowers, and above him, somewhere, are stars.

Greg said nothing when I told him this—they never do, these client-centered boys, but after that session I went to the net and started the hunt for Tendeléo Bi. The Freedom of Information Act got me into the Immigration Service's databases. Ten had been flown out on a secure military transport to Mombasa. UNHCR in Mombasa had assigned her to Likoni Twelve, a new camp to the south of the city. She was transferred out on November Twelfth. It took two days searching to pick up a Tendeléo Bi logged into a place called Samburu North three months later. Medical records said she was suffering from exhaustion and dehydration, but responding to sugar and salt treatment. She was alive.

On the first Monday of winter, I went back to work. I had lost a whole season. On the first Friday, Willy gave me a print-out from an on-line recruitment agency.

"I think you need a change of scene," he said. "These people are looking for a stock accountant."

These people were Medecins Sans Frontiers. Where they needed a stock accountant was their East African theater.

Eight months after the night the two policemen took away Ten's things, I stepped off the plane in Mombasa. I think hell must be like Mombasa in its final days as capital of the Republic of Kenya, infrastructure unraveling, economy disintegrating, the harbor a solid mass of boat people and a million more in the camps in Likoni and Shimba Hills, Islam and Christianity fighting a new Crusade for control of this chaos and the Chaga advancing from the west and now the south, after the new impact at Tanga. And in the middle of it all, Sean Giddens, accounting for stock. It was good, hard, solid work in MSF Sector Headquarters, buying drugs where, when, and how we could; haggling down truck drivers and Sibirsk jet-jockeys; negotiating service contracts as spare parts for the Landcruisers gradually ran out, every day juggling budgets always too small against needs too big. I loved it more than any work I've ever done. I was so busy I sometimes forgot why I was there. Then I would go in the safe bus back to the compound and see the smoke going up from the other side of the harbor, hear the gunfire echo off the old Arab houses, and the memory of her behind that green wired glass would gut me.

My boss was a big bastard Frenchman, Jean-Paul Gastineau. He had survived wars and disasters on every continent except Antarctica. He liked Cuban cigars and wine from the valley where he was born and opera, and made sure he had them, never mind distance or expense. He took absolutely no shit. I liked him immensely. I was a fucking thin-blooded number-pushing black rosbif, but he enjoyed my creative accounting. He was wasted in Mombasa. He was a true front-line medic. He was itching for action.

One lunchtime, as he was opening his red wine, I asked him how easy it would be to find someone in the camps. He looked at me shrewdly, then asked, "Who is she?"

He poured two glasses, his invitation to me. I told him my history and her history over the bottle. It was very good.

"So, how do I find her?"

"You'll never get anything through channels," Jean-Paul said. "Easiest thing to do is go there yourself. You have leave due."

"No I don't."

"Yes you do. About three weeks of it. Ah. Yes." He poked about in his desk drawers. He threw me a black plastic object like a large cellphone.

"What is it?"

"US ID chips have a GPS transponder. They like to know where their people are. Take it. If she is chipped, this will find her."

"Thanks."

He shrugged.

"I come from a nation of romantics. Also, you're the only one in this fucking place who appreciates a good Beaune."

I flew up north on a Sibirsk charter. Through the window I could see the edge of the Chaga. It was too huge to be a feature of the landscape, or even a geographical entity. It was like a dark sea. It looked like what it was . . . another world, that had pushed up against our own. Like it, some ideas are too huge to fit into our everyday worlds. They push up through it, they take it over, and they change it beyond recognition. If what the doctor at Manchester Royal Infirmary had said about the things in Ten's blood were true, then this was not just a new world. This was a new humanity. This was every rule about how we make our livings, how we deal with each other, how we lead our lives, all overturned.

The camps, also, are too big to take in. There is too much there for the world we've made for ourselves. They change everything you believe. Mombasa was no preparation. It was like the end of the world up there on the front line.

"So, you're looking for someone," Heino Rautavaara said. He had worked with Jean-Paul through the fall of Nairobi; I could trust him, Jay-Pee said, but I think he thought I was a fool, or, at best, a romantic. "No shortage of people here."

Jean-Paul had warned the records wouldn't be accurate. But you hope. I went to Samburu North, where my search in England had last recorded Ten. No trace of her. The UNHCR warden, a grim little American woman, took me up and down the rows of tents. I looked at the faces and my tracker sat silent on my hip. I saw those faces that night in the ceiling, and for many nights after.

"You expect to hit the prize first time?" Heino said as we bounced along the dirt track in an MSF Landcruiser to Don Dul.

I had better luck in Don Dul, if you can call it that. Ten had definitely been here two months ago. But she had left eight days later, I saw the log in, the log out, but there was no record of where she had gone.

"No shortage of camps either," Heino said. He was a dour bastard. He couldn't take me any further but he squared me an authorization to travel on Red Cross/Crescent convoys, who did a five hundred mile run through the camps along the northern terminum. In two weeks I saw more misery than I ever thought humanity could take. I saw the faces and the bands and the bundles of scavenged things and I thought, why hold them here? What are they saving them from? Is it so bad in the Chaga? What is so terrible about people living long lives, being immune from sickness, growing extra layers in their brains? What is so frightening about people being able to go into that alien place, and take control of it, and make it into what they want?

I couldn't see the Chaga, it lay just below the southern horizon, but I was constantly aware of its presence, like they say people who have plates in their skulls always feel a slight pressure. Sometimes, when the faces let me sleep, I would be woken instead by a strange smell, not strong, but distinct; musky and fruity and sweaty, sexy, warm. It was the smell of the Chaga, down there, blowing up from the south.

Tent to truck to camp to tent. My three weeks were running out and I had to arrange a lift back along the front line to Samburu and the flight to Mombasa. With three days left, I arrived in Eldoret, UNECTA's Lake Victoria regional center. It gave an impression of bustle, the shops and hotels and cafés were busy, but the white faces and American accents and dress sense said Eldoret was a company town. The Rift Valley Hotel looked like heaven after eighteen days on the front line. I spent an hour in the pool trying to beam myself into the sky. A sudden rain storm drove everyone from the water but me. I floated there, luxuriating in the raindrops splashing around me. At sunset I went down to the camps. They lay to the south of the town, like a line of cannon-fodder against the Chaga. I checked the records, a matter of form. No Tendeléo Bi. I went in anyway. And it was another camp, and after a time, anyone can become insulated to suffering. You have to. You have to book into the big hotel and swim in the pool and eat a good dinner when you get back; in the camps you have to look at the faces just as faces and refuse to make any connection with the stories behind them. The hardest people I know work in the compassion business. So I went up and down the faces and somewhere halfway down some row I remembered this toy Jean-Paul had given me. I took it out. The display was flashing green. There was a single word: lock.

I almost dropped it.

I thought my heart had stopped. I felt hit between the eyes. I forgot to breathe. The world reeled sideways. My fucking stupid fingers couldn't get a precise reading. I ran down the row of tents, watching the figures. The digits told me how many meters I was to north and east. Wrong way. I doubled back, ducked right at the next opening and headed east. Both sets of figures were decreasing. I overshot, the east reading went up. Back again. This row. This row. I peered through the twilight. At the far end was a group of people talking outside a tent lit by a yellow petrol lamp. I started to run, one eye on the tracker. I stumbled over guy-ropes, kicked cans, hurdled children, apologized to old women. The numbers clicked down, thirty-five, thirty, twenty-five meters . . . I could see this one figure in the group, back to me, dressed in purple combat gear. East zero. North twenty, eighteen . . . Short, female. Twelve, ten. Wore its hair in great soft spikes. Eight, six. I couldn't make it past four. I couldn't move. I couldn't speak. I was shaking.

Sensing me, the figure turned. The yellow light caught her.

"Ten," I said. I saw fifty emotions on that face. Then she ran at me and I dropped the scanner and I lifted her and held her to me and no words of mine, or anyone else's, I think, can say how I felt then.

Now our lives and stories and places come together, and my tale moves to its conclusion.

I believe that people and their feelings write themselves on space and time. That is the only way I can explain how I knew, even before I turned and saw him there in that camp, that it was Sean, that he had searched for me, and found me. I tell you, that is some thing to know that another person has done for you. I saw him, and it was like the world had set laws about how it was to work for me, and then suddenly it said, no, I break them now, for you, Tendeléo, because it pleases me. He was impossible, he changed everything I knew, he was there.

Too much joy weeps. Too much sorrow laughs.

He took me back to his hotel. The staff looked hard at me as he picked up his keycard from the lobby. They knew what I was. They did not dare say anything. The white men in the bar also turned to stare. They too knew the meaning of the colors I wore.

He took me to his room. We sat on the verandah with beer. There was a storm that night—there is a storm most nights, up in the high country but it kept itself in the west among the Nandi Hills. Lightning crawled between the clouds, the distant thunder rattled our beer bottles on the iron table. I told Sean where I had been, what I had done, how I had lived. It was a story long in the telling. The sky had cleared, a new day was breaking by the time I finished it. We have always told each other stories, and each other's stories.

He kept his questions until the end. He had many, many of them.

"Yes, I suppose, it is like the old slave underground railroads," I answered one.

"I still don't understand why they try to stop people going in."

"Because we scare them. We can build a society in there that needs nothing from them. We challenge everything they believe. This is the first century we have gone into where we have no ideas, no philosophies, no beliefs. Buy stuff, look at stuff. That's it. We are supposed to build a thousand years on that? Well, now we do. I tell you, I've been reading, learning stuff, ideas, politics. Philosophy. It's all in there. There are information storage banks the size of skycrapers, Sean. And not just our history. Other people, other races. You can go into them, you can become them. Live their lives, see things through their senses. We are not the first. We are part of a long, long chain, and we are not the end of it. The world will belong to us; we will control physical reality as easily as computers control information."

"Hell, never mind the UN . . . you scare me, Ten!"

I always loved it when he called me Ten. Il Primo, Top of the Heap, King of the Hill, A-Number-One.

Then he said, "and your family?"

"Little Egg is in a place called Kilandui. It's full of

weavers, she's a weaver. She makes beautiful brocades. I see her quite often."

"And your mother and father?"

"I'll find them."

But to most of his questions, there was only one answer: "Come, and I will show you." I left it to last. It rocked him as if he had been struck.

"You are serious."

"Why not? You took me to your home once. Let me take you to mine. But first, it's a year . . . And so so much . . ."

He picked me up.

"I like you in this combat stuff," he said.

We laughed a lot and remembered old things we had forgotten. We slowly shook off the rust and the dust, and it was good, and I remember the room maid opening the door and letting out a little shriek and going off giggling.

Sean once told me that one of his nation's greatest ages was built on those words, why not? For a thousand years Christianity had ruled England with the question: "Why?" Build a cathedral, invent a science, write a play, discover a new land, start a business: "Why?" Then came the Elizabethans with the answer: "Why not?"

I knew the old Elizabethan was thinking, why not? There are only numbers to go back to, and benefit traps, and an old, gray city, and an old, gray dying world, a safe world with few promises. Here there's a world to be made. Here there's a future of a million years to be shaped. Here there are a thousand different ways of living together to be designed, and if they don't work, roll them up like clay and start again.

I did not hurry Sean for his answer. He knew as well as I that it was not a clean decision. It was lose a world, or lose each other. These are not choices you make in a day. So, I enjoyed the hotel. One day I was having a long bath. The hotel had a great bathroom and there was a lot of free stuff you could play with, so I abused it. I heard Sean pick up the phone. I could not make out what he was saying, but he was talking for some time. When I came out he was sitting on the edge of the bed with the telephone beside him. He sat very straight and formal.

"I called Jean-Paul," he said. "I gave him my resignation."

Two days later, we set out for the Chaga. We went by matatu. It was a school holiday, the Peugeot Services were busy with children on their way back to their families. They made a lot of noise and energy. They looked out the corners of their eyes at us and bent together to whisper. Sean noticed this.

"They're talking about you," Sean said.

"They know what I am, what I do."

One of the schoolgirls, in a black and white uniform, understood our English. She fixed Sean a look. "She is a warrior," she told him. "She is giving us our nation back."

We left most of the children in Kapsabet to change on to other matatus; ours drove on into the heart of the Nandi Hills. It was a high, green rolling country, in some ways like Sean's England. I asked the driver to stop just past a metal cross that marked some old road death.

"What now?" Sean said. He sat on the small pack I had told him was all he could take.

"Now, we wait. They won't be long."

Twenty cars went up the muddy red road, two trucks, a country bus and medical convoy went down. Then they came out of the darkness between the trees on the other side of the road like dreams out of sleep: Meji, Naomi and Hamid. They beckoned: behind them came men, women, children . . . entire families, from babes in arms to old men; twenty citizens, appearing one by one out of the dark, looking nervously up and down the straight red road, then crossing to the other side.

I lived with Meji, he looked Sean up and down.

"This is the one?"

"This is Sean."

"I had expected something, um . . ."

"Whiter?"

He laughed. He shook hands with Sean and introduced himself. Then Meji took a tube out of his pocket and covered Sean in spray. Sean jumped back, choking.

"Stay there, unless you want your clothes to fall off you when you get inside," I said.

Naomi translated this for the others. They found it very funny. When he had immunized Sean's clothes, Meji sprayed his bag.

"Now, we walk," I told Sean.

We spent the night in the Chief's house in the village of Senghalo. He was the last station on our railroad. I know from my Dust Girl days you need as good people on the outside as the inside. Folk came from all around to see the black Englishman. Although he found being looked at intimidating, Sean managed to tell his story. I translated. At the end the crowd outside the Chief's house burst into spontaneous applause and finger-clicks.

"Aye, Tendeléo, how can I compete?" Meji half-joked with me.

I slept fitfully that night, troubled by the sound of aircraft moving under the edge of the storm.

"Is it me?" Sean said.

"No, not you. Go back to sleep."

Sunlight through the bamboo wall woke us. While Sean washed outside in the bright, cold morning, watched by children curious to see if the black went all the way down, Chief and I tuned his shortwave to the UN frequencies. There was a lot of chatter in Klingon. You Americans think we don't understand Star Trek?"

"They've been tipped off," Chief said. We fetched the equipment from his souterrain. Sean watched Hamid, Naomi, Meji and me put on the communicators. He said nothing as the black-green knob of cha-plastic grew around the back of my head, into my ear, and sent a tendril to my lips. He picked up my staff.

"Can I?"

"It won't bite you."

He looked closely at the fist-sized ball of amber at its head, and the skeleton outline of a sphere embedded in it.

"It's a buckyball," I said. "The symbol of our power."

He passed it to me without comment. We unwrapped our guns, cleaned them, checked them and set off. We walked east that day along the ridges of the Nandi Hills, through ruined fields and abandoned villages. Helicopter engines were our constant companions. Sometimes we glimpsed them through the leaf cover, tiny in the sky like black mosquitoes. The old people and the mothers looked afraid. I did not want them to see how nervous they were making me. I called my colleagues apart.

"They're getting closer."

Hamid nodded. He was a quiet, thin, twenty-two year old . . . Ethiopian skin, goatee, a political science graduate from the University of Nairobi.

"We choose a different path every time," he said. "They can't know this."

"Someone's selling us," Meji said.

"Wouldn't matter. We pick one at random."

"Unless they're covering them all."

In the afternoon we began to dip down toward the Rift Valley and terminum. As we wound our way down the old hunters' paths, muddy and slippery from recent rain, the helicopter came swooping in across the hillside. We scrambled for cover. It turned and made another pass, so low I could see the light glint from the pilot's heads-up visor.

"They're playing with us," Hamid said. "They can blow us right off this hill any time they want."

"How?" Naomi asked. She said only what was necessary, and when.

"I think I know," Sean said. He had been listening a little away. He slithered down to join us as the helicopter beat over the hillside again, flailing the leaves, showering us with dirt and twigs. "This." He tapped my forearm. "If I could find you, they can find you."

I pulled up my sleeve. The Judas chip seemed to throb under my skin, like poison.

"Hold my wrist," I said to Sean. "Whatever happens, don't let it slip!

Before he could say a word, I pulled my knife. These things must be done fast. If you once stop to think, you will never do it. Make sure you have it straight. You won't get another go. A stab down with the tip, a short pull, a twist, and the traitor thing was on the ground, greasy with my blood. It hurt. It hurt very much, but the blood had staunched, the wound was already closing.

"I'll just have to make sure not to lose you again," Sean said.

Very quietly, very silently, we formed up the team and one by one slipped down the hillside, out from under the eyes of the helicopter. For all I know, the stupid thing is up there still, keeping vigil over a dead chip. We slept under the sky that night, close together for warmth and on the third day we came to Tinderet and the edge of the Chaga.

Ten had been leading us at a cracking pace, as if she were impatient to put Kenya behind us. Since mid-morning, we had been making our way up a long, slow hill. I'd done some hill-walking. I was fit for it, but the young ones and the women with babies found it tough going. When I called for a halt, I saw a moment of anger cross Ten's face. As soon as she could, we upped packs and moved on. I tried to catch up with her, but Ten moved steadily ahead of me until, just below the summit, she was almost running.

"Shone!" she shouted back. "Come with me!"

She ran up through the thinning trees to the summit. I followed, went bounding down a slight dip, and suddenly, the trees opened and I was on the edge.

The ground fell away at my feet into the Rift Valley, green on green on green, sweeping to the valley floor where the patterns of the abandoned fields could still be made out in the patchwork of yellows and buffs and earth tones. Perspective blurred the colors—I could see at least fifty miles—until, suddenly, breathtakingly, they changed. Browns and dry-land beiges blended into burgundies and rust reds, were shot through with veins of purple and white, then exploded into chaos, like a bed of flowers of every conceivable color, a jumble of shapes and colors like a mad coral reef, like a box of kiddie's plastic toys spilled out on a Chinese rug. It strained the eyes, it hurt the brain. I followed it back, trying to make sense of what I was seeing. A sheer wall, deep red, rose abruptly out of the chaotic landscape, straight up, almost as high as the escarpment I was standing on. It was not a solid wall, it looked to me to be made up of pillars or, I thought, tree trunks. They must have been of titanic size to be visible from this distance. They opened into an unbroken, flat crimson canopy. In the further distance, the flat roof became a jumble of dark greens, broken by what I can only describe as small mesas, like the Devil's Tower in Wyoming or the old volcanoes in Puy de Dome. But these glittered in the sun like glass. Beyond them, the landscape was striped like a tiger, yellow and dark brown, and formations like capsizing icebergs, pure white, lifted out of it. And beyond that, I lost the detail, but the colors went on and on, all the way to the horizon.

I don't know how long I stood, looking at the Chaga. I lost all sense of time. I became aware at some point that Ten was standing beside me. She did not try to move me on, or speak. She knew that the Chaga was one of these things that must just be experienced before it can be interpreted. One by one the others joined us. We stood in a row along the bluffs, looking at our new home.

Then we started down the path to the valley below.

Half an hour down the escarpment, Meji up front called a halt.

"What is it?" I asked Ten. She touched her fingers to her communicator, a half-eggshell of living plastic unfolded from the headset and pressed itself to her right eye.

"This is not good," she said. "Smoke, from Menengai."

"Menengai?"

"Where we're going. Meji is trying to raise them on the radio."

I looked over Ten's head to Meji, one hand held to his ear, looking around him. He looked worried.

"And?"

"Nothing."

"And what do we do?"

"We go on."

We descended through microclimates. The valley floor was fifteen degrees hotter than the cool, damp Nandi Hills. We toiled across brush and overgrown scrub, along abandoned roads, through deserted villages. The warriors held their weapons at the slope. Ten regularly scanned the sky with her all-seeing eye. Now even I could see the smoke, blowing toward us on a wind from the east, and smell it. It smelled like burned spices. I could make out Meji trying to call up Menengai. Radio silence.

In the early afternoon, we crossed terminum. You can see these things clearly from a distance. At ground level, they creep up on you. I was walking through tough valley grasses and thorn scrub when I noticed lines of blue moss between the roots. Oddly regular lines of moss, that bent and forked at exactly one hundred and twenty degrees, and joined up into hexagons. I froze. Twenty meters ahead of me, Ten stood in one world . . . I stood in another.

"Even if you do nothing, it will still come to you," she said. I looked down. The blue lines were inching toward my toes. "Come on." Ten reached out her hand. I took it, and she led me across. Within two minutes walk, the scrub and grass had given way entirely to Chaga vegetation. For the rest of the afternoon we moved through the destroying zone. Trees crashed around us, shrubs were devoured from the roots down, grasses fell apart and dissolved; fungus fingers and coral fans pushed up on either side, bubbles blew around my head. I walked through it untouched like a man in a furnace.

Meji called a halt under an arch of Chaga-growth like a vault in a medieval cathedral. He had a report on his earjack.

"Menengai has been attacked."

Everyone started talking, asking questions, jabbering. Meji held up his hand.

"They were Africans. Someone had provided them with Chaga-proof equipment, and weapons. They had badges on their uniforms: KLA."

"Kenyan Liberation Army," the quiet one, Naomi said.

"We have enemies," the clever one, Hamid said. "The Kenyan Government still claims jurisdiction over the Chaga. Every so often, they remind us who's in charge. They want to keep us on the run, stop us getting established. They're nothing but contras with western money and guns and advisers."

"And Menengai?" I asked. Meji shook his head.

"Most High is bringing the survivors to Ol Punyata."

I looked at Ten.

"Most High?"

She nodded.

We met up with Most High under the dark canopy of the Great Wall. It was an appropriately somber place for the meeting: the smooth soaring trunks of the trees; the canopy of leaves, held out like hands, a kilometer over our heads; the splashes of light that fell through the gaps to the forest floor; survivors and travelers, dwarfed by it all. Medieval peasants must have felt like this, awestruck in their own cathedrals.

It's an odd experience, meeting someone you've heard of in a story. You want to say, I've heard about you, you haven't heard about me, you're nothing like I imagined. You check them out to make sure they're playing true to their character. His story was simple and grim.

A village, waking, going about its normal business, people meeting and greeting, walking and talking, gossiping and idling, talking the news, taking coffee. Then, voices; strange voices, and shots, and people looking up wondering, What is going on here? and while they are caught wondering, strangers running at them, running through, strangers with guns, shooting at anything in front of them, not asking questions, not looking or listening, shooting and running on. Shooting, and burning. Bodies left where they lay, homes like blossoming flowers going up in gobs of flame. Through, back, and out. Gone. As fast, as off-hand as that. Ten minutes, and Menengai was a morgue. Most High told it as casually as it had been committed, but I saw his knuckles whiten as he gripped his staff.

To people like me, who come from a peaceful, ordered society, violence like that is unimaginable.

I've seen fights and they scared me, but I've never experienced the kind of violence Most High was describing, where people's pure intent is to kill other people. I could see the survivors—dirty, tired, scared, very quiet—but I couldn't see what had been done to them. So I couldn't really believe it. And though I'd hidden up there on the hill from the helicopter, I couldn't believe it would have opened up those big gatlings on me, and I couldn't believe now that the people who attacked Menengai, this Kenyan Liberation

Army, whose only purpose was to kill Chaga-folk and destroy their lives, were out there somewhere, probably being resupplied by airdrop, reloading, and going in search of new targets. It seemed wrong in a place as silent and holy as this . . . like a snake in the garden.

Meji and Ten believed it. As soon as we could, they moved us on and out.

"Where now?" I asked Ten.

She looked uncertain.

"East. The Black Simbas have a number of settlements on Kirinyaga. They'll defend them."

"Three days?"

"That woman back there, Hope. She won't be able to go on very much longer." I had been speaking to her, she was heavily pregnant. Eight months, I reckoned. She had no English, and I had Aid-Agency Swahili, but she appreciated my company, and I found her big belly a confirmation that life was strong, life went on.

"I know," Ten said. She might wear the gear and carry the staff and have a gun at her hip, but she was facing decisions that told her, forcefully, You're still in your teens, little warrior.

We wound between the colossal buttressed roots of the root-trees. The globes on the tops of the staffs gave off a soft yellow light—bioluminescence, Ten told me.

We followed the bobbing lights through the dark, dripping wall-forest. The land rose, slowly and steadily. I fell back to walk with Hope. We talked. It passed the time. The Great Wall gave way abruptly to an ecosystem of fungi. Red toadstools towered over my head, puff-balls dusted me with yellow spores, trumpet-like chanterelles dripped water from their cups, clusters of pin-head mushrooms glowed white like corpses. I saw monkeys, watching from the canopy.

We were high now, climbing up ridges like the fingers of a splayed-out hand. Hope told me how her husband had been killed in the raid on Menengai. I did not know what to say. Then she asked me my story. I told it in my bad Swahili. The staffs led us higher.

"Ten."

We were taking an evening meal break. That was one thing about the Chaga, you could never go hungry. Reach out, and anything you touched would be edible. Ten had taught me that if you buried your shit, a good-tasting tuber would have grown in the morning. I hadn't had the courage yet to try it. For an alien invasion, the Chaga seemed remarkably considerate of human needs.

"I think Hope's a lot further on than we thought."

Ten shook her head.

"Ten, if she starts, will you stop?"

She hesitated a moment.

"Okay. We will stop."

She struggled for two days, down into a valley, through terribly tough terrain of great spheres of giraffe-patterned moss, then up, into higher country than any we had attempted before.

"Ten, where are we?" I asked. The Chaga had changed our geography, made all our maps obsolete. We navigated by compass, and major, geophysical landmarks.

"We've passed through the Nyandarua Valley, now we're going up the east side of the Aberdares."

The line of survivors became strung out. Naomi and I struggled at the rear with the old and the women with children, and Hope. We fought our way up that hillside, but Hope was flagging, failing.

"I think . . . I feel . . ." she said, hand on her belly.

"Call Ten on that thing," I ordered Naomi. She spoke into her mouthpiece.

"No reply."

"She what?"

"There is no reply."

I ran. Hands, knees, belly, whatever way I could, I made it up that ridge, as fast as I could. Over the summit the terrain changed, as suddenly as Chaga landscapes do, from the moss maze to a plantation of regularly spaced trees shaped like enormous ears of wheat.

Ten was a hundred meters downslope. She stood like a statue among the wheat-trees. Her staff was planted firmly on the ground. She did not acknowledge me when I called her name. I ran down through the trees to her.

"Ten, Hope can't go on. We have to stop."

"No!" Ten shouted. She did not look at me, she stared down through the rows of trees.

"Ten!" I seized her, spun her round. Her face was frantic, terrified, tearful, joyful, as if she in this grove of alien plants was something familiar and absolutely agonizing. "Ten! You promised!"

"Shone! Shone! I know where I am! I know where this is! That is the pass, and that is where the road went, this is the valley, that is the river, and down there, is Gichichi!" She looked back up to the pass, called to the figures on the treeline. "Most High! Gichichi! This is Gichichi! We are home!"

She took off. She held her staff in her hand like a hunter's spear, she leaped rocks and fallen trunks, she hurdled streams and run-offs; bounding down through the trees. I was after her like a shot but I couldn't hope to keep up. I found Ten standing in an open space where a falling wheat-tree had brought others down like dominoes. Her staff was thrust deep into the earth. I didn't interrupt. I didn't say a word. I knew I was witnessing something holy.

She went down on her knees. She closed her eyes. She pressed her hands to the soil. And I saw dark lines, like slow, black lightning, go out from her fingertips across the Chaga-cover. The lines arced and intersected, sparked out fresh paths.

The carpet of moss began to resemble a crackle-glazed Japanese bowl. But they all focused on Ten. She was the source of the pattern. And the Chaga-cover began to flow toward the lines of force. Shapes appeared under the moving moss, like ribs under skin. They formed grids and squares, slowly pushing up the Chaga-cover. I understood what I was seeing. The lines of buried walls and buildings were being exhumed. Molecule by molecule, centimeter by centimeter, Gichichi was being drawn out of the soil.

By the time the others had made it down from the ridge, the walls stood waist-high and service units were rising out of the earth, electricity generators, water pumps, heat-exchangers, nanofacturing cells. Refugees and warriors walked in amazement among the slowly rising porcelain walls.

Then Ten chose to recognize me.

She looked up. Her teeth were clenched, her hair was matted, sweat dripped from her chin and cheekbones. Her face was gaunt, she was burning her own body-mass, ramming it through that mind/Chaga interface in her brain to program nanoprocessors on a massive scale.

"We control it, Shone," she whispered. "We can make the

world any shape we want it to be. We can make a home for ourselves."

Most High laid his hand on her shoulder.

"Enough, child. Enough. It can make itself now."

Ten nodded. She broke the spell. Ten rolled on to her side, gasping, shivering.

"It's finished," she whispered. "Shone . . ."

She still could not say my name right. I went to her, I took her in my arms while around us Gichichi rose, unfolded roofs like petals, grew gardens and tiny, tangled lanes. No words. No need for words. She had done all her saying, but close at hand, I heard the delighted, apprehensive cry of a woman entering labor.